T0116783

immechanica

immechanica
a novel

e. f. coleman

Luminastra Press

immechanica
© 2023 by E. F. Coleman

Luminastra Press, LLC
5305 River Rd N Suite B
Keizer, OR 97303
press@luminastra-press.com

Cover illustration © 2021 by James Lincolnshire
Cover and interior design by Sonia Williams

Publisher's Cataloging-In-Publication Data
(Provided by Cassidy Cataloguing Services, Inc.)

Names: Coleman, E. F., author.
Title: Immechanica : a novel / E.F. Coleman.
Description: Identifiers: Subjects:
Keizer, OR : Luminastra Press, [2023]
ISBN: 979-8-9860637-0-6 (paperback) | 979-8-9860637-1-3 (ebook)
LCSH: Corporate state--California--Los Angeles--Fiction. | Corruption-
-California--Los Angeles--Fiction. | Climate change--Fiction. | High
technology--California--Los Angeles-- Fiction. | Electronic surveillance--
Fiction. | Hacking--Fiction. | Betrayal--Fiction. | LCGFT: Dystopian fiction. |
Cyberpunk fiction.
Classification: LCC: PS3603.O4342 I46 2023 | DDC: 813/.6--dc23

Library of Congress Control Number: 2022948078

10 9 8 7 6 5 4 3 2 1

Printed in the United States of America.

For the activists

PART 1
UNDERGROUND

1

Starlight in her Hair

S HE PICKED HER way down the cramped alley, decaying shipping containers on one side, rust-stained corrugated metal buildings on the other. A pulsing green arrow hovered ghostlike in front of her, directing her toward the dark silhouette of a long-abandoned warehouse erupting from cracked concrete. Feeble light leaked from the edges of a small window carelessly plastered over with yellowing newspaper. Beyond the warehouse, closer to the water, the shattered wreck of the *Georgina Maersk* lay broken, speared on the jagged metal fingers of the old docks by a freak storm nearly eight years ago. The area had been up for renewal ever since, but something always held it up. Toxic waste, last she'd heard. Cheaper to move the harbor a few miles than clean it up.

Heat shimmered in the evening air like vitriol after an argument. Sweat clung to her face and arms. The glowing arrow brought her to a massive wood and metal door in the side of the warehouse. "You have reached your destination," a synthetic voice said in a programmed British accent.

She hammered on the door. A small panel flipped open, sending cold blue light streaming around her. "Yeah?"

"Pterodactyl, man."

"Name?"

"Nadine."

The panel slammed shut. A moment later, the door slid partway open with a metallic shriek. She squeezed through into a small room paneled off with temporary partitions. A gaping doorway in the far wall led into a dark tunnel. A large, barrel-chested man in stained work pants and a leather vest glowered at her. Black and red tattoos, jagged and spiky, decorated his neck, spread across his chest. He folded his arms. "You a cop?"

"You know cops don't have to tell you if you ask, right?"

"So are you?"

"Do I look like a cop? No, I'm not a cop. Jesus."

He slid a flat black paddle from his belt. Nadine raised her arms. He grunted as he ran it along her body. An all-clear hologram flashed green. He tucked the paddle away and produced a small flat rectangle of grease-stained white plastic, chipped on one corner. "Thirty." Nadine pressed her thumb to it. He waved her toward the dark opening, eyes already drifting past her. "Have fun."

She made her way through a tunnel of heavy black felt draped over corroded metal scaffolding. Beneath her feet, cracks spiderwebbed through stained concrete. She pushed through the curtain at the end of the makeshift corridor, strobing multicolored light washing over her. The center of the warehouse had been mostly cleared of junk, leaving an open space for a makeshift dance floor, jammed beyond reasonable capacity with twisting bodies. Along one wall, a bank of gasoline-burning generators purred, venting exhaust through holes chopped in the corrugated metal. Tangles of thick cables ran to an elaborate mixing deck, where a man in a gaudy sequined trench coat swayed back and forth, eyes half-closed, running practiced hands over the controls. Lasers sliced the air around him. Banks of colored spotlights swept the center of the warehouse, where the eager crowd danced in eerie silence among abandoned pieces of heavy equipment.

Nadine's implant chimed. Words appeared in her vision, floating ghostlike over the surreal scene. "Signal found: d4nc3p4rty0602. Accept?"

"Yes," she said.

Music poured through her, thumping bass and deep, driving percussion. The warehouse lit up with brilliant cartoon animals floating in hallucinatory color over the heads of the dancers: a white unicorn with long eyelashes and a rainbow-colored tail cavorting obscenely with a grinning hippopotamus as a menagerie of animated squirrels, foxes, and chickens leered. "Get you something, hon?" came a voice at her arm.

Nadine turned. The voice belonged to a slender woman, dark skin and dark eyes, black hair that fell in multiple rows of braids to her waist. She wore a leather miniskirt and spiky stiletto heels that still didn't bring her as high as Nadine's shoulder. Loops and whorls of fluorescent green decorated her bare chest. "Get you something?" she repeated. "Beer? Whiskey? Vodka?"

"Vodka sounds good."

"Eighteen."

The woman held out a blank white square. The edge lit up green when Nadine touched it. "Be right back, hon." She disappeared into the gloom and returned a moment later with a small plastic cup. "Enjoy."

Nadine wandered farther into the warehouse, watching dreamlike figures dance beneath the sweeping lights.

"Heyyyyyy." A gangly, blond-haired kid, barely old enough to shave, appeared grinning at Nadine's elbow. Long, waxed ribbons of hair in blue, green, orange, and red hung over his face. "P-p-p-party supplies? I have it all. Latest designer empathogens from D-d-doctor Happy hisself. Uppers, downers, synthetic cannabis analogues, anything you want."

"What's your name?"

"T-t-terry."

"Terry. I'm Nadine. Got any Strake?"

"Yeah!" His eyes, pale blue somewhere behind the hair, lit up. "How much you want?"

"Depends. Is it good?"

He looked hurt. "Only the best for my c-c-customers."

"Then you won't mind showing me."

Terry pulled a fat wad of plastic strips dotted with little blisters from the pocket of his baggy jeans. He sorted through them, untangled a strip, and shoved the rest back in his pocket. From another pocket, he produced a small black cylinder with a lens on one end and a row of buttons up the side. He peeled open the strip and shook out a bright pink pill flecked with green. A smiley face printed in black ink stared back up at him. Intense green light shone from the end of the tube. A moment later, a hologram appeared over it, lines on a grid showing spectral peaks. Nadine nodded. "How much for two?"

"Sixty. Cash only."

Nadine pushed a handful of crumpled bills at him. He handed her the naked pill and another just like it, still trapped in its plastic blister. Nadine tucked the plastic-wrapped pill in her pocket and let the other dissolve on her tongue. The vodka chaser burned her throat. She closed her eyes and let the music envelop her.

The drift came on slow, like a warm fuzzy blanket gently drawn over her, smooth, no jitters. Only the best, just like Terry promised. Rainbows swirled behind her eyelids. Drumbeats thumped in her head, tinged with blue and green. She stood for a time, swaying gently while the music swirled through her.

When she opened her eyes, a vision of beauty floated before her, so aching her breath caught. She danced with sensual grace, tiny LEDs woven through her long black hair, pulsing with the beat of the music. Her black dress clung to her like a second skin, faintly shimmering in the roving spotlights. Complicated straps crisscrossed her back, exposing sweat-glossed skin.

Nadine flicked off the feed. The music stopped. The pornographic cartoons overhead evaporated without a trace. She watched the woman dance in uncanny silence, captivated by her effortless grace. The woman turned, hands over the top of her head, moving to music Nadine could not hear. Their eyes met. In slow motion, the woman reached out to take Nadine's hand. Her skin buzzed when they touched. "I'm Anna."

"Nadine."

"Nadine." Anna draped an arm over Nadine's shoulder. Laser light slashed the air around her. "Dance with me, Nadine."

Nadine switched on the feed. The music folded around her like an old friend. She closed her eyes and let it carry her, following in Anna's wake.

They danced for hours through a shifting tapestry of light, heat, scent, and sound. They spiraled in toward each other, closer and closer, until Anna's body moved against her, sweat-slicked and sensual. Nadine drifted away into a soft haze, where nothing existed except the music in her head and Anna's skin warm against hers. The LEDs in Anna's hair glittered, edged with hallucinatory color. Electric currents raced along Nadine's skin. By the time the Strake started to recede, releasing her as gently as an outgoing tide, most of the crowd had already cleared out.

Anna led her to a small round table of battered gray metal flanked by two rickety folding chairs, where she plopped down gracelessly, panting. Nadine sat beside her. "I saw you looking at me," Anna said.

"I'm sorry. I know it's rude to stare."

"I'm not." Anna regarded Nadine with heavy-lidded eyes. "Wanna trip with me?"

"I—sure."

Anna took a round pink pill from a compact metal case. She placed it on the tip of her tongue, then leaned across the table to kiss Nadine, slipping tongue and pill between Nadine's lips. The pill disintegrated on Nadine's tongue.

The kiss stretched out to eternity. When it finally ended, Anna ran her fingertips over Nadine's arm. Nadine's skin glowed at the touch.

"You kiss nice," Anna said. "If I blow in your ear, will you follow me anywhere?"

Nadine caressed her face. The warehouse tilted to one side, edges blurring. "You're so beautiful."

"That's the drugs talking."

"No, I mean it."

"Aww." Anna nuzzled her hand. "You're sweet. Stay here. I'll be right back."

Nadine leaned back with her eyes closed and turned up the music until it pounded through her. Seconds or hours later, she wasn't sure which, a hand caressed her shoulder. Nadine opened her eyes. "Where did you go?"

Anna held up a long plastic strip. Eight small pink pills lay trapped within. "Party favors. I'm taking you home with me. Cab's on the way."

The room fuzzed around Nadine. "I told my roommate I'd be home tonight."

"Is he going to mind if you stay out?"

Nadine shook her head. "She. Olivia."

"Olivia. That's a pretty name. Would you rather go home to Olivia?"

Nadine gazed into Anna's face. The LEDs wreathed her in a shimmering, unearthly glow. "No."

Anna took Nadine's hand. Red and green lasers strobed across her skin. At the curtain, the server in the miniskirt stepped up to her, body paint glowing under the lights and the second dose of Strake. "Here," she said, handing Anna a hoodie printed with dozens of cartoon faces, mad grins beneath large eyes.

"Thanks, hon." They embraced warmly. Anna pulled on the hoodie and slipped the hood over her head.

"Friend of yours?" Nadine said as they made their way back through the fabric tunnel toward the door.

"Ex-lover. That bother you?"

"Just curious. She's cute."

They waited outside as a battered black Tesla made its cautious way up the alley, lights blue-white in the gloom. The front wheels whined as it inched between the storage containers and the sheds. It stopped in front of Anna. The rear doors popped.

They climbed into the grubby back seat, upholstery cracked and torn. The cab was old enough it still had a full-size steering wheel and a complete dashboard in the vacant driver's seat. A cracked screen lit up on the scratched Plexiglass divider between front and back. "LA transit police investigate all reports of Booker cab vandalism," the cab warned in a bored synthetic monotone. "Vandalism may adversely affect your Booker score. Acceptance of transit implies assent to these conditions."

Anna and Nadine mashed the "Accept" button. "Thank you," said the synthetic voice. The doors closed. The cab rolled backward down the narrow alley, retracing its path.

Anna was in Nadine's arms in an instant. Her lips touched Nadine's, warm and soft. "Think anyone ever looks at the camera logs?" Nadine said.

"If they do, let's give them something worth watching."

They made out on the stained upholstery, hands roving unfamiliar bodies, until the cab pulled up in front of a faded cookie-cutter mansion surrounded by near-identical twins, monuments to bland conformity. Potholes littered the street like bomb craters. The sounds and smells told Nadine the ocean was not far off.

The doors popped open. "Nice place," Nadine said, looking up at the balcony a story overhead.

"Used to be, until the storm. After that, nobody could get insurance any more. Banks called in their loans, lot of people lost their shirts. Whole neighborhood sat empty for, what, four years, something. Developer came in, bought all the houses for pennies on the dollar, divided 'em up into apartments, home sweet home." She presented her eye to a scanner in the door jamb, then fiddled with a heavy-looking deadbolt.

"Anna." The voice came from the darkness behind them.

"Night off," Anna said without looking up.

"Sorry." A man stepped out of the shadows, dressed, like Anna, in a dark hoodie printed with lolling cartoon faces. Beneath the hood, Nadine got a quick glimpse of dark-colored goggles. "Here." He handed Anna a fat manila envelope tied closed with thin red string. "Who's your friend?"

"Nadine," Anna said. She unwound the string and looked inside the envelope. "Nadine, Dan-boy. Dan-boy, Nadine. We just met."

"Pleased, I'm sure. Can I talk to you?"

"If you must." Anna gave Nadine a quick kiss. "Make yourself at home, darling. I'll be right in."

Lights flicked on as Nadine slipped through the door. She found herself in an expansive living room, peaked ceiling two stories above her head. A crudely-fitted gypsum-board wall divided it rudely in half. Paint peeled from the decorative trim along the edges of the ceiling. In one corner, a cheap IKEA desk held a sleek, top of the line laptop surrounded by three large holographic monitors, all rendering different pastel screensavers. A soldering iron sat atop the desk in its spiral holder, a set of precision screwdrivers and a fiber optics tap beside it. Voices drifted in from somewhere outside, his angry, hers placating.

After a while, the voices softened to some sort of resolution. Anna came in and locked the deadbolts behind her. "Sorry."

"Boyfriend?"

"Ha! He wishes."

"Ex-boyfriend?"

"He'd need to be a boyfriend first." She tossed the envelope onto the desk, where it skidded to a stop against the curved foot of one of the monitors. Neatly-banded bundles of cash slid out. She draped her arms over Nadine's shoulders. "Where were we?"

"Right here, I think." Nadine kissed her lower lip.

Without breaking the kiss, Anna half-led, half-dragged Nadine through a door that hung slightly askew in its ornamental frame into a large bedroom with a vaulted ceiling. A battered fan with wide black blades rotated slowly overhead. She pulled Anna down onto a huge, rumpled bed, scattered with unmade sheets and old clothes. Wherever they touched, Nadine's skin buzzed. "Come into my parlor, said the spider to the fly," Nadine murmured.

"Hmm?"

"Nothing."

Their lips met again. Electricity crackled. Anna hooked one leg around Nadine's and pushed her off-balance. Nadine thumped down onto her side, flailing. In an instant, Anna rolled atop of her. Nadine pressed a finger to Anna's lips. "Aren't we moving kind of fast?"

Anna's eyes searched her face, pupils enormous under the effects of the hallucinogen. "You prefer the slow approach? Casual meetings separated by periods of longing? Furtive glances over restaurant tables? Gradual accumulation of erotic tension, building up to explosive release in one wild night of unrestrained carnality?"

"When you put it like that," Nadine said, "it sounds like a lot of work."

"My thoughts exactly. Now come here."

NADINE WOKE THE next morning to an empty bed. Cheerful humming floated in through the open door. She searched around for her tank top, pulled it on, fished her panties out from between the bed and the wall, and followed the sound.

She followed oddly-shaped hallways, their geometry distorted by the ruthless carving of the house, into a spacious, well-appointed kitchen.

Another unpainted gypsum-board wall chopped the kitchen in half, extending from the counter to the far wall, bisecting an island appointed with a granite countertop that had probably once been expensive but now looked somewhat tawdry.

Nadine leaned against the door and watched Anna go about fixing a simple breakfast of eggs and bagels. She'd unwound the LEDs from her hair, which now fell loose around her shoulders. Anna moved with uncommon grace, body hard beneath a simple lace teddy of white silk. She hummed to herself as she worked. "Hi!" she sang when she noticed Nadine. "Can I get you anything? Coffee? Tea?"

"You're beautiful."

"You're still high."

Nadine held her hand in front of her face. A faint blue glow crackled around her fingers, chemically induced St. Elmo's fire clinging to her skin. "True. But in a few hours I'll come down and you'll still be beautiful."

"Aww." Anna lowered her gaze coquettishly. "You don't have to, you know."

"Have to what?"

"Come down. I brought plenty of supplies."

"What if I want to explore you without chemical help?" Nadine stalked into the kitchen, where she trapped Anna against the half-island in a cage of her arms. "What about that, hmm?" She kissed the tip of Anna's nose.

Anna blushed. "Aren't we moving a little fast?"

"If you like," Nadine said, "we can try furtive glances across a restaurant table. You might have to explain how to do that, though. I'm not sure I've ever been furtive."

"Who has that kind of time?"

Several hours, two toasted egg sandwiches on bagels, and uncounted orgasms later, they lay together on the bed, tangled in poly-silk sheets. Anna stroked Nadine's cheek. "Nadine," she said. "Isn't that French? You don't look French."

"No?" Nadine propped herself up on one arm. "What do French people look like?"

"You know what I mean!"

"My mother is French Canadian. My father is Chinese. Hong Kong, not mainland. He ended up in Vancouver, BC after the thing, then in Montreal after Vancouver flooded. Met my mom there."

"How'd you end up down here?"

Nadine laughed without humor. "How does anyone end up here? I wanted to be a movie star. Gotta come to LA to be a movie star, right? That or Bangalore, and I don't speak Kannada. My father helped me swing a work visa. Easy to fix if you know who to bribe. He told me it would be the last thing he'd ever do for me until I gave up this foolishness and came back. Haven't talked to him since."

"Did you make it in Hollywood?"

"No. Damned if I'm crawling back to tell him that, though." She rolled over onto her back and studied the ceiling, peeling paint above the dusty fan. "What about you? How did you end up..." She waved an arm at the room around them.

"Ah, well, see, that's complicated." Anna rose and wrapped a bathrobe around herself. "You want some coffee? I want some coffee."

"Was it something I said?" Nadine wondered aloud to the empty room.

2

Economy of Motion

OLIVIA RAISED AN eyebrow. "You're home late."

Nadine stood blinking in the doorway to the small apartment. The battered screen door slammed shut behind her with a metallic rattle. "What time is it?"

"Tuesday. It's Tuesday."

"Ah. Right." She blinked again, running absent fingers through tangled hair. "I suppose it is, isn't it?"

"Did you call off work yesterday?"

A slow, irrepressible smile spread across Nadine's face. "Yeah, I did."

"There's a funny smell coming from your room."

"Ah. Sorry." Nadine squeezed past Olivia into her small, untidy room. The smell came from a bowl of hammered copper on her dresser, filled with the sludgy remains of oranges gone fuzzy. She bowed to the black and white photograph in its battered frame behind the bowl, a young woman smiling unselfconsciously at the camera from beneath an ornamental hat many decades out of style, before she carried the bowl to the kitchen. She dumped the decaying fruit into the compost, then carefully washed the bowl. Olivia followed her into the kitchen. "Did you have a good time? Is she hot? Tell me everything!"

"I, um...I did, yeah."

"What's her name?"

"Anna." Nadine rolled the word around in her mouth, savoring it. "Anna."

"So dish it, girl! When do I meet her? What's she like?"

"She's beautiful. And she smells like heaven. And I need a shower, and maybe a nap. She didn't let me sleep. Went in to work today totally ragged." She looked down at herself. "I hope nobody noticed I was in the same clothes I wore on Friday."

Olivia snorted. "Nobody cares what you wear. That place you work, they barely know you're a person."

Nadine fished several new oranges from a plastic net and arranged them in the bowl. Olivia followed her back to her room, where Nadine genuflected three times to the photograph before she restored the bowl to its proper place. She lit a match, cupped the flaring thing in her hand, touched it to a stick of incense. Sweet-smelling smoke drifted up from the orange glow. She placed it in front of the photograph and bowed again. Olivia frowned. "Kinds seems like idolatry, the way you give offerings to that picture."

"Says the woman who wears a necklace of Saint Leonard around her neck," Nadine said without turning around. "You Catholics know all about the idols, hey?"

Olivia glowered. "You should not blaspheme against the saints or the Holy Spirit."

"You shouldn't talk about my grandmother." Nadine slipped into the cramped bathroom with its rust-stained tub and faded shower curtain decorated with wavy lines, where she stripped out of the clothes she'd worn for three days and closed her eyes beneath a spray of hot water.

Olivia poked her head through the door. "So what does she do, this Anna of yours?"

"Dunno. Something with computers, I think."

"She's not a narc, is she?"

"Pretty sure she's not a narc."

"How do you know? You can never be too sure."

"She gave me some Strake."

"That's how they do it. It's called entrapment. You're far too trusting."

Nadine rolled her eyes. "She's not a narc."

"If you get arrested, don't come crying to me!"

"Olivia," Nadine said, "if I get arrested, I promise you'll be the last person I'll call."

Nadine floated through the next week, and the one after that. Anna's smile drifted in her wake. Her life split, two separate tracks that felt, almost, to belong to two separate versions of herself, parallel-universe Nadines with little in common, one who moved through a world of underground dance parties and carnal excess, the other who lived in a place of corporate drudgery. The workdays blurred, tedious tasks for tedious people, placeholders between the weekends, when she came alive, dancing with Anna in dingy, abandoned spaces while lights strobed around her and Strake softened the world.

Olivia became the gatekeeper between the real world and her strange, surreal underworld, sending her off Friday evenings with "Have fun! Get laid! At least one of us should," then greeting her on Sunday night or, more often, Monday morning with a mix of surly snarkiness, well-concealed concern, and inquisitive probing into what new things Nadine had learned of Anna.

The man, Dan-boy, made himself absent. Nadine learned not to ask what Anna did for a living, as any question, however delicate, invariably sent Anna away somewhere else, somewhere cold and distant where Nadine was not invited.

She learned her way around the strangely bifurcated house, or at least Anna's part of it, which became, if not a home exactly, at least somewhere comforting and familiar. The part Anna lived in included what had once been a luxurious master bath, dominated by an absurdly oversized tub with water jets in it, some of which still worked. Heat and humidity had corroded the edges of the mirror over the fancy pedestal sink. "You should see the other side," Anna told her the second weekend she'd spent there, as they lay together in the tub. Anna ran her fingers down Nadine's back. "Bathroom's the size of a closet. Nice stove, though."

Bit by bit, a slow accretion of Nadine's things accumulated in Anna's space, like the detritus left on a beach at low tide. Each time Nadine visited, she arrived with more than she left with. Olivia, alarmed by the drift of Nadine's worldly possessions, started making noises about legally binding rental agreements. "Relax," Nadine grumbled one Monday morning. She hadn't slept the night before, her head hurt, and the prospect of another day of purposeless office work filled her with a sense of sick dread. "I'm still paying rent. You get the best of both worlds. My money and the house to yourself."

"She must be some piece of ass," Olivia said.

"You jealous?"

"Just feeling like a hotel maid these days. The weird smell from your room is back!"

Olivia's prodding lingered in Nadine's mind as she lay with Anna weeks later, Nadine on her back staring up at the fan that circled slowly overhead, trailing cobwebs and dust, Anna curled on her side beside her. Street hallucinogens lent a slight rainbow shimmer to the edges of the fan blades, a tiny edge of surrealism that could, almost, make Nadine believe she was dreaming. Outside, an uncharacteristic rainstorm hammered against the window. The air conditioning wheezed as it struggled to keep the muggy heat at bay. "How would you feel," Nadine said as Anna's finger traced small circles around her nipple, "about me moving in here with you? Officially, I mean."

"Isn't that awfully clichéd?"

"What?" Nadine frowned.

"You know the joke. 'What do two women bring on a second date? A U-Haul.'"

Nadine rolled on her side to face Anna. "I have no idea what you're talking about."

"Maybe it's an American thing."

"Maybe you're high."

"Maybe *you're* high."

"Maybe I am, but I'm serious." Nadine touched Anna's face. Faint colors swirled around her fingertips.

Anna's expression went blank. "I don't think that's a good idea." Nadine's heart plummeted. "Oh, darling, don't look at me like that," Anna went on. "It's not you. It's...my life is complicated."

"Maybe it wouldn't be so complicated if you didn't shut me out!"

Anna shook her head, lips pressed tight together. "At least let me think about it. This...this is a big thing for me."

"For me too!"

"All the more reason to think about it." Her expression softened. "Look, I'm not saying no, okay? I just need to process some things."

Despite Anna's reluctance, Nadine's possessions accumulated in Anna's house, drawn there by the gravity of their mutual attraction. Slowly, gradually, without any acknowledgement from either of them, Nadine spent more and more of her time in the decaying mansion by the sea. The last thing to make the move was the portrait in its frame, the woman out of time frozen in a moment of unguarded joy. "I guess it's official," Anna said when Nadine placed the bowl in front of the portrait on the nightstand.

"I'm still paying rent to Olivia," Nadine said, a trifle defensively.

Anna laughed. "Oh, darling. Welcome home."

Weeks later, Nadine woke to lingering dreams of Montreal, memories of a carefree childhood spent swinging in the park a few blocks from the sprawling suburban house where she grew up. She hadn't appreciated, then, her father's wealth, or the luxury it afforded.

She rolled over. Anna was already awake, as usual, regarding her with eyes made luminous by the morning sun slanting through the window. "Good morning!" Nadine said. "You're beautiful."

"You say that every morning."

"It's true every morning." She pulled Anna close, burying her face in her neck. "How did I get so lucky to find you?"

"You say that every morning, too."

"Not every morning. Only on mornings you're here."

Shutters slammed behind Anna's eyes. "We agreed we won't talk about—"

"Shit, I'm sorry. I didn't mean it like that. I just meant I'm grateful for the days I wake up with you. You don't need to tell me anything you don't want to."

Things had changed since Nadine moved the portrait, and therefore her sense of home, into the shabby mansion. The window, for one. Nadine had cleaned away a decade's worth of grime. Anna complained, in a faux-grumbly kind of way, about the light it let in. "The better to see you with, my dear," Nadine laughed. They eventually compromised on filmy blue curtains that sent ripples of sunlight across the bed.

The bed, too, changed. It was far too large for one person. Anna had developed the habit of using half of it to store assorted piles of laundry. After Nadine moved in, dirty laundry ended up on the floor where it belonged.

Anna rose and rummaged through discarded clothing on the floor, eventually settling on a pair of panties in neon pink and a pale blue chemise that had seen better days. Nadine settled back in a mound of pillows and watched her. Anna did everything with an economy of motion that made even the simplest actions look like a dance. She caught Nadine looking at her. "What?"

"Just you."

"Breakfast? Coffee?"

"Both."

Nadine showered and dressed. She lit a stick of incense, placed it in front of the photograph, and bowed three times to the faded memory of a woman. That done, she wandered into the weirdly bisected kitchen, still pulling a black sleeveless tank top over her head. Anna had already laid out a couple of plates: bright pink sheets of thin-sliced fish of some sort on toasted bread. The smell of coffee filled the air. "Mm, this looks wonderful." Nadine nuzzled Anna's neck. "Positively good enough to—"

A loud crash from the front of the house interrupted her, followed by a frantic thumping that rattled the door in its frame.

Anna tensed, still as a praying mantis, head cocked just a little. Then, in a sudden flurry of motion almost too fast to follow, she flashed out of the kitchen. In one graceful turn, she yanked open a narrow closet full of sheets and heavy winter blankets, slid a small, nasty-looking handgun from beneath a pile of linens, and crouched by the door.

Nadine followed after her. "Anna—"

"Get down." Anna gestured without looking. More hammering at the door.

"Anna—"

"Down!"

Anna flipped the deadbolt. She spun in eerie silence, bringing the gun up before the knob started to turn.

"Anna—"

The door slammed open. Three people stumbled through, all wearing gaudy hoodies, hoods pulled up in defiance of the oppressive heat. Nadine caught a quick impression of faces obscured by strange, angular makeup, stark jagged lines of black and white, splotches of bright color. "Jesus, Dan-boy, you scared the shit out of me." Anna lowered the gun. "I almost blew you away. What did I tell you? Never bring anyone here. Never."

"Got no choice." Dan-boy glared at Nadine. "What's she doing here?"

"Guess you aren't keeping up. She lives here now." A groan dragged her attention away from him. "What's going on?"

"Marcus. He's hurt bad."

Dan-boy and a woman Nadine didn't know, thin and gangly with fluorescent pink hair beneath her hoodie, rolled a short dark-haired man onto his back. The front of his hoodie had been shredded, leering cartoon faces torn apart. Blood flecked his T-shirt. Nadine blanched and looked away. "What happened?" Anna said.

Dan-boy shot a side-eyed glance at Nadine. Marcus convulsed. Blood oozed from hair-thin flechette darts sticking from his chest like spines on a cactus. "For fuck's sake," Anna said. Marcus howled, a desperate, keening sound of raw agony that raised the hairs on the back of Nadine's neck.

The pink-haired woman spoke up. "We were up north. Combined Chemical Supply. Heard stories, something new." Dan-boy glared at her and gestured, hand across his throat. She shook her head. "Security saw us. Shot at us. Thought it was a tear gas grenade, maybe, something, but..." She jerked her head toward the wounded man writhing on the floor, his face contorted into something almost inhuman beneath the strange patterned makeup.

Nadine touched one of the fine spikes protruding needle-like from his chest. Fiery pain lashed through her, blinding in its ferocity. She snatched back her hand with a scream. "What is it?" Anna said.

"It burns!" Nadine's face flushed. She fell as if axed, curled around her hand. "It's like fire!" Her voice rose into a cry of agony. "Oh, God, it hurts!"

"Let me see." Anna knelt beside Nadine. She forced her to uncurled her fingers, contorted into a tight fist. A tiny splinter glinted in her index finger.

Nadine pushed her away. "Don't touch it!"

Anna grabbed her purse, a cheap knockoff of a designer brand popular three years ago, from behind the bedroom door and dumped its contents to the ground. She sorted through the junk—department store cosmetics, a crumpled packet of tissues, a tangle of plastic hair bands in bright neon colors—until she found a compact nail kit. With fumbling hands, she fished out a pair of tweezers. "Give me your hand."

It took three tries to pluck the sliver from Nadine's finger. Marcus convulsed on the floor beside her. Anna fished around the pile of junk from her purse until she found a small bottle of over-the-counter painkillers. She dumped them out, small red pills scattering on scuffed hardwood. The sliver went in the bottle in their place. "Does it still hurt?"

"Yes!" Nadine cried.

The pink-haired woman stepped back, staring at the mess of Marcus's chest. "If one sliver does that..."

"We need to get him to a hospital," Anna said.

"No," Dan-boy said.

"Look at him!" Nadine said through clenched teeth.

"Out of the question. No hospital."

"Dan-boy." The woman whose name Nadine didn't know spoke in a flat, tight voice. "I don't think you fully appreciate the situation." Nadine examined her for the first time. A hardness lurked in her eyes, incongruous in her waifish face.

Marcus howled, an animal cry stripped of all humanity. For the first time since they'd burst through the door, Nadine forced herself to look at him. He was young, maybe four years younger than Nadine. Eyes of dark brown, open and staring sightlessly at the ceiling as if the solution to his pain lay hidden in the peeling paint. Dark hair cropped close to his skull. His hands, twisted into claws, curled in what was left of his shredded rock band T-shirt. Blood smeared his chest, but Nadine saw no major wounds, just a sea of small, glittering thorns protruding jagged from his skin. He screamed again. The sound pierced her, a raw cry of agony like nothing she'd ever heard before. "I'm calling an ambulance."

"No!" Dan-boy's face flushed with rage.

"You brought him to my place," Anna said, arctic chill in her voice. "I told you, but you did it anyway. He needs a hospital."

"But—"

"My place, my rules. Shouldn'ta brought him here if that isn't what you wanted. I'm calling the ambulance now." Her lips moved, subvocalizing to her implant.

"No ambulance. I don't want him traced back here. Call a cab. We take him ourselves."

"Fine." Anna's eyes went glassy for a moment. "Cab's on the way. Nadine. Bandages in the bathroom. Get them. Scissors, too. Lena, help me get him on the sofa. Dan-boy, watch for the cab."

Nadine retreated to the bathroom, grateful to be out of the room with the screaming man and the smell of blood. She fumbled through the large medicine cabinet, edged with curlicues in tarnished bronze. A bottle of alcohol tumbled into the sink. She found the roll of bandages and scissors, grabbed a tube of antibiotic for good measure.

Lena helped Anna cut the scraps of shirt from Marcus's chest. Marcus spasmed, screaming like someone possessed. A sleepy voice came through the crude wall, somewhere above them: "Everything okay down there?"

"Yes!" Anna called back. "Everything's fine." She pulled the last scraps of Marcus's shirt away. His skin bristled with needle-thin slivers. "I don't know what to do," she said. "I want to bandage him, but—"

"Cab's here," Dan-boy said.

"Nadine. Get his feet. Help me get him into the car. Nadine!"

Spurred by the sharpness in her voice, Nadine grabbed Marcus's feet. His foot slammed into her sternum, knocking the wind out of her. Pain flared in her hand. The cab waited for them in front of the building, once-black paint faded to dull gray, filmed over with dirt and years of saltwater spray. Numbers on peeling yellow squares clung to the bumper. Nadine and Anna wrestled Marcus into the back seat.

"LA Transit police investigate all reports of Booker cab vandalism," the cab said. "Vandalism may adversely affect your Booker score. Acceptance of transit implies assent—"

"Fine!" Anna mashed the button on the glowing touchscreen. "Who's going with him?"

"I'll go," Dan-boy said.

"Good." Anna backed out of the cab, leaving a thin smear of blood on the door jam. The smooth mechanical "chunk" cut off Marcus's cries. Electric motors whined. The cab sped away.

Anna sagged. Lines of tension appeared around her eyes. "Lena. Wanna tell me what the fuck is going on?"

Over the next two hours, as Nadine wrapped her hand in bandages, fragments of the story emerged. Nadine pieced together some kind of surveillance thing, but for who or what, she wasn't clear. "Combined Chemical Supply," Lena said. "They're a contractor. They make riot gear for police and military, tear gas, less-than-lethal weapons, shit like that. Stun batons, tasers, flash-bangs. You wanna fuck up someone's day without, you know, actually killing them, they're your one-stop shop. We heard a rumor they had something new. Sat and watched for days. Found a place just outside the perimeter, saw a bunch of trucks going in at odd hours, big tankers."

"Why?" Nadine said through gritted teeth. Waves of pain seared her with each heartbeat. "Why were you even there?"

Anna's eyes unfocused. Her lips moved. "Dan-boy says he dropped Marcus off in front of the emergency room and hightailed it out. I'll need to fix the taxi logs."

"Dan-boy, he said he wanted to get a closer look," Lena went on. "Thought he saw a way over the fence, place where the guards couldn't see. Said it would be easy."

"Something went wrong?" Nadine said.

"Fuck yeah, something went wrong. Fucking drone spotted us. Tiny, no bigger'n your palm. Didn't see it until it was too late. Next thing we knew, security all over us. One of them shot Marcus."

"With what?" Anna said.

"Dunno. Only saw the result. He screamed like his soul was being ripped out of his body, went down right where he stood. We grabbed him and ran."

"Did they follow you?"

"No. Let us go."

"Weird," Nadine said.

Lena shrugged. "Bureaucracy is the ultimate persistence hunter, you know? You think you've gotten away, week later, year later, they show up on your doorstep."

"Think they got your IDs?"

"We were wearing scramblers, dazzle, the whole thing. Who knows? Probably not. You know how it is." Another shrug. "Arms race. They make better recognition AI, we make better countermeasures. Game goes on."

"Dazzle?" Nadine said.

Lena touched her face. "Confuses facial recognition. Breaks up lines and contours and such. They got clever for a while, used infrared, looks right through the patterns, sees the contour underneath. This stuff, it's new, got some kinda metal flakes in it, something, I dunno. Confuses IR."

Nadine abruptly bent over double, keening, holding her hand protectively. Anna touched her shoulder. "What's wrong?"

"My hand is on fire! Feels like the sliver is still in there. Did you get it all?"

"Let me look." Anna took her hand, forced her fingers to unclench. The skin was smooth and unmarked. "There's nothing there. Think it's poison or something?"

"I don't know!" Tears of pain glistened in the corners of her eye.

"Whatever it is," Lena said, "Marcus got a chest full of it."

3

Your Girlfriend is a Criminal

FTER LENA LEFT, slipping furtively into the late afternoon sunshine, Anna fussed over Nadine like a protective mother hen. Nadine grumbled as Anna wrapped her hand and pressed a cold pack into it. "How's it feel?"

"Like someone's jabbing me with a hot needle," Nadine said. "Little electric shocks. Like nothing I've ever felt before."

"Maybe the hospital will figure something out."

"Maybe."

"Got something I gotta do."

"What do you—"

"I don't have a lot of time." Anna rose and sat in front of the expensive computer atop the flimsy particle-board desk. It came to life, holographic displays hovering in front of her, sectioned up into little windows scrolling rows of cryptic information.

"What are you doing?"

"Let me work. Please."

As Nadine watched, Anna's hands danced over the machine. She muttered to herself, lips moving. Glyphs strobed across the display almost too fast to see. Nadine imagined them as sorcerer's incantations, unreadable by anyone without the right training, calling up strange and forbidden powers...

A new panel appeared on the screen, a grainy fisheye view of the inside of a taxi, Marcus lying on the back seat convulsing, mouth open in a silent scream; Lena holding his hand; Dan-boy looking grim beneath his dazzle makeup. A faint rainbow fringe surrounded the edge of the view, distortion from a cheap plastic lens. The time glowed in the lower left of the image.

"Here it is. UCLA Medical." Anna's fingers danced. The video vanished, replaced with a blank black rectangle with "FILE NOT FOUND" in white letters in the center.

Her fingers danced again. Logs scrolled by: times, dates, pickup locations. One by one, they vanished behind labels of FILE NOT FOUND. About ten minutes later, she hit a switch on the edge of the computer and rose. Flowing screensavers rippled across the monitors. "There," she said. "Best I can do."

"You hacked the cab company?"

"Yeah. Long time ago, actually. Left myself ways in for exactly this kind of contingency. You'd be surprised how handy it is."

"What about the cab? Won't Marcus's DNA be all over it?"

She shrugged. "Nothing I can do about that. But there's a lotta cabs in LA, lotta DNA. Would take a long time and a pile of money to test 'em all. And they'd have to know what they were looking for."

Nadine curled her hand into a fist. "Ow."

"We should get you to a hospital, too."

"I think it's time you tell me what's going on," Nadine said. "Whatever it is, you can trust me."

Anna's lips pressed together in a tight line. "It's not about trusting you!" Something flared in her eyes, gone too quickly to recognize. "You're the best thing to happen to me in a long time. I'm not trying to protect me from you, Nadine, I'm trying to protect you from me."

"So explain it to me."

Anna closed her eyes. "Okay, listen. I met Dan-boy two, maybe three years ago. We had some connections in common. I was hustling, selling electronic intrusion, data hacking, that sort of thing. Also other stuff. Moving money too. Lot of that." She shrugged. The movement against Nadine, the feel of Anna's warm skin on hers, set a shiver through Nadine's body. She shoved the thoughts away, irritated. "Anyway," Anna went on, "guy I knew said hey, this guy he knew was into something, might want to pay for my services, was I interested?"

"A guy you knew," Nadine repeated flatly.

"Yeah. Your girlfriend is a criminal. Sorry. You can probably guess the rest. I did a job for him. Easy work, paid well. After, he asked me if I wanted more. I said yes. Been doing jobs for him and his crew ever since."

"So what is he? Like, organized crime?"

Anna laughed without humor. "Nothing that simple. You familiar with the PRG?"

"The Peace Resistance Group? Yeah, I've heard about them. You're a Peacer?"

"I'm a hacker. Dan-boy and the others, they're Peacers."

"You work for terrorists?" Incredulity tinged Nadine's voice.

"I work for a lot of people. But yeah, I work for the Peacers, if you can call them terrorists."

"What else would you call them?"

"Kids, mostly. Idealistic kids on a crusade." Tiny lights danced in Anna's eyes. "Speaking of. Hey." Pause. "Taken care of." Pause. "Goddamn right I'm sure, how long we work together?" Pause. "Okay." Her eyes cleared.

"Dan-boy?"

"Yeah. Wanted to make sure I took care of the taxi records."

"Listen, we need to talk."

The shutters had already gone down behind Anna's eyes. "No. The less you know about what I do, the better."

"Okay." Nadine touched her shoulder. "I'm in this with you, one way or the other. When you're ready to talk, I'm ready to listen."

"How's your hand?"

Nadine flexed her fingers. Little shocks of pain jolted up her arm. "Feels like touching a live electrical wire. Starting to fade a bit."

"We should get you to a hospital—"

"I'm fine."

THE CRY OF gulls dragged Nadine from her sleep. At high tide, water raged at the seawall right behind the house, sending crashing spray against the window. Even at low tide, the ocean was always there, patiently nibbling away at the edge of the doomed row of crumbling mansions. Soon, Anna had told her, the water would start rising over the seawall when the tide came in. City planners kept talking about building the walls higher against the encroaching ocean, but the money never materialized.

Nadine called a cab, lips moving as she subvocalized to her implant, then dressed and made breakfast. Anna, already up, sat naked in front of her computer, damp hair wrapped in a towel. Her fingers flew. Windows appeared and disappeared on the holographic displays too fast for Nadine to follow. Nadine didn't bother trying to talk to her. When Anna worked like this, she'd go hours at a time without acknowledging Nadine, lost somewhere in a world of abstracts.

A soft beep from Nadine's implant told her the cab waited for her outside. She waved in Anna's general direction. "Heading to work!" she called. Anna didn't respond.

The cab deposited Nadine at the foot of the bland glass tower where she worked. Generically sleek company ads shifted across wide plate glass windows. The moment she closed the door, the Tesla slotted with mechanical precision into the early-morning flow of traffic and was gone. A compact, vaguely dog-shaped robot trotted by, painted LAPD blue. White italic letters on its side read "To Protect and To Serve." The black barrel of a sniper rifle jutted from its snout, just below the dark glass lens of night-vision optics. Overhead, a FedEx drone carrying a large canister descended toward the receiving platform that jutted from the top of the building, lights blinking. Far above drifted the vast black bulk of a police surveillance platform. Oppressive heat hung heavy and humid in the air, covering Nadine's body with a thin film of sweat.

The moment she stepped into the lobby, a blast of Arctic air from the laboring air conditioning system turned the sweat chill. She flashed her badge at a bored security guard behind an enormous U-shaped desk of off-white Formica and rode the elevator to the thirtieth floor. The noise and bustle of a sprawling cubicle farm, identical compartments with identical desks and identical computers as far as the eye could see, washed over her.

"...don't care what he says," an angry voice raged. The angry voice belonged to an angry man in an angry shirt with thin blue pinstripes, sweat-stained despite the best efforts of the air conditioning. "Tell him payment's due on the first or I'll have his ass in a sling on the second." He snapped his fingers at Nadine. "You. Coffee. And bring me the lease agreements for Sunnyside." Tiny lights glittered in his contacts.

He stomped off between rows of cubicles. Nadine sighed, shook her head, and made her way to the cramped break room stuck as an architectural afterthought between a broom closet and a bank of air handlers for the servers on the floor below.

Eight hours and two minutes later, Nadine stepped out into the early evening heat. Mirages shimmered above the pavement. The surveillance platform had moved on and was now nowhere to be seen, but small delivery drones bustled about picking up last-minute packages before the offices closed.

She summoned a cab. Less than a minute later, a battered black Tesla with a cracked headlight purred up to the curb. The back door popped open. Nadine slid across the scuffed seat. The car pulled into traffic with a faint whine. Its climate control battled the heat to a barely-tolerable stalemate. "Stop," Nadine said, leaning forward abruptly. "Change of plan."

"Do you wish to change your destination?" the cab asked.

"Yes. UCLA Medical. Take me there."

"Booker is not liable for passengers in need of medical attention. Should you require urgent care, please exit the cab and call 9-1-1," the car said primly.

"I don't need medical care! I just want...never mind. Just take me there."

"Change of destination requires fare modification," the cab informed her. "Please indicate your assent to the new fare."

"Fine!" Nadine mashed her thumb on the screen. She settled back on worn leather and watched out the window as the cab navigated itself through traffic. There was a mathematical precision to the flow, a mechanical correctness unruffled by the vargarities of human drivers with human emotions. The car whisked her calmly through the shabby streets lit by the harsh yellow glare of the merciless sun.

They pulled up in front of the hospital. The car made its way to a cab stop. "Wait for me," Nadine said.

"Waiting incurs charges as explained on the screen. Failure to return within twenty minutes without releasing the cab may adversely affect your Booker score. Exiting the vehicle indicates assent to these conditions," the car said in its bored synthetic monotone.

"Fine. I'll be back. Wait here."

The hospital lobby smelled of antiseptic and stale sweat. Cameras in every corner kept a watchful eye on the people huddled around uncomfortable molded plastic chairs in institutional green. A large ceramic pot squatted in one corner, holding a mournful-looking plastic ficus with a bent stem, artificial leaves fluorescent green beneath LED panels. A security guard in a black bulletproof vest looked her over with lecherous eyes. Nadine glared at him until he scratched his ear and looked away.

She shuffled behind the line waiting to talk to the nurse, acutely aware of time passing and the cab waiting in the parking lot with its meter running. Eventually, she found herself face to face with a man in a rumpled white lab jacket that looked slept in. "Can I help you?" he said in a disinterested monotone.

"I'm here to see a friend. He would've been brought in yesterday afternoon."

"Name?"

"Marcus."

"Last name?"

"I—I don't know."

The man sighed. "You don't know your friend's last name? Do you know his Booker ID at least?"

"No."

"I see." He gazed levelly at Nadine until she looked down. "What do you know?"

"His name is Marcus. He came in yesterday afternoon with a chest wound."

"That's something, I suppose." The man's eyes grew vacant. He stared at a point past her shoulder, lips moving slightly. Nadine fidgeted. Finally, he returned his attention to her. "No."

"No I can't see him?"

"No, he isn't here. Nobody with a first or last name of Marcus or Mark or Matt or anything like that has been admitted in the last 48 hours for any reason. Definitely not with a chest wound."

"There must be some mistake. I know he's here. Can you look again?"

"No."

"Please!" Nadine said. "I know he's here, he must—"

"Your friend is not a patient at this hospital. There are people waiting behind you."

"But—"

His eyes went vacant again. The security guard started forward from his corner. "Fine," she said. "Thanks for your time."

She left the hospital under the watchful eye of the security guard. The cab unhooked itself from the charger and popped its door at her approach. She gave it the address and slumped in the seat as the hospital disappeared behind them.

Back home, she found Anna sitting in the living room winding a cold compress around her hand. Anna waved. "Hey, lovely! You're home late today."

"Yeah. Stopped at the hospital to check on Marcus. They say nobody with that name has been admitted."

"You asked about him at the hospital?"

Nadine blinked. "Yeah, is that a problem?"

"I don't know. Maybe." Anna sat and rolled her chair in front of the cheap IKEA desk. The computer came to life. Glyphs glowed and danced across the monitors. Nadine held her breath.

A few moments later, Nadine watched a fuzzy, jerky image of herself waiting in line in the shabby reception room, shuffling toward the nurse behind the counter. The screen froze. A window appeared over it. Lines of text scrolled across.

"He's right, Marcus's not in the admissions log," Anna said, more to herself than Nadine. "Huh. Hello, what's this?"

"What's what?" Nadine said.

"Deleted record."

"Does that mean—"

"I need to focus."

Nadine watched as Anna played the machine, muttering under her breath to herself. "I wonder if they deleted it from the backups, too. Let's just see..." Her fingers flew. "Internal cameras, they're recorded on a different system. How thorough are you guys?" The information on the monitors changed too fast for Nadine to follow. Anna's eyes glittered, tiny bursts of light from her lenses writing data directly onto her retinas.

Nadine watched over her shoulder for a while. Anna seemed unaware of her, lost in whatever world she retreated into when she worked. Information flickered across the screen, too fast to follow, feeding directly into Anna's implant somehow—Nadine didn't understand how Anna did what she did, or even what it was she did.

Eventually, boredom drove Nadine into the bifurcated kitchen. She rooted around in the refrigerator and was midway through assembling a roast beef sandwich when things went sideways.

"Nadine." Anna's voice cut through the air, sharp and cold. "Pack some things. Now."

"What—"

"Move!" The word exploded from her, driven by a flat sense of urgency Nadine had never seen before. Nadine bolted. Somehow, Anna beat her to the bedroom, already moving with the same eerie, surreal grace that had taken her when Dan-boy made his unexpected appearance at the front door with Marcus. She looked like a video played at the wrong speed, frame rate screwed up, dancing across the room with her face set in an expression of absolute calm, every motion precise but too fast by half.

"What's going on?"

"Pack a bag. Only what you need. Clothes. Cash."

"For how long?"

"Assume we aren't coming back."

"I don't unders—"

"*Move!*"

Nadine jolted into action, prodded by the sharp urgency in Anna's voice. She shoveled a handful of clothes at random from the bedroom floor into her travel suitcase. Her keys, several boxes of disposable contacts tuned to her implant, her meager collection of jewelry, and her passport followed them in. She zipped it shut and wheeled it out to the living room, where Anna had collected a duffle bag from the closet, already packed and ready to go. The hilt of a compact pistol protruded from the back of her jeans.

The thin wail of distant sirens drifted in on the humid air. Anna cursed. "Out of time. Stay with me." She pressed her thumb against the computer on the desk. The rolling screen savers on the monitors flickered out. Something hissed and spat. Smoke curled up, carrying the acrid smell of burnt electronics. She grabbed Nadine's arm and dragged her out the back toward the seawall. Behind them, the sirens grew louder.

"Close," Anna muttered. She unlatched a long box of black fiberglass bolted with stainless steel straps to the cracked concrete wall. A black bundle lay wadded up inside it. She pulled a red cord. The bundle started to unfold with a loud hiss. A short curved steel ramp jutted from the seawall over the angry, stormy water below. Waves lashed at concrete. Salt spray beaded in Nadine's hair. Anna shook her head. "Gonna be close."

"What are you doing?"

"Get down!"

Tires squealed out front. Nadine heard shouting voices, followed by a dull *thunk thunk thunk*. A row of metal balls about the size of her fist rose over the top of the house. They froze impossibly in midair at the peak of their trajectory, then spread out like glittering birds of prey. "Fuck," Anna said.

The black bundle unfolded itself into a long wedge shape in front of Nadine's eyes. Overlapping plates slid into place in the bottom. Nadine heard glass shatter from the direction of the house, followed by two ear-splitting explosions. She clapped her hands to her ears. "They're shooting at us!"

Anna shook her head. "Flash-bangs." The hissing stopped. The black bundle finished expanding into a long, narrow boat with a rigid floor and inflatable sides. Anna grabbed Nadine's hand. "In!"

"But—"

Anna seized Nadine's jeans and flung her bodily into the boat. Three men trotted around the side of the house in a tight group, shadows in black riot gear and helmets. "Over here!" one of the men called. "You! Stop!"

Anna half-leapt, half-crawled into the Zodiac after Nadine. She tugged frantically at a thick knotted rope that lashed the end of the boat to a steel ring on the ramp. The knot resisted her. One of the three men knelt and leveled his rifle at them. The other two came fast, flanking the sides of the boat.

The rope came free. Nadine's stomach lurched. The boat slid down the ramp. Behind them, she heard a sharp series of shots, earsplittingly loud. She screamed. Then they were falling, plummeting toward the water below.

They hit with a sickening impact that flung Nadine from the boat. Her vision went black. Water closed around her. She forced her way to the surface, still clutching her suitcase, gasping and choking. A second volley came from above and behind her. Something small and fast struck the water around her.

Nadine caught a handle on the side of the Zodiac with one hand. Her bag dragged at her. Anna folded down a compact electric motor and hit the throttle. The boat leapt forward as if kicked. Nadine spun around, her face smashing into its rubber side. Her arm screamed in agony. She inhaled a mouthful of seawater and coughed violently. Bullets carved bubbling channels in their wake.

"Hang on!" Anna cried. The tiny boat bounced across the waves, each jarring thud threatening to rip Nadine's arm from its socket. The shoreline fell away.

Anna didn't slow until they were far enough out they could no longer make out the men on the seawall. The Zodiac bobbed when she cut the motor. Anna dragged Nadine aboard, exhausted and coughing. The skin on Nadine's hand had been rubbed raw where she clung to the handhold. Her arm shrieked pain at her. She dragged her small suitcase aboard. Her fingers refused to unclench from its neoprene-coated handle. "Are you okay?" Anna said.

Nadine choked violently. Her eyes stung with salt water. She nodded.

"Good. We're not out of this yet. Look." She nodded. Overhead, a fan of drones raced out toward them, forming a net of gleaming silver balls across the harsh blue sky, each drone a small round ball at the corners of an array of hexagons.

Anna slammed the throttle. The Zodiac jumped as if kicked. The drones raced after them, the hexagons growing larger as they sped out to sea. "We can't outrun them!" Nadine said.

"We don't have to. They're part of a mesh network. Each one relays information to its neighbors, then on to their neighbors. We just have to get out far enough the mesh can't reach the shore."

"What happens then?"

"Right now, they'll be retasking a surveillance platform. That takes time. Twenty minutes if we're lucky, ten if we're not. Until then, they'll want to keep an eye on us. So they'll be taking measures to stay in contact with the drones."

"What measures?"

"There." Anna pointed. Nadine followed her finger to where something glinted in the sky. "Communications hub. Powerful radio, big batteries. That'll let them stay in touch with the drones until they can task a platform and get some boats out here."

"What are we going to do?"

"Take it down."

Anna turned. As she did, she seemed to speed up. She moved with the easy grace of a ballet dancer, drawing the gun from the back of her jeans in one smooth motion as she spun toward the oncoming drone. She stood still as a statue, waiting, arms outstretched, holding the gun in both hands in front of her, her body still as a statue as the Zodiac rocked beneath her.

"Anna—"

"Not now."

The drone grew closer. The hex grid overhead rippled as the smaller drones moved out of the way. The large drone came closer, six arms extending from around a flattened body, a small propeller on the end of each one. Nadine could see stubby antennas sticking from its upper side.

Anna held her breath. She held her aim at it, unmoving. Nadine's nerves jangled. "Anna—"

The gun roared. The drone exploded into a thousand fragments. Instantly, the neat hexagonal pattern above them collapsed. The small drones swirled in a long funnel that swooped almost to the water and then climbed again, reminding Nadine of a flock of starlings. "What happened?"

"They're cut off. We have a few minutes."

"Why are they doing that?"

"Fallback routines built into their firmware. They have no command and control link, so they revert to flocking behavior, keep from crashing into each other or piling into the ground. You don't want to lose a whole cluster of drones just because they've been disconnected from the network." She shoved the throttle. The Zodiac darted forward. "If we're really lucky, and we don't make any mistakes, we might wake up tomorrow outside of a prison cell."

Nadine lay on her back, fingers still clutched around the handle of her small suitcase, clothes and hair soaked with salt water, shaking violently as the adrenaline ebbed. Her shoulder screamed at her. She felt a bruise rising where her face had planted against the Zodiac. Anna did not speak as she piloted the Zodiac in a broad arc parallel to the shore. Nadine stared up at the featureless blue sky. The drones looped and swirled aimlessly without pursuing them.

Eventually, Anna cut the small motor. She unzipped her bag and stowed the gun inside. "Give me your terminal," she said.

"What?" Nadine shook her head. Her clothes clung to her body, the saltwater already starting to itch. Her hair hung down in her eyes. The last dregs of adrenaline made her shaky. She stared at the swirling cloud of drones without comprehension.

"Your terminal. Can I see it?"

"Um, sure." Nadine fished the compact portable computer from her bag.

"Thanks." Anna dropped it on the bottom of the boat and stomped on it. Jagged shards of polycarbonate scattered across the floor.

"Anna!" Nadine gaped at her. "What the hell are you doing?"

"Keeping us out of prison." Anna tossed the terminal overboard. It sank with a dull splash. "Look, I'm really sorry. Contacts too. And any other electronics you have."

Anna knelt in front of Nadine's bag and rummaged through it. The contact lenses followed the computer into the water. Nadine's watch, a gift from her mother, was the next to go, stomped flat and thrown overboard. "Anna! Stop! Anna!"

Anna touched Nadine's cheek. "I am so, so sorry. You've been kind to me, and now I have ruined your life."

"Anna, what's going on? Talk to me!"

Anna shook her head. She unzipped her duffle bag and pulled out a round loop of metal attached to a handle studded with switches. "Hold still."

"Anna, what are you doing?"

Anna raised the loop to Nadine's head. "I promise this won't hurt."

"Anna! What—"

Anna pressed a button. Nadine heard, or felt, a sensation like a heavy ringing of a bell, so low she could only barely perceive it, then a sudden absence, as though a sound that had whispered in her ear for so long she'd stopped paying attention to it suddenly ceased. "Anna, what have you done?" she cried.

"I've disabled your implant."

"Anna!" Nadine said. "Stop!" Tears blurred her vision. "You have no right! What are you doing? You destroyed—destroyed my—"

Anna caught her up in a close hug. Nadine beat her hands on Anna's back as she wept. "I'm so, so sorry," Anna murmured. "This is my fault. I wish I could go back in time, stop you from getting involved in all this. With me."

She held Nadine while Nadine screamed and raged, until eventually Nadine's cries spent themselves into small quiet sobs. "We have to go," Anna said. "We don't have much time." Nadine sat shivering in the bottom of the boat, clutching the handle on her bag, as Anna revved the tiny electric motor.

Anna sat silent in the back of the tiny boat, piloting them in a broad arc that curved until they roughly paralleled the shore. Merciless sun beat down on her. Every bounce and jolt sent a blast of salt spray into her face. Nadine stared numbly at the water sloshing in the bottom of the boat. Without her implant, she felt cut off, some vital part of herself torn away. She could not call anyone, could not summon a cab or look up directions, could not make notes, could not record or replay what happened around her.

The sun hung low when Anna finally steered them toward the shore. "Hang on. This might get a little rough." She revved the engine and pointed the boat toward the shore. A deluge broke over the bow as they plowed through the surf. The small boat skidded onto the beach, scattering tattered scraps of seaweed. Rotted stumps of palm trees jutted from gray sandy dirt. Anna hopped out and offered Nadine her hand. "Take off your clothes."

"What?"

"Here." Anna zipped open her duffle bag. "Put these on." She pushed a nondescript T-shirt and dark jeans into Anna's hands. "Your clothes are wet. This too." She handed Nadine the hoodie she'd worn the night they met. Cartoon faces leered at her.

"It's too hot."

"Wear it anyway. It confuses facial recognition."

"Anna—"

"Crash course in your new life as a fugitive. Part one, cameras. You'll need to learn to hide your identity. Dazzle, camouflage, confusing clothing. The cartoons register as faces to facial recognition AI. Put it on. Keep the hood up."

Nadine dressed in silence. Anna took her wet clothes from her unresisting fingers. She threw them into the Zodiac and hauled out her duffle bag and Nadine's sodden suitcase. She stripped down to her underthings. "I'll be back in a bit."

"Where are you going?"

Anna put her hands on Nadine's shoulders. "I think I've always known this day would come. For a while there, I'd hoped..."

"Hoped what?"

Anna shook her head. "It doesn't matter. You don't need to stay. There might be a way out for you, I don't know. If you can convince them you weren't involved, you didn't know anything about my life..." She shrugged. "Your parents are rich, right? They can afford good lawyers. There's only one way forward for me. That might not be true for you." She placed an achingly gentle kiss on Nadine's lips. "If you aren't here when I get back, I'll understand."

She pushed the Zodiac back into the water, then paddled after it. Nadine watched her go without expression. Once she'd passed the surf, she climbed into the boat and gunned the engine. The Zodiac vanished into the setting sun.

Nadine sat heavily on her suitcase. Salt water squished around her. A breeze blew in from the ocean, heavy with the smell of things that lived and died in the sea. Anna receded until she was a dark dot in the distance.

Nadine sat sweltering in the early evening heat, feeling a yawning chasm opening beneath her. She wrestled with her impulse to flee, turn herself in, find some way to make the black-uniformed police and the people behind them believe that she wasn't part of whatever Anna was part of. Her eyes swam. The tears came on slowly but implacably until her chest heaved with wracking sobs. She wept until her nose ran and her eyes turned red and raw, huddled into herself on that open shoreline. Several times she stood to go, and several times she stopped, slumping back onto the suitcase to wait.

Beyond the line of surf, the tiny black dot of the Zodiac bobbed, still and silent. Anna arced gracefully into the water. Nadine's heart hammered. She held her breath, waiting for Anna to surface. Her chest ached. In the distance, the boat seemed to sag as it collapsed in on itself.

An agonizing eternity later, Anna's head broke the surface of the water. She swam back toward shore with strong strokes, and hauled herself onto the seaweed-strewn beach.

"What did you do?"

"Bought us some time." Anna stripped, opened her bag, and dressed quickly. She shrugged into a dark-colored hoodie decorated with random bars, lines, and splotches of color. "I slashed the boat. It should drift for quite a ways. It'll take them a while to figure out where we came ashore. They might even assume we drowned." She grinned without mirth. "Not that I expect to be that lucky. Come on, let's go."

"Where?"

"You wouldn't believe me if I told you."

Scary Ninja Shit

NADINE DRAGGED HER suitcase up the beach behind Anna. The wheels dug into soft sand and jammed on scraps of half-rotted seaweed. Eventually, they found a dirt trail that gave way to pavement. They walked until long after sunset, along cracked and potholed streets fronted by decaying convenience stores. Windows papered over with flickering holographic ads flashed with color, hidden behind black iron bars and thick layers of overlapping electronic graffiti. Weed-choked lots yawned in the gathering gloom, littered with wrecked cars and unidentifiable bits of rusted metal. Infrequent streetlights cast small pools of blue-white light separated by long stretches of growing shadow.

"Keep your hood up and your head down," Anna said. "Don't look at any cameras. Don't look up. There aren't usually drones or surveillance platforms out here, but you never know. Take longer steps."

"What? Why?"

"Behavioral gait analysis. It's still not very good, lotta false positives, but they use it when they can't get a facial match. Try not to walk the way you normally do."

"You're serious."

"Yes."

The shadows grew longer. Light spilled out onto the darkened street from the open door of a dingy, one-story bar. Flickering neon advertised cheap beer. Dark shapes moved in the gloom. Raucous laughter drifted into the hot, humid air. A wolf whistle came out of the darkness to their right. A dark figure paced them across the street. Another fell into step behind them. On the other side of them, another figure matched their pace. Nadine took Anna's arm. "Anna..."

"I see them. Get behind me." Anna walked faster, muscles tense, face grim. She slipped one hand into the front pocket of her hoodie.

The figure to their right whistled, a shrill sound that pierced the night. He altered course to intercept them. "Hey, *chiquitas*!" he said. "Looking for a good time, hmm?" The figure behind them sped up.

Anna stopped, so abruptly Nadine nearly ran into her. She unslung her duffle bag and let it fall to the ground. "No," she said quietly. "I'm not looking for anything you have to offer."

"Aww, you sure?" He stepped close, his stained white muscle shirt reeking of stale sweat. "You haven't given us a chance!" His dark eyes flicked from under a tangle of greasy black hair toward his friends, who closed in on them from all sides. "You look like you need friends, out here all alone. I think we can be friends. Would you like to be friends?"

"No." Menace edged her voice. "Look, I've had a really bad day, and I'm not in the mood for your bullshit. Why don't you do us all a favor and just fuck off wherever you came from, okay?"

"We'll make your day better, won't we?" the man said. Sweat clung to massive arms.

The figure behind them grabbed Nadine by the arm. He stank of beer. He licked Nadine's face. Nadine's stomach knotted. "Anna—"

"Okay," Anna said. "Okay. We'll do it your way, then." She rocked forward on her feet like a dancer. "Let's see what you've got."

"Ah, now that's more like it," muscle-shirt guy said. "Now just relax, and we'll go easy—"

Anna drew her hand from her hoodie and spun, fast and graceful as a professional boxer. She flicked her wrist. A rod flashed out, three nested cylinders of spring steel telescoping silently, and caught the man holding Nadine across the side of his head. He staggered, cursing, and released her. Anna spun, diving low beneath muscle shirt's fist. The rod in her hand flashed again, catching his knee with a sickening crunch. He screamed as he fell.

"Ah, ah, ah. You shouldn't have done that." The third man pressed the barrel of a small black handgun to Anna's head. "We might have taken it easy on you, but now..." He licked his lips. "I'm going to enjoy spreading your brains all over the street." Muscle shirt cursed and swore on the ground in front of her.

Anna raised her hands slowly. "Listen, before you kill me," she said, "there's something you should know."

"Yeah?" He glanced behind Nadine. "What's that, honeydew?" The man behind Nadine chuckled.

"Guns are ranged weapons." Anna blurred into motion. A brilliant flash split the dark. An explosion staved in Nadine's ears. She clamped her hands to her head and screamed. The club sliced the air. Another scream joined Nadine's.

The spots in front of Nadine's eyes faded. Anna stood eerily still, holding the gun in one hand and the spring steel club in the other. Two would-be attackers lay on the ground. The third considered the new odds, then turned and fled.

Anna spat at muscle shirt. She stood over him for a moment, as if considering what to do with him. He shuffled backward away from her, face white.

"Let's go!" Nadine said. "Let's get out of here!"

Anna nodded. The tension drained from her. "Yeah." She picked up her bag and kicked muscle shirt in the ribs. "Your lucky day. My girlfriend doesn't want me to kill you." He curled into a ball. She stepped over him. "Come on." She took Nadine's hand and led her away from the two men.

As the adrenaline drained away, Nadine staggered. Her body shook violently. Her ears rang. "Anna, where are we going? What's happening? They tried to kill us!"

"Tried," Anna said. "Failed." In the darkness, her face looked hard, almost inhuman. She collapsed the club and slipped it into her pocket. As they walked, Anna ejected the magazine from their would-be attacker's gun and flicked the cartridges one by one onto the pavement. She flung the empty magazine into an empty lot, ejected the last round from the chamber, then with a few quick motions disassembled the gun and tossed the pieces aside.

"How did you do that?" Nadine said.

"I got lucky."

"Anna, I was there. That wasn't luck. That was scary ninja shit." Nadine stopped dead in her tracks. "Who are you?"

"You know who I am!"

"No, I don't."

Anna sighed. "You know the important parts. I love you. I'm still the same person I was yesterday."

"I don't know—"

"This isn't the time or place for this. Please, trust me just a little bit longer, okay? We're almost there."

"You won't even tell me where we're going! Why won't you tell me anything?"

Anna caressed Nadine's face. "Just a little while longer. I promise."

Nadine followed Anna silently along the crumbling asphalt road. The groans of their would-be assailants faded behind them.

They walked until Nadine's feet ached. Her hair dried into a salt-crusted tangle around her face. The suitcase dragged at her arm, wheels frequently catching on cracks and potholes. Her throat burned. Anna stayed in front of her, one hand in her pocket, hood up over her head, bag slung over her shoulder, tense and alert. Off in the distance, a thin trail of fire rose from ground to sky, a suborbital passenger rocket on its way to New York. It lit up the clouds for a few moments, so remote and unreal it might have come from another world.

Fatigue dragged Nadine down. She stumbled after Anna, gradually moving slower and slower. Anna made no effort to hurry her. Finally, Nadine stopped beneath a streetlight. Insects chirped around her. The muggy air clung to her, stifling beneath the absurd hoodie with its printed faces. Sweat pooled beneath her borrowed clothes. "Anna, I can't keep going."

"We're almost there. Just a little bit farther."

Nadine staggered a few more steps. "I'm sorry, Anna. I can't."

"Okay." Anna scanned the street. On one side, the graffiti-sprayed, steel-shuttered faces of a row of closed shops lurked in the shadows between the intermittent streetlights, garishly bright ads just visible around the edges of the shutters. On the other, an auto repair shop squatted behind a chain-link fence. A glowing yellow sign read "A&J CHE P AUTO R PAIR U BREAK IT WE FIX IT" in peeling black letters. Rust-stained gasoline-powered cars clustered like crows behind the fence. "Listen. Just one more block, okay?"

"Okay."

They set off once more, slower this time. The promised one more block became two, then three, before Anna found what she was looking for. "Wait here. I'll be right back."

Nadine dragged her suitcase to the curb and sat on it. Anna disappeared through the door of a small convenience store wedged between a closed pizza shop and an RV park with a hand-painted "No Vacancy" sign. A shrill electronic chime announced her entrance.

She came back a few moments later with a plastic bag. Inside, Nadine found a box of granola bars, an energy drink, and bottles of water. "I got you some coffee, too," Anna said.

Nadine's heart melted. "Thank you. You're the best."

Anna's face tightened. She looked away. "If that were true, I would never have dragged you into this."

"I'm in this with you. Whatever this is."

Anna shook her head, lips pressed tight together.

Nadine sat on the curb and drank two bottles of water, one right after the other. She was halfway through the coffee and several granola bars when a large man with a pot belly barely contained by a dark polyester shirt with a corporate logo embroidered near the collar stuck his head out the door. He peered down at where Nadine sat, the darkening bruise on her face obvious in the light of the shifting ads. "You ladies okay? You need help?"

"We're fine," Anna said. "Let's go."

Nadine reached for the time. The gaping void where her clock should be reminded her she'd been separated from her implant. She forced herself to her feet. "Lead on, white rabbit."

The moon had set when they reached their goal. Anna stopped in the shadows of a derelict industrial park, broken windows gaping holes into long-abandoned buildings. A massive concrete wall a block in front of them blazed with light from a row of floodlights on tall, spindly metal towers that rose like skeletal fingers from cracked asphalt. Ramshackle wood buildings sprouted like fungus above the wall. "Tijuana town."

"What?"

"We'll be safe there. Safer, anyway." Anna adjusted her duffle bag. "Maybe. I hope."

She set off across a vast parking lot, now mostly empty, toward the wall. Weeds pushed up through fissures in the asphalt. A row of cars clustered in a neat line near the wall, elaborate paint jobs gleaming in the harsh lights. A handful of electric cars sat in the line, but most of them seemed to be antique gas-burners, lovingly restored and cared for. Some of them bore the hallmarks of self-driving conversions: small, discreet sensor pods tucked into the immaculate bodywork, tiny mesh antennas projecting just above the windshields.

A road led through a wide opening in the wall, closed by a steel gate on a long metal track. Two cameras over the gate glared down at them. A heavily tattooed kid dressed in black, scarcely older than sixteen, rose from a battered folding chair at their approach. "¿Que pasa?" he said, one hand not quite touching the sleek black semiautomatic tucked in his jeans.

"Just lookin' for a place to crash, man," Anna said.

He shook his head. "No room at the inn."

"Look, I've had a day you just won't believe, and I am not in the mood."

He spread his hands. "Maybe you come back later."

"Maybe you want to reconsider and let us in."

He folded his arms. "Why would I do that?"

"Because," Anna said, "I can be pretty persuasive." She leaned forward and whispered in his ear.

"Why didn't you say so before?" he said. "Hey, welcome to Tijuana-Town."

"So we have a deal?"

He stuck out his hand. Anna shook it. He whistled, a shrill sound that tore the night. The gate rumbled and clanked, sliding aside just far enough to let them through. Anna slung her bag over her shoulder. "Thank you."

"Welcome," the kid said as they walked through. "You ladies have fun."

"What did you say to him?" Nadine whispered as they passed through the gate.

"I told him I have a hundred dollars in my hand."

"Do you?"

"Not anymore."

On the other side of the wall, they found an open courtyard fronted on two sides by warehouses and on the third by a long building made of cinder block almost completely hidden beneath layers of graffiti. Light streamed out through large openings with metal doors rolled into the ceiling. Cacophony slammed through the air, half a dozen different bits of music competing with the clang and buzz of machines. Nadine flinched as the noise washed over them.

Ramshackle wood structures sprouted from the roofs of the warehouses, supported where they overgrew the edges by long pilings that reached to the ground. A complex web of wood and steel staircases, some covered by slanted plywood roofs and some open to the elements, clung to the hodgepodge façades. Narrow catwalks with wooden rails spiderwebbed overhead.

In the open space between the buildings, a beat-up gasoline-powered panel van that had once been white but was now a uniform shade of grime sat incongruously next to a gleaming, brand-new electric pickup. A little further on, a group of four women in brightly-colored plaid shirts that hung open over halter tops huddled around a firepit made of cinder blocks, chatting loudly in Spanish as they cooked something in a large cast-iron pot. Their conversation died when they saw Anna and Nadine.

Another boy of perhaps sixteen materialized out of the darkness. He wore all black, with a black ballistic vest over the top despite the sweltering heat. He carried a handgun in a holster at his side. "Mayor wants to see you."

"Now? It's three o'clock in the morning! I was hoping to bed down, maybe talk to him in the morning—"

"Now," the boy said.

"Fine. Nadine, wait here for me."

"Her too," the boy said.

"Look—"

"It's okay," Nadine said. "I'm here with you. If this guy wants to talk to us, let's talk."

"Leave your bags here," the boy said.

Anna tensed. "I'd really rather not."

"I'd really rather you did."

"If anything goes missing—"

"Nobody going to mess with your stuff." He leered at them.

"That's how it is, huh?"

"That's how it is."

Anna unslung her bag and dropped it to the ground. "Leave your suitcase," she told Nadine.

"But—"

"Leave it. If things go smoothly, it will still be here when we come back. If they don't, it won't matter."

A younger boy in black, perhaps fourteen years old, appeared like a ghost from the shadows. His ballistic vest hung from his shoulders, two sizes too big. Silhouettes drifted along the roofs of the jumbled pile of crude buildings above them. "Follow me," the boy said. "Bossman's in the penthouse."

They followed him up a steep metal staircase clamped to the side of one of the warehouses with crudely welded brackets. At a small landing made from what looked like a metal grille salvaged from a storm drain, Nadine saw a Plexiglass window fitted into a hole in the warehouse. Inside, the walls were painted in a two-tone color scheme, teal on the top half, burgundy on the bottom. Framed photos covered the walls: the Blessed Virgin, pictures of people Nadine didn't recognize, symbols that meant nothing to her. On the other side, four men played cards around a wobbly table with a leg that had been broken and repaired with duct tape. All wore sleeveless shirts, bare arms covered in elaborate, colorful tattoos. Music thumped out of the room, a woman singing in Spanish to a driving percussive beat. One of the men saw her and pulled a faded curtain over the window. The kid gestured impatiently. "Come on."

They climbed to the flat roof of the warehouse, where a sprawling conglomeration of crude makeshift structures had grown over time, accumulated piecemeal as the needs of the residents changed. Nadine heard indistinct voices through the plywood walls. Smells of food cooking, stale coffee, and a heavy odor like the combination of sweat and unwashed laundry drifted on the muggy air.

Their guide pulled open a heavy steel door in a plywood wall that opened directly into a staircase, carpeted with worn red carpet that had clearly seen better days. Naked LED panels screwed to the plywood walls cast a harsh blue-white glow.

They trudged up the steps, surrounded by the smells of plywood and old carpet and too many people living too close together, until at last they came into a small, boxy, windowless room with an ornate door of carved oak embedded incongruously in the far wall. The same red carpet covered the floor. An enormous, muscular man sat in a folding chair at a desk much too small for him, attention focused on the pieces of a large handgun spread out across the desk. His long hair and beard were braided, once black but now going salt and pepper. He wore black pants and a scruffy black sleeveless shirt. The chair creaked as he rose to his feet. He picked up a wand and gestured to Anna without a word.

She stood with her arms apart. He ran the wand around her body. It squealed. A glowing red X floated in the air in front of it. Anna reached slowly, two-fingered, into the pocket of her hoodie and pulled out the telescoping club and a rugged knife with a folding blade. She reached behind her and passed over the compact black handgun. After he took them, he wanded her again. With a grunt of satisfaction, he did the same to Nadine. When he'd finished, he sat back down. "What now?" Nadine said.

"Now we wait," Anna said.

The man turned his attention to the pieces of his gun, cleaning them with practiced motions. When he finished, he reassembled it and shoved the magazine into place with a satisfied grunt. Anna stood as calm and still as a statue. Nadine fidgeted. Her feet ached. Her eyelids dragged down.

Finally, after what felt like an eternity, the man looked up. "Mayor will see you now." Without standing, he reached out and opened the door.

The room beyond was, by the standards of what Nadine had seen so far, opulent. Polished oak paneling covered the plywood walls. A window to the right looked out into darkness. Rich red carpet in much better shape than what was outside covered the floor. An enormous desk filled half the room, so large Nadine wondered how they'd managed to get it up here, its surface gleaming beneath antique lights in the walls and ceiling. A large computer, several messy piles of paper, and a carbon fiber folding knife covered the table.

A tall, muscular man with a shaved head sat in a high-backed chair with his boots up on the desk. He wore a black leather vest and black BDUs. Tattoos covered his arms down to his hands, his neck, and the sides of his head: a stylized skull with wings, a hooded figure holding a long curved scythe, two nude women with exaggerated breasts kissing. Five black squares had been tattooed above his left eyebrow. Nadine wrinkled her nose.

He flicked open the knife and looked at his fingernails critically. "Anna," he said at last. "Anna, Anna, Anna. *Mi mala.*" He dug under his thumbnail with the tip of the knife. "You look..." His eyes swept her up and down. "You look like shit. What do I do with you, eh? You bring problems to my door."

"I didn't figure you for a low-problem kind of guy, Tony."

"Ah, ah, ah!" He waggled the tip of the knife at her. "Mayor Tony, please." He shook his head. "My life is complicated now. Gangs north and west threatening war, I'm managing our delicate arrangement with the police, the Police Commissioner is always squeezing me for more. My life is nothing but headaches. And you, Anna...what have you got mixed up in? Television says you're a terrorist! You and your *pedazo de culo* here." Nadine bristled.

"You shouldn't believe everything you see on TV," Anna said.

"Anna." A moment passed. Nadine tensed. Then, abruptly, he set the knife down and rose, grinning, arms open. "I'm just fuckin' with you! *Mi casa, su casa*, hey? And your *onna*, too." He embraced Anna warmly, then gave Nadine an exaggerated bow. "Mayor Antonio Delgado, at your service."

"We're in a bit of a bind," Anna said.

Tony gestured expansively. "Nobody comes to T-Town unless they got nowhere else to go. Were you followed?"

"No. We left in the Zodiac just ahead of LAPD SWAT."

"Always the dramatic exit with you. Where's the boat now?"

"Slashed it up and left it to float away. Surface current goes south. They'll find it south of my place, maybe figure we headed that way. Left Nadine's clothes in the wreck. Maybe they'll think we drowned."

Tony snorted. "Uh-huh. When you moving on?"

"I figured when things die down—"

"Ah, Anna, you aren't watching the news! You're a wanted terrorist. You know, secret rendition? Guantanamo Bay? This...this is not something that dies down. I don't want to sound ungrateful for everything you've done for me, especially with the guy in the you-know, but..."

"I get it. We're too hot even for Tijuana Town."

He shrugged, palms up. "Nothing personal. I have responsibilities now. You are free to stay for...shall we say a week? Then I would be grateful if you make other arrangements."

"Tony, man." Anna spread her hands. "You're killing me."

"Best I can do, *chiquita*. Go. Get some sleep. You look like you need it."

Back out in the other room, Anna recovered her knife, club, and gun. The large musclebound man grunted when he handed them over. They disappeared into the pocket of Anna's hoodie. "Keep those there," he rumbled. "Bossman likes you, but not so much he'll let it go if you cause trouble."

The kid who'd brought them upstairs reappeared at some secret signal. "Follow me."

They followed him back out into the muggy evening air. He conducted them along the roof of the warehouse to a bright green door hacked incongruously through a wall of overlapping sheets of plywood. "Mayor's guest quarters," he said. "Home sweet home."

Anna and Nadine found themselves in a small room paneled with cheap sheetrock walls painted in turquoise and green. Brilliant paintings of religious figures hung in gilt-edged frames on the walls. A simple curtain of dark fabric hung over a small plexiglass window. The floor beneath their feet was bare wood. On the far wall, a narrow door opened into a small bathroom with a rust-stained sink and a tiny shower with a leaky showerhead. A large bed and two shabby but comfortable chairs made up the whole of the furnishings. Anna's bag and Nadine's suitcase already sat on the floor.

Nadine sat on the bed, drained and numb. She stared unmoving at the floor for a long time. She was dimly aware of Anna bustling about, unzipping her bag, going through its contents, dragging her suitcase off into a corner, but it seemed remote, disconnected from her. She realized with a sudden aching flash of clarity that the black and white photo in its tiny frame, unique and irreplaceable, still sat on the dresser in the decaying mansion by the sea, the one she would never go back to. The digital copies, stored in patterns of electrical charge on the smashed remnants of her terminal, drifted toward the bottom of the sea, surrendering to entropy.

Nadine's shoulders quivered. Her sobs started slowly, but grew and grew until her body shook. Anna sat on the bed beside her. "Oh, hey," she said. Nadine clung wordlessly to her while she wept until her tears ran out.

SHE DID NOT remember going to sleep that night. She woke, still in Anna's clothes, with the sun streaming around her from the curtain in the small window. Anna lay behind her under the cover, arms wrapped protectively around her. The small, stuffy room felt like an oven in the oppressive Los Angeles heat.

Nadine stirred. Anna came awake with a gasp. She looked around wildly for a moment, then relaxed. Nadine turned to face her. "You're beautiful."

"You say that every day. I don't believe you today."

"Why not?"

"I'm dirty, I'm smelly, and I have salt in my hair."

"You're still beautiful."

Anna looked away. "Do you still feel lucky to have found me?"

"I...that's a big question."

"I feel like a monster," Anna said, voice low.

"Why?"

"Because I ruined your life. Our prospects...well, they're not good. I should have told you. I was afraid you'd leave me, and..." Her voice trailed off.

"Hey." Nadine caressed her face. "I knew something was up with you. I mean, I didn't know it was this, exactly, but I knew something was up. I chose to stay." She rose from the hard mattress. Her back creaked. "I'm hungry. Where do you suppose I can find some breakfast around here?" She frowned. "I'm still not entirely sure what 'here' is. What is T-Town?"

"That's a story."

"So come tell me while I get cleaned up." Nadine stripped out of Anna's clothes and stood beneath a modest spray of room-temperature water, grateful to scrub the salt spray from her body.

Anna followed her into the tiny bathroom. "Brief history of Tijuana Town," she said. "Used to be an industrial park. Closed down when the economy collapsed. Tony was just another gang-banger then, maybe with more ambition than most. He moved in, set up a chop shop, quietly started consolidating his power. Kinda became Switzerland, you know? Neutral in gang politics. People started moving in because it was safer than where they were, and..." She shrugged. "Must be two hundred people call this place home now."

"He said something about cops?" Nadine said as she washed her hair.

"Yeah. He pays them to leave him alone. Truth is, he keeps the peace, so they're happy to do it. Rumor is the LA police commissioner's on his payroll."

"Huh." Nadine stepped from the shower and looked around for a towel. "Um, shit. Well." She shook herself vigorously. Her bangs dripped in her face. "Sounds expensive."

"Probably." Anna took her place in the tiny, rust-stained shower. She washed briskly, then quickly dressed, still damp. She unzipped her bag. The gun went into the waistband of her jeans; the telescoping club went into her pocket. She pulled a hoodie on despite the heat.

"What happens now?" Nadine said.

"We get your implant taken care of, meet with Dan-boy and the others, and figure out what happened to Marcus. First, though, we get breakfast."

5

Anthropology

BREAKFAST TURNED OUT to be problematic.

Anna opened the door to find the same kid who'd escorted them to their meeting with Tony standing outside, hands clasped behind his back. Heat shimmered above the asphalt below them. The gate stood open, and a group of three men pushed a late-model electric car toward one of the bays in the long, low concrete building. The boy turned when the door opened. "Huh-uh. You stay inside. Bossman says so."

"Excuse me?" Anna said.

The boy shrugged. "Sorry, *chiquita*. Orders."

"Are we prisoners?"

"Bossman says you stay inside during the day, you stay inside during the day. Call it what you want."

"So we're supposed to starve?"

"Bossman, he said let him know when you're up. You're up. I just let him know." Another shrug. "Rest ain't up to me."

"What if I try to leave right now?"

The kid shook his head. "Don't abuse Mayor Tony's hospitality." He pushed the door shut.

"Now what?" Nadine said.

Anna flopped onto the hard bed. "We wait. Again."

"Why does everyone call him Mayor Tony?" Nadine asked.

"He fancies himself the benevolent leader of his own little city, I think. I—"

A knock at the door interrupted them. Anna opened it. Tony grinned at her. "May I come in?"

Anna swung the door wide and sat down on the bed next to Nadine. Tony closed the door behind him. "You are settling in well? The accommodations are to your liking?"

"Could do with some air conditioning," Anna said. "It's a bit stuffy in here."

"I am sorry to hear that. I brought you something." He set two paper cups and two plastic bags on the table. "I hope I am not interrupting."

"Anna was just getting ready to tell me how you two met," Nadine said.

"Was she? Ah. That is not as interesting a story as you think."

"Maybe I have unusual ideas about what's interesting."

"More useful to talk about the future than the past, yes? Things are not going so well for you." He spread his hands. "I have to ask, what are you doing, Anna? Where will you go?"

"Oh, I don't know. I was thinking, when this is all over, maybe Nantucket. You know, buy a house, settle down. I hear the weather's nice."

Tony shook his head. "You're not as funny as you think. I don't know if you get it. This is not the sort of thing that is ever over."

"You think I don't know that?" Anna passed one of the bags to Nadine. She opened the other and pulled out a sandwich, limp lettuce and lunch meat on white bread. "Tony, you're acting like you think I have a plan. I don't have a plan. Right now I'm putting one foot in front of the other. There are some things I need to do—"

"What things?"

"Nadine's implant. I've disabled it. I need to change the UUID. Get a new computer. Get new documents for Nadine. Meet with Dan-boy and the others."

"You still running with him? No wonder you're in the shit."

"Yeah, that's me. I associate with the wrong people. Bad habit." She bit into the sandwich. "This whole thing started with Marcus. Tell me something, Tony. You know anything about an outfit called Combined Chemical Supply?"

Tony leaned back and looked at her through narrowed eyes. "Yeah, I know it. They make tear gas and pepper spray for *los cerdos*. What about it?"

"Dan-boy and Marcus were up there. Said something about some kind of new chemical weapon or something, I don't know. Marcus got shot. We took him to the hospital. Next thing, he's snatched and LAPD SWAT drops by for coffee."

"So you think whatever got you on the wrong side of a terrorist warrant, it goes back there?"

"Yeah, I think it goes back there," Anna said around a mouthful of soggy sandwich. "I got a feeling if we find Marcus, we find the source of all our suffering. But I can't do that locked inside this room."

"*Mi mala,* you are not locked inside."

"Your boy out there says we can't leave. Your orders, he says."

"I'm just looking out for what's best for you. We have people coming in and out during the day, people who might not respect friendship and family the way I do. Lot of money on your head, Anna, yours and your friend's. Stay inside. Take care of your business at night. Keep out of sight. If there is anything I can do to make your stay more comfortable, just ask." He rose. "If you will excuse me, I must attend to business."

"You could maybe bring us something better than a shitty sandwich," Anna said. "And a towel would be nice!" she called after him as the door closed.

"Do you think he was telling the truth?" Nadine said.

"About what?"

"A reward for us."

"Probably."

"Will he turn us in?"

Anna shook her head. "Tony? I don't think so. He has some weird but strong ideas about honor, and no love for cops."

"Yeah, but he thinks of himself as a mayor now."

"Mm."

"What do we do?"

"Wait for Dan-boy. Take care of your implant. If he turns us in we're fucked, so might as well not sweat it, right?"

"Anna, how do you do it?"

"Do what?"

"Stay calm like this."

Anna smiled a tight, brittle smile. "I'm only calm on the outside. Tonight I need to introduce you to a friend of mine."

"What kind of friend?"

"The best kind. The kind I pay."

A WIRY KID in an ill-fitting ballistic vest arrived just after sundown to escort them. "Keep your faces covered," he said. "Bossman's orders."

Clad in long pants and hoodies, they followed him into the evening heat. He brought them down the spidery framework of stairs to the concrete building with its noise and lights. They passed through a large steel roll-up door into a long garage where people swarmed around four cars, three antique gas-burners and one electric, in various stages of disassembly. To Nadine's eye, it seemed a dance of carefully choreographed efficiency. A heavyset woman in stained coveralls caught Nadine's eye and turned away. A half-dozen different styles of music blatted out at them from portable players resting atop boxes and crates, competing with the sounds of air-powered tools. In one corner, a tarp lay draped partway over a car with an angular 1950s shape. Nadine leaned close to Anna. "Why don't they play music on their implants?"

"Not everyone here has implants."

Nadine gaped. "What? Why?" Anna shrugged.

Their escort led them through a curtain made of flat sheets of clear plastic that formed a sort of office and workspace in the far end of the building. A workbench squatted against one wall, groaning under the weight of a huge mound of electronics parts, electric motors, viewscreens, and less identifiable bits of flotsam that overflowed its confines and spilled in heaps on the floor. Battered, dented test equipment Nadine couldn't identify rose like islands from the sea of junk.

A small, thick Japanese man with broad shoulders and hair cut in a military style rose from a round stool in the approximate center of the mass of electronic detritus. He wore a black sleeveless shirt and faded black shorts. Elaborate, colorful tattoos covered both arms. "Anna!" he said. "Always good to see you. I hear you're in a bit of trouble."

"Takeru!" Anna embraced him. "You could say that. Need your talents."

"Implant mods playing up?" Takeru looked her up and down. "I warned you. I said those mods were experimental. I told you I'd do the best I could, but—"

"No. Mods are fine. It's for my friend here." Anna hooked a thumb at Nadine. "I disabled her implant. I need you to change the ID number so it's not linked to her any more and turn it on again."

"No secret military software? No experimental hardware? Anna! This is unlike you. How..." He paused, searching for the word. "Pedestrian." He poked his head out through the plastic sheeting and yelled something in rapid-fire Spanish. The woman in stained coveralls waved.

"Follow me." He led them back out into the sweltering night. They followed him up a flight of rusted iron stairs salvaged from some tenement building somewhere to a plywood shack on the roof. He pulled open a heavy oval metal door that looked out of place lashed to the crude plywood wall. Inside, they found a space nothing like what Nadine expected, glossy white walls and recessed LED panel lights in the ceiling. A large medical bed surrounded by intimidating-looking equipment filled the center of the space, with a small office desk squeezed coyly into the corner. The chilly air carried the tang of antiseptics. "Standard rates, of course," Takeru said as he closed the door behind them.

"Of course."

Takeru gestured to Nadine. "On the bed, please."

Nadine swallowed. Anna squeezed her hand. "You'll be fine. Takeru takes good care of me." She shot him a sideways glance. "Well, mostly."

"You wound me." Takeru sat on a tiny chair with rollers beside the bed and pressed a button. A curved clamp padded in peeling black neoprene rose from the head of the bed. "Lie down, please."

Nadine took a deep breath, fighting back sudden tears. She sat gingerly. Anna held her hand. "Relax," Takeru said. "Rest your head there."

Nadine leaned back. Takeru brought a strap around her forehead. Nadine felt suddenly like a sacrifice laid out on an altar. "Lie still," Takeru said. "You probably won't feel anything."

"Probably?" Nadine said.

"No talking." He pushed a large white box on green plastic wheels over to the bed. A screen lit up atop it. A thin rod with a loop of wires on the end slid out of its side toward Nadine's head. She trembled. Anna squeezed her hand.

Takeru sat in a wheeled chair and rolled over to the box. "Okay, let's see what we can...mm, fancy. Neuralink, top of the line. Not what I expected. Very nice. Not as nice as what's in Anna's head, but top-shelf for consumer kit. You rich, Anna's friend?"

"My name—"

Takeru held up his hand. "Don't need to know. Don't want to know. Your name is Anna's friend, okay?"

"No, I'm not rich."

"No? Expensive hardware in your head for someone not-rich."

"My parents are rich. They live—"

"Don't want to know."

"So what does that mean?" Anna said.

"Tricky. Neuralink, see, they care about security. Very hard to tamper with their firmware. It's all encrypted, code-signed, boot loader checks—"

"But can you do it?"

"Anna! It's me. Going to be expensive, though."

"Are you taking advantage of me?"

He shrugged. "I have tools to pay for, hey? And word is, you have nowhere else to go."

"Just do it."

"Anything for you." He unfolded a small keyboard from the front of the box. A holographic display sprang to light atop it. "There's a whole community that gets all over every new firmware update. Neuralink makes good kit but they don't like letting people hack it. So folks find ways around, jailbreak, add new features, you name it. I make a point to keep up. God bless the street, hmm?" He winked at Anna. "Now let's see...uh oh."

"Uh-oh? What uh-oh?" Nadine said.

"When Anna disabled it, she disabled OTA update too. Got to do it manual."

"What does that mean?"

"You know I said you won't feel anything? Well, yeah, change of plan." He opened a drawer beneath the compact keyboard and took out a long, thin drill bit sealed in plastic. At the touch of a button, another rod slid from the box. Takeru fitted the drill bit to the end.

Nadine's heart pounded. "Anna—"

Anna took Nadine's hand in both of hers. "It's okay. I promise. I've done this before. Lots of times."

Nadine swallowed and stared at the ceiling. "So Anna says a lot of folks here don't have implants?"

"Yeah." Takeru brushed the hair away from Nadine's temple. He used a tiny electric clipper to shave a small spot on the side of her head, then sprayed her with something that smelled of alcohol.

"So why are you here, then, with all this?" She waved with her free hand to take in the small room with its gear.

"Officially? I'm a value add for Mayor Tony. He makes money sending people to me. People needing to change the IDs on their implants like you, people wanting augments like Anna, people wanting—" He hesitated. "Other stuff. Unofficially, think of me as an anthropologist." He scooped some blue gel from a tiny round plastic pot with a long cotton swab and rubbed it on Nadine's temple. "Almost ready."

"An anthropologist?"

Takeru grinned. "Haven't you noticed? The human species, *Homo sapiens,* is dividing. Species evolve to fit the environment, hey? Our environment is our society, and our society is technological. Two species startin' to emerge. Call them *Homo mechanica,* mechanical man, and *Homo immechanica.* I'm an anthropologist observing a tribe of *Homo immechanica.*"

"Don't think Tony's crew would much like hearing you call them a 'tribe,'" Anna observed dryly.

Takeru shrugged. "Tribe, family, whatever. Used to be more than one species of *Homo*. You know what happened to them? We did. We don't share. You a betting woman, Anna's friend? My advice, put your money on *Homo mechanica. Immechanica* goin' to lose, you see." He touched a button. The drill spun with a mechanical shriek. Nadine swallowed and squeezed her eyes closed. Anna held her hand tightly.

Nadine flinched when the drill touched her skin. She felt a sensation of twisting and pulling. A loud grinding sound reverberated through her head, then a sharp spike of pain, white-hot in her skull. She cried out. Anna held her hand tightly. "It'll be over in a second. Breathe. You can do this. I know it sucks, but it's better than rotting in jail. You're okay. Just a little bit more. Three, two, one..."

The grinding and the pain stopped. Takeru did something Nadine couldn't see. Cold spray squirted across her temple, then the drill retracted and a slender probe tipped with fine wires took its place. "Good contact, establishing communications...ah, good. See? Easy. Now we just cozy up, trick this beautiful piece of hardware into accepting a new update. I'll disable future OTA updates, so the factory can't undo what we're about to do. Loading some highly unauthorized software, way outside warranty. Just lie still, all automatic from here."

Nadine stared at the LED panel in the ceiling, trying to steady her breathing. Her heart pounded. "Anything else you want, long as I'm in here?" Takeru said. "Won't charge you much, seein' how I'm elbow-deep anyway."

"Like what?" Nadine said.

"You still have that Newton package I sold you?" Anna said.

"Yeah," Takeru said. "Nice bit of work, that."

"She have enough processing grunt to run it?"

"Specs are a little low, but yeah. If she didn't have such a fancy implant, no, but with this? I can make it work."

"Put it in."

"Put what in?" Nadine said.

"Custom CQB software, milspec, cutting-edge." Takeru said.

"Weapons alert?" Anna said.

"Done." His fingers danced. "Okay, you might hear some sounds. Don't sweat it."

"Sounds? What kind of sounds?" Nadine said. A long, low tone with no apparent source filled her head and was gone. "Oh."

"You just hear a beep?"

"Yeah."

"That's your implant sayin' it's ready for new firmware. Don't move. I mean it."

Nadine closed her eyes. Anna ran her fingers over the back of her hand. Minutes ticked by, each longer than the one before, then the low tone came again from all around her.

"And that's it," Takeru said. The probe drew away into the bowels of the machine. "Easy. Ish. You call people now, your name will show up as 'Melody Landry.'"

"Melody? I look like a Melody to you?"

"You want to go back to whoever you were, Anna's friend?"

"No."

"Your name is Melody Landry." He scooped a small amount of white paste onto another swab and pressed it against the side of Nadine's head. "Biocompatible filler," he explained. "Plugs the hole to prevent infection. You're good, Anna's friend." He unstrapped her head. "Can you access your implant?"

Nadine reached for it. "Find me a pizza."

The voice came instantly inside her head. "I found four pizza shops in your area. Which one do you want?"

"Yeah," Nadine said. "Thank you."

"Don't need nothin' but the thanks that matter." He rummaged around in the desk drawer and came out with a white cube with a small gooseneck camera attached. He fiddled with it for a moment.

Anna whistled. "You are gouging me."

"Man's gotta eat."

"Fine."

Takeru held up the camera. "No, other eye," Anna said. "Biometrics attached to my other identity."

A light flashed inside the lens. Takeru grinned. "Pleasure doing business with you, Anna's other identity."

Back in their small room, Nadine said, "What did he mean by custom software?"

"It's a predictive and analytic program," Anna said. "Military. Here." She tossed Nadine a box of contacts. "Put these in. Pair them up with your implant and I'll show you."

When the green light blinked in the corner of Nadine's vision, Anna took the telescoping club from her bag. With a flick of her wrist, she snapped it open. "Tell me what you see." She swung it at Nadine, the tip swishing by just centimeters from her skin.

"Whoa," Nadine said. "What was that? It was like a green fan."

"Newton's laws of motion," Anna said. "Your implant will look for moving objects near you and draw an arc showing the most probable path. Solid color means high certainty, fades out as it gets harder to predict. Green means won't hit you. Yellow means might hit you, red means will hit you if you don't get out of the way. Lets you see a second into the future, kind of. You still need to practice to make the best use of it. You ever take judo classes?"

"No."

"Want to?"

"You telling me I have a choice?"

"You'll have an advantage if you do." She snapped the club shut and reached into her bag. Nadine jumped. "What do you see?"

"A yellow triangle with an exclamation mark floating in the air."

"Your implant can recognize weapons faster than you can. Machine learning, big data set." She slid her gun out of the bag. "Implant recognized the edge of the gun before you did. You see that, look out."

"You have this stuff?"

"Yeah."

"And other stuff?"

"Yeah."

"What did Takeru mean about experimental hardware?"

"He meant experimental hardware." Anna grinned. "Cutting edge of *Homo mechanica*, babe. I'm hungry. Let's go see what our *immechanica* friends have on the menu. Strangers in a strange land, hmm?"

Corporativos

A LOUD ARGUMENT THE evening of their third day in T-Town announced Dan-boy's arrival. The kid assigned to protecting or imprisoning them, depending on how you looked at it, rapped on the door.

"Yeah?" Anna said.

"Friends of yours outside." He scratched under his ballistic vest. "Don't wanna give up their guns. Mayor wants to see them, but they're saying no. Askin' to talk to you."

Anna rolled her eyes. "Jesus. Really? Fine." She shrugged on her hoodie. "Stay here."

Nadine sat fidgeting on the bed. Loud voices came from somewhere down below. Eventually, the voices quieted, reaching a consensus of some sort. The kid parked outside opened the door to hand Nadine a large backpack. "Your friends say you look after this while they see the mayor."

"They're not my friends," Nadine said.

The boy flashed her a genuine smile. "Good choice."

Nadine slung the backpack in a corner. She paced back and forth, chewing her thumbnail. After what felt like an eternity but was probably less than twenty minutes, Anna returned with Dan-boy, Lena, and two men Nadine didn't recognize. All of them wore sullen expressions. "I don't see why we couldn't talk to him tomorrow," Dan-boy complained.

"His place, his rules," Anna said.

Dan-boy glared at Nadine. "What's she doing here?"

"Haven't you heard? She's a wanted terrorist."

"She's—"

"She's in this," Anna said. "She's part of this, whether you like it or not."

"It's her fault what happened!" Dan-boy said. "If she didn't insist on bringing Marcus to the hospital—"

"If you didn't insist on bringing Marcus to scout out that chemical company," Anna interjected, "we might not be here. We still don't know what's happening. Pointing fingers won't get answers or help Marcus, so do me a favor and stow that shit."

"But—"

"Nadine's lost as much as I have. Maybe more. She didn't sign up for this. You don't like it, go away."

"I need you."

"Then Nadine stays. This is her life too."

Dan-boy bristled. One of the men put his hand on Dan-boy's shoulder. "Fine. What now?"

"Jacob." Anna nodded to the second man. "Kev. Lena. Dan-boy. How many others are left?"

Kev and Lena exchanged glances. "Nobody," Kev said. "Everyone else has disappeared or been arrested in the past 48 hours."

"Fuck."

"Yeah."

"How?"

"Dunno. They must've squeezed Marcus."

"That or Anna screwed up and they traced the cab."

Anna clenched her fists. "I didn't screw up."

"So you say."

Lena held out her hand again. "This isn't helping. We need a plan."

"We go underground," Jacob said. "Take new identities. Disappear."

Anna laughed bitterly. "They're calling us terrorists." She shook her head. "Something very weird is going on. This all goes back to Marcus and whatever you saw in that factory. Someone took Marcus out of that hospital, and it wasn't the police."

"How do you know that?" Lena said.

"Because the police wouldn't tamper with the records to make it look like he was never there."

"If not the police, then who?" Dan-boy said.

"Dunno. Dunno. We need to find out. I fried my computer on the way out. Didn't want LAPD to have it, but I'm blind without it. I need to get a new one. Tonight, I think."

"Where are you going to get a computer tonight?" Dan-boy said.

"There's a mall in Santa Monica. Computer store right next to a chocolate place. Figure we could go there, maybe get some nice dark chocolate while we're out. The fuck you think, Dan-boy? I know a guy who knows a guy, he'll hook us up. I want you and Kev with me. Jacob, you and Lena stay here with Nadine."

"So now you're giving orders?" Dan-boy said.

"You're the one got us into this," Lena said. "I'm okay with trying it her way."

"Good," Anna said. "We head out after nightfall."

WHEN NIGHT CAME, Anna unpacked her duffle bag and repacked one of the backpacks Dan-boy had brought with him. She took a sealed bag of black plastic from her bag and cracked it open. Nadine goggled. A solid brick of cash, neatly bundled and shrink-wrapped in clear cellophane, lay inside. Anna slit open the cellophane wrapper and transferred the bundles of bills to the backpack. "I had no idea you had this kind of money," Nadine said.

"I won't after tonight," Anna said. "Gonna be an expensive trip." Lena caught Anna's eye and smirked. Anna zipped up the backpack and slung it over her shoulder. "Let's go."

"What if someone mugs you?" Nadine said.

Anna smiled thinly. "I'd like to see them try. Stay here, darling. We'll be back soon." She kissed Nadine's cheek and disappeared into the muggy night air, Kev and Dan-boy at her back.

"How long have you known Anna?" Nadine asked Lena in the silence that followed.

"Why? You jealous?"

"Just making conversation. Should I be?"

Lena shrugged. "We had a thing for a while. I'm okay with that if you are."

"Why wouldn't I be?"

"No reason. Some people, they just get funny around their main squeeze's ex."

"Are you jealous?"

"Nah. We were pretty casual about it. I'm more into guys, truth said."

"You two go back a ways."

"Yeah. Met her when I signed on to Dan-boy's crew."

"I don't really understand..." Nadine waved her hand. "All of this. Who is Dan-boy? What do you do?"

"Hasn't Anna told you anything?" Lena said.

"No."

"Huh. So you're in the shit and you don't even know why?"

"That's about the way of it."

"Where did you meet?"

"Underground dance party."

Lena leaned back on the bed, regarding Nadine like she was waiting for a punchline. "You're serious."

"Do I look like I'm joking?"

Lena laughed. "Oh, that's rich. Honey, you have no idea what you've gotten yourself into."

"So enlighten me."

"Not my place, sugar-pie. That's between you and your squeeze."

Jacob shook his head. "I have a bad feeling about this."

"Only because you aren't keeping up." Lena snorted. "We're way past bad feelings." She produced a small metal tin from her pocket. "Card game, anyone?" She leered at Nadine. "We can play strip poker if you like."

Anna arrived back hours later, carrying a large, multi-pocketed case in place of the backpack. Dan-boy wore a surly expression. Nadine embraced her. "Listen," Anna said. "I'm going to try to nail down what happened to Marcus. Whatever's going on, it all starts with him."

"How do you know that?" Kev said.

"There are no coincidences. Everything went to shit after he got shot."

"Wouldn't have happened if your girlfriend wouldn't have insisted on taking him to the hospital," Dan-boy said.

Anna whirled. "Don't. You don't get to have this conversation with me. You brought him to my place. What did I tell you? I told you never. Never do that. Don't you even pin this on her. This is all on you."

"I still think—"

"Think it somewhere else. I have work to do."

Dan-boy opened his mouth. Lena stepped smoothly between them. "C'mon. She's right, and I'm hungry."

When they left, Anna seemed to deflate. Nadine sat on the bed beside her. "You okay?"

Anna turned tired eyes to her. To Nadine, she seemed beaten. "No." She pressed something small and hard—a key, its round barrel indented with irregular cutouts—into Nadine's hand. "Santa Monica Storage, locker 531. Insurance in case something happens to me."

"What?"

"Santa Monica Storage, locker 531. Say it."

"Santa Monica Storage, locker 531."

"Again."

"Santa Monica Storage, locker 531. Is this really necessary?"

"Don't lose it."

"Do you think something's going to happen to you?"

"Nature of the business. I should never have dragged you in."

"Bit late for that now. I'm sorry," Nadine added at Anna's wounded expression. "I didn't mean it like that."

"Still true," Anna said softly. She stared into space for a moment, then blinked and shook her head. "I better get busy."

"Is there anything I can do?"

Anna squeezed Nadine's hand. "No. I expect to be under for a while."

"What should I do?"

"Stay inside. Don't talk to anyone. Don't call anyone. I'm sorry, but that's all I got."

FOR THE NEXT three days, Nadine paced in the stuffy, airless room while Anna immersed herself with her terminal, coming up only occasionally to eat the limp sandwiches that Tony or one of his people brought. A tangle of music thumped and boomed through the walls. Sounds of machinery, power tools, and occasional raised voices drifted in nonstop from outside at all hours of the day or night. Dan-boy, Lena, and the others stopped by occasionally, only to be chased away when Anna growled that she had nothing to report.

The routine changed on the fourth day. Anna, who'd taken to rolling straight out of bed to her computer without bothering to dress or shower, surfaced in the late afternoon. Nadine offered her a cold sandwich and a bottle of lukewarm water, courtesy of Mayor Tony. Heat shimmered in the air, turning the small room into a muggy hotbox. A film of sweat covered Anna's skin. Her eyes, red and baggy, peered out from beneath unkempt bangs. "Found him," she said.

"What? Where?" Nadine said.

"Let's wait for everyone else."

By the time Anna had showered in a weak stream of tepid water and dressed in what little clean clothing she had, Dan-boy, Lena, Kev, and Jacob had gathered in the stifling room. Tony was there also, flanked by two teenage boys in sweat-stained, badly fitting body armor. "You look like hell," Dan-boy said without preamble.

"I'm in good company, then." Anna looked him up and down. "Company, anyway." Lena sniggered.

"So what you got, *mi mala?*" Tony said.

Dan-boy spun. "What's he even doing here? This is private business." He glared at Tony. "You understand? Private business." The boy to Tony's right, a gangly kid of perhaps fifteen with dark eyes and scraggly, unkempt hair, bristled.

Tony folded his arms. "I understand you are a guest in my house, and you disrespect my hospitality. You and your friends here, I don't think you appreciate the magnitude of your situation. The police, they say you're a wanted terrorist. All of you. They have video. It's all over the news. You, Anna here, all of you. Building bombs, they say. Radiological. Even Anna's lovely friend. There's a reward, you know. Hundred and fifty large. That's a lot of money, *mi amigo.*"

Dan-boy lunged at Tony. The two boys flanking Tony tensed. Nadine blinked. Her vision blurred. A quick flash of color floated in front of her, green arcs fanning out from Dan-boy's hands and from the two people flanking him. She shuddered. Tony raised his hands. "Relax. We're all friends here, right? Anna is family."

The boy to Tony's left, a skinny brown-haired kid whose arms were decorated with complex tattoos of half-naked women, scratched his head. "Dunno, boss, that's a lot of money."

Tony shook his head sadly. "For shame, Enrico. What does it profit a man to gain the whole world, yet lose his soul? These people are family to us." He glared at Dan-boy. "Even if they don't always act like it."

Dan-boy tensed. Kev put his hand on his shoulder and shook his head slightly. Dan-boy turned away with a look of disgust. Nadine shivered. Adrenaline she hadn't even felt drained from her. "What do you mean, they have video?" she heard herself say.

"On the news," Tony said. "Surveillance footage, they say. You and Anna, SWAT team raiding your house, bombs, barrels with radiation symbols painted on them." He turned toward Anna. "Something I should know? You makin' bombs?"

"You know me better than that," Anna said.

"Ah, I hope so, *mi mala.* What news about your missing friend?"

"Taken from the hospital," Anna said. "Whoever did it erased the patient records. Far as they're concerned, he was never there."

"So it's a dead end?" Kev said.

"No. Harder than you think to erase anything completely," Anna said. "Big corporations live and die on data, see? Everything is replicated, backed up, tucked away into duplicate databases. Sometimes the people who run the systems don't even know how it's all set up."

"Get to the point," Dan-boy said.

"They thought they were clever. I am more clever." She dragged her computer onto her lap. A glowing rectangle hovered in front of it. "They record video all the time, in every hallway. Video goes to an off-site contractor. Contractor subcontracts backups to a data replication service. All seamless, all real-time, very expensive. Video got erased from local storage and the contractor's main data store, but not before it got replicated." Her fingers danced. An image of a long, wide hallway floated ghostlike in front of her. "Watch."

A door opened. Two men dressed in black wheeled a gurney into the hall. Nadine leaned forward. Blankets covered the man strapped to the bed. He wore a transparent breathing mask over his face. One of the men caught his foot on the door and cursed silently. Anna's fingers moved. The image froze.

"That's your friend?" Tony said.

"Marcus. Yes."

"Are you sure?" Lena said. She walked over to study the floating image. "It's hard to tell."

"It's him."

"Can you enhance it?"

Anna shook her head. "Not without magic. Cheap-ass camera. It is what it is."

"How do you know it's him?" Dan-boy said.

"I've watched this footage a hundred times. They bring him into that room. The next day, these two take him out. It's him."

"Who are those guys?" Tony said. "Orderlies?"

"No. And they aren't hospital security or police, either. I think they're private security."

"Back up a little," Tony said.

Anna wound the video back. Tony walked over to Lena, frowning. The two boys shifted nervously. "I know these uniforms," Tony pointed. "See that patch? Black Tiger. Corporate security. Why are *corporativos* taking your friend?"

"Why, I don't know. Where, on the other hand..." Anna's hands tripped gracefully across her computer. A new video floated in the air. "Look here. Three minutes and twenty-eight seconds later, external cameras catch this van pulling out of the back of the building. It's the only vehicle big enough for a stretcher in the eight minutes after they took him from the room. Unmarked, no windows, but..." The video zoomed in. "I got your license tag!" she sang. "From there it was easy. Just a matter of hacking LAPD automated tag and transponder recorders—"

Lena snorted. "Easy."

"Easier than you think," Anna said. "LAPD outsources the whole network to outside contractors on a lowest-bid basis. Place in Hyderabad. Their security is shit." The image changed again, an overhead view of the city's streets. A row of red dots overlaid the map. "Each of these dots is an automated snapshot of the tag or transponder signal," Anna said.

"*Hermano Mayor les está vigilando*, hmm?" Tony said.

"*Hermana Mayor*, perhaps." Anna zoomed in on the map. "The van disappears somewhere in here. Industrial park. No transponders or license cameras. Doesn't appear again for another twenty-eight hours." She stabbed her finger at the glowing image. "Here. They took him here. I'd bet money on it."

"Okay, so what now, hmm?" Tony said. "You ride in, guns blazing, rescue your friend?"

"It's a thought," Jacob said.

"A stupid one," Lena said.

Nadine withdrew from the conversation. As the sun settled outside, she wrapped Anna's hoodie with its cartoon faces around herself and wandered down to the sweltering courtyard, where a heavyset woman with face and shoulders decorated with simple geometric tattoos offered her some kind of roasted meat over a bed of yellow rice. The others argued for hours. The voices of Anna and Dan-boy frequently rose above the rest.

Nadine wandered into the garage and settled on a narrow round stool of cracked wood, where she watched the relentless, frenetic activity. The place ran night and day, people in sweat-stained overalls swarming over cars as they were brought in, reducing them to piles of parts. Electric motors were stacked neatly in the corner. Computers and sensors were carefully wrapped and placed in scuffed fiberglass bins. Battery sleds went in one of the garage bays, piled on pallets with blocks of wood between, awaiting their fate. Harsh, merciless white work lights glared down from above. Three different stereos pumped competing music into the space, loud and discordant. The workers paid no attention to her.

Anna found her, late that night, wandering aimlessly between the wall and the rear of one of the warehouses, trailed by a dark-eyed kid in a badly-fitting ballistic vest who looked slightly embarrassed to be following her. "Hey," she said.

"Hey," Nadine said. "Did you make a decision?"

"We've come to a consensus, or near enough to," Anna said. She wiped a film of sweat from her forehead. "Listen. I want to say I'm sorry—"

"Don't." Nadine held up her hand. "I knew something was off the first night we met. Normal people don't get envelopes full of cash in the middle of the night. I stayed. I'm here. You can't undo what's happened."

Anna kissed Nadine's hand. "I'm still...I wish things had been different."

Back in the small, stifling room with its plywood walls and scratched Plexiglass window, Anna undressed Nadine and led her by the hand to the bed. They lingered over each other for hours, patient and gentle, until eventually they both fell into a fitful sleep, coiled around each other despite the heat.

7

It's Not Magic

"**I**'M GOING WITH you."

"No. Out of the question."

"I'm part of this now. I have the right to go."

Anna shook her head. "It's not about what you have the right to do. I don't want you to get hurt."

"I'm already in the middle of this. The police are looking for me. What am I going to do, stay here? What if you get caught? Mayor Tony owes me nothing. What happens to me then? You can't protect me by leaving me behind. I'm going with you."

Anna ran her hand through her hair with a sigh. "Okay. Fine. You're right. I don't think Dan-boy's going to like it."

True to her prediction, Dan-boy folded his arms, face set in a grim scowl. "No. Absolutely not."

The entire group—Anna, Nadine, Dan-boy, Kev, Jason, and Lena, together with Takeru, Mayor Tony, and two of his crew—crowded into the small room with its plywood walls. Four different kinds of music thumped and pulsed outside. An hour past sunset, the heat still lingered.

Kev put his hand on Dan-boy's shoulder, but he was only getting warmed up. "She's not coming. She's a liability. If shit goes sideways, she'll screw us all, or worse. I don't know why you've bothered to drag her along with you. You should've cut her loose a long time ago. No way is she coming with us."

Anna shrugged. "Wherever she is, I am. If she doesn't go, neither do I. You need me. I say she goes with me."

"You can't—"

"I can. I am. This is the way it is."

"Why?"

"I dragged her into this. I'm responsible for her."

"Fine. You're responsible for her. Make sure she doesn't screw up."

"Do you have a plan?" Tony said.

"Yeah. But you'll hate it."

"Ah, *mi mala,* I haven't liked anything you've done since you arrived at my door with your girlfriend. Why change now?"

"I need wheels. Clean, spoofed transponder, no plates. Something big enough for all of us, plus Marcus if we find him. A van, something like that."

Tony nodded. "I can find you something. Expensive, but doable. I need the full value up front."

"Tony. You know I'm good for it."

"Any other time, *mi mala,* yes. This time..." He shook his head. "I'm not so sure you're coming back. You or your friends."

"Fine. Money up front, then. I also need four, maybe five of your boys, young. Young enough to look like kids getting into trouble, to create a distraction."

Tony's eyes narrowed. Chill silence descended on the cramped room, broken only by the cacophony of music outside. "Anna," he said at last. "Anna, Anna, Anna. You presume on my hospitality. I welcome you and your friends, I take you into my home, and you do what? You take advantage of our friendship?"

"Tony, please."

"Anna. You trespass on my good nature."

"I can pay."

"I don't want your money. Not for this."

"It's not for you," Anna said. "It's for them. You know me. You know I have it. Enough to make a real difference in their lives."

"What good is money if you get them killed?" He shook his head. "No. No, Anna, you presume too much. Tijuana Town is my home. The people here are my family. I look after my own."

"Let me help."

One of the boys next to Tony shifted uneasily on his feet. "I dunno, boss. I'll do it."

Tony's mouth set in a grim frown. "No."

"But boss, I—"

"You see?" Tony said. "This is what you do. You undermine my authority in my own home..."

Anna sighed and spread her hands. "I don't want to cause problems—"

"Too late for that."

"—but I need your help. Marcus is family. Family is important."

Tony regarded her through narrow eyes for a long moment. Finally, he nodded. "We agree on that. Family is important. Okay, *mi mala,* say I will give you my boys. Payment in advance. For everything. What then?"

"I've been digging," Anna said. "Whoever set up this office park is careful and smart. Lots of data going in. Big fiber optics trunks. I found the permits. No way in from the outside, though. Firewalled, top-shelf, good design. I need physical access." She touched a stud on her computer. A building plan appeared, blueprints overlaying the site map. "The fiber optics come into an underground junction here. Room here with lots of power and AC, has to be the server room. I looked at the street view. There's a manhole cover right here that leads to a tunnel underneath for cable and data. I need to get down there, splice in myself."

Dan-boy shook his head. "No way. No way. Guards, cameras, who knows how many drones—"

"Right. That's where Tony's boys come in. Here's what I'm thinking…"

They talked until far into the night. When at last they'd reached consensus, Tony and the others filtered out into the muggy heat. Music thumped through the plywood walls, muted and cacophonic. Insects buzzed and chirped in the night. When at last the others had left, Nadine burrowed beneath a thin sheet, arms wrapped tight around Anna despite the heat. "Do you really think this will work?"

"I don't know. We have to try."

"We might get killed."

"We might."

I don't understand," Nadine said. "Why not—why not just go to the police? Tell them everything. What happened to Marcus, the people at the hospital, everything."

Anna shook her head. "Oh, darling. I love you. It doesn't work that way. We're already wanted terrorists, remember? Besides, we're little people. The police don't work for us."

"But if—"

"No." Years of bitterness colored Anna's voice. "We aren't rich. We don't have daddy's money to protect us. This is Los Angeles. If you're little people, you're dog food. Nobody in the system will listen to us. Things here aren't like what you're used to. Here, they decide if you're guilty or innocent, then they have the trial. Maybe. If you're lucky. If not, you disappear from a hospital and there's no record you were ever there."

"If you explain to the police, there's no way they'd allow—"

"You're naive. I love you, but you're naive."

"That's not fair," Nadine said.

"No? Tell me something. You ever been arrested?"

"No."

"Know anyone who's been arrested?"

"Not really, no."

"When you've had as much experience as I have, you can tell me what the police will or won't listen to."

"Are you angry with me?"

"With you?" Anna studied Nadine's face. "No. But you're not in Wonderland any more. You're in a world you know nothing about, and this shit is real."

Nadine turned away. "Don't talk down to me."

Anna gave her an exasperated sigh. "In my world, you're a babe in the woods."

"Stop treating me like a child!"

"Stop acting like one!" Anna cried. "You don't know what you're talking about. If we go to the police, we'll be disappeared faster than you can say 'extraordinary rendition.' There is nothing about this you're ready for!"

"Then why did you agree I could come?"

"Because I got you into this!" Anna cried. "This is my fault. Every bit of this. I—I wanted to have you. I convinced myself it was possible. I should have known better. Now I've ruined your life through my own selfishness." She turned away.

"I chose to be here!"

"It wasn't an informed choice, was it? That night we met, I didn't exactly say, 'Come home with me, I'll destroy your life and turn you into a wanted criminal,' did I?"

Nadine reached out to touch Anna's shoulder. Anna flinched violently. "Don't. I'm sorry. I can't. Not right now. Don't you get it? I might get you killed tomorrow."

"Then why did you argue to let me come with you? Why not just do what Dan-boy says and tell me not to go?"

"Because you have the right to be there, if that's what you want. I dragged you into this. I just wish...I wish I had never met you."

Nadine rolled away, her heart a lump of stone in her chest. They slept fitfully that night, in the Los Angeles heat, while music in several languages thumped around them.

THE SUN SAT low on the horizon when Anna shook Nadine awake, sending red fingers of light through the scratched Plexiglass window. Nadine mumbled sleepily. "Showtime," Anna said. "Get dressed and follow me." She slung her backpack across her back and picked up the duffle bag. "Bring your suitcase and anything you have of value. Anything that might identify you, too. Can't bring it with us."

Nadine dressed quickly. Anna led her out across the courtyard. A small group of teenage boys stood in a loose circle, talking in low voices in Spanish. One of them loaded long cans into a battered gray backpack. Glowing yellow triangles with exclamation points hovered over them, warnings from the new software in Nadine's implant.

Nadine dragged her suitcase behind Anna to the same building where they'd first met Mayor Tony. They slipped through an ill-hung door into a large windowless room paneled in white-painted drywall. A small air conditioner wheezed in one wall. A bare LED overhead flooded the room in harsh blue-white light. Rows of heavy locked cabinets squatted along three of the walls, all painted the same drab institutional green. The air smelled of paper, dust, and fatigue. A low formica table extended across nearly the entire length of the space, chopping it in two.

"Mateo, this is my friend," Anna said. "She has need of your services."

The man Anna addressed could have stepped right off the stage of some community college theater group. He was tall, thin to the point of being gaunt, with angular cheekbones, dark skin, and wide, dark eyes. He wore a severely formal suit that had been out of style for at least two centuries and a tall, immaculate top hat. He and Anna exchanged a flurry of words, hers in Spanish, his in a mix of Spanish, French, and some other language Nadine didn't recognize, then he bowed and tipped his hat to her. "Always pleased to make a new customer," he said.

"What is it you do, exactly?" Nadine said.

"I safeguard that which is most precious to you." His voice, soft and mellifluous, carried a hint of an accent Nadine couldn't place.

"Give him anything you don't want to lose," Anna said. "He'll look after it."

"Do you trust him?"

Mateo clasped both hands to his heart. "Anything you entrust to my care, I will look after as if it were my very soul."

"Means yes," Anna said. She hoisted her duffle bag onto the counter, unzipped it, counted out a sheaf of crisp bills, slid them to Mateo. "Me and her."

Mateo nodded gravely. He scribbled something on a small slip of cardboard and passed it to her, then placed her bag in a locker which he shut with a combination lock. "And you?" he said to Nadine.

Nadine slung her suitcase onto the battered formica. "Weird to think this is everything I have left in the world."

He nodded in sympathy. "People often drift ashore in Tijuana Town carrying only that which the world has not yet taken from them. This is it?"

Nadine hesitated, then dug into her pocket and slid him the key Anna had given her. She slipped off her ring and passed it over as well. "Take care of this. My mom gave it to me."

He bowed. "*Très bien*. I will look after it, *dalaga*."

Back in the early-morning heat, the boys had finished packing their backpacks and now were clustered over a collection of battered electric scooters plugged into an ancient gray charger fed from a wire that descended from one corner of the large warehouse, chatting excitedly in Spanish. Yellow triangles floated in Nadine's vision, clear and bright. Nadine blinked. "Will I ever get used to that?"

"To what?" Anna said.

"The little triangles."

"Depends who you hang out with, I imagine. Ah, here we go." She stepped forward and waved to Dan-boy, who steered a nondescript white electric panel van cautiously in their direction. A logo on the side read "Consolidated Facilities Services" in neatly stenciled letters that looked brand-new. From the passenger seat, Lena blew a kiss in their direction.

Dan-boy pulled the van to a halt in front of them and hopped out. He opened the back of the van, where Jason and Kev waited. A triangle with exclamation points hovered over Jason, a ghost in the machine warning her of the potential for mayhem.

The van had been stripped to bare white metal, no seats, not even a carpet. A hospital stretcher, legs folded beneath it, occupied a third of the rear. "Gift from Takeru," Anna said to Nadine's questioning look. "In case we find Marcus."

One of the boys whistled. They all dragged their scooters to the van and climbed in, jostling for space. "Get in," Anna said, mouth set in a tight frown.

Nadine climbed up into the van. Anna squeezed in after her and pulled the door shut. The cramped space smelled of cleaning products and sweaty bodies. One of the boys, barely in his teens, leered at Nadine. "*¿Te gustan las chicas*, hmm?" He brought his hand to his face, fingers spread in a V, and flicked his tongue between them. Anna glared at him without expression until he looked away.

The van moved off. Nadine watched the four boys, none of them over fourteen. Yellow triangles rotated over them, hovering near the left side of one boy's vest, the pocket of another boy's baggy jeans. "Anna?"

"Yeah?"

"How does my implant know to put up alerts? It can't look through clothes, can it?"

Anna shook her head. "No. It's all pattern matching. Expert system, trained neural network, looks for shapes in clothes, body language, all that."

"There's room for that in my implant?"

"Thank your parents. Neuralink's seriously overengineered. Rich people buy 'em because the specs look good. Not that they understand what the specs even mean. Bigger numbers must be better, right? Including the price tag." She grinned without mirth.

"So what else can it do?"

"I'll teach you when we get back. If we get back."

"You really think we might not?"

"Kind of, yeah."

Kev laughed. "Tell me why you're here again?"

Nadine shook her head. "I feel responsible."

"For Marcus?"

"Yeah."

"Wanna blame someone, blame Dan-boy. It was his idea that started all this."

"I heard that," Dan-boy said from the front.

"I know." Kev leaned forward. In a lower voice, he said, "I hear you got some upgrades in your implant. What does it tell you about me?"

Nadine looked him up and down. He wore baggy cargo pants in a generic beige color, probably straight off the discount rack at Walmart, and a battered and shapeless hoodie that had seen better days, covered with leering Japanese anime faces. "Nothing."

Kev lifted his leg, causing two of Mayor Tony's boys to shift and grumble in the cramped space. With the stretcher, the pile of scooters atop it, and the people, the van's cargo area left little room. Beneath his pant leg, a black nylon holster strapped to his ankle carried a compact revolver. A yellow triangle sprang into existence in Nadine's vision, hovering just above the handgun. "What did you just learn?"

"You tell me."

"Tech's an aid. Don't let it become a crutch. It's not magic." He lowered his pant leg. "It does the best it can. Software's trained to look for patterns, see? Bulges in fabric. Really good with hip holsters, a bit shit at more concealed stuff. If it tells you someone's armed, believe it, but if it doesn't, that doesn't mean they aren't. Get it?"

"Got it," Nadine said. "You got this software too?"

"Ha! I wish. My implant's not that good." He tapped his head. "Best software's still the old Mark I brain."

Nadine glanced over at Anna, who nodded. "He's right. Keep it in mind."

"So why'd you even have Takeru put it in?"

"Because you don't have the benefit of a lifetime on the street and it's better than nothing. Mark I brain takes a long time to train. Besides, we were already in there anyway, and the gear you got in your head, it'd be criminal to let it go to waste." She smirked. "Maybe I wanted something for you to remember me by."

"I doubt anyone could forget you," Jason said.

Anna smiled a genuine smile. The van pulled to a bumpy stop. One of Tony's boys fell against the back of Lena's seat with a curse. "Showtime," Dan-boy said.

"You know what to do?" Anna said.

"Ain't rocket science, *chiquita*," the boy who'd been rude to Nadine said. Anna opened the back of the van. The boys pushed out, dragging electric scooters with them. The one who'd spoken made a show of squeezing past Anna, backpack pressing uncomfortably into Nadine. Anna glared at him. He grinned, then pulled up his hood. The other boys crowded around as he pulled cans from his backpack and passed them out.

"Don't engage," Anna said. "You're just looking to draw them off."

"We got this, *chiquita*." He flipped a switch on his scooter and jumped onto the footboard. The thing rocketed off, faster than Nadine would have expected. The other boys followed after, hoods over their faces, laughing and calling to each other in Spanish.

Anna pulled the back doors shut. "Same goes for you," she told Kev and Jason. "Don't engage. Just cover our backs, warn us of trouble."

"Got it." Jason shrugged out of his hoodie and into a work vest, brilliant Da-Glo colors and reflective tape. A hard hat and dark wraparound sunglasses hid his face. Beside him, Kev did the same.

Kev touched the center of his sunglasses. Words floated in front of Nadine: "117xc34rtz would like to share a stream with you. Accept?"

"Yes," she said. Instantly, a ghostly, hallucinatory image floated translucent in front of her, like the reflection on a pond: herself, dressed in baggy clothes and a hoodie far too warm for the daytime heat, eyes tired and a little bloodshot, face haggard.

The image centered on her breasts, what little could be seen of them beneath the shapeless, distinctly unflattering clothes. "You getting this?" Kev said.

"Yeah," Anna said. "Eyes forward, flyboy."

Kev spread his hands. "Guy can window shop."

Jason laughed. Anna rolled her eyes. "Jesus. This is why I don't shag men."

"S'okay," Lena sang from up front, "more for me! Hey Anna, we get back, you think maybe—"

"No."

The van reacquainted itself with the flow of traffic. Horns blared. Autonomous cars swarmed around them. Nadine realized with a jolt of surprise Dan-boy was driving, manual control, not letting the van pilot itself. She looked quizzically at Anna. "No telemetry," Jason said. "No GPS, no record of where we're going, no nothing. We aren't even transmitting VIN and registration. Just like the old days." He flicked his fingers in the air. "We're a ghost."

"That place we stopped just now—"

"Closest place to the industrial park where there's a dead spot in surveillance," Anna said. "Bitch to find. Won't be a record of us dropping off our passengers."

"You eat?" Jason said.

"Huh?" Nadine realized he was looking at her.

"This morning. Breakfast. You eat? You look hungry."

"No."

He fished a protein bar from his discarded hoodie and passed it across to her. "Here."

"Thanks." She unwrapped it and chewed automatically without tasting it.

A radio crackled from the front of the van. "Splinter." The voice rode in on a burst of static. "Donatello here. We ready when you are."

Dan-boy keyed an old-fashioned microphone. "Donatello, Splinter. Just getting there now. Give us a sec."

"Right. Give April my love." Nadine cocked her head. Anna shrugged.

Nadine craned to look forward. Through the van's windscreen, she saw a generic entrance to a generic industrial park, neatly sculpted shrubbery in a curve swooping around a concrete slab painted eggshell pink, pitted bronze street numbers riveted to its face. A large wooden sign behind it bore a map of the buildings, each neatly labeled. "How many companies here?" Nadine said.

"Officially? Five. One big, four small. Things you'd expect. One installs IP cameras, one does wireless high-broadband telemetry, that kind of stuff."

"Unofficially?"

"Funny thing, that," Anna said. "Every tenant is owned by a shell company that's part of a conglomerate that all has the same parent. Landlord that owns the park, too. Parent company is a subsidiary of a defense contractor out of Texas, place called Terracone Research. Security here's provided by Black Tiger, same outfit Mayor Tony says snatched Marcus."

"This is insane."

"Bit late for cold feet," Jason observed.

Dan-boy pulled the van up to the curb on the main road into the park and stopped. "Place we're looking for is a manhole cover on the other side of those bushes," Anna said. "There's one camera with a good view of it. We should be parked right in front of it. Drones and other cameras, too. Turtles will take care of those."

"Turtles?" Nadine said.

"Old cartoon or something, I don't know. Radio's scrambled, but it's still better than using real names." She turned toward the front. "Let 'em loose."

Dan-boy spoke into a clunky-looking handheld radio with a stubby black antenna, its plastic case scuffed and battered. "Donatello, Splinter. Go go go."

The radio crackled. "Gotcha, Splinter, there in a flash."

It ended up taking a bit longer than a flash. Dan-boy and Lena sat in the front seats, hoodies pulled up, while Nadine huddled with the others in the back. "Aren't they going to see them on the camera?" Nadine said with a nod toward the front seat.

"Nope. Security film on the windows. Reflects infrared or something, very hard for cameras to see through," Jason said. "Polarized in weird ways, too."

"Expensive?"

"It is if you don't have Mayor Tony's crew stealing it from a shipment that was supposed to end up at a BMW plant in South Carolina," Anna said. "Very resourceful man, Mayor Tony."

"How do you know about it?"

"Who do you think fudged the shipping order at the factory?" Anna flashed her a toothy grin.

"And here we go," Lena said. As she spoke, Tony's four boys sped up the driveway and flashed by the van, whooping and hollering in a mix of Spanish and what sounded to Nadine's ears like Japanese, traveling so fast Nadine marveled that the wheels on the scooters didn't melt. They all held metal cans in one hand. They separated at the parking lot in front of the largest building, still yelling, pressing the nozzles as they raced along smooth pavement. Bright streamers of DayGlo fluorescent spray paint bloomed on expensive Teslas and Audis in the parking lot. One of the boys hopped his scooter expertly over the curb and raced along the sidewalk, scrawling something Nadine assumed was probably vulgar in Spanish on the windows.

Shouts rose after them. Two men in black uniforms took off on foot in pursuit. Four palm-sized drones swooped from the sky after them. "We good?" Dan-boy said.

"Give it another few seconds," Lena said, fiddling with a compact device on her lap. A flat screen showed a series of dots superimposed over a green-on-black schematic of the industrial park. "And...we're good."

Lena opened the side door and ducked out. Dan-boy crawled across the cabin and went out through her door after her. "Go," Anna said. "They won't be able to see us."

Nadine squeezed between the front seats and out the door. Lena was already ten meters out, making for a large clump of surrealistically well-manicured bushes. "Keep your head down," Anna hissed. Behind her, Kev and Jason opened the back of the van and hopped out, orange vests bright in the California sun. Kev carried a clipboard. Jason uncoiled a long, thick hose from a well beneath the van's floor. "Anybody asks," Anna explained, "they're cleaning the storm drain. Work order and everything. Paperwork's on file with the landlord." She flashed the same toothy grin again.

"Isn't the landlord owned by the same company that owns that building?"

"Yep. That's the nice thing about holding companies and shell companies. Left hand never knows what the right hand's doing." When they reached the hyper-groomed bushes, Lena had already produced a tool, metal T-handle at one end, hook at the other, that she used to pull aside a manhole cover. As soon as the cover was clear, Dan-boy descended into darkness. Lena followed him down, catlike. Nadine peered over the edge. U-shaped metal rods bedded in a concrete shaft made a ladder going down into the gloom. "Go," Anna hissed. "Tony's boys won't be able to keep them distracted for more than another couple minutes."

Nadine climbed down, considerably less graceful than Lena. Anna followed after, dragging the manhole cover back more or less as it should be behind her. Without the sun, the only light in the shaft came from small flat-panel LEDs epoxied at irregular intervals to bare concrete.

The shaft didn't go down far, barely three meters by Nadine's reckoning. She got to the bottom and found herself in a horizontal tunnel also lit by the same LEDs stuck along the ceiling. A thick pipe about twenty centimeters across made of black PVC ran along the wall, held in place by brackets bolted to the concrete. A second, thinner pipe ran over their heads, feeding the LEDs with power.

"Cameras?" Nadine said.

"Not down here," Anna said. "Go."

Nadine stumbled behind Lena, eyes still dazzled from the daylight above. As her vision adjusted, she saw red stenciled markings along the thicker pipe, triangle around a circle with lines radiating from it, "Invisible Laser Radiation" written below in Helvetica bold.

"So, we cut into the fiber optic, something like that?" Nadine said.

"Nope. Housing's pressurized. Cut into it, pressure drops and sets off an alarm. There's a patch panel up ahead, probably used for testing when they were installing everything. That's why we have to be here in person."

"All of us?"

"You're the one who wanted to come with." She squeezed past Danboy and Lena. "Junction's right here." She stopped at a box of dull gray plastic fastened to the curving wall with large steel bolts just below the fiber optic trunk. An armored conduit snaked from the box into the trunk line. A faded sticker, wrinkled with age, clung to the front of the box. At some point in the past, someone had written a series of numbers on it in ballpoint pen.

Anna set her backpack on the ground and pulled out a compact cordless drill with a small star-shaped bit. "Security screws." The screwdriver whirred. "Also a switch lets someone know the panel's been opened."

"So they'll know we're down here?" Nadine said.

"Nope." Anna set down the screwdriver with a grin and produced a long, thin piece of spring steel and a roll of tape from her backpack. She tore off a piece of tape, stuck it to the wall, then pried the front of the box open just enough to slide the flat steel through the gap. Only when it was in place did she pop the cover off completely. "See? Switch is this little thing right here." She pointed to a flat black plastic rectangle with a short silver lever on its side. "Just stick a bit of tape over it, and they'll never know. The better patch panels have a little ridge inside the cover that fits into a notch on the security switch. All photoelectric, take off the cover and the beam is no longer blocked. Big pain in the ass."

"So why is this one so simple?"

"It's two dollars cheaper. Company buys a few thousand of these, it adds up. Nobody really expects someone to sneak down here and start popping covers, right? Okay, let's do what we came here to do." She took two bundle of aluminum tubes connected by canvas from her pack and, with a deft flick of her wrist, unfolded them into a compact table and a squat camping stool. Her new computer went on the portable table. She plugged one end of a slender black cable into the back of the computer and the other end into a small round depression in the patch panel. A holographic display materialized. Her fingers danced. A small window appeared showing a live video feed of a corrugated plastic pipe sliding down a storm drain. "You look like you're having fun."

"You know it," Kev's voice said.

"Anything?"

"Not yet. Drones are back. Expect someone to come have a chat with us soon. Got the paperwork right here."

Anna's fingers flew over the compact computer. Windows filled with green text on a black background sprang up. Lena peered over Anna's shoulder. "What is it with you and green on black?"

"What can I say? I'm retro. Let me work."

"God, you're hot when you do nerd stuff," Lena said.

"I'm hot all the time," Anna said absently.

"Just find Marcus," Dan-boy snapped.

How Remarkable

HOLOGRAPHIC CODE SCROLLED over Anna's computer. The ghostly green glyphs might as well have been Egyptian hieroglyphs for all Nadine knew. She got the sense she was only seeing part of what was going on, the rest relayed directly to Anna's retinas via her contacts, the commands scrolling on the laptop's display more a sideshow than the main event. In their little corner of the window, Kev and Jason maintained their pretext of legitimate facilities management. *Just cleaning the storm drain, nothing to see here...*

Dan-boy stood at the end of the tunnel like a statue, calm and implacable. No, not like a statue, Nadine thought, more like an ambush predator, waiting for prey to wander close: unmoving but wound tight, ready to spring without warning. Lena, for her part, shuffled her feet, somehow managing to look simultaneously tense and bored.

Her attitude seemed contagious. Nadine found her mouth dry, her heart pounding fast. The LED panels along the tunnel glowed with constant light, a strip of luminescent squares forming a chain that extended along the length of the tunnel. The tunnel itself traveled at least as far as the largest building in the little industrial park, probably a hundred meters or so, until it curved gently out of sight.

"How long is this supposed to take?" Nadine said.

Lena shrugged. "As long as it takes. Your girl, she's good. Maybe best I've seen. If there's anything to find about Marcus, she'll find it. But how long? Who knows?"

Minutes ticked by. Nadine found herself more and more jittery. She placed back and forth across the tunnel until finally Lena told her to stop. "You're making me nervous."

"Is there anything I can do?" Nadine said.

"Not for this bit. We find Marcus and need to bust him out, might be all hands on deck. For now, we wait and see what your girlfriend finds. Ask you a question?"

"You just did."

"Why'd you want to come along? Real talk here. You say you feel responsible for Marcus getting grabbed, but you don't even know him. What's it to you?"

"That is the real reason," Nadine said. "That and my life got turned upside-down. What am I supposed to do, sit in the background and somehow hope it all gets sorted out for me? At least this way I might be able to do something to affect what's happening."

Lena looked thoughtful for a moment, then nodded. "Makes sense. Somebody put me in your place, I don't know what I'd do. Bad luck, huh?"

Nadine watched Anna, who stood nearly as still as Dan-boy, fingers flying over her computer. "Luck of some sort, I suppose." She shook her head. "Parts of it are good."

"Man, she's really got her claws into you, hey?" Lena said.

"You know I can hear you, right?" Anna said without looking up.

"Just keep doing that thing you do, hon," Lena said. "Don't let us distract you."

Nadine vibrated in place. "How do you stand it?"

"Stand what?" Lena said.

"The waiting."

"Coffee. Lots of coffee. Preferably black. Maybe some energy drinks."

"I need space," Nadine said.

"Suit yourself. Not like there's far to go down here."

Nadine turned her back on the three of them and set off down the tunnel. The LEDs overhead splashed stark shadows across gray concrete. "There's nothing down there," Lena called after her.

"Good. Nothing to worry about then."

The gray, featureless tunnel offered nothing but blank concrete. No currents disturbed the still, stifling air. Nadine wandered halfway to where the tunnel bent toward its appointment with some server room somewhere. Sixty meters or so down, the fiber optic trunk split at another box similar to the one Anna had tapped into. A smaller trunk, no bigger around than Nadine's hand, extended upward through the concrete tunnel.

"Huh, this is weird." Anna's distant voice came down the tunnel to her, reverberating oddly off the concrete walls.

"What's that?" Dan-boy's voice, equally distorted.

"Something called 'Project Mirage.' Whatever it is, they're spending a lot of money on it. I mean a lot of money. Crazy money. Can't figure out where it's all coming from, but it's all going through here to that company in Texas. Weird shit."

"Anything about Marcus?" A note of urgency tightened Lena's voice.

"Not yet. I—"

Everything happened quickly after that.

Nadine turned back toward Anna and the others. Kev's voice came through the speakers in Anna's computer, thin and tinny: "What's that? Look out! There's something—"

A burst of static filled the air. The feed cut out. Anna's head snapped up, alarm written on her face. Dan-boy came to life, spinning toward the ladder. From somewhere up above, Nadine heard dull sounds, pop-pop-pop, muffled by earth and concrete.

She started down the tunnel. More sounds filtered through the ground, five sharp reports. "Fu—" Dan-boy said, one hand on the rung of the ladder, pitted metal extending from concrete. His word cut off mid-cry. He dropped as if axed, hands clasped over his ears, screaming as he curled into himself.

The manhole cover scraped open. Something small tumbled end over end. A yellow triangle with an exclamation mark flared in Nadine's vision, dotted line connected to the small, beige-colored thing. The cover slammed closed with a metallic crash.

Anna was already up, moving with that inhuman catlike grace, twisting away from her computer, racing impossibly fast toward the tiny thing that tumbled lazily toward the ground. Two green arcs slashed across Nadine's sight, one tracing the path of the falling thing, the other fanning out from Anna: Newton's laws of motion written in augmented reality, intersecting just above the ground.

The thing dropped into Anna's hand as she pulled it into herself, curling around it. Lena opened her mouth, arrested in the instant. A hard, bright flash strobed in Nadine's vision, over before she was fully aware of it. Pink mist filled the space where Anna had been. Lena blinked, surprise on her face, then an invisible hand slammed her to the floor. A split-second later, the world cracked apart with the loudest sound Nadine had ever heard, pile drivers crushing her ears. That same invisible hand slapped her, huge and hot, its force irresistible. She fell backward. Darkness swallowed her.

SOME TIMELESS TIME later, she opened her eyes. She lay on her back, her ears ringing. Brilliant light glared down at her, moved away, glared down again. A blurred, indistinct shape swam into view. "Squeeze my finger."

"Wha—"

"Squeeze my fingers. Come on, there's a good girl."

Nadine tightened her fingers. "Good, now the other one. Good." The blurred shape moved away. "Nothing broken, no shrapnel wounds. Mild concussion, no neurological damage beyond that. X-rays look good. You can talk to her now."

"Wha—" Nadine said again. She tried to sit. Wide straps around her arms, legs, and chest bound her to whatever was beneath her. "Where—"

The world cleared. Four tiled walls closed around her, a compact room filled with the sharp tang of antiseptics, a large round light overhead, switched off. Two people in white jackets, faces covered by disposable masks, stood at the end of the long, narrow stretcher beneath her. A man in a black uniform stood beside her, ramrod straight. *Security,* Nadine noted vaguely through the fading haze. An earpiece dangled from his ear. Three yellow triangles danced around him. "Miracle she survived," one of the masked figures said, a woman's voice, clinically disinterested.

"She wasn't supposed to." The other figure, a man's voice.

"He wants to see her," the security man said.

The woman shrugged. The two masked figures undid her straps. The security officer watched, alert and wary, one hand on his holster.

"Can you sit?" The man this time. He slipped one hand under her back and lifted her upright without waiting for an answer. Nadine shook her head, dizzy. Her vision wavered. "Good." The security officer closed a pair of handcuffs around her wrists, black brushed steel gleaming in the light of the flat-panel LEDs overhead.

In one motion, he hooked his hand under her arm and pulled her to her feet. Her clothing, she realized, was gone, replaced with a thin gown, open in the back, lime green squares printed on cheap, flimsy cotton. One of the masked, jacketed figures, she couldn't tell which, passed a card over a flat square of gray plastic in the wall. The plain steel door unlatched with a mechanical rattle. "Go."

He propelled her through the door into a hallway lit by the same flat panel LEDs in the ceiling, smooth linoleum under her bare feet.

"Where are you taking me?"

"Shut up." He shoved her, hard enough to make her stagger. They stopped in front of a steel door painted pale institutional green. He swiped a card over a blank plastic square. The door buzzed.

Inside, Nadine found a plain square room, bare except for a steel table bolted to the floor in the center, with a steel chair on each side. A camera looked down at them from a mount on the ceiling in one corner, red light glowering steadily. A single square LED panel in the ceiling gave the room a featureless, unforgiving blue-white glow.

"Sit." He took her by the arm and wrestled her into one of the chairs. He pulled a set of manacles connected by chain from a pocket, threaded them through a U-shaped steel rod welded to the table, and closed them around Nadine's wrists. Only then did he unlock the cuffs. He swiped his card again. The door buzzed, and Nadine was alone. Cold air prickled along the nape of her neck as she waited. She tugged on the manacles. Chain rattled against metal. She glared at the camera, which stared back at her with its unwavering glass eye. A tiny red LED glowed steadily. Her heart hammered. A hot flush spread through her body.

Minutes ticked by. Nadine curled her shaking hands into fists. Her legs trembled. Her heart pounded. Blood roared in her ears. The scene replayed in her head over and over: the look of surprise and confusion on Lena's face, Anna leaping through the air, hands outstretched to catch the falling grenade.

She jolted back to the present when the door buzzed to admit three people: the security guard she'd seen before, another who could've been his brother, and a man in a perfectly fitted tailored suit, immaculately-groomed hair just starting to silver at the edges, neatly trimmed beard that couldn't quite decide if it wanted to be a goatee. The man in the suit turned the unoccupied chair around and sat, draping his arms casually across the back. The two guards set up tripods with cameras atop them in the corners of the room, then took station on each side of him.

They stared at each other, Nadine in her thin hospital gown, the man in his expensive suit, for a long minute. Neither of them spoke. Finally, the man turned to the guard who'd escorted her here. "Uncuff her."

"Sir—"

"We aren't savages." His voice, mild and cultured, carried an undercurrent of absolute confidence, an expectation of obedience.

"Yes, sir." He unfasten Nadine's cuffs, coiled the chain, and tucked them in his pocket.

"Wait outside."

"Yes, sir." With a swipe of his card over gray plastic, he left.

"Well, well, well," the man in the suit said. "You defied the odds. My people have run multiple simulations of the...situation in the tunnel. You die in fifty-four percent of them. How remarkable."

"Where are my friends?" Nadine said.

He studied her for a long moment before he spoke again. "My name is Martin Taylor. You are Nadine Beatrice Jiang, daughter of Mun Fong Jiang and Romy Gauthier, age twenty-nine, failed actor and until recently gainfully employed as an administrative assistant at Dynamics Commercial Realtors. Your current legal troubles have, of course, impacted your employment status. Engaged in a licentious affair with Annette Chaparala, who has rather a long history of unfortunate legal entanglements of her own. Had, I should say. Known associations with members of the Peace Resistance Group, which I've always found to be an ironic name. So now we have been introduced." He regarded her levelly. Nadine stared back at him. "What? No surprise? No 'how do you know all this about me'? Hm. Interesting."

"What do you want?" Nadine said.

"Want?" Mild surprise showed in his eyes. "From you? I came here to get a look at you, nothing more. You did beat the odds, after all. You should be dead with the rest of your friends."

"Murderer!" Nadine spat.

"Murder is the unlawful premeditated killing of one human being by another. Under the laws of the State of California, bona fide security personnel of a duly registered corporation have the legal authority to use lethal force to defend corporate assets from an imminent threat." He shook his head. "I must say how disappointed I am. Did you believe you could, what, ride in here and save the day? Lift your friend from our villainous clutches? Did you think for even half a second that we would not have resources in place at the hub of an organized criminal gang so near to our sphere of operation? Though you have given us an unexpected opportunity in that regard. Projections suggest Antonio Delgado's influence might grow to the point where it begins intersecting with ours in a financially deleterious way within the next five to seven years, so your unexpected survival might be fortuitous. We'd already written a press release. 'Terrorist cell killed by private security forces.' But perhaps with one of you at large, the narrative might be 'Fugitive terrorist escapes, believed harbored by known gang leader.' His participation in this expedition should not go unchastised."

"What have you done with Marcus?"

"He enjoyed our hospitality for a time. He is no longer with us."

"You monster!"

"Me?" Genuine surprise, quickly smoothed away. "On the contrary. I represent one of the last remaining forces for order and stability. The work I do is vital to a safe, prosperous society. We live in a world beset on all sides by disorder and chaos. We create the means by which everything our forefathers have built can persevere."

"What is Project Mirage?"

"Where did you hear that? I must have a discussion with our information security team. Do you imagine that here, now, at the end of your life, I'm going to explain everything to you? I am not a villain from some spy movie, Ms. Jiang. There are no black and white baddies here."

With a scream of rage, unaware of what she intended to do until the moment her legs uncoiled explosively beneath her, Nadine launched herself across the table at him, arms out. She saw him move to react, saw him bring up his arms to ward her off, saw the blurred arcs that predicted where his hands would be, saw the path through. Her fingernails raked his face, leaving two gouges in his cheek. The security officer beside him sprang into action, already moving before her nails reached his skin. He slammed heavily into her, knocking her sideways from the chair. Her head met the floor with a crack. Darkness closed in from the corners of her vision for a moment. By the time her vision cleared, he had already hauled her up, arm twisted painfully behind her. He slammed her face into the table, leaning heavily against her, his other arm across her neck.

Martin unfolded a handkerchief from his pocket and dabbed at his cheek. He examined the square of white cloth critically. "She'll make an excellent bogeyman. Her escape is, I think, likely to prove useful for the indefinite future. We should have plenty of video to deepfake some convincing sightings. Deal with her in the usual manner. Let me know when it's done."

"Yes, sir."

Martin rose and swiped a card across the plastic square, handkerchief pressed to his cheek. The door buzzed. Martin turned to look back at her. "How very frustrating it must be for you, Ms. Jiang, to die without ever knowing what any of this is about."

As he left, the other security guard came in, one hand on his holster. "Get up."

The first guard grabbed her arm, painfully tight. Nadine's heart thudded. "Listen—"

"Shut up. Move."

The second guard stood aside as he marched her through the door, hand still on his holster, wary. Yellow warning triangles glowed in Nadine's vision, three of them, thin lines pointing to his belt. The door shut as he took up station behind them. They brought her down a long, sterile hallway, doors with blank gray rectangles along both walls, that eventually ended at a T-junction with a large black roll-up door latched with a padlocked lever. The security guard behind her unlocked the padlock and rolled the door up. The man holding her arm pushed her through into a small loading dock, down a ramp to where an unmarked van—the same one from the video captured at the hospital, or one just like it—waited in a space marked off by painted yellow lines.

"Nice ass," the guard behind her said. "Shame. I like Asian girls."

"This one doesn't take the D," the guard holding her arm said. He steered her toward the back of the van while his friend unlocked the driver's side door.

"Maybe that's just because she hasn't met the right D yet." He climbed into the driver's seat.

"Okay, end of the line," the guard holding Nadine's arm said. He shoved her toward the open doors in the back of the van. "Get in." From up front, the van chimed to life. The lights came on.

Nadine turned toward him, heart pounding so fast her entire body vibrated. She raised her hands. "Please—"

"Now."

She flashed into motion, kicking him square between the legs with a bare foot. "You bit—" he started to say, but she was already reaching for his belt, following the line from the glowing triangle where it terminated at his holster. He grabbed for her, yellow arcs slicing out from his hands, a preview into a future that might be. She grabbed the gun and leapt backward, realizing as she brought it up, surprisingly heavy in her hands, she had no idea how to use it, or even how to turn off the safety. She squeezed the trigger, halfway expecting nothing to happen, her last desperate act of bravado to end in futility.

The gun kicked in her hand. A roar shattered the stillness in the cramped loading dock. The man started to fall, shock and disbelief battling on his face.

Nadine spun. His partner turned his head to look between the seats. "Jesus, did you have to do it he—"

She pulled the trigger again with a small, desperate prayer. The gun jerked, three more times, every kick accompanied by a sound that drove icepicks into her ears. His face changed, the same shock and disbelief written across it. The first two shots produced round holes edged in a lacework of cracks in the van's windshield. On the third, a jet of red, impossibly bright, sprayed across the front of the van. The man's head jerked back at a strange angle, then he went limp as a ragdoll.

She heard a groan behind her. She turned. The security guard lay on his back, hand clutched to his stomach. Something sticky and red pooled around him. He stretched out his other hand toward her. "Please—"

The gun kicked, without any conscious intent on her part. Her ears rang. Where his eye had been, there was now...now... She blanched and looked away.

Nadine ran to the driver's door. Her gorge rose. She grabbed the slain security guard by his belt and pulled. He fell to the ground at her feet like a sack of potatoes, head lolling. She threw the gun into the van and scrambled over him. The windshield had two round holes in it, surprisingly small, cracks spiderwebbing from them. A thin film of something sticky dripped down the central touchscreen. Behind her, the huge gate leading up and out to freedom began to scroll closed.

"Fuck!" Nadine swore. "Fuck fuck fuck!" She hopped into the driver's seat and shifted into reverse, slamming the door as she stomped on the accelerator. The van shot backward as if fired from a cannon. Blood obscured the rearview display. "Fuck!" Nadine craned her head behind her, aiming for the narrowing sliver of blue. She struck the concrete pillar beside the gate with a glancing blow. The van kicked sideways. The gate came down on the roof. She floored the pedal. With a shriek of metal, the van shot out into the driveway.

Nadine stood on the brakes. Hands shaking, she fumbled at the shift lever. She yanked the steering wheel around and hit the accelerator again. The van obliged, flinging itself forward with gusto. She sped past the place where Dan-boy had parked Tony's borrowed van. No trace of it or Jason and Kev remained. Then she was out on the street in the hot, humid Los Angeles afternoon, cars honking around her as she cut through the flow of traffic.

Tears stung her eyes. She wiped them away impatiently with the back of her hand and realized she was shaking. She gripped the wheel with both hands until her knuckles turned white.

A plan. She needed a plan.

Santa Monica Storage, locker 531. Anna's voice.

Nadine shook her head violently. "I must be in shock."

Santa Monica Storage, locker 531.

Nadine reached for her implant. "T-town. Take me there." She glanced around the bloodied wreckage inside the van, the hospital gown she wore. "Avoid traffic." It responded with gratifying promptness, a green arrow superimposed over her vision, translucent. She kept her eyes fixed straight ahead, willing herself invisible. Riders gaped at her. A couple of cars honked. She ignored them, following the green arrow with grim focus. Her ears rang. Afterimages of muzzle flashes hung in her vision with every eyeblink.

She saw a surveillance platform, off to her right, fifteen minutes before she reached T-town, and of course cameras sprouting from every pole and cell tower and, in some cases, tree, but apparently a woman in a hospital gown driving a van with bullet holes in the windshield didn't rise above the background of everyday Los Angeles weird. She drove through the parking lot with its mix of rusted-out hulks of ancient internal-combustion cars and lovingly customized rides and stopped in front of the gate, where two of Tony's boys stood in ill-fitting body armor. Yellow warning triangles hovered over them.

One of the boys, a dark-haired, dark-eyed kid of perhaps eighteen or nineteen with rippling muscles on bare arms, shook his head. "No admittance."

Nadine rolled down the window. "It's me! Let me in."

"No admittance," he repeated.

"I need to see Tony. Anna and the others are gone."

"Anna?" This precipitated an excited flurry of Spanish with the other boy. They both approached the driver's door, eyes suspicious and wary. "Where is Anna?" He registered the bullet holes and blood. "What happened?"

"Mayor Tony. Right now."

The kid keyed a microphone clipped to his collar. More rapid Spanish, then he nodded. The gate clanked into life and slid aside.

Tony was already coming out into the courtyard when Nadine drove through, three more boys at his back. Nadine opened the driver's door and jumped out. Her bare feet met hot, hard-baked dirt. *"Chiquita,"* Tony said. His eyes narrowed. "Where is Anna?"

Nadine bent over double and threw up. Bile and the remnants of Jason's protein bar splattered wet to the ground. She kept heaving even when nothing more would come.

Tony barked in Spanish. One of the boys pushed past Nadine and flipped the switch to open the hood. A flat battery panel and a row of diagnostics connectors lay beneath. The boy moved around to the front of the van, pulling a compact folding tool of some sort from his pocket as he did. Tony shook his head. "Where is Anna?"

Nadine straightened. "Dead. They're all dead."

"And you bring this van here, to my crib? With GPS and transponders?"

"It doesn't matter. They knew we were coming. They were waiting for us. They said they have someone here, in your crew. Said they plan to teach you a lesson. Punish you for sending us their way."

Tony's expression turned grim. He turned to the boy at the front of the van, who straightened, holding a small silver device at the end of a severed bundle of cables like a fisherman holding up a giant bass. "We need to talk."

"We don't have time to talk." Nadine set out toward the building with Mateo and his room of cabinets.

Tony whistled, a shrill sound that shattered the air. Every eye in the courtyard swiveled toward them. "*Chiquita.* We need to talk."

"I need clothes," Nadine said without turning.

"Whose blood is all over this van?"

"Former occupant."

"You did this?"

"Yes. Gun's on the passenger seat. I don't want anything to do with it." She started walking again. One of Tony's boys ran around her and planted himself in her path, hands on his hips. Triangles flared. Nadine spun. "So talk."

"You do not disrespect me in my home."

"Fine. I'm sorry. Did you hear what I said? They were waiting for us."

"That could be. Or maybe you aren't who you say."

"So my plan is, what? I kill my girlfriend and her friends? I come back here in this?" She plucked at the flimsy hospital gown. "Not even wearing shoes? We don't have time for this."

"For you to say I have a *soplón* in my crew, this is a serious accusation."

"Yeah, well, it's been a serious kind of day."

The boy in front of her stepped out of her way, responding to a small gesture from Tony. Through the door, up the stairs, plywood coarse beneath her feet, plywood walls vibrating with the cacophony of music she'd come to accept as the background noise of Tijuana Town, labored wheeze of an air conditioner struggling to keep the temperature manageable. Tony and his boys followed close behind. Mateo waited for her in his room of steel cabinets. He touched his hat when she came in. "*Dalaga.* You are here to make a withdrawal?"

"Yes."

"Ah. Some new clothes might be in order, I see."

"I don't have the paper you gave me."

"*N'importe.* I remember everyone." He unlocked a cabinet, slid her suitcase to her. "Your ring. Your key."

"Thank you." She opened the suitcase, pulled on a pair of panties and the faded black jeans Anna liked on her, shrugged an oversized shirt over the hospital gown, untied the gown, and slithered out of it. She balled the gown up and put it on the counter. "Can you—? I don't want to touch it any more."

Mateo nodded slightly. "*Très bien.*"

"And now," Tony said, "we need to talk."

Nadine looked at her toes, curled against cheap industrial carpeting. "I don't have any shoes."

"Now."

She followed him to his office, dragging her suitcase up the stairs behind her. The same bodyguard who'd been there the night they arrived sat in the small chair in front of the door. He glowered at her as she went past. With all three of Tony's boys crowded into the space, it seemed less expansive than it had the first time she'd been here. A gangly-looking kid with glasses who would not have seemed out of place at a high school math olympiad, closed the door behind them. Warning triangles floated around all of them. Tony settled into the chair behind his desk, hands folded in front of him. He stared through Nadine. "Talk."

Nadine related the entire story: the ambush in the tunnel, waking up in the small sickbay, her interview with Martin, her escape. He listened, face growing grimmer and grimmer as she spoke. When she finished, he looked at her for a long time. A vein in his temple throbbed. Nadine swallowed.

At last, he said, "You have given me lots to think about. One of my crew, betraying me..." He shook his head.

A radio on the belt of the gangly kid crackled. Excited Spanish poured out. Tony stood, so suddenly Nadine flinched. "It seems you were right. You—" he pointed at the kid, startled expression made owlish by his glasses. "Take her downstairs. Give her the car. You know the one. You," he said to Nadine, "take it and get out of here. Get rid of it when you are away. Cloned transponder, shows up as LAPD to drones and receivers.

It will do for a quick glance, but any deep search will attract attention you don't want. Go."

"Thank you," Nadine said.

Tony shook his head violently. "No. You told me of a problem in my house. After this, we are even. Make sure I never see you again."

"What's happening?"

"*¡Puerta!*" he barked.

The kid propelled Nadine out the door by her elbow. He urged her down the stairs, taking them two at a time into the courtyard. A shadow eclipsed the sun. Nadine squinted and shaded her eyes with her hand. The great bulk of a surveillance platform drifted toward them, looking somehow predatory as it floated through the air. Nadine stopped and gawped. The boy at her elbow prodded her on. "*¡Señorita!*"

Nadine allowed herself to be propelled into the garage, where a row of cars in various states of disassembly awaited their new lives as black-market parts. The kid pulled the tarp off a car in the corner, a white late-model GM sedan with a spotlight on the door, all-electric. He fumbled with the charging cable. "Go, now!"

"The platform—"

"It will ignore you!" He opened the driver's side door and pushed her in. "Go!" Without waiting for her to belt herself in, he bolted across the courtyard toward the gate, waving his arms over his head and yelling in Spanish.

Nadine threw her suitcase into the back seat. The car came to life. "Please fasten your seat belt," a feminine voice announced primly. "This vehicle is equipped with self-driving functionality, but you are responsible for safe driving at all times. Always pay attention to the road ahead and stay prepared to take immediate corrective action. Failure to be aware of road hazards may result in serious injury or death. Please touch CONFIRM to accept these conditions."

Nadine jabbed at the button on the front panel. The car chirped, satisfied. She pulled out into the courtyard, where the gate was already opening, chain rattling in its groove. The moment she was clear, the gate closed behind her. Once past the cars in the lot and onto the street, she risked a look back at the dun wall of Tijuana Town behind her. The bulk of the surveillance platform drifted closer. From somewhere in the distance, she heard the dull whup-whup-whup of helicopters.

Three blocks away, she pulled over as a string of police cars and SWAT vans screamed by, sirens wailing. Her heart leapt into her throat. As Tony promised, they sped past, paying her no mind. Nadine huddled in the GM with its cloned transponder, waiting them out. As the adrenaline finally burned itself out, the sobs tore through her, screams of anguish and loss ripping themselves from her throat until nothing was left. When at last they spent themselves, she dried her eyes, put the car in gear, and navigated back into the street.

PART 2
BESTIA EX MACHINA

9

Field of Poppies

S ANTA MONICA STORAGE turned out to be a long, drab building in beige, a row of sun-bleached orange roll-up doors facing a parking lot behind a dilapidated chain link fence. Entry was afforded through a small gate guarded by a length of PVC pipe painted with yellow stripes that swung obligingly out of her way. She saw no cameras anywhere.

Nadine pulled the nondescript car up to the tinted glass door. Only two other cars sat in the parking lot: a beat-up Tesla with a cracked front quarter panel and an antique Mini Cooper, an obvious aftermarket electric conversion, as pristine as if it had just rolled off the showroom floor. Through the door, an arctic blast of cold air greeted her. A woman looked up at her from behind a scratched and battered counter, bubblegum-pink hair framing a face studded with piercings. She wore a skintight shirt decorated with bright pink stripes and brilliant yellow neoprene shorts. "Yeah?"

"Locker 531?"

The woman jerked her thumb down one of several rows of lockers, crowded claustrophobically tight. "Thanks," Nadine said, but she had already gone back to the video display on her lap, face blank with disinterest.

Locker 531 was near the end of the row farthest from the counter. An emergency fire valve that had probably once been red protruded from the wall, so stained with rust it seemed unlikely a prybar could move it. Nadine knelt on the cracked concrete floor and opened the locker. Inside, she found a large duffle bag of black ballistic nylon with two large straps. Nadine dragged it from the locker and slung it over her shoulder. The key stayed in the lock. The straps, long enough to let the bag bang against the back of her legs, dug into her skin. She waved to the woman behind the counter, who didn't look up as she left.

Back in the GM, she set the bag on the passenger's seat and unzipped it. A large shrinkwrapped cube of $20 bills filled most of its space, faded and worn beneath the transparent overwrap. On top of the bundle of cash sat a black handgun, several magazines, two boxes of ammunition, an old-fashioned handheld cell phone of the type Nadine saw in low-budget crime thrillers, and a neatly folded sheet of paper.

With shaking hands, she unfolded the sheet of paper. A bank chip slipped into her lap. She put the chip in the bag and read the elegant handwriting that flowed across the heavy, cream-colored paper in crisp black ink.

> *My darling Nadine:*
> *If you're reading this, I'm in jail or worse. God, that's such a cliched thing to write, isn't it? Ah well. You probably won't ever read this, so my ramblings won't matter anyway.*
> *The phone is untraceable, or near enough. It contains one number. You can trust the person it leads to. He will help you. Go somewhere else. Start a new life.*
> *I love you, my dearest. More than you will ever know. You have been such a blessing. I feel guilty dragging you into the muck and chaos. I know it wasn't what you signed up for. I think about it late at night when I watch you sleep. You make little happy sounds when I wrap my arms around you in your sleep, did you know that? I don't think I ever told you.*
> *I'll stop before I get any more maudlin. I guess I can say it all here, since you'll probably never read these words. Thank you for being who you are, my love.*
> *Anna xoxox*

Tears blurred Nadine's vision. She wiped them away with the back of her hand and picked up the phone. As promised, it had one number in the contacts list, labeled J. She fumbled at the buttons with clumsy fingers. The phone rang.

"Yeah." A man's voice, clipped, brusque.

"I'm...uh, I don't know what I'm supposed to say. I'm Nadine. Anna gave me this phone."

"Where is Anna?"

"She—" Nadine's throat closed. "Gone."

"We don't have a lot of time, so I need you to listen to me and do exactly as I say. Got it?"

"Yes."

"Get out of the car."

"How do you know I'm—"

"Do it now." His voice carried a hard edge of command.

Nadine stepped out into the heat, leaving her suitcase and the black nylon bag behind, phone still to her ear. "Turn around," the voice said. "Face the gate."

Nadine complied. "I don't see anything,"

"Look down." A bright red dot, hard-edged, danced on her chest. "So we understand each other. If you are who you say you are, we'll get along fine." A pause. "Why are you barefoot?"

"Long story."

"Car next to you. Reach under the left front wheel well." Nadine fumbled around in the wheel well of the Mini and came up with a black plastic box, clipped in place with a magnet. "Good. Open it." A wireless keyfob lay inside. "Unlock the door. Take everything you need out of your car and put it in the back seat."

Nadine complied, aware of the red dot that remained on her as she transferred her suitcase and the bag into the Mini's compact rear seat. "Get in the driver's side. Leave the door open. Hang up the phone. Put both hands on the wheel. Don't take your hands off the wheel, understand?"

"Yes." Heart pounding, Nadine did as she was told. Sweat clung to her skin. The mirror showed motion behind her. She gripped the wheel tightly, scarcely breathing. A moment later, a man stood next to the door, holding a strange, foreshortened rifle, a squat thing with a black scope, in his left hand, not quite pointed at her. To Nadine's eye, it looked more like a sci-fi movie prop than a real weapon, compact and angular, magazine in the back. It and his cloak were the same mottled green. "Anna's friend, I presume," he said. "Jake Fox. How'd you meet her?"

"Underground dance party," Nadine said. "Terminal Island."

"What was she wearing?"

"I don't remember. Uh...LEDs in her hair."

He nodded. "This your car?"

"No. Mayor Tony gave it to me. Said it had a cloned police transponder."

"Clever. Dangerous, but clever. Okay, here's the deal." He reached in through the window to tap the dashboard. His right hand ended in a mechanical claw, titanium prosthetic partly encased in mottled green plastic. Servos whined. "Start the car. Navigation is already programmed. Motel, room 114, bottom floor, near the back. Key's in the glove box. I'll meet you there."

"Where are you going?"

"To get rid of this car. You have the fob?"

"I, um...it's in the car."

"Good. Don't call anyone. Don't talk to anyone. Follow the navigation. Go straight into the room. Take all your stuff with you. Lock the door. Wait for me."

The Mini took her on a circuitous route, avoiding major roads, frequently turning down side streets for no reason Nadine could see. Eventually, they drove east, away from the heart of the city, through an endless jungle of strip malls and run-down industrial parks. The car pulled into the parking lot of an anonymous, generic motel and chimed. "You have reached your destination. Please assume manual control for parking."

Nadine parked near the back next to a scratched, dented charger. The Mini beeped. A charging probe extended blindly from the battered charger.

As promised, the glove box contained an old-fashioned metal key attached to a large diamond-shaped tag of green plastic. She dragged her suitcase and the duffle bag into the room. Two double beds, a small refrigerator, coffee maker atop a scuffed particle board desk, a chair upholstered in hideous red with stuffing leaking from the corner. Nadine's stomach rumbled. She opened the refrigerator to find it empty.

She looked around the room. Other than what she'd brought in, it contained no luggage, no sign that anyone else had been here. A folding door opened onto a tiny closet, empty hangers dangling from a wooden bar. She sat gingerly on the edge of one of the beds, its covers the same hideous red as the chair. A poster of a bland country scene rendered in oil paints hung on the wall in a simple wooden frame covered with peeling gold paint. On one wall, a narrow air conditioner hummed beneath heavy blackout drapes.

The day's terror drained, leaving her blank and numb. She stared dully at the painting, a woman in a hat with a tiny blue parasol leading a child through a field of red flowers. The colors blurred and faded before her eyes, nothing more than shapes and brushstrokes. Part of her felt trapped in the tunnel, watching the grenade fall, the surprise on

Lena's face, the spray of red filming gray concrete over and over, a low-resolution loop of horror. "I wish—" she said aloud.

Wish what? Anna's voice, startlingly clear inside her head.

"Wish I had never said to take Marcus to the hospital. Wish I'd never gone to see him and brought the police back to you. Wish none of this had happened."

Wish you'd never met me?

"I—" Tears leaked from her eyes. "No. Not that. Never that."

Your life is ruined. And for what?

"I don't know."

"Don't know what?" The voice came from a shadow in the doorway, briefly eclipsed by the sun. Nadine blinked. Jake carried a small travel bag in one hand. He pushed a white bag toward her, held in the clamp on the end of his prosthetic. A cartoon animal decorated its front. "Food. Hope you like hoagies. Got some soda too. Or coffee, if you prefer. Who were you talking to?"

Nadine shook her head. "No one." She opened the sandwich. Her mouth watered.

Jake sat in the chair, eyes narrowed. "Your face is all over the news."

"Do you believe what they're saying about me?"

"Does it matter?" He looked levelly at her until she dropped her gaze. "No. Not that it makes a difference. Anna paid me to get you out of the country in the event something happens to her, so that's what I'm going to do." He reached into his pocket and produced a passport. "Here. Melody Landry. Canadian citizen. You live in Toronto. Pass back and forth a few times a year on business, this time you were down here to see your grandparents. Your flight leaves in eight hours. Economy class, I'm afraid. Now, tell me everything."

Between bites of sandwich, Nadine related the entire story: Marcus and the others arriving at the door, her visit to the hospital, the SWAT raid, the desperate flight to Tijuana Town, what happened after. "That fills in a few details," he said when she'd finished. "Martin Taylor. Nasty piece of work."

"You know him?"

"By reputation. Ex-military. Marines. Went private sector, ran a security company for a while. Some kind of CEO now."

"He sure didn't like it when I scratched his face."

"You did what?"

"I gouged him pretty good."

Jake leaned forward. "Have you showered?"

"What?"

"Showered. Bathed. Have you showered?"

"No. Why?"

"Let me see your hand." He held out his mechanical arm. Nadine reached for him, hesitant. He took her finger gently between metal fingers, examined it closely. "Don't move." He pulled a folding knife from his pocket and flicked it open.

"What are you doing?"

"You managed to get his DNA. Careless of him." He dug beneath her nail with the point of the knife, then took a small plastic bag from his suitcase and carefully sealed the scrapings in it. "Could be useful."

"For what?"

"Don't know yet." He grinned unpleasantly. "This guy Marcus. What was wrong with him?"

"They said he got shot. His chest was covered with these little bristles, like cactus spines or something. I kept one."

"Do you still have it?"

"Maybe." She opened her suitcase, dug through her purse. "Yes. It's in here." She opened the pill bottle. The tiny sliver still lay inside. "Don't touch it. The burning lasts for ages."

"Interesting. Whatever that is, someone thought it was important enough to do a snatch and grab from a hospital. Risky. I would very much like to know why. May I have that? I know some people who know some people who might be able to analyze it." He produced a bottle of pills from inside his pocket. With a few deft motions of his prosthetic arm, he shook out a couple of plain white tablets and handed them to her. "Take these."

"What are they?"

"Beta blockers. Inhibit formation of emotional associations. You're headed for PTSD if you don't."

Nadine swallowed the pills with a mouthful of warm soda. "Who are you?"

"Friend of Anna's. That's all you need to know."

"Why do you care about any of this?"

"Because I'm a friend of Anna's. I want to find out what happened to her. Call it professional curiosity. Get cleaned up and get some sleep. I'll take you to the airport in six hours."

Nadine showered under a real proper shower, rather than a tepid drizzle, for the first time since she'd fled Anna's. Unreality settled around her. The day's horror faded like the clinging remnants of a dream. She dried her hair with a towel and padded back out into the room. Jake sat with his back to her, the parts of his rifle spread out on the small table. Instantly, the fear and trauma poured over her again. She reeled.

"You should try to sleep," he said without looking up. "You look like shit. It'll be dark soon. You're on the redeye to Toronto."

"No," she said.

"No what?"

"No, I'm not going."

"Something wrong with Toronto?"

"I need...I need to know why. Why all of it. Why Marcus, why...why everything."

He set down the part he was cleaning and turned to face her. "There is no why. It just is. There's no grand design. There's no great secret that will make any of this make sense. There's just people doing shit. You and your friends did some shit that got you caught up in shit other people were doing, that's it. Nothing you learn will make you feel any better. Best outcome you can hope for is to walk away, try to start a new life, maybe one day stop looking over your shoulder." He shrugged. "Shit happens."

"Why are you here?"

"Anna paid me. She said if you show up looking for help, I'm to get you out of the country by any means necessary. I saw you on the news, figured you'd be calling, got to the storage place ahead of you. Now it's time for you to go."

"What will you do?"

"I will admit to a certain curiosity. You've landed in something weird and dangerous. Might shake some trees, see what falls out."

"Does the word 'mirage' mean anything to you?"

"You mean like water in the desert that isn't really there?"

"No. It's something Anna said, right before...before she died. Project Mirage. She found it in their computers. Texas, she said."

"No idea."

"Take me with you."

He shook his head. "No. Out of the question. Do you even know how to use that gun in your bag?"

"You went through my stuff?"

"Of course I went through your stuff. I'm sticking my neck out for you. Have you ever used a gun before?"

Heat flared in Nadine. "You mean besides shooting two people today?" The hot spike of anger faded as quickly as it had come. "I honestly didn't think it would work. Isn't there supposed to be a safety or something?"

"Glock," Jake said, as if that answered it. "Look, I'm not criticizing. You handled yourself well. But you're standing here breathing right now because you were lucky. That, and Anna saved your life. That grenade, she hadn't done what she did, it would've cut you to ribbons. Even with that, if you were standing any closer, you'd have gone white butterfly."

"White butterfly? What does that mean?"

"Blast lung injury. The shockwave would've killed you. Point is, you got lucky. You capitalized on your luck, sure, but it's luck that kept you alive. You aren't trained for this."

"Yeah?" The anger was back, a tiny ember of rage hot in her belly. "Those men I shot, were they trained? How about Dan-boy's crew, were they trained?"

He spread the fingers on his left hand. "Listen, I was paid to do a job."

"So do it. I'm not leaving. Fuck Canada, fuck Toronto. I don't care, get it? My life is over. I will never stop looking over my shoulder. The world believes I am a terrorist. So what, I settle down? Buy a house in the suburbs? Get married? Wait for the cops to show up at my door one day? The last thing Martin said to me is I would die without ever knowing why. Well, fuck him. I need to know why. I'm not getting on that plane. I can either do this myself, and probably get killed, or do it with you, and maybe get killed. There is no path that leads to me getting on a plane to Toronto and trying to pretend none of this ever happened. You want to do the job you were paid to do? Keep me out of harm's way? Take me with you or get out of my way."

He spread his arms in a gesture of surrender. "Your funeral."

"Fine. Where do we start?"

"We start with getting you shoes."

THE SHOES TURNED out to be more complicated than Nadine expected. Jake refused to allow her to leave the hotel room. "There's a hornet's nest out there," he said. "One camera identifies you and we're done. Stay here. Don't open the door for anyone and for God's sake don't talk to anyone." He flicked open his knife, slit the plastic wrapping the brick of cash, and pulled out several bundles of bills. "I'm going to make some passes at some people I know, maybe get a line on an organic chemistry lab that understands discretion. Don't go anywhere."

Nadine paced the small room, shoulders tight with anxiety. She thought about Toronto and the promise, however implausible, of a new life. Toronto seemed a mirage, a phantasm of a life that had been taken away from her.

She flipped on the news feed. The same story dominated every channel. Police and SWAT cars surrounded a wall, colored lights crashing against dun stucco, as flames billowed from a warehouse behind it. The same footage played over and over again: cops swarming the encampment like angry ants, a brilliant arc of fire from ground to sky, the surveillance platform crashing through the roof of the largest building. "Gang leader with terrorist ties killed in police raid" scrolled beneath the video carnage.

Nadine shook her head, unable to grasp what she was seeing. Images flashed through her mind: Mateo in his top hat, Takeru in his room crammed with medical gear. Had they made it out? Were they dead? Were they in prison?

She jumped when the door came open. Jake came in with several large bags hung from his titanium arm and a large worn Army rucksack slung over his shoulder. He dumped them on the bed. "Got you some shoes. Hope you like Doc Martens. You need to dump that suitcase, it's a giant screaming target on your back. Here." He shoved the black rucksack and a smaller white plastic bag toward her embossed with the logo of a beauty supply company.

"What's this?"

"Need to change your hair. Cut it shorter, dye it. Also a few wigs in there. Dazzle makeup. You'll need to learn to use it."

"Won't that make me stand out even more?"

"Lotta people use it. It's not that big a deal. You'll stand out a lot less than you will surrounded by cops because facial recognition tagged you. Getting harder and harder to slip under the radar these days. You want to cut your hair or you want me to? Won't fool computers, but you'll be less likely to get noticed by human beings."

"I can do it."

A couple hours later, Nadine emerged from the room's tiny bathroom, long black hair transformed to a short bob. Jake nodded in satisfaction. "You look like an anime girl."

"I hate it."

"You'll hate prison more. Got you some new colored contacts. Ditch the ones you're wearing and pair these to your implant. Get some sleep."

Nadine curled up beneath the hideous red cover. In the space between blinks, the image cycled itself again and again: the tiny grenade falling, Anna leaping in that surrealistically graceful way she had, pink mist. Eventually, sleep dragged her down.

10

Off Plan

NADINE WOKE CONFUSED, not sure for a moment where she was. Sleep tugged at her, slowed her mind. "Anna?" she mumbled, reaching out beside her.

"Get dressed. Got a call." Jake's voice sent cold water down her spine. Sick memory curdled in the pit of her stomach. Nadine curled up, knees pressed to her chest, willing it to be over, a bad dream... "Got a lead on someone who can maybe tell us what that sliver is," he went on. "All starts there. Someone was willing to go through a lot of trouble to get your friend. You're so hot to find out what happened, that's the thread we pull first."

Nadine crawled out of bed and dressed without a word. Jake handed her an egg and sausage muffin wrapped in green cellophane and a paper cup filled with coffee that burned a hole in her stomach. "Here." He dropped a tiny, coarse rock in her palm. "Put this in your sock."

"What?"

"You'll have to walk carefully to keep it from digging into your foot. Messes up gait detection software."

"You're serious," Nadine said.

"As a heart attack. Think of it as asymmetric warfare, people versus the Panopticon. Police, military, they spend tons of money on AI surveillance systems, defeated by the simplest things. Rocks and makeup."

"Doesn't that piss off the politicians?"

"Nah. Gives them an excuse to spread more money around, help their friends get richer. Appropriate more and more taxpayer cash every year finding ways to work around the street's workarounds. Perpetual arms race means a perpetual river of money."

Nadine cracked the seal on the high-end contacts, more expensive than the ones she usually bought. The tiny LED array glittered on the inside of the curved surface, a high-resolution matrix that promised higher fidelity graphics than she could normally afford. They also made her brown eyes green. Between that and the hair, she looked even more like a refugee from an anime movie. "You've already turned off network connectivity on your implant, right?" Jake said.

"What? No."

"Fuck. Okay, that moves up the timetable a bit."

"How come?"

Jake sighed. "You were in the same room with Martin. You may have changed the ID on your implant, but you can bet he probably scanned it. I've had a jammer running since we got here, but there's a chance you may have been tracked this far. Or at least to the storage place. Nothing for it now, but from now on you leave your network off. Let's hide your identity."

Jake, yellow triangles hovering around him, taught her to use the dazzle. "The thing you want to do," he explained, "is break up the contours the machine learning systems use to identify your face. Shape of your cheekbones, height of your eyes, like that. Your hoodie is good. Confuses facial recognition, makes it hard for it to identify your face. Okay, good as it's going to get," he said when he'd finished. "Hood up. Grab your stuff. Let's go."

The sun had barely risen, but the morning air already felt like an oven. Nadine slid her new rucksack and Anna's bag into the back of the Mini, then slipped into the passenger's seat. Jake brought the car to life. "This friend of yours," Nadine said, "you trust him?"

"We have history. I did him a favor years back, helped get his family out of a tight spot. Another country, another life." The lines of Jake's mouth settled into something grim.

"Who is he? Ex-military? Spy?"

"Not quite." He stared off into space for a moment, lips moving slightly. "I checked us out. Let's go."

The Mini navigated them to a small coffee and cannabis shop near the place where the interstate discharged into University Hills. Nadine hobbled after Jake, trying her best to look inconspicuous, stone digging painfully into her arch. At this hour, the shop had only a few patrons, all of them college age, more interested in caffeine than cannabis. Jake headed to a table in the back, where he sat down beside a middle-aged man who looked vaguely Middle Eastern, silver hair pulled back in a ponytail, cheap suit jacket draped over the back of his chair. "Doctor Abdullah," he said. "Pleasure to see you again."

The man examined Nadine through a pair of silver wire-framed glasses. Light flitted across the lenses, though Nadine couldn't read whatever it was he was looking at. "This your friend?"

"Client. Melody, meet Dr. Fazel Abdullah, professor of molecular biology at California State University. Professor, this is Melody."

"How..." he started. "Never mind."

"We have a favor to ask."

"Yes, of course you do. Otherwise you wouldn't be here." He raised a tiny ceramic cup to a wry smile. "Always business with you."

"This is an interesting one. Appeals to your skill set." Jake opened his jacket, took out Nadine's pill bottle. "There's a sample in here. We need to know what it is. Be careful with it. Don't touch it."

Fazel leaned forward, interested in spite of himself. "What can you tell me?"

Jake looked at Nadine. "Took it from the chest of a...friend," she said. "He'd been shot. Had a whole forest of these needle-like things sticking out of him. Screaming like crazy. I touched one. It hurt. Bad, for a long time."

"Interesting." He tucked the bottle in his pocket, finished the last of his coffee. "That's it? Just tell you what it is?"

"And anything else you might find out," Jake said. "Got another thing for you too."

"Wonderful."

Jake passed him the small bag with the scrapings from beneath Nadine's fingernails. "There's a DNA sample in there. Need the sequence. Please. And a major histocompatibility analysis, too, if you can."

"Anything else? A kidney, perhaps?"

"Why, you got an extra one?" Jake rose from the table. "I'll be in touch. Give Tayeba and Razia my regards."

"Of course."

Nadine followed Jake back out into the heat. "What happens now?"

"Now he does his job. Meantime, I want to dig up more on Martin Taylor. And we need to find a new place to stay." He pulled the Mini out into traffic under manual control.

"Mind if I ask you something?" Nadine said.

"What happened to my arm?"

"Yeah."

"Belarus."

"Shit. You were there?"

"Yeah. Made it out alive, but not exactly in one piece. Lot of folks weren't so lucky."

"How'd you know what I was going to ask?"

"Your expression. People always have that same look when they ask. Like they're horrified and fascinated and worried they're saying the wrong thing, all at once. Saw you watching the news back there, in the motel room. Guess you saw what happened to T-Town."

Nadine shook her head. "It doesn't seem real."

"Anything strike you as weird?"

She turned to look at him. "You're kidding, right? Everything about my life seems weird since Marcus and them came crashing through the door."

He nodded curtly. "Okay, yeah. My sense of normal occasionally needs recalibration. Anything about it seem especially weird to you?"

"Besides people I know dying and the place going up in flames?"

"Besides that."

She sat back, exasperated. "Is there something you're getting at?"

"The police surveillance platform got shot down. Crashed through the roof of one of the buildings. Started the fire, lotta people died."

"Yeah? And?"

"Official story is a criminal gang hiding fugitive terrorists shot it down. No matter how many times I watch, I can't make it make sense. Shot that splashed it came from outside the wall."

"So?"

"So why would the people inside the wall be hanging out with a rocket launcher outside the wall? I don't think it was your gangster friends."

"Who, then?"

"That's a question, isn't it? I think there was another player on the board, not LAPD and not your friends in Tijuana Town."

"Taylor's people?"

"Hadda be. Hadda be. They wanted to make sure LAPD wasn't recording what went down."

"So, what, they took down surveillance? Why?"

"At a guess? So they could whack you. No attempt at arrest, just walk up and shoot you."

"Cops had body cams, though, right?"

"Sure, in theory. In practice, you'd be surprised how often they seem to malfunction. Not that it would matter if it wasn't a cop who did the axing. You said Taylor told you he had someone inside, right?"

"Yeah."

"There you go. That, or a crooked cop on his payroll, or one of his own people. This guy really wants you dead."

"Yeah, well, feeling's mutual."

"I can't imagine he's ingratiated himself with the police. Those platforms are expensive. They're blaming it on Mayor Tony's crew, but they know that's bullshit. They gotta be upset. You don't just roll up to a police bust with a rocket launcher without someone seeing it. Someone knows, count on it."

"That help us?"

"Probably not. Just a thing that's been bugging me. Anyway, weird."

They drove for a while in silence. After a time, Nadine said, "Where are we going?"

"Wish I knew."

"What?"

Jake sighed and closed his eyes. The little Mini navigated its way down the street, palm trees all around, oppressive heat outside. "I don't have a plan. Not any more. My plan was to get you a new identity and bundle you off to Canada. You screwed that up, so now I'm making this up as I go along."

"What's the idea?"

"We need some place to go to ground. We need to get our heads around this, all this, what's going on. We've started that second bit already. The first bit, I have some ideas, but it'll take some prep work. Like that duffle bag you're carrying. That was supposed to be your get-the-fuck-out-of-Dodge cash. Now that you aren't getting the fuck out of Dodge, you can't exactly walk the street with a bag full of cash. The bank chip, probably connected to one of Anna's troves somewhere, who knows. That'll come in handy, open some doors, maybe help us find some things out. A big brick of cash might become more liability than asset. We need a place to stash it."

"Why couldn't we stay in the motel? Police?"

He shook his head, expression grim. "Ain't the police I'm worried about. Our friend Mr. Taylor needs you off the game board. He'll be looking for you too, through side channels. Figure he's got ins with the cops—I would, in his place—plus his own people as well. Who, I might add, might be inclined to take things personal, on account of you killed two of them."

"So where are we going?"

"Let me think."

"Pull over," Nadine said.

"What?"

"Pull. The fucking. Car. Over." Unexpected steel in her voice.

Jake took a breath, opened his mouth, then took manual control and flipped on the signal. He guided them into a parking lot near a small park. A gaggle of kids swarmed over a molded plastic jungle gym, its bright colors bleached by long exposure to UV. A jogger ran by, small remote held in his left hand, a compact white drone following overhead. A pole near the edge of the park bristled with cameras. Jake stopped in a space not quite in direct line of sight of any of them, with practiced ease that seemed automatic. The car dinged. He turned to face her, expectant.

Nadine closed her eyes, gathered her thoughts, then opened them again. "Okay. Number one. I'm tired of being a passenger on this ride. If this is my life now, I think I need a say in what happens."

"Okay."

Nadine blinked in surprise, mouth open. She'd geared up for a fight, and now the adrenaline fizzed and churned inside her with nothing to do. "Right." She took a deep breath to recalibrate. Her brow furrowed as she thought. "Where would you go, if you were in my position? You must have some plan, some place to lie low, disappear for a while."

He leaned back, amusement in his eyes. "What makes you think that?"

"Oh, please."

"Fine." He spread his hands. The prosthetic, she noticed, had two curved pincer-like steel hooks and a retractable segmented thumb that extended with a whine of servos. The thumb reminded her a bit of the neck on a gooseneck lamp. "Yes, I have a contingency plan. You won't like it."

"I haven't liked anything that's happened this week."

"Fair. We can go to ground for a while, somewhere neither the cops nor Martin Taylor's private security forces can find us. There are limits, though. All it takes is one mistake, one look at a camera at the wrong time when you aren't disguised, one person you pass on the street who recognizes you. Hiding isn't a long-term strategy."

"Right." The shape of an idea started to coalesce in Nadine's mind, a faint glimmering outline of a plan lurking somewhere in the cold gray mist. "I assume the cops and Martin's goons are looking for me."

"Most definitely."

"What will they do first?"

"Talk to your friends, known associates, past lovers if they can find them, known associates of Anna's. Your parents—that's harder, international jurisdictional crap, but you can bet they'll be monitoring any communications with them."

"I don't want to bring my parents into this. They're probably wrecked enough as it is."

"Yeah."

Nadine dragged Anna's bag from the back into her lap. She opened the zip. The gun went into the Mini's glove box. The bank card and note went into her pocket. "You got that knife of yours?"

Jake fished it out of his pocket and handed it over, still with that look of amusement in his eyes. Nadine carefully sliced the shrink-wrapped brick of twenties in half, wrapping up half the cash in the now more flaccid plastic. She twisted around and tucked it one-handed into the rucksack . "You know, I don't think I've ever held this much money in my life." She fluffed the remaining pile of bills in the bottom of the duffle bag. "You know anyplace in San Pedro that's easy to get to but has no cameras?"

"I can find one." He tapped the side of his head. "Why?"

"I want to stash this somewhere, call my old roommate, have her pick it up for me."

Jake shook his head. "Bad idea. The cops will already have talked to her. Taylor's people too, if they're any good. You trust her?"

"I trust her greed." She fished out the tiny padlock that once belonged to her suitcase and locked the duffle bag shut.

"You going to offer her money?"

"Not exactly."

"Okay." Jake touched the power button on the dash. The Mini chimed to life. "Got a place that might work."

"Just like that, huh? You're going to listen to what I say?"

Jake set the car in motion. "Consider this your chance to show me what you're made of. You handled yourself well when it mattered. That's worth something. And I figure you've already smashed the plan to hell and gone anyway." He flashed a disquieting grin. "Taking a big chance, calling your old roommate."

"Taking a chance no matter what we do." Nadine leaned back with her eyes closed.

Pink mist.

They made their way through surface streets, city's decay all around them, until they came to a bus stop on the corner of a street next to a run-down dinery that had closed some time ago. Graffiti in a dozen colors covered the diner's windows. "There," Jake said. "Trash can. Let me."

He parked a block away. "Give me the bag." He squashed the duffle bag as flat as he was able, stuffed it under his shirt, then dug his sunglasses from the glove box. "Wait here."

Nadine watched him walk toward the diner, hunched over, looking like any random street person, all trace of military bearing gone. He walked past the trash can, stumbled for a moment, moved on. A moment later, he vanished behind the diner.

Nadine waited for him to reappear. The minutes stretched out. That same tense anxiety she'd felt in the tunnel stole over her again. Her heart gradually sped up. When the door opened, she nearly jumped out of her skin. "Whoa! You scared the shit out of me. What went wrong?"

"Wrong? Nothing."

"I was watching. I didn't see you put anything in the trash."

Jake winked. "Make the call."

Nadine held up the manual phone, the one that had been in the bag. "This thing untraceable?"

"Right up until you use it to call someone who's being monitored. It's clean, if that's what you mean. No GPS, no phone company records. Can't be tracked back to you."

Nadine settled back into her seat, eyes closed. She breathed deeply, lips moving slightly. "What are you doing?" Jake asked.

"Getting into character." She took a deep breath, let it out, dialed.

The phone rang. A woman's voice came through, tinny from the cheap speaker. "Hello?"

"Olivia?" Nadine put a quaver in her voice. "It's me."

"Nadine? Holy shit! You're all over the news! What's going on?"

"I can't talk about it." More quaver. "Please, Olivia, I need your help." A tear rolled down her cheek. "There's nobody else I can trust."

"Okay, okay, calm down. What can I do?"

"I need you to keep something for me. It's really important. I can't come by the apartment. I'll leave it for you at—" She turned to Jake and lifted an eyebrow. He stared off into space for a moment, then mouthed the words to her. "The bus stop at 5th and Gaffey. Look in the trash can. Big black duffle. It's really important to me. I'll call you in a bit, when things cool down, come and get it from you, okay?"

A pause, then Olivia's voice again: "Okay. What's going on? A guy came by last night asking about you. Late, like I was almost ready for bed late."

"A guy?"

"Yeah. Big guy. Lots of grafted muscle. An ogre, like in the movies. I've never seen one in real life before. He said there's a reward out for you."

"What did you tell him?" Nadine pitched her voice up, slightly breathless.

"I said I hadn't seen you since you moved out."

"Good. Don't tell anyone you've talked to me. Keep the bag for me, okay? Only for a week or two. Keep it safe. I need it back." More tears flowed. "Thank you, Olivia. You're my only friend."

"What's going—"

"I gotta go!" Nadine squeaked. "I'll call you in a bit, okay?" She hit the button to end the call.

"Think she'll show?" Jake said.

"Oh yeah." Nadine stuck the end of the knife in the cheap 3D printed plastic shell of the phone and twisted until it popped apart. She dug out the battery, unplugging the wires with another twist of the knife. "We going to wait to make sure?"

"Can't. No cameras here now, but if anyone was listening to that call, and I'll bet you money someone was, they'll be sending drones here as fast as they can. Maybe a surveillance platform."

"Think they'll let her get the bag?"

"Depends who was listening. If they don't, they'll tell her to wait for your call. Either way, our next steps are the same. Clever, putting some cash in there. Makes it easy to believe you'll be highly motivated to get it back."

"Show me this bolt-hole I'm not going to like," Nadine said.

"We'll need to stash the car," Jake said. "How do your new shoes fit?"

"They're okay. Why?"

"We're gonna be doing some walking."

He drove to a small, dilapidated building near the ruins of what had once been Holly Park in the southwestern edge of South Central Los Angeles. They arrived in the early afternoon, when the harsh sunlight lent a dry, bleached-bones look to what Nadine assumed had once been a gas station and mechanic's shop for internal-combustion cars. The rusted-out hulks of gas pumps, silent tombstones of obsolete technology, marched in rows beneath an awning that had started to collapse at one corner. Jake stepped out into the muggy heat to unlock the padlock on a graffiti-sprayed roll-up door. He pulled it open with a shriek of complaining metal. The Mini, on some hidden command, pulled itself into the gloom. Jake followed it through and pulled the door shut. LED panels flicked on overhead, casting harsh blue light onto oil-stained concrete. A charge probe extended, blind and serpentine. The Mini opened its access hatch obligingly. "This your place?" Nadine said.

"In a manner of speaking. Belongs to a company that exists only as a piece of paper and a registration in a government database. Folks who used to own it tried to convert it to a speed-charging station a while back. Had grand visions of serving delivery drones for a big warehouse not too far from here. Put a bunch of solar panels on the roof, that was as far as they got. Storm destroyed the panels, warehouse moved, owners walked away. I did some work with Anna a couple years ago, set up a corporation, bought the place for back taxes. Restrictions on development, hazardous waste, leaking gas tanks, so nobody wanted it."

"How come you bought it?"

"In case I ever need to stash my car for a while and disappear." He gave her a look she couldn't read. "It's hot out there. Don't want to move until evening. Plus I have some things to collect."

"Things?" Nadine felt stupid the moment the word left her lips.

"Things. Make yourself at home, such as it is. There's a little refrigerator in the office. Get some food. You'll need it."

Nadine explored the small space. The scent of oil, brake fluid, and coolant permeated the building's pores. She stepped injudiciously and yelped as the rock dug in. Cursing, she undid the Doc Martens and took the rock out of her sock.

As promised, she found a compact refrigerator in the manager's office, behind a warped and oil-stained wooden door. All the windows had been covered with dark tinting, now peeling at the corners, then papered over with fading yellow newsprint. Nadine was surprised they hadn't been smashed. "They're hardened polyacrylate," Jake explained over cold sandwiches and bottled water at the front reception desk, its glossy surface covered with scuffs and scratches. "Difficult to break. Plus the cameras all over the front discourage people from trying too persistently. Most of them are fakes, of course. Some of them are painted to look like LAPD, some like municipal cameras. Couple of different private security cameras, too. All dummies. There are real ones on the front door, back parking lot, and garage, but they aren't networked. Local recording only. The fakes keep the city from trying to install more."

"Wouldn't LAPD know they don't have a camera here?"

Jake laughed. "You assume a lot from their record-keeping."

Nadine ran her hands over scuffed laminate, skin weirdly bluish in the glow of the LEDs. "Why can't we stay here?"

"Not safe." Jake finished his sandwich, crushed his empty water bottle. "There's a little shower in the back. I suggest you use it. Might not have an opportunity again for a while. Then get some sleep. I'll set up a sleeping bag in the office. Not comfortable, but the best I can offer."

The shower turned out to be a claustrophobically small fiberglass prefab tucked behind the service bay, with what looked like a solid decade's worth of grime caked around the showerhead. An obscenely cheerful shower curtain decorated with brightly-colored fish hung from a collapsible curtain rod wedged against the open side. At least the water was hot, and strong. Nadine closed her eyes under the stinging spray.

Pink mist.

The tears came then, rolling silently down her face, lost in the pouring water.

11

The Beast

NADINE DRIED AND dressed in worn jeans and a simple T-shirt with a logo on the front of an electronic music band she knew nothing about except that they'd been popular years ago. She put the small, jagged rock in her pocket. The bank card went into her sock, then she went out to find Jake spreading a battered green sleeping bag one-handed on the floor. His prosthetic sat on the desk where they'd eaten, a thin cord snaking to a charger plugged into the wall. A red light glowed somewhere deep in the complicated elbow joint. Jake wore a thin green T-shirt; he'd dumped his jacket in a heap next to the prosthetic. His right arm ended above the elbow in a complex mechanical socket that looked permanently affixed, studded with small gold connectors.

He looked up when she came in. "Keep meaning to put a cot in here. Never have gotten around to it. I learned to sleep just about anywhere, just about any time, so..." He shrugged apologetically. "Not really set up for company."

"I don't think I can sleep anyway."

"Suit yourself. I still have some things to pack up."

Nadine followed him into the garage bay, where he lifted the back of the Mini and took several bundles wrapped in brown paper from the space where she imagined a spare tire might be kept if the car had a spare tire, which apparently it didn't. He produced a dark-colored nylon backpack from a large repurposed tool chest in the corner and transferred the brown bundles to it, working one-handed with practiced efficiency. Next went several bottles of water and several more cans of energy drinks from the small refrigerator, followed by a pile of small packages in uniform olive drab with black writing on the side. The oddly short rifle went into a case, which Jake tucked into the space formerly taken up by the bundles. "Can I ask you a question?" Nadine said.

"Shoot."

"What do you know about ogres?"

"You don't want to arm wrestle one. Custom engineered growth hormone plus grafted muscle tissue grown from stem cells. Russian tech, bootlegged over here, popular with a certain flavor of hyper-masculine asshole you're best not tangling with. Sometimes employed by private security forces, especially overseas. Why?"

"Olivia—my roommate—said an ogre came by the place asking about me."

"Working for Taylor, no doubt. Might need to take out a special kind of insurance."

"What do you mean?"

Jake flashed a nasty grin. "Pack up. We move out before sunset."

They had a simple dinner of energy bars and bottled water that night, as the sun sent slanting rays around the edges of peeling newspaper. The unwavering cold LED glow gave Nadine a surreal sense of timelessness, like they'd temporarily slid sideways, away from the world.

After they ate, she rearranged the few things she had hastily transferred from her suitcase to the rucksack. At Jake's insistence, she stashed the gun and some of the remaining cash in a tight bundle in the bottom of the bag. The rest went beneath the floor mats in the Mini and in a hidden compartment in Jake's belt. She rolled up her clothes, a trick her father had taught her to make packing easier, and tucked them and Anna's note back into the rucksack. A third of the space remained empty, silent testimony to how abruptly she'd fled her life.

Exit, pursued by LAPD SWAT.

She slipped the stone into her sock before they set out. Jake rolled up the sleeping bag, tied it atop his backpack, and slung it over his shoulders. Nadine followed him along streets that hung suspended in that place of light and shadow, beneath the red haze of sunset, the world lost in that timeless moment before the streetlamps came to life. The stone dug painfully into her sole at every injudicious step.

They walked for nearly an hour in the gathering gloom. The lights flicked on above them, signaling the transition from day to night. Cars raced by, each darkened capsule a hermetically sealed, untouchable world, ordinary people going about ordinary lives far from Nadine's extraordinary misery. The rucksack hung on her shoulders, heavier with every step as she followed Jake's dark outline. Uncanny déjà vu stole over her, fragments of her flight to Tijuana Town with Anna. Tears stung her eyes. If Jake noticed her self-absorbed silence, he didn't comment.

They passed a row of telephone poles, each with a lonely blue-white light extending like some sinister mechanical anglerfish's lure from atop it. Nadine stopped in the pool of light at the base of one of the poles, snared by a sheet of paper tacked slightly crooked to zinc-plated metal. "Come on," Jake said.

"Hang on." Nadine stared at the poster. The word "WANTED" stretched across its top in black san-serif type. Beneath it, Anna's face and her own stared back at her. She didn't recognize the photo of Anna, gazing directly at the camera with a scowl on her face, a nondescript beige wall behind her. Olivia had taken the photo of Nadine, leaning against a streetlamp in downtown Los Angeles. The two-dimensional version of herself looked happy.

Jake beckoned, impatient. On some impulse she didn't understand, Nadine carefully peeled the poster from the telephone pole. She folded it up and slipped it into her pocket before she caught up with him.

The shadows grew darker. Eventually, they came to a large, flat field, surrounded on three sides by silent roadway. The moon shoved itself into the sullen sky. Jake shouldered his way through a gaping rent in a rusted chain-link fence. Dense thorny scrub clawed at Nadine's Doc Martens, the newest things she owned. They climbed a small dirt rise covered with a thick mat of hardy grass, to a large square of concrete with a hinged door of dull gray metal set in it. Jake heaved the gate open. A ladder disappeared into darkness. Nadine shuddered, heart thudding. "What is this place?"

"Way back in the 20s, LA started work on a new subway extension down south almost as far as Terminal Island," Jake said. "Plan was to extend the Green Line and add a whole new line. Supposed to be up and running by 2040, not that that was ever likely. It was always more about moving money into certain contractor's pockets than moving dirt. Still, they dug a bunch of tunnels, even put in some infrastructure."

"And then?"

"Remember that storm, the one that beached the container ship?"

"Before I got here."

"Well, it flooded the tunnels, too. Smashed things up pretty good. Construction halted, accusations were made, the city launched an investigation, then the state launched an investigation of the investigation, some low-level assholes fell on their swords to protect the high-level assholes, and, well, this is it. Your tax dollars at work." He took a small L-shaped light from the top strap of his backpack, slipped it down the front of his shirt, where it clung to his collar with a metal clip. Blue-white light puddled in the dense dark. "Give me your bag."

Nadine handed it to him. Bag slung over one shoulder, he stepped up over the top lip and started down the ladder, alternating his good hand and the mechanical claw. From somewhere far below, Nadine heard faint voices. She hesitated at the top of the ladder. Jake looked up at her. "You coming?"

"Sorry. It's just...last time I stood at the top of a ladder like this, the woman I loved and all her friends died." Nadine shook her head, surprised at her own detachment. "Let's go."

Jake's dark bulk descended the ladder, the pool of light glancing off concrete. Nadine watched herself stand at the foot of the ladder, dreamlike, watched the way she put her foot on the first rung, careful of the rock in her shoe.

The shaft descended much deeper than the one outside the industrial park. Jake's voice came back up to her, muffled by the backpack that filled most of the space. "Friend of a friend of mine showed me this place. Not sure how long people have been using it. Hard to find if you don't know what you're looking for. This was supposed to be a maintenance and ventilation shaft. The main entrances into this part of the subway got sealed up when the city walked away. Here we are. Mind your head."

Jake stepped out into a cramped tunnel with a low roof. Mud and tangled debris covered the ground. Regular columns of dull gray concrete clung to the tunnel walls, casting razor-edged shadows in the light of Jake's flashlight. "This was going to to be a pullout from the main tunnel," Jake said. "This way."

Nadine started after him. Blackness closed around them. Jake's flashlight concealed as much as it illuminated, creating a world of brilliant light and hard shadow. A yellow triangle flared in her vision, line pointing into darkness. Nadine froze. "What?" Jake said.

"There." Nadine pointed. "There's something—"

Jake swiveled the flashlight. A shadow detached itself from the column, became a large, heavyset figure dressed in black. Yellow triangles floated around him. Jake held out his good arm. The two men embraced. "Lucas!" Jake said. "Good to see you, man."

"Likewise. Who's your friend with the good eyes?"

"Lucas, meet Melody Landry. Melody, this is my friend Lucas. He helps keep an eye on things down here." They clapped hands. "Lucas is a good man to know."

"What brings you here? Bit late for you."

"Same old, same old. Gotta see Catman. He here?"

"Yep." Lucas gestured down the shaft. He melted back into the shadows as they moved past, becoming nothing but a yellow triangle glowing ghostlike in Nadine's vision.

The sounds grew louder, a murmur of voices somewhere ahead. Nadine stumbled over a gleaming rail half-embedded in the sludge that clung to the bottom of the tunnel. A cacophony of smell reached her nose, mud and decay mixed with a tang of human waste and something like grilled meat. A dim glow against the wall faintly suggested light ahead.

The tunnel curved slightly to join with a much wider tunnel, its roof high enough overhead it was lost to Jake's flashlight. The ground underfoot was slightly less muddy, and smelled of a beach at low tide. The susurration came to her again, louder but still distant, oddly amplified and distorted by the still air of the tunnel. The glow ahead brightened as they slogged through the tunnel. Nadine limped along behind Jake, ever mindful of the rock in her shoe. They curved left, gradually, with the glow growing brighter ahead of them, cold and blue. Jake picked up his pace. The tunnel shifted abruptly, curving back to the right, then met up with another that opened into...

Nadine blinked.

They stood in a cavernous space with an arched ceiling so high its peak was lost to the gloom. Light from a string of square LED panels along the far wall lit the space well enough to see a wide platform, a bit more than waist-high, floored in tile covered with a layer of grime. Massive marble columns marched along the far wall. Someone had set up a ramp made of plywood from the tunnel up onto the platform. Jake urged her up.

Tents and improvised shelters of every description crowded the space, from small triangular one-person backpacker's affairs in bright colors to large tarps draped over plywood cubes. Cables snaked along the ground, connecting the LED panels like a demented string of Christmas lights. Someone had whimsically fastened a convenience store OPEN sign to one of the columns with twine. The letter E didn't work, so it blinked OP N OP N on an endless loop.

At the far side of the platform, across from where they stood, another ramp led down into another tunnel. At the top of that ramp sat a chaotic pile of small electric scooters, all connected by a snarl of cabling to a dented, badly-scuffed electric charger. A green light glowed atop it.

People crowded the space, glaring out from the tents, sitting on the edge of the platform with their legs dangling over the edge. A man who looked in his late 70s knelt in front of a small camp stove, heating something in a round tin. Another man, perhaps in his 40s, sat in a wheelchair near the ramp, wearing a shabby green Army jacket covered with holes large enough to suggest he had no shirt beneath, and a pair of dirty combat pants with the legs tied off at the knees. Startling blue eyes stared from beneath bushy eyebrows at some point beyond the far wall. His mouth, hidden behind a shaggy overgrowth of filthy, unkempt beard, did not change expression when Jake and Nadine passed.

"Uncle Jake!"

The voice came from somewhere behind a large tent of grubby olive-drab nylon, illuminated from within by a warm yellowish glow. "Uncle Jake!" A short, distinctly androgenous figure, clad in searing orange shorts of tight Spandex and a lime-green shirt that fit as though it were painted on, threw an arm around Jake. Brilliant green eyes with horizontal slits—custom contacts, Nadine assumed—peered out from a delicate face surrounded by a bob of hair so yellow it seemed unlikely to be anything close to a natural color. He was of an indeterminate age probably greater than mid-twenties but less than mid-thirties, though where it might be in that range, Nadine couldn't guess. He wore a headband with two cat ears, fuzzy with orange faux fur, atop it. The jaunty triangles swiveled with a faint whine of servos.

No, she realized, looking closer, not a headband. The ears seemed anchored to his skull, protruding like rock formations from the sea of his surrealistically yellow hair.

"Melody, Catman. He's an old friend. We go back." Jake draped his good arm around his skinny shoulders.

"You're here late," Catman said.

"Brought something for you." Jake unslung his backpack, unzipped the top. "Here." He pulled out one of the paper bags with his claw, carefully unrolled it, and took out several large bundles of white and blue pills wrapped in a dense layer of clear cellophane.

"Thanks, man," Catman said. "You're a lifesaver." He turned to Nadine. "This man is a hero."

"We need a place to stay." Jake slung the bag back over his shoulders. "Lie low for a while, away from prying eyes."

"You got it, man. Anything. Anything you need. You can have my bed. You and your friend." He gave Nadine a look, intense and direct, tongue at the corner of his mouth, that made her blush. A long tail, covered with the same orange faux fur as his ears, twitched back and forth.

Nadine gawped. "What's with the ears and tail?" she heard herself say before she could stop the words. Her face burned. "Sorry. That was rude. I'm...I haven't had a lot of sleep."

"Don't sweat it. I have a specialized clientele. They pay extra for a genuine cat boy, get it? Call it my competitive advantage." The tail flashed out from behind his leg again.

"So you can control them?"

"Not directly. They react to mood and stress." Twitch, twitch. One of the ears rotated backward with a faint whine. He tucked the bundle of pills under his arm. "Gotta jet. Thanks for the stuff."

Jake led her through a maze of people and tents to a tile-covered wall at the end of the platform. A woman sat just outside a tiny blue dome-shaped tent, white hair a snarled rat's nest atop her head. She wore a black shawl that reminded Nadine in some vague way of funeral attire. She had laid out a large square of black velvet on the ground in front of her, with a glittering array of obviously hand-made necklaces and brooches spread out on it beneath the cold glare of a small battery-powered work light. She held a bit of blue glass in her hand, perhaps the bottom of a bottle worn smooth by the action of wind and waves until nothing remained but this flat disc. She rocked back and forth as she engraved a design on it with a battery-powered hand tool, ignoring the crush of humanity around her.

"Come on." Jake indicated a small alcove between a crude barrier made of wooden planks gone silver with age and the wall of the subway station itself, where a tangle of clothes, bits of fabric, and a futon from Ikea formed a sort of nest. Jake unslung his backpack again, unfastened the sleeping bag, and unrolled it on top of the futon. Nadine let her worn rucksack fall with a thud, suddenly regretting not taking the opportunity to nap back in the gas station.

"If you need to pee," Jake said, "keep going down the tunnel we came in. There are lights every ten meters or so. About fifty meters down you'll find a side tunnel. Smells bad, I'm afraid. If you need to do more than pee, hold it, or if you must, bury it."

Nadine sat heavily on the sleeping bag. "Those pills you gave Catman. What are you, a drug dealer?"

"Manner of speaking. I have a contact at the VA. I give him cash, he gives me what I need, I bring it here. He has a friend makes off-books deliveries for him, fudges the inventory records."

"Oxy? Fentanyl?"

"No."

"What, then?"

"It's a long story."

Nadine shook her head violently. "No. I need to know what kind of person you are. Tell me."

Jake looked at her for a long time, eyes black in the dim light. Finally, he said, "Antiretrovirals, mostly. Reverse transcriptase inhibitors, viral polymerase blockers."

Nadine hugged her knees to her chest while that sank in. "You mean—"

"Yeah. Budget cuts hit the people here especially hard."

"But why? What's your connection to these people? What's it to you?"

Jake leaned back against the tiled wall. He fished through his backpack and passed Nadine a pair of earplugs, two blunt-tipped cones of green memory foam. He took a small bottle from his pocket, shook out a white tablet. "Next dose of beta blockers. You'll need to keep taking these, if you don't want to bug out and end up in a psych ward, or worse. Get some sleep. Good idea to do that whenever you can, here on out. Likely to be a bumpy ride for a while."

Nadine swallowed the tablet with a mouthful of water from a bottle. "Where does this end?"

"Don't know yet."

A dizzy wave of blackness threatened to overwhelm her. She shook it off, fingers curled in the cheap sleeping bag. "Am I going to be okay?"

"You can still go to Toronto."

"No."

"Get some sleep."

The day caught up with her all at once. Nadine watched from somewhere outside herself as someone with her hands wrapped the sleeping bag around her, and then she tumbled down a gaping void into blackness. She dreamed sharp fragments of sorrow and loss until they, too, were swallowed by empty nothingness.

Nadine jolted awake all at once, clutching at the sleeping bag. Jake sat with his back to the wall, arms draped over his knees in a loose-limbed, marionette stance, vibrating with watchful readiness. The cold glow of improvised LEDs gave jagged shadows to the landscape of his face.

Nadine rubbed her eyes. "How long—"

"About nine hours."

"Have you been there the whole time?"

"Yes."

"Did you sleep?"

"No." He reached into his pocket and held out his hand. A round red pill lay on his palm. "Custom synthetic phenethylamine. Like amphetamines without the nastiness. Used 'em in Belarus. We all did."

She shook her head. "I need to pee."

The dank tunnel turned out to be every bit as revolting as she feared. When she finished and returned to the platform, she saw no sign of the man in the wheelchair. It occurred to her to wonder how he'd managed to get down there, and for that matter, where the electric scooters had come from. People moved about the platform, fewer than there had been the night before. "What's the plan?" she said to Jake.

He grinned mirthlessly. "Plan? Best I can offer is an intention."

"Okay, what's the intention?"

"I got some errands to do. Need to see about getting that insurance policy, in case we meet your ogre. I'll need some of your get out of Dodge cash, given that we aren't in fact getting out of Dodge. If you don't mind."

"Will it help us find out what's happening?"

"Dunno. But it might keep us alive."

"Take as much as you need."

"Here." Jake dug in his backpack and passed her a slim package, dull-colored vacuum sealed plastic.

"What's this?"

"Combat ration, CR2A1, ready to eat, with self-heating coffee substitute. Everything you need except texture or flavor. You be okay here for a bit? I'm going to be gone for a while. Should be back before sundown, not that sunup and sundown make much difference here."

"I haven't been okay since all this started."

"Fair. You manage?"

"Yeah." Nadine ripped open the combat ration to find something a bit like an energy bar. The coffee substitute, self-heating, turned out to be a drab green tube with a cap on one end and a pull tab on the other, COFFEE SUBSTITUTE BEVERAGE PULL TAB TO HEAT printed in black along the side. Something in the tube hissed when she pulled the tab.

"You know," Jake said, "most people would shit themselves in your shoes."

"That supposed to be a compliment?"

"Best I got. Thank you for not shitting yourself."

"No promises," Nadine said. "I still might, once all this catches up with me." She raised the tube to her lips. The liquid inside was hot, black, and more like coffee than she expected. "This isn't half bad."

"Soldier fuel."

"None of this feels real." Nadine waved her arm, taking in the platform, the tents, the broken humanity clinging to the edges of their lives. "It's like, I don't know, I'm in a video game or something. Some end-of-the-world, fall-of-civilization thing."

Jake regarded her through half-closed eyes. "I think civilization is falling. It's just a slow-motion thing. We always thought the end would be some big apocalypse. Nuclear war, supervolcano, something like that. Instead we got the death of a thousand cuts."

"How did you and Anna meet?"

He clapped his good hand on her shoulder. "If you want to go wandering, there's another encampment about half a klick down the tunnel we came in. They don't much like company. Recommend you steer clear. Take a left down the other tunnel, it'll eventually lead back out to the surface—easier climb but more cameras. Right takes you to... well, somewhere else." He handed her his flashlight. "I'll be back." With that, he disappeared down the tunnel across from where they'd come in.

After he left, Nadine curled into herself in the tiny nest between the wall and the crude wood planks. People moved about in the unvarying gloom, paying no attention to her.

When she finished the meal bar, which was exactly as tasteless as Jake promised, Nadine rose, restless. Without anything better to do, she took his oblique suggestion to explore her new environment. Flashlight in hand, she made her cautious way down the long, silent tunnel, identical to the one that had brought them to the platform. Shadows fled across damp concrete from the harsh beam of light. Thick, foul-smelling mud sucked at her boots. A crust of salt on the tunnel wall suggested the peak of previous floods. Graffiti covered the walls, a dense tangle of symbols she couldn't understand. Small scurrying things ran out of her way, gone before she could identify them.

Nadine wandered down the abandoned subway tunnel until she came to a place where another tunnel split off, dark signal lights jutting from the wall. Someone had sprayed the word "BEAST" in crude letters, red against gray concrete, with an arrow pointing into darkness. She shivered.

She followed the arrow, finding an odd solace in the isolation, the dark pressing still and silent around her. She could, for a moment, pretend she was a child again, exploring the cave beneath the Island of Montreal with her father.

The tunnel curved. A huge hulk loomed suddenly in the light of Jake's flashlight, impossibly immense, a vast machine of white and yellow metal that filled the entire tunnel. Walkways ran along its flanks, their rails pitted and corroded. Massive cables hung silently from twisted steel channels. A crust of salt clung to the base of the thing, glittering in the light.

Something glowed on the catwalk along the abandoned machine's side. Intrigued, Nadine moved closer. A tiny LED powered by a coin-sized battery, blue-white light feeble in the gloom, shone on a framed photograph. A face smailed out through grimy glass, a woman of perhaps sixteen or seventeen, wearing a bright red headscarf. The photo looked spontaneous, unstaged, caught in a moment of unguarded joy, cars blurred in the background.

Next to it, she found another photo, a small cheap printout from an office supply store, colors faded: a dark-skinned man in an Army uniform, a shattered building pockmarked with holes behind him. Grim, serious eyes stared straight through Nadine. Beside that, another photo, and another, and drawings as well: a pencil sketch of an elderly man's face on lined notebook paper; a watercolor of a woman with flowers in her hair, a clump of shriveled, desiccated flowers in front of it. Hardened wax drippings from dozens of candles hung like colorful stalactites from the edge of the catwalk. The head of the machine, an enormous round mass of solid metal, filled the entire tunnel, blocking off any hope of passing.

Nadine turned away, unexpected tears in her eyes. A voice came out of the gloom behind her: *Why are you crying?* Anna's voice, Anna's words.

Nadine froze, then turned slowly, slicing the darkness with Jake's light. She was, to the extent she could tell, alone in the tunnel, with only the silent machine for company. "I miss you," she whispered.

What do you suppose it means?

"Jake's magic no-trauma pills aren't working. I'm losing my mind."

Not me, the machine.

"I don't know." A pause. "You aren't real."

Perhaps I am. Perhaps I left some fragment of myself in your implant. A literal ghost, as it were, in the machine.

"Did you?"

You tell me. Maybe you are losing your mind, here in the dark.

"Anna?"

Yes?

"Why did you do it? Why did you jump on that grenade?"

I needed you to make it out. Make it worthwhile. Make my death mean something. We couldn't all die down there.

"Why are you here? Why are you talking to me?"

When you save a life, you become indebted to the life you save. You're responsible for it.

Nadine walked back down the tunnel, away from the machine. She paused at the junction with its enigmatic warning, the letters sprayed by a hurried hand. She played the flashlight over the word. "Beast. What do you think it means?"

No answer came.

Back at the station, Nadine found the woman with the brooches and necklaces had reappeared in her absence. She sat crosslegged near the wall, the black cloth laid out in front of her like a prayer mat. Jewelry adorned it, all made from found objects: broken bits of glass, little gears, pieces of cast-off machinery from who knew what. She wore the same funeral attire she'd been in the night before, with the addition of a hat with a small fragment of black veil that hung over one eye. She rocked back and forth as she worked on a necklace made of green stone wound with wire hung with what looked like gears from a mechanical watch. Nadine squatted in front of her and examined the wares spread out on the black cloth, gleaming like otherworldly artifacts in the cold glow of her battery-powered light.

They sat in silence for a time. Then the woman's hand darted out, snake-rapid. She clutched the necklace Nadine had watched her working on last night, a smooth lump of sea-tumbled blue glass, now engraved with a fanciful design that reminded Nadine of something that might be found in a medieval codex of religious symbols. "This, for you. For the Beast."

"What?"

"For a prayer. For an offering. Twenty dollars. It speaks to you." She held it out to Nadine, dangling on a black thong wrapped with silver wire. "Twenty dollars."

"I don't know what you mean."

"You have lost!" She rocked back and forth, clutching the necklace. "We have all lost! All of us who are here! You must take it. It is yours. Twenty dollars."

Nadine, carried helplessly along the currents of a conversation she didn't understand, watched herself fish a battered bill from her sock, hand it to the woman. She dropped the necklace in Nadine's hand. The bill disappeared somewhere in her shawl. "You wear it."

Nadine saw herself slip the thing over her neck, feeling as though she watched a character in a television show she'd turned on in the middle. The woman met her gaze for just a moment, her eyes a deep, rich brown, then she returned her attention to the green stone she'd been working on. "May I see that?" Nadine said.

The woman shook her head, still rocking back and forth. "Not for you, not for you."

"I see you've met Mama Mary."

"What?" Nadine turned. Jake had crept up on her quietly enough she hadn't heard him coming.

"That's what the people down here call her. She won't tell anyone her real name. Did she get you to buy anything?"

"For her!" Mary shrieked, voice thin in the cavernous station. "It was for her!"

"Um, yeah." Nadine curled her hand around the necklace.

Jake whirled on Mary, a dangerous, feral look in his eyes. "Leave her alone. You hear me? You don't take her money, you don't sell her your crap. You don't talk to her. You don't go near her." He leaned close, claw snapping in front of her face. "Leave her alone!"

"It was for her!"

"Leave her alone!" Jake yelled. "Save your scams for the rubes, you hear me? Run your racket on her again and so help me—"

"Jake!" Nadine said. "Jake, what the hell is wrong with you? Stop it!"

"Hey, hey, hey, it's okay." Lucas materialized like a ghost from nowhere. "He just gets that way. Lot of Army folks do, ain't that right, Jake?" He grabbed Jake by the arm. Rage flared on Jake's face, gone as quickly as it had come. "Lot of folks been through what he's been through, they just forget sometimes, you know? War stays with them. Jake, man you cool?"

Jake shook off his arm. He glared at Lucas for a long moment, body tense, hands curled into fists, breathing hard. All at once, the rage drained from his face. He looked around as if he wasn't quite sure where he was. "Yeah. I'm cool." He turned toward Nadine. "Don't give her any more money."

"Fine." Nadine shook her head. "Hey, listen, those pills you're giving me, do they make you hear..."

"Hear what?"

Nadine shook her head. "Never mind. You want to talk about what just happened?"

"What just happened when?"

"Now!"

"Nothing to talk about."

"Did you find what you were looking for?"

Jake raised his finger to his lips, a quick flicker of motion almost too fast to catch. He jerked his head toward Catman's little alcove. Nadine followed him, chastised. He settled himself atop the sleeping bag. "I had to call in a few favors."

Nadine sat beside him. "From who?"

"People you're best off not knowing. But I got us an edge over that ogre."

"What's that?"

The nastiest grin Nadine had ever seen slashed across Jake's face. "Maybe you want to give your roommate a call."

"Ex-roommate."

"Whatever. We can't keep hiding. Time to get proactive. We need to leave. Tonight."

"Why?"

"Basics of life on the run, which is what you're doing. Don't stay in the same place for more than a day or two."

"Do you have another place in mind?"

"We'll find something."

Nadine made an exasperated sound. "I know a place. It's a ways from here. Might need your car. But it's secure and nobody will think to look there."

"Good. Saddle up."

Nadine closed her eyes. "Something I gotta do first. Something private." She flicked on Jake's flashlight. He nodded.

Nadine walked down the tunnel to the spray-painted word, where she stood for a time, tracing the letters with the flashlight, trying to understand what had driven someone to scrawl the random graffiti. Was it a warning? A prayer? A conjuring?

Eventually, she followed the tunnel to the great silent hulk of the boring machine, repurposed into a cast-off altar by cast-off people. She climbed onto the catwalk, the rail cool and slicked with moisture beneath her hand. Careful not to disturb any of the tiny shrines, she searched for a vacant spot on the walkway, a place not yet occupied by a silent offering to someone's grief. When she found what she was looking for, she squatted and took the Wanted poster from her pocket. She smoothed it out and placed it carefully on corroded metal. She slipped the necklace from her head and hung it in front of the poster, looping the thong around the metal handrail. After a moment's hesitation, she placed Anna's letter, the one she'd found in the duffel bag in the storage locker, next to the poster. "I miss you, Anna," she said out loud. Tears blurred her vision. "I miss you so much."

She wiped her eyes with an impatient hand and went back down the tunnel.

12

Make It Worthwhile

OCK IN HER shoe, hoodie pulled up over her head despite the heat, shoulders hunched against the weight of the rucksack, Nadine set off after Jake. He seemed to possess some nearly supernatural sense of where to find cameras and how to avoid them. They followed a circuitous route along desolate streets. They kept off major roads, often cutting through neighborhoods Nadine would, in her previous life, never have ventured into.

At one point, as they walked a pothole-strewn street through what had once been a nice neighborhood, surrounded by the dark shapes of decaying houses, Nadine shivered and ran up beside Jake. The rock dug painfully into soft flesh, one small drop of misery in a driving rainstorm. Somewhere in the distance, a dog barked, over and over. "Ask you a question?" she said.

"Sure."

"Why are you doing this? You don't even know me. I put a monkeywrench in your nice, tidy plan. Anna hired you to get me out. I didn't go. Why are you still here?"

Jake stopped and turned toward her, face hollow and craggy in the shadows. "You want the truth?"

"Please."

"I'm not doing this for you. None of this is for you."

"Why, then?"

Something flitted across his face, gone before Nadine could identify it. "I'm doing this for her."

"For Anna?"

"Yes. We were friends for a long time. Maybe I'm hoping..."

"What?"

"Nothing." He adjusted the straps on his pack and moved off again. "Doesn't matter. Consider this my last gift to her."

They walked in silence for a time. The distant barking grew fainter. A long, sleek Mercedes swished by, nearly silent, black against the dark night. Someone leaned out the back window and yelled, his words ripped away by the wind of his passing.

"Jake?"

"Yeah?"

"What would have happened, if I'd have gone to Toronto?"

"If you played your cards right, you might have carved out a bit of time. Ten years, if you kept your head down and didn't make any mistakes. Enough time to settle down, find a nice home in the suburbs, get a job in some office somewhere. Maybe find a husband or a wife or something."

"It wouldn't last."

"Nothing lasts. Thing is, the government is like a spider, see? It can afford to be patient. They'd never stop looking for you. One day, when you were sitting in your kitchen with a bagel and a cup of coffee, they'd kick down your door and that would be that. Arrested, maybe. Shot while resisting arrest, more likely. They'd never stop looking."

"Did Anna know that?"

"Yes."

"So what...what would be the point, then?"

"Because those years, however many of them you got, would be years you didn't spend in a cell or in the ground. That's the thing. You never know what's going to happen, see? We might both be hit by a car tonight and that's it, that's the end. Every day you wake up outside a cell is another day you have. When you live on the edge, every day's a gift. Anna knew that. You keep going until you can't anymore."

"You always have this attitude?"

"Had my attitude adjusted in Belarus."

"What do we do from here?"

"Keep going until we can't anymore." That nasty grin slashed his face again. "Take some of them with us."

"You don't expect to survive this."

"And? You afraid of dying?"

"Not any more," Nadine said. Several moments passed. "Are we going the right way?"

"Depends on where you think we're going." Amusement glinted in Jake's eyes.

"Back to that gas station?"

"Too risky."

"Where, then?"

"Right here." He sat down on the curb. Nadine sprawled gracelessly beside him, relieved to be off her feet.

Scarcely a minute later, a car pulled up alongside them. Nadine shielded her eyes from the glare of its headlights. The Mini's doors popped open. "Get in," Jake said.

Nadine threw her rucksack in the back. Jake settled into the driver's seat. "Manual control," he said. The car chimed. "Get in the back," he told Nadine. "Keep your head down. Where to?"

"Commercial park. Southwest." She gave him an address. He pulled the car away from the curb.

Half an hour later, they arrived at a sleek white three-story building, round-edged and anonymous. Black letters along the top proclaimed "TRSW, Inc." Lights glowed in the windows, looking out over an empty parking lot. "You sure this is the place?" Jake said.

"Yeah."

"What is it?"

"Place my old company gave up on. They've been trying to lease it for years after the tenants went under. No takers."

"How come?"

"Basement floods every time it rains. Cost of fixing it is more than the building's worth. They keep the lights on to deter squatters and use the whole thing as a tax write-off."

Jake slowed the Mini as he drove by. "Alarms?"

"Too expensive. Disconnected years ago. Cameras too."

"How do you know?"

"I'm the one who canceled the contract. Pull around back. Door in the middle."

Jake snuggled the car against the rear of the building. Nadine punched a number into the keypad of a windowless steel door. Electronic latches rattled.

The space beyond was a single long room with plain white walls. Marks on the floor showed where cubicle walls had been removed, leaving cables sprouting like strange plants from recessed bronze plates set through holes in the nondescript industrial carpeting. Two doors on the far side of the space, marked with a black silhouette of a figure in a triangular dress and another in pants, stood slightly ajar. "Water's on," Nadine said. "City requirements."

"How often do people come by to check on the place?"

"Not often. Once a month or so. We have a couple weeks."

"Home sweet home." Jake carried everything from the car into the abandoned cubicle farm, rifle case last. They sat on the gray carpet. Jake tossed Nadine a brown box and opened another one himself. "Macaroni with chili and meat substitute, self-heating. Jackpot!"

Nadine pulled the tab on her foil pack. "Beans, rice, and chicken substitute, self-heating," she read. "You ever get used to eating these?"

"Nope. Okay, first order of business. We need some place contained, some place we can set up an ambush to deal with this ogre of yours. If he visited your old roommate, you can bet your last dollar Martin Taylor and the LAPD are keeping an eye on her. That's our in."

"I might know a place. What's your plan?"

"You ever see a zip gun before?"

"No."

"Improvised firearm, made from bits of pipe and other stuff. Nail, spring, shotgun shell, pretty much all there is to it. Add a tripwire and it's a booby trap. Some extra sauce for our ogre and it's just the thing. We'll only have one shot at it, though."

They talked long into the night. Exactly at 1 AM, the lights flicked off. Jake jumped in the dim glow of the EXIT sign over the door. "It's on a timer," Nadine said. "The lights in front stay on, keep up the illusion people still use this place."

Jake passed Nadine another tablet and a bottle of water. While she swallowed it, he spread out his sleeping bag on the floor. "You going to be okay?" Nadine said.

"I should be asking you that. I can sleep anywhere." He rolled onto his back on the carpet with his duffel bag under his head. "This is far from the least comfortable place I've slept."

NADINE DREAMT THAT night of her childhood home in Montreal, somehow made larger, more ominous. She ran through the house searching for someone she knew with dream-logic wasn't there. Every door opened onto another empty room, faded curtains over the windows, a film of dust on hardwood floors. Somewhere far away, she heard a voice: *Make it worthwhile.*

"I don't know what to do!" she cried.

Make it worthwhile.

A hand reached out from a wall to grab her. She thrashed, screaming. "Hey, easy," Jake said. He let go of her arm. "You sounded like you were having a bad dream. Here." He gave her a bottle of water. "Time to move."

"What time is it?"

"About an hour before sunrise. We got a few hour's sleep. You good?"

"Yeah." Nadine gathered herself, arms hugged tight around her. "I'm good. Gimme one of those coffee substitute things and I'll be great."

"That's the spirit."

Over tasteless food bars and hissing cylinders of coffee substitute, Jake said, "Tell me about this place you might know."

"Old elementary school near Watts," Nadine said. "City closed it down a while back. Sat vacant for a while, then some folks petitioned to turn it into a community center. Didn't go so well. Someone else tried making the auditorium into a community theater. That's how I know about it. Did a couple of shows there."

"Performing?"

"Yeah, among other things. Community theater lets you be the star and the custodial staff all at once. Not sure who owns it these days. Hasn't been a production there since...I don't know. 2051? '52, maybe? There won't be anyone around."

"Okay. We lure the ogre there, take him off the board—"

"No."

"What?"

"I want to talk to him first."

"Why?"

"You ever watch the news, Jake?"

"Yeah. What of it?"

"Know any journalists might want to hear a conversation with a private security goon about using deepfakes of a supposed terrorist for political purposes?"

"You want to record him."

"I want to record him."

Jake gave her a long look. Eventually, he said, "I see what Anna saw in you. Okay, let's go. Pack your stuff in the car."

The sun had just peeked above the horizon when they arrived. The old school squatted within spitting distance of the most exuberant, extravagantly baroque interstate interchange Nadine had ever seen, its bizarrely improbable stacks of looping, whorling asphalt a tribute to a bygone age, when everyone bought their own cars at great expense so they could enjoy the freedom of hours trapped in massive traffic jams that stretched to the horizon.

Jake drove cautiously around the block, the Mini mostly on autopilot, scoping the place out. Three long connected buildings arranged in a U-shape, the open end facing a parking lot, surrounded a small open courtyard filled with half-dead trees and brown grass. A weathered iron fence enclosed the old school, rust-pocked and dented. Small square windows like blank eyes peered out from walls painted institutional beige and covered with dense, overlapping graffiti. One of the windows had a construction-paper jack-o-lantern taped to the inside, orange sun-bleached nearly white. A faded residential neighborhood closed tightly around the place on all four sides, dilapidated houses with overgrown yards. A handful of cars, mostly internal combustion, meandered down the street. The parking lot sat empty. "Where's the entrance?" he said.

"North side."

He took manual control and steered the Mini around the block again. "Door locked?"

"Probably, yeah."

"Key?"

"No."

"Okay." Jake made one more pass around the block, scanning the sun-baked street, eyes alert. On the third trip past the entrance, he touched a control on the Mini's touchscreen. "Let's go."

The car rolled to a stop. Jake opened the door, hauled out his bag and the oddly stunted rifle in its case, and gestured for Nadine to follow. As soon as they were clear, the Mini rolled off. "Where's it going?" Nadine said.

"Safe parking, a bit from here." Jake trotted quickly to the entrance, protected by a square roof held up by metal poles. He fished something small and flat from his pocket and slipped it in the keyhole. His claw gripped the knob. A moment later, the door opened into darkness. Jake flitted through, silent as a ghost. Nadine followed. The air inside had a dusty, disused smell, like it had somehow gone past its sell-by date. Scuffed linoleum beneath their feet, vanishing into darkness when the door closed behind them with a boom. Jake flicked on his flashlight. "Where to?"

"Left, then left again."

In the blue-white beam of Jake's light, the hallways, wide and empty, had a haunted air that made Nadine shiver. They pushed through an enormous set of double doors that opened into the cavernous auditorium. Tiers of vacant seats covered in worn, grubby red fabric faced the blank blackness of the stage. "You did plays here?" Jake said.

"Yep."

"Come to LA to be an actor?"

"Of course. Why else would anyone come to this Godforsaken shithole? Vancouver looked set to steal Hollywood's thunder for a while, but after the floods..." She shrugged.

"Ever get in any movies?"

Nadine laughed. The vast space swallowed the sound, echoed back a dry rustle. "I was an uncredited extra in a couple of movies. Made it into the credits once. 'Woman on sidewalk with ice cream.'"

"Anything I might've seen?"

"Doubt it. Movie didn't exactly set the critics on fire. *Lost City Showdown.*"

Jake stopped dead. "No shit. You were in that? I love that movie!"

"You and two other people." She edged cautiously toward the stage in the gloom, halfway expecting yellow triangles to flare up in her vision, the bootleg software in her head warning her of things that go bump in the night.

Nothing.

The circuit breaker panel, a great dull box of gray metal rusted on one corner, clung to the wall just behind the narrow door that led backstage. She flipped a few breakers. A handful of the cracked lights flickered on, sending dusty rays of colored light through faded cellophane onto the stage.

Jake flicked off his flashlight and looked around. The stage, almost shoulder high, curved outward into the auditorium, its floor scuffed wood. Shabby, threadbare curtains hung open. A set designed to look a bit like a living room stood partly assembled on it, opaque plastic sheeting hanging from a false wall covered in hideous green wallpaper. A dilapidated couch and equally scruffy easy chair faced each other across a small coffee table that looked to be a refuse bin rescue. Overhead, trusswork covered with spotlights, many dented and battered, straddled the faux living room. Ladders, cans, an empty wheeled clothes rack with a few sad wire coat hangers hanging from it, and other bits of detritus cluttered the stage and the space in front of it.

More junk lay against the wall near the door: an old IKEA shelving unit with a broken top; a large, heavy tripod, minus a leg; a lighting truss, stripped of its spotlights. Bits of furniture shrouded in plastic like funerary garb had at some point been pushed against the far wall, blocking the emergency exit. "Nice place for an ambush," Jake said.

"That's good, right?" Nadine said.

Jake twitched an asymmetric shrug. "Maybe, if your ogre is arrogant enough. Thankfully, he's probably operating on the assumption that you're alone and scared."

"Well, the scared part is true."

"He'll have an implant, of course."

"What do we do about that?" Nadine said.

"Leave that to me. Time to get to work."

"What do you need me to do?"

"Stay out of my way."

Nadine watched Jake set about turning the not-quite abandoned community theater in the husk of the abandoned school into...something else. A killing field, she realized. They intended for someone to die here, in this space. The thought disturbed her less than she expected it to.

Jake set about his grim task with an efficient economy of motion that reminded her, just a little, of the way Anna sometimes moved. No waste, every movement as precise as a ballerina's. Three doorways offered access to the old auditorium: the one from the hall with its silent rows of vacant classrooms; an emergency exit beside the stage, blocked off with random clutter; and another emergency exit backstage, behind the tidy utility room and the much larger space that now served as a kind of tomb of discarded props and cast-off equipment. Jake made short work barring both emergency exits. "The key to a successful ambush," he said, "is limiting the enemy's path of access. We need to make sure he comes in where we want him to. He won't be expecting me, and he certainly won't be expecting a trap. He probably figures you kept the gun you used to shoot his friends. Did you, by the way?"

"No," Nadine said. "I gave it to Tony to get rid of."

"He'll expect at worst a scared girl with a handgun. Dangerous, to be sure, but he'll assume he has the upper hand. Which, if that were true, he would." Jake wedged a bit of truss under the doorknob behind the stage. Having only one good arm didn't seem to slow him down. "Keep out of sight, when he comes in."

"Where will you be?"

"In the lighting platform above the stage with my rifle. The minute, and by that I mean the nanosecond, anything comes off the rails, I'm shooting him in the head. Only reason we're not doing that on sight is your buck-wild desire to talk to him." He grunted as he dragged the gutted remnants of a sound mixing board in front of the wedged door. "Wish we had some boards and nails, but that's as good as it's gonna get. Not even an ogre is getting through there. I think I saw some mannequins backstage. Help me drag them on stage?"

"Why?"

"Confusion. Disorient him for a second, make him think there are more people here."

Nadine helped him position three mannequins, one of them missing a leg, partly concealed at the edge of the stage. Jake put a fragment of truss in one of the mannequin's arms. "Looks a bit like a rifle barrel," he explained. "If your ogre comes in guns blazing, I'd rather have him shooting at our plastic friend than us." He patted the mannequin's back with his claw.

Nadine did her best to stay out of his way. The last thing he did was lash the thing he'd called a "zip gun" to the side of a heavy cabinet he'd dragged next to the door. Nadine examined it curiously. It looked like a bit of junk—a short piece of pipe, a nail, a hinge, a spring. He mounted a small electronic box below it and ran a tight cable from that to the spring. He attached a small, square thing that looked a little like a bicycle reflector to the wall across from the door. "Don't want to use a tripwire," he explained. "Our friend will probably see it. This will shine an invisible laser across the door about knee high. Watch." He waved his hand in front of the door. With a snap, the hinge slammed the nail into the pipe.

"Jake?"

"Yeah?"

"Is this going to work?"

Jake tilted his head sideways. "Better than even odds," he said eventually. "Odds would be better still if you'd let me shoot him in the fucking head as soon as he turns up, instead of talking to him first. Not to say I think yours is a bad idea, if it works," he added hastily. "Could give us some leverage. But it's dangerous. Adds complexity. We're making this up as we go along, and we're catastrophically under-resourced. Still, we do have one thing going for us."

"What's that?"

"He's almost certainly underestimated you. Both of them, really. Taylor and our ogre. That gives us just the tiniest edge of possibility, which is why I agreed to this. See what we find out. Take an enemy piece off the board. Keep going until we can't anymore." He reset the zip gun and held up a shotgun shell. "We only have the one. It wasn't easy to source. Had to burn a half-dozen favors to get it." He slipped the shell into the zip gun. "Do not, and I cannot emphasize this enough, under any circumstances use this door. One mistake and it's game over, forever. Got it? Here." He handed Nadine a small box with two short antennas protruding from the top and a compact solid-state recorder.

"What's this?"

"Short-range signal jammer. Turn it on when he comes through the door. Not before. If he loses comms before he's in, he'll know something's up. It's time. Make the call."

Nadine fished the phone from Anna's storage locker out of her bag. She reconnected the battery, closed her eyes, and took a deep breath.

She dialed. The phone rang. "Hey, it's me," Nadine said. "Listen, did you pick up that bag I left for you?"

Olivia's voice came distorted and tinny through the phone's cheap speaker. "Yeah."

"Did you look inside?"

A pause. "No."

"Good. Listen, I know this is a huge, huge favor to ask, but I really need it back. I'm leaving town. Can you bring it to me?"

Another pause. "Sure. Anything for you."

"Thank you." Nadine put relief into her voice. "Um, hey, don't tell anyone, okay?"

"I won't. Where are you?"

"I'm at...um, do you remember the place I played in that rewrite of *Rosencrantz and Guildenstern Are Dead*? You know, the one directed by the guy with the beard you said looked like a used mop?"

"Yeah, I remember."

"I'm there. And Olivia?"

"Yeah?"

"You're the best." Nadine ended the call and disconnected the battery. "Think she bought it?"

"Be surprised if she didn't." He unslung his odd-looking rifle, checked the magazine. "They should've given you a bigger part."

"What?"

"*Lost City Showdown*. They wasted your talents. I bet she's calling Taylor right this minute, not that she needs to since they've almost certainly bugged her phone. Why the long face?"

"It still hurts," Nadine said.

"What?"

"Olivia. Knowing that she's ratting me out to Taylor and his goons."

"This whole idea kinda depends on that."

"Yeah, I know." Nadine shook her head. "That doesn't make it hurt any less."

"Not like she has a lot of choice."

"Maybe. What now?"

"Now we wait."

13

No Point Flattering the Dead

Rifle slung, Jake climbed up into the trusswork above the stage, where he settled down and seemed, by some sleight of hand, to disappear. She couldn't see him, when she looked away and then back again—just a yellow triangle with an exclamation point and a line going to what looked like a bit of truss. "Jake?" she said.

"Yeah?" His voice came somewhere from the shadows above the stage.

"How long do we wait?"

"Hard to say. Taylor has a bit of a hard-on for you, so I suspect he'll send his ogre soonest, but it depends on how far away he is and how soon he can be tasked."

"Do we know he'll send the ogre?"

"No."

"What if he doesn't?"

"Then I kill whoever he does send. Get up on the stage like we said. Stay under cover. When he comes through the door, pull back behind the stage."

Nadine crouched behind an improvised shelter Jake had built on the stage, behind the sofa. He'd unzipped his black bag and lined the back of an overturned table with it. "Kevlar," he said. "Not great, but better than nothing."

Long minutes went by. Nadine heard nothing but her blood roaring in her ears. She looked up. Other than the yellow triangle, she saw nothing. "How do you do it?"

"Do what?"

"The waiting."

No answer.

"Hello, this is interesting." Jake's soft murmur sounded like a shout after the long, tense silence.

"What's that?"

"Newsfeed. Got my implant set to tell me if anything comes up about you. Apparently there's been a sighting of you. San Jose. Surveillance drone caught you trying to rob a convenience store. Biometrics and facial recognition confirmed. Oh, you naughty girl! You stabbed the owner and fled on foot."

"What's that about?"

"Taylor's taken the bait. He's clearing the game board. Getting the Feds to pull out, head to San Jose post haste. He must've had that video dummied up and ready to go. Betting there will be limited police response to the shenanigans here tonight. Almost showtime. You scared?"

"Yes."

"Good. That might help keep you alive."

"Did a shopkeeper really get stabbed?"

"Dunno. Maybe. Maybe the shopkeeper's one of his. Maybe there is no shopkeeper. This kind of shit, who can tell?"

You aren't really, you know. Anna's voice, somewhere behind her.

"Really what?"

Scared. Not as much as I thought you'd be. Knew I saw something there, that night at the rave.

"You aren't real."

"What?" Jake said.

"Nothing," Nadine said. "Hey Jake, you ever hear things?"

"What kind of things?"

"I don't know, things. Things like—"

She never finished the sentence. The wall across from her exploded with a roar. Jake just had time to shriek as the lighting trusswork atop the stage caved in. The front of a large vehicle protruded, angular and brutal, through the ruined wall for just a moment, then withdrew. Headlights shone through the massive cloud of dust that billowed through the room. She heard a cough, then silence.

A door slammed. A moment later, a dark-clad figure darted catlike through the hole, outlined in yellow triangles. A quick flicker of motion. One of the yellow triangles detached from the figure and floated toward her, following a red arc splashed in microscopic LEDs across her vision. Nadine dove to the floor, hands over her head, eyes tightly closed.

An explosion to shatter worlds smashed ice picks into her ears. Nadine screamed, the sound lost behind the shrill ringing. Her stomach heaved. She backed up frantically, disoriented and half-deaf, scrambling on hands and knees. She lifted her head to see the figure turn away from her, stepping over the rubble, scanning the wreckage of the trusswork. A corner of the ceiling had come down, and now lay in ruin, pinned by the cold blue glare of the headlights through the ruined wall.

Run! Anna's voice in her head.

"What?"

Run or die. Now!

Nadine exploded from a crouch, running for the door, driven by an impulse she didn't understand. The figure turned. Yellow triangles danced in the corner of her vision as she raced up the walkway between rows of shabby dust-covered seats, silent and empty. At the door, she jumped, praying she remembered where the laser tripwire was, dreading the bang that would end all of this.

She hit the scuffed linoleum flooring in the hallway off-balance, skidded, then picked herself up and kept going. A wave of vertigo sent her staggering against the wall, long rows of metal lockers painted institutional orange marching in rows down the still, dark hallway. Through the shrill ringing in her ears, she heard sounds behind her, then a distant pop, no louder than a firecracker. She collapsed to her knees, retching, stomach heaving.

"You bitch! You'll pay for that."

Nadine slumped against a metal locker, paint peeling, corrosion eating a hole in the corner of the door. The chrome-plated latch pressed painfully into her back. She looked up at the figure silhouetted in the doorway, surrealistically muscled, a cartoon caricature of a bodybuilder, arms so enormous Nadine wondered if he could even cross them. He wore black pants and a black shirt with a black vest over it, open at the sides, a plate of angular black metal mounted in a kind of cloth pouch in front and held in place with black Velcro. He wore a helmet, too, black matte, and a pair of silver shades over his eyes that looked a bit like a cross between wraparound sunglasses and welder's goggles. He leaned against the edge of the door, blood on his face and the side of his neck. The shot had shredded his shirt along his side, where his vest didn't cover. Blood dripped down one bulging arm.

He reached into his belt and pulled out a baton. A yellow triangle floated above it. It whined like the charger on an old-fashioned camera flash. "Yeah," he said. "I'm coming for you."

Three loud bangs sounded behind him, all in a row, pop-pop-pop. The ogre was moving before Nadine even registered what happened, inhumanely fast, as agile as a hunting cat and graceful as a dancer despite his enormous bulk. Something small and fast whined through the doorway, ricocheted off the locker across from her. Nadine had just enough presence of mind to reach into her pocket and flip the switch on Jake's jammer.

Run! Anna's voice again, startlingly loud.

Nadine dragged herself to her feet and fled down the hall. Somewhere behind her, something detonated, a sound beyond all possible sound, a piledriver crushing her head. The hallway lit up with a blazing light brighter than the noonday sun, bleaching the row of lockers into a jumbled abstract impression of white radiance and black shadow, and then was dark again. She clamped her hands over her ringing ears and screamed.

She staggered on, past doors that opened on both sides of the hall into long-abandoned classrooms. More sounds from behind her, muffled beneath the ringing in her ears, dull firecracker pops, ceasing abruptly. Three left, three right, then a row of narrow doors all close together, bathroom stalls, then three right and two left, one opening into the kitchen, the other into the cafeteria. She flung her shoulder against the door to the cafeteria, which slammed open without resistance, then kicked it closed behind her, panting. She half-ran, half-staggered past rows of tables to a long stainless steel serving line, empty holes for trays of industrial food open like eye sockets in a skull.

From some endless distance away, she heard a door slam open. A thick growl: "*Bitch!*" A crash as another door slammed open. "I'm going to *find* you." Crash. "And I'm going to *fuck you up*." Crash. "Did you really think you could take me?" Crash. "You have no *idea* what you're dealing with." Crash. "Your *boyfriend* can't hide from infrared." Crash, worryingly close. "Come out, come out, wherever you are!" Another door, slammed or kicked open. "Running outta places to hide, little girl..."

The door to the kitchen slammed open. Nadine curled into a tiny ball on the cafeteria side of the serving line, a long, solid rectangle of stainless steel between her and the ogre in black.

Keep low. Anna's voice, in her head.

Nadine's lips moved silently. "Anna, you're dead."

You will be too, if you don't keep low.

Nadine curled tighter. The late evening sun sent razor-edged shadows through the gloom. The ogre brought his baton down with a crash on the stainless steel shelves behind the counter. Nadine jumped, fist stuffed into her mouth. "That little booby trap of yours *hurt!*" he called.

Nadine edged backward, keeping under the long serving tray, heart hammering. *I'm a bit disappointed in Jake,* Anna's voice noted, so close Nadine could almost feel her breath on her ear.

"Why?"

He underestimated this guy. That's not like him. You both did, but at least you have an excuse. This isn't exactly your wheelhouse.

Another crash. The ogre kicked open the walk-in cooler, long unused. An unpleasant smell rolled out.

You need to survive this. Being dead's no fun. Trust me.

"I must be losing my mind," Nadine muttered to herself.

That's a distinct possibility. You're under a lot of stress. Psychotic break. Well, technically, brief reactive psychotic episode. Why did you leave that picture of us on that machine in the tunnel?

"I don't know. Seemed the thing to do. Maybe I was praying."

You're not a believer.

"Yeah, well, I've never been wanted for terrorism before, or hunted down by some kind of augmented assassin freak. Maybe I'm broadening my horizons."

No need to be snarky. I'm just saying. I wonder why they do it?

"Who?"

The people who leave pictures on that thing.

"My old art history professor would probably call it a communal semiotic expression of persistent low-grade trauma or something."

Something's happening.

Nadine held her breath. The classroom door across the hall smashed open.

Go. Now.

Nadine reached up to unfasten the latch beneath the counter. Part of the counter swung aside. She crawled noiselessly through into the kitchen and closed the counter behind her.

Nice. How'd you find that?

"Long story. I stayed late cleaning after a show, one thing led to another, I ended up on my back beneath one of the other performers."

In the cafeteria?

"I said it was a long story."

Did you have fun?

"She was okay, I guess. Not as much fun as you."

No point flattering the dead, babe.

Nadine crawled backward, hands and knees, around a large steel prep table, back toward the massive stainless steel ovens, left here after the school closed because they were simply too cumbersome to take. She wedged herself in a narrow space between stove and wall. The door to the cafeteria crashed open. "The longer you hide, the angrier I get!" the ogre called. "Please, keep hiding. It will be more fun when I find you."

I wonder if Jake's still alive.

"So do I."

You're pretty buggered if he's not.

"Thanks for the vote of confidence."

Call it fatalism. Get it?

The ogre kicked over a table. Nadine flinched. *He seems pretty angry,* Anna's voice observed mildly.

"Tell me something I don't know."

If I'm your manifestation of a psychotic break, I literally can't.

"What do you mean 'if'?"

Shadows scuttled across the ceiling, toward the door. Nadine heard the door across the hall smash open.

Speaking of Jake...

"Yeah, I know, I know."

Another door slammed open. "This is *fun!*" her pursuer said. "I haven't had a good chase in ages. Oh, I'm going to *enjoy* you."

Nadine crawled on hands and knees to the door. *What's your plan?* Anna's voice said.

"I'm making this up as I go along. Find out if Jake's okay. See if we can get out of here."

You should've brought my gun.

"I don't know how to use a gun. He does. If I play his game I lose."

Still, might have come in handy.

"Shush. I need to concentrate."

Another crash, farther down the hallway. *Did you just shush your dead girlfriend?*

"My dead girlfriend is being unusually chatty." Nadine reached up to the doorknob. Holding her breath, she cracked the door just enough to peer down the hallway. The classroom doors past the cafeteria gaped open, wide yawning rectangles in the walls.

Good a time as any.

Nadine took a deep breath, then slipped silent as the gray shadows through the hall. She sped as quickly as she could toward the auditorium, heart pounding, afraid to look behind her. If he saw here, out in the open, there'd be nothing she could do...

Can't think like that. It'll make you crazy.

"I already am crazy." Nadine flashed through the doorway. The smell of cordite hung in the air. She hopped over the last row of seats to the corner of the stage, where she could just make out Jake's head amid a pile of debris. She crouched next to him. "Jake!" she hissed. "Jake!" Her fingers sought a pulse at his neck. "Jake! You okay?"

He opened one eye and gave her a lopsided grin. "Unless you're a Valkyrie here to carry me off to Valhalla."

"To Freyja," Nadine corrected absently. She wormed her hands under the edge of a long piece of truss, straining to lift it.

"What?"

"The Valkyries. They take you to Freyja. Freyja chooses who goes to Valhalla and who stays with her in Fólkvangr."

"Now I know I'm still alive. No real Valkyrie would be having this conversation with me in the middle of a firefight." Jake's face contorted as he struggled to wiggle out from under the stubborn piles. He huffed in frustration.

"Can you move?"

"No. Gimme ten or twenty minutes and I might be able to dig myself out."

"We don't have ten or twenty minutes."

"You do. The hole in the wall is clear enough. Get out of here."

"And then what?" Nadine whispered. "You've seen how fast he is. In an open space I'm dead. Besides, I'm not leaving you behind."

"Why not?"

"You didn't leave me behind."

"Yeah, but I was being paid."

A shadow loomed in the doorway. "Here, kitty kitty!" the ogre growled. "I see you!"

"Fuck!" Nadine looked around frantically. "Where's your gun?"

Jake shook his head. "Don't know. He took it. Backup piece is in an ankle holster, I can't reach it."

"Fuck," Nadine said again. She stood, edging toward the stage, keeping the rows of seats between her and the black-clad man.

The ogre spun his baton between nimble fingers in an intricate whorl. "Let's play."

Nadine glanced sideways at Jake, then back at the ogre. "Come get me."

"With pleasure."

Nadine bolted onto the stage. In a series of fluid bounds, the ogre came after her, leaping effortlessly over the rows of seats. Nadine fled through the curtain that led into the horseshoe-shaped backstage area with its dense clutter of long-dead junk. Long, janky painted canvas backdrops hung in still rows from the ceiling. The gutted remnants of a light panel lay on its side, spilling electronics. A warren of tiny, narrow spaces wormed through the remnants of years of amateur productions.

The ogre burst through the curtain, breathing heavily. "Surprise!" He licked thin lips below mirrored glasses. Something dark flowed down his side. "You've given me the best run I've had in a long time, but you must've known you couldn't win. Show's over, girl."

Nadine leapt over the defunct lighting panel. She darted between two sun-dulled canvas scenes hanging from their cables. The sour scent of dry dust and old paint filled her nose.

"You just don't know when to *quit*," the ogre snarled. A knife blade flashed through the canvas inches from her face. Nadine dropped to the floor and scrambled beneath the row of silently hanging backdrops.

He shoved after her without finesse, slashing through the decaying canvas. She rolled and sprang to her feet, making for a dressing room, sound of his heavy breathing right behind her. She darted through the door. His arm came after her, knife gleaming in his grip, a red fan-shaped arc of light extending in front of it. She twisted away. The red turned green. The knife slashed through the air where she'd just been.

She kicked the door shut on his arm and was rewarded with a bark of pain. He kicked back. The door blurred red. Something smashed into her side. Nadine threw herself backward, rolling as she hit the floor. The knife slashed again, a blur of green just above her.

"You're fast. Good. You know what? Don't give up. This is fun."

For a second, Nadine saw his bulk filling the doorway, then she exploded off the ground, leaping with every ounce of desperate strength at the door connecting the two dressing rooms. She heard a curse behind her.

Her shoulder hit the door. She grabbed for the knob, praying silently that it wouldn't be locked. It turned. The door opened, spilling her into the darkness of the second dressing room. She groped for the fire extinguisher that should be mounted by the door. Her questing fingers found an empty frame.

A yellow triangle flared. A quick flash of red. She dropped. The red turned green. Air swished past her face.

Nadine ran for the corridor. Fingers brushed her shoulder. Adrenaline slammed through her. She flung herself against the door and out into the corridor again. She kicked the door shut behind her. It slammed on the side of his face. He punched through the cheap, flimsy material.

Splinters erupted. "Ow," he said mildly. He staggered, leaning against the wall. "That hurt."

Heart hammering, lungs burning, Nadine threw herself into motion. She darted back onto the stage, dragging a metal wheeled garment rack into the space beside her. The ogre crashed clumsily into it. It crumpled beneath his momentum.

Nadine sped across the stage, its faux living room now covered with a thin layer of gritty white dust. The headlights from the ogre's car sent strange angular shadows through the auditorium. She heard footsteps behind her, the sound of his labored breathing in his ear.

She risked a quick glance backward. A dark shape filled the space behind her, surrounded by yellow triangles. She stumbled gasping across the front of the stage, both arms wrapped tight around her. Every muscle burned. She struggled to pull enough air into her aching lungs. She doubled over, only the wall on the far side of the stage holding up her shaking body. Her knees buckled.

The ogre slowed, chest heaving. "Congratulations," he said. "You drew first blood. I'm impressed. But now it's time to fin...to fin..." He reeled drunkenly. "I'm going..." His knees gave out. He collapsed heavily onto the rickety couch in a cloud of dust.

Nadine, still gasping, forced herself to straighten. Fire traced paths through her body. She turned toward him. The knife fell from his fingers, followed on its path to the floor by a yellow triangle. "What..." he wheezed. "What's happening? What did you do to me?"

Yeah, Anna's voice said, *what did you do to him?*

Nadine crept cautiously toward the man. He slumped unmoving on the couch, eyes concealed behind his glasses. She kicked the knife away. More yellow triangles floated in the air around him. She slipped his baton from its holster. He twisted toward her, his movements clumsy and uncoordinated. She flung the baton off the stage. "What...what..." he gasped.

Nadine unsnapped the holster of his gun. He flung himself at her, hand moving in a yellow arc. She evaded him easily and slid the gun free, marveling at its weight. Without taking her eyes from him, she settled cautiously into the chair across from him. "What did you do?" he croaked.

"Synthetic tetrodotoxin." She over-enunciated the unfamiliar word. "Friend of a friend had some on hand. Packed it in the shotgun shell. Nasty little paralytic. Just the thing for someone with jacked-up muscles. You're going to die. Unless..."

"Unless what?"

"Unless you get an antidote. Sooner rather than later, I think."

"What do you want?"

Nadine took the recorder from her pocket and set it on the table between them. "I want to talk."

"I don't know anything."

"I'm certain that's not true. So what's it going to be? Are we going to have a talk, or am I going to walk away and leave you to suffocate alone in that fancy augmented body of yours?"

"He'll kill me—"

"You're dying now. Better decide fast. Pretty soon your throat will stop working and then you'll be no use to me."

"Okay! Okay!"

"I knew you'd see reason." Nadine pressed a button on the recorder. A small arm rose with a mechanical whirr, a tiny lens on each side of it. She leaned forward, bracing the ogre's gun across her knees, barrel pointed shakily at him. "My name is Nadine Jiang. I am accused of terrorism, and the police are looking for me. Other people, too." Her voice quavered. "I don't know what's happening or why everyone thinks I'm a terrorist. I haven't done anything. This man just tried to kill me. He's not police. Who do you work for?"

"Martin," the ogre wheezed. "Martin Taylor. He contracts with me to do...security work."

"I know him!" Nadine said. "He murdered my friends. He took video of me. He told me he would use it to make deepfake videos of me committing crimes. He *laughed* when he said it." A tear leaked from the corner of her eyes. "Why is he doing this? Why does he want me dead?"

"You know why." Sweat beaded on the man's forehead. "It was that kid. That kid in the hospital. We snatched him from the hospital. You came after him."

"But I'm not a terrorist!" Nadine wailed.

"Doesn't..." He dragged in a long, shuddering breath. "Doesn't matter. You got close. You and your friends. You had to go. The terrorism part was easy. Video is no problem. Taylor..." Another long, labored breath. "Taylor has connections with the police. Easy to slip them intel. Some of it is real. Some, not so much."

"But why me?"

"Wrong place, wrong time."

"How come the police think there's a confirmed sighting of me in San Jose at the same time I'm in Los Angeles?"

"I told you. Easy to fake. Taylor has video footage of you, more than enough."

"Is that why he was filming me when he had me captive in that office park, before he ordered his security team to murder me?"

"Yes."

"Why make fake video of me?"

"Money. Why do you think?" He took another wheezing breath. "Can't...can't breathe..."

Nadine touched the recorder. The tiny arm retracted. "Thank you," she said. She set the gun on the floor and relaxed back in the cushions of the cheap armchair, watching him curiously.

"What about..." The sentence ended in a strangled cough.

"What about what?"

"The antidote?"

She leaned forward. "I want to see your eyes." She slipped off his glasses. "You have pretty eyes. Brown. Gentle. I like them. What's your name?"

"Thomas," he gasped.

"Thank you, Thomas, you've been very helpful. I don't want to lie to you. You're going to die. Right here, on that sofa. There is no antidote."

"But..." His chest heaved. "But you said..."

"I said you're going to die if you don't get an antidote, not that I have one."

His eyes widened, turning from hopeful to desperate. "But..."

"Do you have someone, Thomas? Someone close to you? A wife? A girlfriend? Kids?"

"Girlfriend," he wheezed.

"I'm sorry she can't be here for you, in your final moments," Nadine said. "I had a girlfriend, too. Smart. So very smart. And funny. She made the most amazing grilled ham and cheese sandwiches. It's such a simple thing, but the way she made it, it became something else. Something special, made with love just for me." Nadine closed her eyes. A wistful half-smile drifted across her lips. "I met her at an underground rave. She was so beautiful. Like a goddess, bathed in glittering lights. We danced together, and then she said 'I'm taking you home with me.' I never wanted to leave." Her eyes snapped open. "She died in a shitty concrete tunnel under Martin Taylor's shitty little office park. She died to save me. Do you have any idea what that feels like, Thomas?"

"They...won't stop...They'll carry on coming...until you're dead," he gasped.

Nadine nodded. "I know. Someone told me recently that you keep going until you can't anymore. That's what I'm doing." She leaned across the table toward him. "Do you love your girlfriend, Thomas?"

"What?"

"It's a simple question. Do you love her?"

"Yes."

"I know how you feel. I loved Anna. I loved her so much, just her smile could make my whole day. Seeing her was like being able to breathe when I didn't even know I was holding my breath. I miss being able to breathe. Do you know what that's like, Thomas? A life without that isn't worth living, don't you think?" She clasped his hand in both of hers. "Anna died without anyone to hold her. I won't do that to you. I'll be here, holding your hand when you go. Nobody should have to die alone. It isn't right."

"You...you..." Loathing seethed in Thomas' eyes. His fingers twitched feebly against Nadine's palm.

"Do you miss her, Thomas?" Nadine tenderly stroked a lock of hair out of his eyes. "Your girlfriend, I mean. You'll never be able to hold her again, stroke her hair as you both fall asleep. That's over for you. You'll never be able to watch a sunset with her or look up at the moon with her again. You'll never curl up beside her again. Do you miss her, right now, as much as I miss Anna?" Her eyes searched his face. "I think you do. It hurts, doesn't it, to have that taken away from you. Like acid and ice, all the time, burning and freezing all at once."

A small convulsion ran through his body. He stared helplessly at her, eyes burning with impotent hate. Nadine squeezed his hand, patted it. "Nobody should have to go through that, don't you think, Thomas?"

His lips moved. He convulsed again. Terror filled his eyes for a moment, then they filmed over. Nadine watched patiently as the life drained from them, absently stroking his arm.

When he was gone, she released his hand and slipped the recorder into her pocket. In the corner of the auditorium, Jake's mechanical arm whirred as he worked to extricate himself from the fallen rubble. "What the fuck was that about?" he said.

"What?"

"Nothing. Did you get what you needed?"

"I suppose."

"Good. Give me a hand out of here."

It took almost half an hour before they were able to free Jake from the rubble, one pants leg shredded. Blood slicked his leg and the debris beneath. "You're hurt!" Nadine said.

"I'll live. We need to get rid of that guy and the car."

"Can't we just take it?"

"No. Taylor's people will have it wired six ways from Sunday. Only reason they're not all over us right now is they have no way to know things went off the rails. You turned on the jammer?"

"Yes."

"Good. Then we still have a little time." He hooked his thumb toward the stage. "Help me drag asshole over there to the car."

"What are you going to do?"

"Make him disappear."

Nadine and Jake dragged the ogre's lifeless body out into the evening air. Nadine looked it over. Blue so dark as to be almost black, harshly angular, the windows and windshield unusually thick. "BMW Xi9," Jake said with something like lust in his voice. "Full armor package, all-wheel electric drive, run-flat tires. Beautiful. Goddammit, where's the key?" He patted down the lifeless corpse. "Gotta be here somewhere...ah." He fished something from beneath the corpse's body armor. The car chirped. "Help me get Asshole behind the wheel. Well, would you look at that." Awe colored his voice. "In-vehicle high-resolution Doppler radar. I'm jealous. Asshole here has all the best toys."

"What's that?"

"It's how he knew where I was hiding."

Jake stared off into space. Tiny lights glittered in his contacts. His lips moved soundlessly. "What are you doing?" Nadine said.

"Searching the BMW modder forums. Trying to find...ah, here it is."

He pushed the body out of his way. Thomas' corpse slumped over the center console. Jake hit the power switch several times, then held the shift selector button and the power switch for a long moment, until the car chimed and the power switch started blinking. Nadine peered over his shoulder. "What's that?"

"Service mode. I'm disabling some of the safeties." His finger stabbed at the central console. "Sanity checking."

"Why?"

Jake switched the BMW off and on again. "There." He called up the navigation screen. "I'm telling it to drive to a point about two hundred yards off the end of the last pier on Terminal Island, behind that wrecked ship. Good way to get rid of cars. It'll hit the edge of the map and just keep on going. Be a while before anyone finds it. You still got that jammer?"

"Yeah."

Jake took it from her and tossed it in the front seat. "There. That'll keep Taylor from knowing where it is."

"Won't that block GPS? Screw up the navigation?"

"Nah. GPS is receive-only. Real-time tracking takes the information from the GPS receiver and retransmits it on a different frequency. This'll block the tracking without blocking GPS." He punched a button and slammed the door. The long, predatory-looking car backed away from them. "Bon voyage, motherfucker!" Jake wavered, then collapsed. "Goddammit."

"Hey, you okay?" Nadine looked down. Something dark and slick soaked his tattered pants leg, pooled around his boot.

"Bleeding out. Guess I was hurt worse than I thought. Fuck." He fished a cylinder out of his pocket, unrolled the screen, punched at buttons. "Mini's on the way."

"I'll get you to a hospital."

"Are you insane? No hospital." He shoved the unrolled phone into her hands. "Use this. Call Dr. Abdullah. Get me to him."

"I didn't think he was that kind of doctor."

"He's not. He's a molecular biologist. He was also a field medic in Afghanistan. Not exactly on our side, but not *not* on our side either. It's complicated. Just get—get—" His eyes rolled. He slumped.

"Don't you fucking die on me." Nadine's voice held just a trace of a panicked tremor. She poked at the screen on Jake's phone. While it rang, she tore open what was left of his pants leg, found a long, jagged wound beneath. "Fuck! Fuck!" She looked around the parking lot, then pulled off her shirt and wrapped it as best as she could around his injured leg. Blood flowed around her hands. "Fuck!" she swore. Headlights strobed across her as the Mini pulled itself into a parking space right in front of her. The doors popped.

Still swearing, Nadine hooked her arms under Jake's and dragged him into the passenger seat of the Mini. "Hello?" came a voice.

"Hello, Dr. Abdullah?"

"This is me, yes. Who is this?"

"Listen, I don't have a lot of time to explain." Nadine pushed Jake's legs into the car and slammed the door. "This is Na—Melody. We met a few days ago. I'm a friend of Jake's." She climbed into the driver's seat, called up a navigation map. "Jake's hurt. Bad. He needs medical care. He won't let me take him to a hospital. Says to see you."

"Ah. This is awkward."

"You don't know the half of it. Where are you?"

A pause. "You cannot bring him here. That would be...inadvisable."

"Tell me where, then."

Dr. Abdullah gave her an address. Nadine punched it in. "Are you fucking kidding me?" she said.

"No. Best I can do. I'll be there in twenty minutes."

"Make it ten."

"Very well."

14

Tomorrow We Declare War

HE MIGHT DIE, *you know,* Anna's voice said in Nadine's ear.

"I know." Nadine glanced over at Jake. He looked back at her and managed the barest ghost of a smile. His breathing came fast and shallow. "I'm working on it."

Maybe you should go faster.

"Maybe if I get busted by a traffic enforcement drone, he'll definitely die and then we'll both be fucked."

Did you mean what you said about me to that ogre?

"Every word."

You know I was a criminal, right?

"Yeah, I kinda figured that out early on."

I'm sorry I didn't open up to you sooner.

"I'm sorry too. I really have to drive now." Nadine gripped the wheel until her knuckles turned white. She kept one eye on the blue wedge spearing its way through the digitized version of LA's streets, watching the ETA tick down, keeping just slightly over the speed limit, not enough to catch the attention of a wandering enforcement drone.

I don't remember you cursing this much before.

"I don't remember having conversations in my head with my dead girlfriend before. Uncharted territory for both of us." She reached out to squeeze Jake's good arm. "Don't die," she told him. "If you die I'll never speak to you again."

You sure? Anna said.

Nadine said nothing.

Thirteen minutes and forty-six seconds after Nadine's call to Dr. Abdullah, she pulled into the parking lot of a long, low structure, more an architectural appendage tacked onto a strip mall than a building in its own right. A silver Volvo sat in front of it, the only car in an otherwise vacant lot. He stood next to the car in a business suit, wearing an expression distinctly south of happy. "Dr. Abdullah," Nadine said. "Thank you."

"Fazel. Please."

"Fazel." Nadine looked up at the illuminated sign above the dark door. "A veterinary clinic. You took me to a veterinary clinic."

"You said no hospital."

"He said no hospital." She opened the passenger door. "Help me get him out."

Nadine took Jake's feet, which were saturated with blood. It pooled into the floorboards of the Mini. Fazel hooked an arm across Jake's chest and helped lever him out of the car. "What happened?" he said.

"That is a very long story I have neither the time nor the inclination to get into," Nadine said. "Can you help him?"

"I don't know yet." Fazel opened the door with a key from his pocket. "Get him in here."

"How do you have a key to this place?"

He smiled thinly. "This too is a very long story." He dragged a black shapeless bag with a long nylon strap from the back of his car, slung it over his shoulder. Nadine supported Jake as he limped into the clinic. Fazel elbowed open a door in the back of the small, linoleum-tiled waiting room. LED panels in the ceiling came on. They wrestled Jake onto a large steel table, gleaming in the glow of the lights.

Fazel took a pair of bandage shears from a drawer, moving with the unthinking confidence of one who knew the layout of the place like an extension of his own self. He cut off Nadine's shirt and the leg of Jake's black cargo pants beneath. Nadine's stomach did flip-flops. "This is not good," Fazel said. His voice was calm, detached, like a college professor discussing the history of impressionist painting.

"You should see the other guy," Nadine said.

Fazel examined Jake's leg. "Nothing broken. He's bleeding a lot. Get me a sponge from that drawer. No, not that one, to your right. Wet it. Bring it here. Get some bandages from the top drawer, there." He cleaned the long wound, puckered at the edges, that ran up Jake's inner thigh from knee almost to crotch. "Doesn't look like the femoral artery is damaged, which is good, or he'd've been dead before you got him to the car. He's still lost a lot of blood."

"He didn't seem hurt," Nadine said. "I mean, he seemed fine when he was...anyway, he was moving around okay earlier."

"That's how it is, sometimes. The body reacts strangely to emergencies. I've seen people get an arm blown off, still holding a conversation like they were talking about the weather. Other people, one bit of shrapnel, minor flesh wound, takes them out of action." His brown eyes seemed to turn inward for a moment. "Jake's more the first kind. Here." He laid a bandage over Jake's leg, where blood welled out. "Press. Hard. Both hands."

Sticky warmth flowed over Nadine's hands. "Going to need to stitch him up. He needs blood, too. We really should get him—"

"No hospital," Nadine said. "He said no hospital. After what happened to Marcus, I don't blame him."

"Who's Marcus?"

"Another long story."

Fazel shrugged. On the table, Jake groaned again. "Hypovolemic shock," Fazel noted absently. He threaded a transparent bag of clear liquid through the hook on the end of a tall wheeled stand, unwound a clear plastic tube, pressed a needle into Jake's arm.

"That bag says 'veterinary use only,'" Nadine said.

Another shrug. "No hospital means no hospital. I'm doing what I can."

"How'd you learn how to do this?"

He regarded her for a long moment, brown eyes dark through wire-rimmed glasses. "Afghanistan. The war. A whole different world, a whole different time."

"That where you met Jake?"

"Yes."

"I thought he was in Belarus."

"He was. Nyasvizh. Lost his arm there. Did he tell you that?"

"Yeah."

"Only three people in his unit made it out alive. One of them died in the chopper."

"I saw it on the news. I was still in Canada."

Jake shuddered, gasping, eyes wide. "Hold him down," Fazel dug in his bag, came back with a pair of blue latex gloves and a fat plastic tube, milky white, with a bright orange cap on the end. "I am so very sorry, my friend," he said. He pulled on the gloves, popped the cap off, and shoved the tube hard against Jake's thigh. Nadine heard a loud snap. Jake cried out.

"What did you give him?"

"Morphine analogue. Risky with his blood loss, but what I'm about to do is going to hurt a lot and we can't have him thrashing about."

"So what you just gave him could kill him?"

"Calculated risk. I need you to monitor his pulse. Here." He took her fingers and pressed them against Jake's neck, where she felt his pulse, fast but regular. Jake looked up at her, face contorted, then his eyes rolled back and he went limp on the table.

"So who is he to you?" Nadine said. "He seems to trust you. Why you?"

"He got us out of the country when everything went to shit, me and my family. Helped us resettle. If he hadn't..." He shook his head. "Here I am. I'm going to give him a local anesthetic. I'm sorry, my friend, but this will hurt a lot." He drew a long syringe with a large needle from his bag and set to work. Jake cried out, crushing Nadine's hand tightly. "How is he doing?" Fazel said.

"Pulse is fast. Strong, but fast."

"Come here. Put on some gloves."

"Okay. Now what?"

Fazel took a pair of forceps and a hook-shaped needle threaded with thin cord and sealed inside a flat plastic wrapper from his bag, then tilted the light down. "He needs stitches. A lot of them. Please keep your finger right there. Move it this way as I make the sutures." Nadine blanched when she saw the wound, now cleaned and exposed. With deft motions of the forceps, Fazel started making a row of tiny stitches.

"You're pretty good at that, for someone who's not that kind of doctor," Nadine observed.

"You are very curious, aren't you? I got my doctorate from the Vienna Biocenter. I went back home when it looked like things might finally be going back to normal. I wanted to give back to my country, you know? Then when the shit started again, I was impressed into the army. They found out I was a doctor, studied biology, so they made me a field medic. I tried to tell them what kind of doctor I was, but..." He shrugged. "After the collapse, well...here I am."

"Why'd you go back, if you were in Vienna?"

"I loved my country. I still do, as hard as that might be to imagine. Afghanistan is a beautiful place. Not just deserts like so many Westerners think. In many ways, I still think of it as home. Move your finger, please."

Jake groaned again. Nadine squeezed his hand. Finally, Fazel declared himself satisfied. "These might be the ugliest sutures I've ever seen. Certainly the ugliest I've ever done, but it will work. Help me bandage him."

Fazel wrapped his leg with a bandage. Jake lolled on the hard metal table, crying out occasionally as Fazel worked. "He'll have quite a scar," Fazel said. He replaced the bag hanging above Jake's arm. "He needs a blood transfusion, but that's beyond my capability here."

"Will he live without one?"

Fazel felt his pulse. "Probably. He'll be weak and woozy for a while."

"We need to find a place to hole up. We can't go back where we were. Jake thinks it's a bad idea to go to the same place twice."

"Jake's right," Jake mumbled. He ran his hand over his head. "Where am I?"

"At the vet," Nadine said. "How do you feel?"

"Like a building fell on me."

"What happened?" Fazel said.

"A building fell on me." He struggled to sit and fell back. "I feel like shit."

"That happens to people when buildings fall on them," Fazel said. "You've lost a lot of blood. Your friend said—"

"No hospital," Jake said.

"Yes. She was quite insistent."

Jake shook his head violently. Servos whined in his prosthetic arm. "What did you give me?"

"Morphine. I—"

His face clouded. "You know I can't go near that. You know! What is wrong with you? How could you?"

"I am very sorry." Fazel folded his hands together in front of him and looked down. "Please forgive me. I did not have a choice."

"There's always a choice."

"Yes. I could have chosen to let you die. You will be weak and prone to disorientation for a while."

Jake's face set in a grim line. "Understood."

"I have something for you." He took a large manila envelope from his bag. "Analysis of the sliver you gave me. Gene sequence and MHC profile from the DNA sample."

"And?"

"Have you ever been to Australia?"

"Australia? No. Why?"

"The sliver is a quasicrystal polymer, standard flechette round used in less-than-lethal ammunition. Sharp tip, microscopic grooves to hold the chemical payload. Barbs to make the needle stick in flesh. Nasty. The needle itself carried a payload I've never seen before. Had to look up the spectral analysis. Probably synthetic. The closest match in the literature is moroidin."

"Moroidin?" Nadine said. "What's that?"

"Produced by a plant in Australia. *Dendrocnide moroides*. Locals call it the 'suicide bush.' It activates pain nerves on contact. Small doses can cause agonizing pain that persists for months or years. Those unfortunate enough to wander into contact with a suicide bush often kill themselves from the pain, hence the name."

"Of course it's Australian," Jake said.

"So if you were shot with this..." Nadine said.

"Instant, debilitating agony that does not go away. People who have touched a suicide bush describe it as being electrocuted and burned with acid at the same time. The effects can linger for two, sometimes three years. The toxin is persistent and stable. Plants that have been dried and stored for decades remain toxic. Researchers have been affected by botanical samples."

"Somebody weaponized this?" Nadine said.

"It would seem so, yes."

"Jesus."

Fazel removed his glasses, wiped them on his shirt, tucked them neatly back on his face. "If there were a scale for evil, such a weapon would be very near the top. If you don't mind my asking, how did you come to be involved in all this?"

Jake struggled upright. "Fazel, my friend, it's better for all of us if you don't know."

Fazel handed him a small, unmarked bottle of pills. "Antibiotics. One now, one every six hours until they're gone. Take them all. Drink lots. Don't move."

Jake hoisted himself to his feet, where he stood wobbling, leaning against the table. "Thank you, my friend. You have more than repaid whatever debt you owed me."

The two men embraced. "You can stay with us for a time," Fazel said.

"No way," Jake said. "You can't be anywhere near us. It's not safe. This may be the last time I see you."

Fazel unhooked the bag of fluid from the stand. "Leave this in until it's empty. Take the antibiotics I gave you. Change the dressing—"

"I know. Not my first rodeo, Doctor."

"Of course." Fazel took a thick envelope from his jacket pocket and set it on the counter. "For the man who owns this clinic," he said at

Jake's look. "He serves indigent people with pets. They can't always pay him. We have an...arrangement that helps him stay in business."

"Even after all these years, you still find ways to surprise me with your depth."

"I might say the same about you." Fazel touched his hand to his heart. "*Khodā hāfez*, my friend. Go. I will stay and clean up."

Nadine helped Jake into the passenger seat of the Mini. He wedged the clear bag against his head. "Where now?" Nadine said as she settled into the driver's seat. The screens came to life.

"Out," Jake said. "Out of the city. We can lay low, sleep in the car, figure out what's next."

"No."

"What?"

"No. You're hurt. Sleeping in the car isn't going to work for you."

Jake waved his hands in the air as if chasing mosquitoes. "What do you suggest?"

"Cops think I'm in San Jose, right? And Taylor doesn't know what to think. Last he heard, I should be dead. And they don't even know about you. So that gives us a little breathing room. Find us a cheap motel somewhere just outside town. Someplace you can lay up for a bit. The kind that won't have cameras. I'd do it but I don't want to risk taking my implant online."

He looked over at her for a long moment. Then, "You're probably right." His contacts glittered. His lips moved. "Okay. Got us a reservation. Hope you aren't too picky about accommodations."

"Just tell me where."

Nadine punched in the address. The Mini slotted into the flow of traffic with mechanical precision as it steered itself out into the night. The city whipped by around them. "Ask you a question?" Jake said.

"Yeah."

"What was up with you talking to that guy back there?"

"Thomas?"

"Yeah."

"Didn't think he should die alone."

"Pretty cold."

"Yeah? How many people you kill, Jake?"

"Dunno. Lots. They all needed killin'."

"You think he needed killin'?"

"Yeah."

"So what's it to you then?"

"Just makin' conversation."

"Can I ask you a question?" Nadine said.

"Sure."

"Who was Anna to you? You told me you were doing this for her, not me. Your last gift to her, you said. I assume you weren't fucking."

"Naw, nothin' like that."

"So what, then? What was she to you, that you stick your neck out this far and burn so many favors for me?"

They drove a while in silence. For a moment, Nadine thought Jake had fallen asleep. Then he said, "I was a mess when I got back from Belarus. I was a mess before, truth be told. I went into the army to get away from my parents. When my little brother came out, they kicked him onto the streets. I was a kid, I couldn't protect him..." He stared out the window. "I had to get away. Afghanistan first, then Belarus. Shit went sideways in Nyasvizh, well..."

"Yeah?"

"Lot of vets comin' back, lot of us in pieces. VA budget cuts right about the same time, perfect storm of suck. Not a lot of popular support, Afghanistan or Belarus, lot of folks thought we shouldn't have been there. Can't say I blame 'em. Did some odd jobs, made some connections here and there, started looking for my brother."

"Ever find him?"

"No. Spent what money I had on PIs. Asked around at all the shelters, talked to people, that's how I hooked up with Catman. He's been keeping an eye out for me for years. Always nothin'. Three, four years back, shit got really bad. Pain all the time, VA cut me off painkillers, I started usin'. Told myself it was okay if I was just buying pills, not shooting up, you know?" He laughed bitterly. "Heard that one a bunch of times."

"What's this got to do with Anna?"

"Gettin' to that." He paused for a moment to readjust the transparent bag half-full of clear liquid, shifting the tangled tube that led to the needle in his hand. "Thing is, once you start using, no matter what limits you set for yourself, you're only one bad day from crossing them, see? And I had that bad day. More like a bad several days, really. Then a bad week, bad month. Next thing I knew, couldn't think about anything except that next fix."

"That put you in legal trouble?"

"Worse. Crossed some very unpleasant people, the kind you never want to cross. Needed to get out. Catman knew a guy who knew a guy who knew Anna, said she could get me new IDs, fake biometrics, everything. I had a little bit of money, from the guys I crossed. Figured I could offer it to her as a down payment, get good with a new identity, just quietly skip out, never give her the rest. Never let her know I didn't have the rest." He lapsed into silence.

"And?" Nadine prodded.

"And she saw right through me, of course. Knew I didn't have the money. Fixed me up anyway. Did whatever she does to the databases, helped me drop off the radar. Only payment she wanted, I had to get clean. Kept telling myself I was just playing along, that I could get my fix as soon as she was satisfied. Somehow it never happened."

"Why'd she do it?"

"How would I know? Strange bird, your girlfriend. Maybe she liked to take on charity cases. Maybe she thought she could use me. I still had some friends left, people useful to her, people who owed me favors. Built up my network, after I got clean, met more people useful to her. Wouldn't say we were partners, exactly, but we did things for each other. She had me go back to the VA once, carry a little thing with me, no bigger'n your thumb, plug it into a network jack when nobody was looking. Said she owed me big-time after that. Never did find out why, what it was all about." His voice trailed off.

"Jake?" Nadine said after a while. He didn't answer. Soon muffled snores filled the cabin.

Nadine closed her eyes, suddenly exhausted. She knew better, of course; the public service ads all warned about the dangers of not paying attention when you were in a car that was driving itself. She'd never really understood that—if cars could drive totally empty, like Booker taxis, or drive with passengers in the back seat but nobody up front, what was the big deal?

The car threaded its way through the evening traffic, up along the ridge with the city spread out below like a cracked but glittering jewel. She ignored all of it. It drove them in silence over streets lined with abandoned houses, out past the interstate and then east, through neighborhoods that had seen better days and neighborhoods that had always been sketchy. Eventually, it pulled into a parking spot in front of a long, low single-story motel with a tacky sign out front, rust-stained metal and neon blinking "Economy Motel Stay The Night."

Before the probe even finished negotiating with the car to open the charging port, Nadine had rousted Jake. "Go get the key. No, wait, stop, you're a mess." He grumbled blearily when she pulled the needle from his hand. The plastic bag had deflated like a sad balloon, almost all the liquid gone. "You need to put on some clothes." She looked down, to where she still wore only a bra and jeans. "So do I, but I'm not going with you." She rummaged behind her, fished a shirt out of her bag, dug in Jake's bag for new pants to hide the ruin of his leg. "Jesus, man, you ever wear anything else?"

"Now you're a fashion critic?" Jake sat on the edge of the seat, door open, and pulled on a new pair of cargo pants, same as the old pair. Nadine shrugged into a T-shirt, bright sunflowers printed on stretchy white fabric.

He pulled himself upright and staggered off toward the office. A couple minutes later, he came back with a small plastic card. "Only got the one key."

"Fine."

The key let them into a small room, heavy drapes over the window, that smelled faintly of industrial cleaning products and, beneath that, something musty. Two beds, covered in nondescript brown blankets. A tiny bathroom, two towels, paper cups on the cracked sink. "I haven't showered in forever," Nadine said. "You mind if I—?"

Jake waved at her. She stood under the hot water, eyes closed.

He's right, you know. Anna's voice in her ear.

Nadine jumped. "What?"

That was cold, what you did to that ogre. Thomas.

"I wanted him to have a better death than you got."

That's debatable. What are you going to do now?

"Turn the tables. Kick over a few rocks, shake a tree, see what falls out."

You're getting good at this.

"Thank you. Is it true what Jake said about you putting him back together? Is that why he's doing this for me?"

Silence.

She toweled off, dressed, and came back out to find Jake sitting on the bed in his underwear, rewrapping the bandage around his leg, prosthetic arm whirring. "Ogre destroyed my rifle," he said without preamble. "Going to be a bitch to replace."

"You got a computer?"

"No."

"Don't suppose there's one in the office I can use."

Jake laughed. "As if. Why?"

Nadine held up the tiny recorder. "Want to get this out. Newspapers, online news sites, underground channels, everything."

"You realize if you do, there's no going back, right? They'll see it as a declaration of war."

"We're already at war."

He shook his head. "No. What they're doing to you, it's not war, more like...pest control. You think you have their attention now, wait 'til you start sending that to all and sundry."

"They're trying to kill me. Dead's dead however they view it. Might make their lives harder."

"Might at that."

"So you gonna help me or what?"

"Yeah." He unhooked his arm, set it on the scarred wooden table, plugged the charger in. "Get some sleep. Tomorrow we declare war." He held out a pill. "Here. Take it. Last one."

Nadine swallowed the pill with a mouthful of water from a paper cup. "These things have any side effects I should know about?"

"Like what kind of side effects?"

"I don't know. Headaches, nausea, hearing voices, that sort of thing."

"Why, you hearing voices?"

"Forget it. Good night."

15

Story du Jour

THEY SET OUT in the Mini the next morning, humid heat already shimmering over the asphalt, to buy a computer with some of Anna's money. Nadine wore a brilliant purple wig, one of the ones Jake had brought back to the first cheap motel they'd stayed in. She'd changed her face as much as she could, bold makeup in bright primary colors, like she was auditioning for a burlesque show themed around sparkles and Da-Glo. The purple wig hung down over one eye, concealing half her face. Jake shifted around in the front seat, trying to stretch out his leg. He'd refused any painkillers, had nothing for breakfast but a CR2A1 combat ration with coffee substitute, self-heating. He directed her to a small electronics store in an otherwise deserted strip mall forty minutes' drive from the cheap motel. "Park at the end," he instructed. "Not in front of the door."

Nadine stepped from the car directly onto the rock in her shoe and winced. Jake climbed out the other side, a process that took some time. "Aren't we a pair?" he said.

She looked up at the sign over the shop, COMPUTERS in blue stick-on letters on a white light box. Laptops and small terminals behind dusty glass, armored with a heavy grate. A hologram flickered and strobed over the display: "Great! Prices! Latest! Models!"

"Doesn't exactly look top of the line," she said.

"We don't need top of the line. And they'll take cash."

An electronic chime announced their entrance. Inside, a long glass counter held several more computers resting atop transparent plastic stands beneath fingerprint-smudged glass. "Help you?" said a skinny man with a shock of peroxide hair and a shapeless T-shirt bearing a cartoon character Nadine vaguely recognized as a mascot from a video game. He brightened when he saw her. "Need a computer?"

"Yeah, I think so." Nadine flung out her most dazzling smile, widened her eyes. "Only I don't know which one to get. Can you help me?"

He blinked rapidly. "Um, what do you need?"

"Oh, you know, just to get online, post videos and stuff. I'm not good with technical stuff."

As they talked, Jake quietly faded into the background. The kid in the cartoon T-shirt rattled on about specs and processors and holographic projectors. "They'll all sync up with your implant," he said, "let you do things just by *thinking* about it."

Nadine smiled and giggled and eventually allowed him to talk her into the computer she'd already chosen. She waved aside his offer of an extended warranty, giggled at his suggestion he could help her pair it with her implant, and slid some of Anna's cash across the smudged counter. Box in hand, she stepped out into the heat. Jake had already slipped out the door without setting off the "be-doo, be-doo" of the electronic chime, and sat waiting for her in the Mini.

They returned to the motel by a circuitous path Jake programmed into the Mini's navigation. "Just being paranoid," he said at Nadine's look. "You do have people trying to kill you."

Back at the motel, Nadine balanced the computer on the little stand beside her bed. She skipped over all the setup prompts, clicked past its offer to pair with her implant, and connected to the hotel's network. Jake sat heavily on the bed and dry-swallowed an antibiotic.

Nadine slipped the card from the recorder into the new computer and started typing. "That story you told me about you and Anna true?" she said as she worked.

A long pause. She felt his eyes boring into her from behind. "Yeah."

"So if you worked so hard to get clean, why you taking stay-awake pills when we met?"

"Ah," he said, "see, now that's different. That's being *practical*."

Nadine's finger moved over the keyboard. On impulse, she added a sentence to the end of the message, about the raid on Tijuana Town and the shot that downed the platform from outside. "Okay, I'm sending this video to half a dozen news sites, couple of old-school newspapers, and an anonymizing redirector that'll upload it to a bunch of media sharing sites. Connected to a VPN that'll make it seem like it's coming from New York via Volgograd."

"Clever. Your girlfriend teach you that?"

"Yeah."

"That should create a headache for Taylor."

"Can you think of any reason I shouldn't hit send?"

"You scared of dyin'?"

"Not really."

"Then no." The bed creaked as he leaned back.

Nadine's finger stabbed down. "My turn, motherfuckers." The computer made a little *woosh* sound, like a jet airplane taking off, as the video disappeared into the rushing tide of data that flowed through the world. "And that's that," she said, but Jake was already asleep.

For three days, she paced the tiny room. Neither of them set foot outside the door, just left the little red "Do Not Disturb" light glowing on the latch. Nadine resisted the urge to take her implant online to set up an agent that would notify her if she turned up in the media. She watched the news on the little laptop, gnawing the tasteless contents of the CR2A1 packets and drinking coffee substitute beverage from tubes that fizzed when she pulled the tab. For three days, nothing happened. A sober-looking news reporter with a bad toupee informed them gravely that the police had lost track of her after the sighting in San Jose. Serious-looking men in dark suits and navy ties talked about widening the search, following up on every lead. Breathless reporters broadcasting from the parking lot of the convenience store she'd supposedly robbed said, "If you saw anything, please call..."

On the fourth day, everything exploded.

The serious news sites, the ones that prided themselves on journalistic integrity, bookmarked the reports with disclaimers of "anonymous source" and "unconfirmed identity." The more sensationalistic ones ran it beneath clickbait headlines like COPS INVOLVED IN TERRORIST FRAMEUP? One thing they all agreed on, from the most respectable news outlets down to the whackadoodle conspiracy forums in the far corners of digital space: this was everyone's number-one story. Talking heads argued with other talking heads on streaming video. Anonymous posters screamed in capslock at other anonymous posters on underground forums. Flame wars launched and then burnt themselves out in hours. Media sharing sites ratcheted up views faster than a new video from Lemonayd, the demigirl pop band out of Vietnam.

Jake lay flat on his back on the bed, contacts sparkling as his implant fed him précis of the newsfeeds. "Damn, girl," he said, "you are officially the hot story du jour."

Nadine wandered into the room in a baggy T-shirt and jeans, toweling her hair, currently a disconcerting shade of neon green. "Yeah? Creating problems for Taylor?"

"His lawyers are battling a subpoena. They say it's based on hearsay from, and I quote, 'a slick disinformation campaign engineered by those sympathetic to a radical group's cause.'" He swung his feet to the floor. "Gettin' a little antsy staying here. We should find another place to lay low. Maybe get out of LA. Get out of California altogether. We've been here a long time. Dangerous, that."

"Yeah. Texas."

"Texas?" Jake looked up at her. The scintillating dance of light in his contact lenses faded. "Why Texas?"

Nadine paced back and forth. "Anna found something, right before she died. I don't know what it is, but it was enough for him to try to murder everyone there. I mean, just this chemical thing he's got, this marro—morrow—"

"Moroidin."

"That. Whatever's going on, Anna said it was in Texas. That's where the money's going. That's where Mirage is. People need to know. About all of it."

Jake folded his arms. Servos whirred. "You really want to go into the lion's den," he said, voice neutral.

"Think about it! We found something. Something we aren't supposed to know about. Something Martin Taylor would kill over. Has killed over. That's gotta be important, right?"

"You sound like you're trying to sell me something."

"Are you buying?"

Jake sighed. "We can't stay in this motel. We've already been here too long. Getting out of LA is our best idea, but then, I thought that back when the plan was to get you to Canada." He shrugged. "Okay, look. Every corporation worth anything has dirty secrets it will kill to hide. Taylor's not so different from any other asshole in a suit. So let's say, just for a minute, that he's the kind of asshole whose secrets really ought to be public knowledge. What then? We go to Texas, then what? What do we do about it?"

"Whatever it was Anna found in their database, he seemed surprised she found it." Nadine sat heavily on her bed. "Whoever's in charge of keeping it secret has had plenty of time to bury it deeper. We won't get at it from the outside. But the thing about secrets is, they're only useful if the right people have access, right? Does no good to have a secret project that's so secret nobody can work on it. That means someone knows."

"Martin Taylor probably knows."

"Yeah. Sure would like to get his computer. But we won't get close to him. So, we go to Texas."

Jake leaned back, studying her through narrowed eyes for a long moment. Finally, he said, "You have a narrow window of opportunity here. That recording you sent, it kinda changes the narrative. Tell me something. For real. You scared of dyin'?"

"You asked me that already."

"Humor me."

"No."

"You see," Jake said, "that's the problem. That look in your eyes, I've seen it before. It's the look of someone who doesn't care if they live or die. You know what happens to people like that? They die. More to the point, they take other people with them. We—"

A knock came at the door. Jake jerked his head towards the flimsy bathroom door. "Go," he hissed. "Now."

Nadine darted for the door. Jake whistled and glanced at her bag. She darted back and wrapped her arms around it, hauling it into the bathroom with her.

"Just a minute," Jake called out in a rough voice, "lemme get decent." He grabbed his own bag and briskly upended it on Nadine's bed. A pile of clothes tumbled out.

Nadine closed the bathroom door almost all the way, leaving it cracked just enough to peer out. Jake opened the front door. "Help you?" he said gruffly.

"Um, yes, sorry to disturb you, sir." A man's voice, outside the room, out of Nadine's vision. Young. Nervous. "I'm with the hotel. IT. I just wanted to make sure everything was okay with your stay. We pride ourselves on having the highest standards for all our customers."

"Can't complain," Jake said. "What's up?"

"Well, sir, we've seen unusual patterns of network activity, and we just wanted, that is, I'd like to make sure...is your net access working properly?"

Jake scratched his chin with his mechanical claw. "Well, I think so. Ain't used it a whole lot." He casually removed his arm and draped it in the crook of his elbow. "I mean, I can get on the news sites and all." He scratched absently at his stump, studded with surgically placed contacts. "And shows. I like shows when I'm relaxing. I was just watching *On the*

Beat. You ever watch that show? They take these camera people, see, like producers and stuff, right? Have them ride around with the City's finest. Sort of give you a feel for what it's like, bein' out on the streets keepin' law and order. Sometimes they show us, like, what those robot dogs do, the ones the cops have. Like you can see straight through the dogs' eyes. You'd be surprised how many crimes they stop. They can see in the dark and everything. Kind of amazing, isn't it?" He slipped his arm back on and leaned against the door jamb. "Really makes you wonder how the cops ever did their jobs before."

"Um, yeah, I guess," the unseen man mumbled. "Listen, I won't take up any more of your time. Have a nice day."

"Yeah, you too," Jake said. He closed the door. Nadine exhaled, shoulders slumping, and realized she'd been clenching the edge of the door so tightly her fingers hurt.

"Pack up," Jake said when she came back into the room. "We need to move out. They've tracked the upload here."

"That's impossible!" Nadine said. "I used a virtual network, redirected it—"

"Well, they did. Maybe they just looked for weird traffic, put two and two together. Deep analytics, data analysis, predictive modeling. Egghead stuff. Side channel. They can't follow the upload back, but they can figure what kind of place you might go, look at network traffic at those places. Whatever. It's time to leave."

"Right now?"

"No. I guarantee they have someone watching. That's just the sort of thing they'll be looking for. We go tomorrow, normal checkout time. They know you're in this motel, or at least they think you might be, but they're looking for a scared Asian chick, not a wounded vet who watches too much reality TV. Get your shit together. Get some sleep. We move out first thing AM. We'll finish our conversation after we've found somewhere new."

Nadine swept the mound of Jake's clothes off the bed. She sprawled backward, old springs groaning beneath her. The cheap spray-on texture of the ceiling had little insight to offer. "I'm not sure I can sleep."

"I can give you something."

"For a man with a substance abuse problem, you keep a lot of drugs on hand."

"Call it a moral failing."

"Think I'll pass on the sleep aid."

"Suit yourself."

Nadune curled on her side and pulled the cover over her head. In the darkness beneath, she called up the image of Anna's face, her hair caught in its net of tiny LEDs, the light in her eyes when the sun broke through the window, her lips when she convulsed in ecstasy. "Are you there?" she whispered to herself.

No answer. Eventually, sleep came.

She woke confused, tatters of a dream of home—her old home in Montreal, the big rambling house with its fenced-in yard overgrown with trees. A firm hand clutched at her arm, shaking urgently. "Get up! Now! Up!"

"Anna?" she mumbled.

"Get up. Stay low, away from the window. Don't know if they have infrared or radar. Get your bag."

Nadine snapped awake, the dream already tumbling away, replaced by the horror of the real world. "What's up?"

"Trouble," Jake hissed. He pulled back the edge of the curtain just a little. Strobing blue lights splashed against the walls. Somewhere outside, Nadine heard a shrill, feminine cry, panic beneath the confused anger, gruff voices answering in authoritarian tones.

"What's going on?"

"I think they think they found you. We have to go, now."

Nadine pulled on her hoodie, covered with cartoon faces, tongues lolling in a comedic caricatures of sexual bliss. She pulled the violet wig over her head, fluffing out the bangs to hang over her eyes. She blinked, eyelashes catching on the synthetic strands.

Jake opened the door a crack, hand raised. "Not yet. Get ready." The Mini chirped, doors unlatching with a dull thunk. "Okay, now, move."

Clutching her bag, heart hammering, Nadine followed him out. Three SUVs with private security markings on the doors waited in the parking lot, blue lights flashing. A tight knot of black-uniformed security guards dragged a shrieking, kicking, biting woman into the parking lot, flimsy shirt hanging open over lacy bra and panties, one heeled slipper falling to the ground as she struggled. Another man in the same uniform stood at a door to one of the rooms, thumbs hooked in his belt. As Nadine watched, one of the men drew a taser from his belt and fired at the struggling woman. She convulsed and fell twitching to the ground.

"Fuck me," Nadine breathed.

"That's exactly what'll happen if we don't move." He dove into the front seat. Nadine opened the door, threw her bag in the back, and climbed in beside him. The car was already rolling before she'd slammed the door.

Jake drove slowly past the cluster of security around the convulsing woman. "Glad I'm not her," he said. "Won't take long for them to realize they've got the wrong person. We need to get some distance between here and there before they do."

He pulled onto the street, past a long, low, black limousine with tinted windows. A man in a suit stood in front of it, watching the spectacle in the parking lot with a mildly irritated expression. Nadine's blood froze. She slumped down in the seat as low as she could. "Fuck!" she swore. "Fuck! That's him! Fuck!"

"What?"

"Martin Taylor! He's here!"

"Shit. Did he see you?"

"I don't think so."

"Try again. Did he see you? Yes or no?" Jake pulled out into traffic.

"No. No, he didn't. He was too busy watching—you know."

Jake let out a long, low exhale. "We got lucky. Again. Gettin' awful uncomfortable, how lucky we've been."

"What now?"

"As long as he didn't see you, we're okay. Once he realizes they got the wrong person, they'll start taking a long, hard look at all the comings and goings at that motel. Fact we left right when things went down will ring some bells. They've almost certainly grabbed this car's transponder signal as we rolled out, just routine. Still, that won't lead them very far. Car's registered to an LLC that's owned by another company. Anna set it up. No way to connect it to me. Plus they can't be 100% sure you were even in that motel. That helps. Still, things're getting thin." He glanced at the rearview monitor. "Don't think anyone's following us."

"What now?"

"We find another place to lay low. I try to talk you out of your insanity. You might have a path through this. Your story's getting traction. You take a run at Texas, you're throwing that all away."

"Bullshit. Taylor's never going to stop coming. You get that? Never. Even if the cops exonerate me, he's going to keep after me. The moment the news forgets me, I'm done."

"You can change your identity—"

Nadine folded her arms and stared grimly out the windshield. Palm trees loomed out of the darkness. "You trust any identity to stand up against Martin Taylor's resources and attention?"

"No, I suppose not."

"We finish this."

"You always been this stubborn?"

"No. I had a normal life once. Anna was the stubborn one. Where to now?"

"Little Tokyo. There's a love hotel there—"

Nadine stared at him. "You're serious."

"Don't get any ideas. You're not my type. I like people who aren't being hunted by well-funded corporate sociopaths. It's cheap and it's anonymous and there aren't any cameras."

"After that?"

"We ditch this car."

"Thought you said it couldn't be tracked."

"It can't. But if a car that hightailed it out of a no-name motel in LA right under Martin Taylor's nose turns up in Texas, you'd have to be pretty thick not to connect the dots. I don't think Taylor's thick."

"Okay, so then what?"

"We get another car." Jake sighed. "Then we go to Texas."

16

Local Color

JAKE'S LOVE MOTEL turned out to be a gaudy place with pink fuzzy striped wallpaper, a mirror in the ceiling, and a whirlpool tub wedged into a bathroom too small to accommodate it. Nadine eyed the tub covetously. "You need to be in here? I might be a while."

"Nah," Jake said. "Got some stuff needs doin' if we're headed to Texas. Knock yourself out."

Nadine relaxed in the tub, eyes closed, and let the jets pound the tension out of her. For a moment, she let the horror slip away, and pretended that it was all a bad dream, that soon Anna would come through the door, hold her in her arms...

Living in a fantasy isn't healthy, Anna said.

"Talking to my dead girlfriend in my head isn't healthy."

Touché. What will you do in Texas?

"Try to find out what's going on. Find out why you died."

I died because I'm a criminal and the odds finally caught up with me.

"Maybe that's not good enough."

She rose, dripping, toweled herself off, dressed, and went out into the room. A row of tiny LEDs around the mirror in the ceiling gave the place a surrealist glow. In one corner, a compact minibar of glossy black plastic with a faux wood finish offered tiny bottles of rum and vodka, packages of condoms in bright neon wrappers, and little packets of lube in a dozen varieties. "Only got the one bed," Jake said. "I'll take the floor."

"It's okay. You're still hurt. I'll take the floor."

"Going to be hard to give up my Mini. I love that car."

"Sorry."

"Don't be. Wouldn't ever have had it if it weren't for Anna. Might not even still be here. I got some errands to run. I'll need some more of that cash."

"Starting to run low. What will you do with your car?"

"Been thinkin' about that." Jake scratched his chin, where several days of stubble clung. "Might send it up to Bellingham."

"Where?"

"Washington. Program it to head north, charge itself, find a parking spot right on the Canadian border. That way, if Tayler and his crew decide to chase after it, they'll think we headed to Canada. Meanwhile, we need to find another car, head to Texas."

"Can't we fly or take a bus or something?"

Jake shook his head. "Too risky. It'll be a lot harder for them to follow us if we buy a used car and leave it registered in someone else's name."

"Will it work?"

"You got a better idea?"

Nadine sat on the edge of the bed with her knees hugged to her chest. "No. I'm just...I think I'm going a bit crazy cooped up. And I can't even take my implant online."

"You think this is bad, try prison."

Nadine shrugged. "Something doesn't have to be as terrible as it possibly can be in order to be bad."

Jake gave her a hard look. "I don't understand you."

"I'm allowed to mourn a life that might have been."

Jake sat still and silent for a moment, then nodded. "You're right. I forget you didn't sign up for this. I think I've found a vehicle that'll suit our purpose. You need anything?"

"You want me to go with you?"

"No. Too dangerous."

"But you're all banged up!"

Jake gave her a half-smile. "Been worse. I'll manage."

"Okay." Nadine spread Jake's sleeping bag on the floor and curled up with one of the pillows from the bed, a large, plush thing covered in a fuzzy pillowcase adorned with pictures of lips in garish red. "You do your thing. I'm going to try to sleep."

A blast of heat intruded into the love cell as Jake left. Nadine fidgeted atop the sleeping bag, but sleep would not come. Images danced behind her eyelids: the hulk of the great digging machine, dripping with dampness; Martin Taylor's face, smug disinterest written across it; Anna's smile, lights sparkling in her hair. Eventually, she gave up.

She dumped the contents of her bag on the floor and spent some time sorting and re-packing it all, just to keep the visions away. Fatigue tugged at her—not the ordinary sort, the consequence of poor sleep, but something deeper, more bone-wearying.

Not a lot left, Anna's voice observed.

"Yeah, I haven't spent much time shopping."

What will you do once you find out why I died?

"You seem certain I will."

You've made it this far.

"I don't know," Nadine said. "I haven't thought that far ahead. I suppose it depends what I find out."

Three hours later, Nadine watched, fascinated, as Jake navigated a massive fourteen-year-old RV through LA traffic. "Can't you just turn on self-navigation?" she said dubiously. She ran her fingers over the cracked dashboard.

"Nope!" Jake said cheerfully. "Manual control only."

"Why did you get this?" Nadine turned to look over her shoulder at the expanse behind them. "I've seen apartments smaller than this thing."

"Keeps us from having to stop at hotels, and with as long as this trip is, we can't really sleep in a car," Jake said. "With any luck, by the time they sort out what's happened back at the motel, the Mini will have them running in entirely the wrong direction. I paid cash and left the registration alone, so there's nothing linking this thing's transponder code to us. Good camouflage. We don't need to stop for anything except charging. I got us a prepaid tourist Booker card at a convenience store. Costs more to charge, but the Booker system won't flag that my account is being used in two places. The Mini will charge on my Booker account."

"Do you think Martin will try following the Mini?"

Jake scratched the stubble on his chin. "Dunno. It's a reach. All he knows is I was at a motel that might maybe have been the source of anomalous Internet traffic that might maybe have been connected to the file upload you did. It's a stretch for sure. But if he does, it should lead him on a merry chase, hmm?" He grinned without mirth. "Buckle up. This is going to be a long ride."

"How long?"

"Solid day of driving, not counting charging time. You think you can drive this thing?"

Nadine shook her head. "I don't know how to drive. Never learned. Never needed to."

"Okay. I don't want to drive more than about eight hours or so a day, so let's call it three days and a bit. Oh, by the way, try not to use the bathroom back there. Apparently the black water tank has a leak."

Nadine made a face. "Glad you warned me."

"I live to serve."

The interstate drifted by, a monotonous ribbon of black connecting towns that all looked the same. They left the RV rarely except to charge or eat, and slept on separate folding beds. Jake took the bed above the cab, giving Nadine the larger but only slightly less lumpy bed in the back.

On the second day of the trip, sometime after passing a sign Nadine vaguely remembered as saying New Mexico, Jake's contacts danced with light. He guided the RV onto the shoulder and sat still for a while, lips moving slightly.

Nadine climbed between the front seats and plopped down beside him. "Something wrong?"

"You're driving me a little crazy with the pacing," Jake said.

"Sorry. Last time I was in an enclosed space with no way out, my girlfriend died. You'll forgive me if I'm a little twitchy."

"Sorry," Jake said. "No, I was just talking to Lucas."

"Lucas?"

"You met him. Back in the subway tunnel. Good guy. Old friend. Arranged to have him take up the slack while I'm away, deal with the VA, get the stuff to Catman. My guy in the VA's jerking him around. Raised his price."

"Lovely."

"No honor among thieves, right? I'll take care of it when we get to Houston. Always something." He pulled back onto the interstate. "Sit down or go to sleep or something, would you? Hard to think with all your pacing."

Nadine retired to the back, where she called up a television show about a Korean girl with bright blue hair who played roller derby and, apparently, solved crimes. She couldn't focus on the program, but the sound offered a welcome distraction from thinking too closely about the past or the future.

They spent the night at a rest stop just west of the Texas border. When Nadine rubbed sleep from her eyes the next morning, Jake was already settling into the driver's seat preparing to move off. "Sleep well?"

Nadine pulled the tab on a tube of coffee substitute. "Not even a little."

"Me neither. About ten hours to Houston once we hit the border. So the thing about Texas, they take that whole 'Federation of Free

States' thing real serious-like. Made noise about seceding, enough so Washington gave 'em a bunch of concessions to stay in, now Texas thinks of itself like its own little sovereign empire. Rest of 'em too, but Texas is the one that's most crazy about it. Makes it complicated for us."

"How so?"

"Customs. We need to go through customs at the border. That presents certain...peculiar challenges, what with you a wanted criminal and all. I sure hope your girlfriend did her job with the biometrics and databases and such or this trip is likely to come to a shouty end."

"Can't we just, like, drive off the road? Go around? They can't have a wall around the whole state!"

Jake laughed humorlessly. "You'd think that, wouldn't you? They have cameras on every road, including IR. Vibration sensors, too. Drones and IR cameras and motion sensors all along the border, spot anything bigger'n a house cat. All hooked up to AI that can tell the difference between a deer and a person. Spent more money than you'd believe, most of it with companies cozy to the governor, no-bid contracts. That's how it works in the Federation of Free States. The next few hours depend on how well your girlfriend cozied up to certain high-security databases nobody should be able to touch. Last chance. You still want to do this?"

"Yeah. I still want to do this."

"Somehow, I knew you were going to say that." He pulled on a battered military jacket with a name patch reading J FOX.

"What's that for?" Nadine said.

"Local color." Jake settled behind the wheel and switched on the RV. "Here goes nothin'."

Less than an hour later, Jake slowed for a long mass of cars that inched its way along the freeway in the shimmering morning heat. Soon they were surrounded on all sides. Overhead, a wide yellow sign with flashing lights on each corner read "WELCOME TO TEXAS, CHARTER MEMBER OF THE FEDERATION OF FREE STATES" in black blocky letters. Beneath, a smaller line of type read "Freedom Begins Here - Prepare For Border Inspection". Nadine pulled on a bright blue wig with strands that hung in front of her face and a dark pair of wraparound sunglasses.

"Showtime," Jake said. "You got your passport?"

"Yep," Nadine said.

"What's your name?"

"Melody Landry."

"Where are you from, Melody Landry?"

"Toronto."

"What brings you to Texas?"

Nadine looked out at the wall of cars surrounding them. "To find out more about the corporation that murdered my girlfriend and framed me for terrorism."

"No," Jake said, so sharply Nadine jumped. "These people have no sense of humor. About anything. If we're going to do this, I need your head in the game. Now, try again. What brings you to Texas?"

"I'm sorry." Nadine blinked, shook herself. "I'm here on vacation. My grandma just passed, and I'm using my inheritance to see the United States."

"Better," Jake said. They inched forward, toward a small building of red brick in the center of an immense parking lot. "Plays to Texas pride. If you're on vacation, why not see the greatest state, right? Dead granny is a nice touch." Nadine frowned and looked away.

When they reached the head of the line, a bored-looking man in a black uniform directed them from a small booth into a numbered space in the parking lot. Yellow triangles danced around him in Nadine's vision. Another uniformed man, also surrounded by yellow triangles, directed them to leave the RV, took their keys, then herded them into a long line that snaked around the building. Shimmering heat radiated from the black pavement. Armed men wandered between rows of parked cars, while another officer wrangled a German shepherd to each new vehicle.

Nadine shuffled from foot to foot, restless in the searing heat. "They could make the building bigger," she grumbled. "Or put up sun shades or something."

Jake, unperturbed, gave her a lopsided shrug. "Hostile architecture. The cruelty is the point. See those cameras? They're connected to expert systems doing behavioral profiling. Discomfort causes stress, gets people to reveal more of themselves."

"And here I am a wanted criminal."

"You're the one insisted we go to Texas." He flashed her a toothy grin. "Don't let 'em see you sweat."

At the door, a black-uniformed guard handed out paper cards with spaces for their name, ID number, and affirmation they weren't carrying drugs, undeclared fruits or vegetables, or proscribed biological agents. Inside, people lined up in front of counters enclosed by bullet-resistant glass. A gigantic portrait of Lawton Cabot, Texas governor and head of the Federation of Free States, glowered down at them from the far wall. Video screens flashed messages in white letters on a blue background:

"The State of Texas welcomes you. US citizens form three rows to the left. Non-citizens to the right. Entry implies consent to be recorded. Agents are authorized to use lethal force."

Jake winked as he and Nadine found their separate lines. The line for non-US citizens was mercifully short, and ended in a scuffed black slab of a counter where a man in a black uniform stood behind a thick window of bulletproof glass with a narrow slot for paperwork. "ID and declaration," he said.

Nadine passed her passport and the slip of paper through. He scowled at them, jaw working as if he were chewing something he found mildly unpleasant. "Melody Landry?"

"That's right."

He turned the scowl on her. "You don't look like any Melody I've ever seen."

"My mom was a musician," Nadine said.

"Yeah? What kind of music?"

"Folk music, mostly, some other kinds too."

"What other kinds?"

"You know, traditional stuff."

"Canadian?"

"Mostly, also a bit of—"

"No, I mean you're Canadian?"

"Oh, yeah."

"You don't look Canadian, either."

"My parents are Chinese."

"Huh." His jaw worked harder. "What does a *yak* want in Texas?"

Nadine's face flushed. "I'm sorry, what did you just say?"

The man folded his arms and rocked back on his heels, studying Nadine. "You have a hearing problem? What does one of your people want in Texas?"

Nadine's hands curled into fists. "I heard you just fine."

"Then answer the question."

"I came here," Nadine spat with barely contained rage, "because I'd heard all these stories about how much better and..." Her eyes flicked downward. "Bigger Texas is. Guess you can't believe everything you hear."

He looked at her slip of paper, clenching his jaw so tightly his muscles bulged. "You arrived from Los Angeles?"

"That's what it says."

"Why didn't you stay in California?"

Red mist filled Nadine's vision. "Listen, I—"

Jake put a hand on her back. She jumped. "Hi, honey!" he said, voice chipper. To the man behind the bulletproof glass, he said, "She's never seen the real America before. Wouldn't want her to get the idea it's all like San Francisco, hey?" He winked.

The man grunted. He tapped Nadine's passport to the reader and glowered at a small display for a while. Eventually, a green light came on. "You may go," he said as he passed it back to her.

Jake escorted Nadine away from the counter. "He called me a—" Nadine began.

"Yeah. I heard. Come on." He stopped in front of a row of free-standing kiosks. "I need to get a new Booker card."

"I thought you already had one."

"Need a new account to travel here. The Federation of Free States is its own thing. Booker accounts don't transfer."

"What? Why?"

"Tax. The Federation negotiated some kinda tax deal with the Feds, keep 'em from seceding. Part of the deal was that money that stays here gets taxed different, see? Cheaper for Meta to spin off a Federation subsidiary, that way they don't repatriate profits out to the real United States." He grinned toothily. "Though I'm sure these folks are the ones who'd call themselves the 'real' United States. *E pluribus unum*. Know what that means? 'Out of many, one.' Nice idea, huh? Turned out kinda the opposite."

"Do we need a Booker card? We have the RV."

"It's not exactly low profile." Jake fed a set of bills into the machine, which beeped and disgorged a flat card of blue plastic with a chip carrier embedded in the center of the Meta logo. "Better to have it and not need it than need it and not have it."

"Is everything here this fucked up?"

"Welcome to Texas."

PART 3
TINY DEADLY THINGS

17

Dropping a Card

THEY GOT BACK on the highway. Texas rolled by, endless miles of heat and dust. Nadine sat beside Jake fuming silently.

"So the thing about Texas, see," Jake said, "it's its own little world. It's not like California. Not like anything, really, except Texas. Not even like the rest of the Federation of Free States. Insular, you know? They do things their own way."

Nadine stared out the window. Heat created shimmering pools off in the distance, reflecting the cloudless sky. "And what way is that?"

"They never did let go of the nastiest bits of the twentieth century. Always looking backward, though of course that ain't how they see it. Thing is, this place were looking for..."

"Terracone Research."

"Yeah. Figure there's a reason they're in Texas. I wasn't able to find out a lot about them. Secretive. Most defense contractors, they make a lot of noise, at least in the circles they exist in. This place? Nothing. Weird."

"So what does that mean?"

"Means we're gonna need some local help. I know a guy, in Houston..." His voice trailed off.

"And this friend of yours can help us?"

Jake flashed her a look. "Never said he was a friend. Can he help us? Yeah. Will he, that's a more complicated question."

"So how do you get in touch with him?"

"Well, see, that's another question. Finding him is also complicated. I know a place where some folks who work for him hang out."

"And that's where we're going?"

Jake shot her the look again. "In a manner of speaking. Houston's still a bit of a drive. Figure we'll probably make it as far as Dallas, catch some sleep, drive to Houston tomorrow. Could take some wakey pills and do it in one shot, but I want to be fresh when we go into the lion's den."

"Jake?"

"Yeah?"

"Thanks. For everything. I mean it."

"I'm not—" He stopped and shook his head. "You're welcome. Besides, what else was I going to do? I mean, now that Anna...you know."

As they traveled, a disconnected restlessness settled over Nadine. She floated free, above herself, watching the small, pinched woman hunched in the passenger's seat looking out the RV's side window as she mutated into someone unreal, a character in a movie perhaps. The light took on a strange, flat feel, the world outside the RV fading to a poorly-rendered hologram, color balance all wrong. They drove on, an self-contained world sealed away from the outside, through a monotonous landscape that scarcely changed.

They stopped in a travel plaza just outside a place called Childress to let Jake change his bandages and charge the batteries. The charging station sat in the back, four lonely pylons tucked in the far corner of a sprawling lot, only one of them in use. Nadine raised an eyebrow. "It's Texas," Jake explained. "Oil's still king here. I'm going to get a burger. Want anything?"

"How's your leg?"

"Still attached, which is more than I can say for some bits of me. Itches like a sonofabitch."

"I suppose Thai's out of the question? Indian, maybe?"

"Burger's the best I can offer."

"Burger it is, then."

Jake limped across the parking lot and returned some minutes later with a couple of paper bags and two large Styrofoam coffee cups in a little cardboard carrier. They sat in the back of the RV and ate while the meter on the dashboard slowly ticked up. Nadine bounced her leg up and down. "Why is this taking so long?"

"Not likely to find any ultra-capacity chargers until we hit Dallas."

"I don't like this. I feel like a sitting duck."

"Might as well be a well-fed sitting duck. Eat."

When the batteries finally hit full, they set off again. The landscape sped by, patchwork farms on both sides.

The sun set before they reached Dallas. The city rose gleaming from the darkness, a brilliant fairyland of multicolored light. Knife-edged spires reached toward the blackened sky, hard and bright. Nadine gaped. "Pretty, isn't it?" Jake said. "Huge construction boom about ten, fifteen years ago. Lot of money got trapped here when the deal was signed and the Federation became a thing, so..." He shrugged. "We'll get some shut-eye, be in Houston tomorrow afternoon. Then we get to work."

They spent the night in the back lot of an anonymous truck stop outside the city, near an interstate highway that Jake said would take them on to Houston. This place, at least, had more chargers, and higher power, so the RV batteries would be full well before they planned to go.

Nadine stretched out on her side on the battered mattress and looked at the distant, surreal fairy towers of downtown Dallas. They didn't fit, somehow, with her experience of Texas so far. They seemed magical, luminous, a glittering cityscape belonging more to some distant place like Singapore, still hanging on with its uncanny institutional cheer against the ever-encroaching sea.

She jerked awake to a banging on the RV door. Outside, the far-off skyscrapers still glowed against velvet night. Her implant told her it was 3:42 AM. Her heart leapt into her throat. Jake was already moving, catlike, in the darkness, his silhouette oddly shaped against the truckstop lights that filtered through the curtains. His prosthetic arm lay on the table amidst the detritus of the cheap burgers, plugged into a charger in the wall. "Jake?" she whispered.

"Shh. Stay down," he hissed. He worked the door handle with his hip, foot braced to prevent it from opening more than a crack, hand behind his back. A yellow triangle glowed in Nadine's vision.

She heard a low mutter of voices, his and someone else's, high and feminine. The conversation came to a quick end. Jake closed the door with his foot. "Who was that?" Nadine said.

"Lot lizard."

"What?"

"A woman of negotiable affections who frequents truck stops seeking clientele."

"Jesus, that gave me a scare."

"Go back to sleep."

Nadine lay for a long time, but sleep would not come. The cityscape had lost its fairy-tale glow, somehow, and now seemed to Nadine something cold, remote, and inexplicably hostile. When at last she slipped away, the glowing skyscrapers remained fixed in her dreams, pixelated phosphorescence that loomed over a sinister alien landscape.

She came awake again with daylight streaming around her. Bouncing, swaying motion told her they were underway. She staggered out of the narrow bed in search of a tube of mil-spec coffee substitute beverage. "Good morning!" Jake called from the driver's seat. "You were sleeping pretty hard. Didn't want to wake you. Talking in your sleep, too."

"Yeah?" Nadine carried the hissing, fizzing tube to the front and collapsed gracelessly into the passenger's seat. "What was I saying?"

"Dunno. Sounded like you were having a conversation with someone. You okay?"

"No."

"You as okay as circumstances permit?"

Nadine sipped the coffee-like stuff. "I don't know how to answer that. I've never had my life destroyed before."

"Fair."

She stared out the window. They were on a proper interstate now, not the narrow strip of highway that had brought them to Dallas, but the landscape outside was little different from what it had been: endless flat, parched farms. "This state gives me the creeps."

"First order of business when we hit Houston is to track down someone with better resources than we have. We're also gonna need to sneak a peek at that bank chip of Anna's, only real quiet, in case those accounts are flagged. I doubt they will be, she was pretty good with making money undetectable, but we can't afford to take chances. Might have an in with solving both those problems. But first, we need to get some supplies."

"What kind of supplies?"

"I need to bring you to a meeting."

Houston loomed in the windshield before noon, a grubbier, more monochrome version of Dallas, dominated by a row of identical black skyscrapers with sharply chiseled tops, like great daggers of volcanic glass slicing into the sky. They spent the next hour navigating a maze of interstates, taking a wide circular beltway west around the city center before they finally emerged on a long, straight surface street. Businesses crowded along both sides of the road: a nail center, a music store, a chain 3D printing outlet, all with signs in English and Hindi. Jake muttered to himself, subvocalizing to his implant. Light sparkled in his contacts.

At last he seemed to find what he was looking for, a tiny electronics boutique wedged between a jewelry store and a motorcycle courier. He navigated the RV effortlessly into a street parking space Nadine would have sworn was too small for it. "Wait here," he said. "I'll be right back."

Nadine gnawed her fingernails. *Second thoughts?* Anna's voice came in her head.

She jumped. "Quit sneaking up on me."

Not sure I can.

"What do you want?"

Take care of Jake.

"What? Why?"

He doesn't expect to get out of this alive.

"Why do you care?"

I told you. When you save a life, you're responsible for it.

"How am I supposed to do that?"

The side door opened. Nadine yelped. Jake came in, grinning. "Okay. Meeting's set up. Here." He handed Nadine a small, expensive-looking bag with twine handles and the logo of a Chinese multinational on the side. "You'll need this."

"What is it?" She opened the bag and pulled out a box. Inside, a compact headset nestled in black silk. "We aren't meeting in person?"

"Not that kind of meeting. Still not safe for you to take your implant online, new ID or not, so we do it this way."

Nadine settled the headset across her eyes and touched the power stud. Three chirpy notes played in her ears. The logo materialized in front of her, just out of reach, then vanished to be replaced by a menu. She chose one of the default avatars, a generic, vaguely Asian woman with long pink hair wearing a corporate caricature of a schoolgirl's uniform, something a teen girl might select. A prompt floated in front of her, asking her to join a closed-link connection. The moment she clicked Connect, she was in a minimalist waiting room, plain walls sketched out in faintly glowing lines. Jake sat across from her, elbows on his knees, looking pretty close to the same as he usually did, only with two arms and a cleaner Army jacket, seams crisply ironed. "Now you look even more like an anime character," Jake observed, his words coming to her both in the van and through the headset.

"Is that good or bad?"

"If I were a sixteen-year-old boy, you'd be haunting my dreams. Hang on, I'm dialing in now."

Pixelated noise washed across them, breaking up the waiting room. When the static cleared, she and Jake stood in a long hallway, garishly hung with red and gold drapes, a red carpet beneath their feet. All along the hall, rows of nude women danced suggestively inside glass cages. "Come," purred a throaty feminine voice, "indulge your wildest fantasies with our sexy girls."

Nadine looked sideways at Jake's avatar. "Long story," he said in a side channel. He switched to the main channel and said "I'd like to chat with your girls, please."

One of the red tapestries moved aside to reveal a large door of polished mahogany that opened without a sound. Nadine followed Jake through into a graphic artist's 3D vision of a pornographic Victorian sitting-room, only on a huge scale: paintings of nude women in gilt-edged frames looking down over over-stuffed red chaise lounges, with the same red carpet beneath them. 3D-rendered women in various stages of undress reclined on the chairs, some locked in conversation with avatars in a wild assortment of styles: generic off-the-shelf models of men and women; elaborate custom models with bulging biceps or long black cloaks, hats drawn down over their eyes; a red-skinned cartoon demon with curved horns, a pointed tail, and an enormous erection; vague blurs in place of customers who wanted more privacy. In the corner, a raven-haired woman in a complicated skin-tight outfit of shiny black latex spoke to a man wearing nothing but a harness of leather straps around his chest and a black leather pouch over his junk. A whip-like thing with red and black lashes hung from her waist. As Nadine watched, they both disappeared in sprays of color.

Jake settled into a lounge. A dark-haired woman with absurdly large breasts barely concealed by a translucent robe slipped onto it beside him. "You looking for a good time, hon?" she said in a side channel. "I can make your evening more interesting. Yours and your friend's."

"I had something else in mind," Jake said in the main channel. "I'm looking for a friend of mine. His name's Safan. If I'm not mistaken, I think he runs this place. Let him know Jake's looking for him."

"I'm sorry, hon, you've got the wrong place." The woman rose and walked away.

Jake stood. "I need to talk to my friend Safan. He's about so tall—" He held his hand palm down a bit below his own eye height. "Bosnian chap, sharp nose, black hair, likes Irish whiskey neat, the more expensive the better. Haven't talked to him in years. Really would like to catch up. Anyone know where I can find him? Anyone?"

Several of the avatars winked out. A disembodied voice came in on a side channel: "I don't know who you think you are, friend, but you're making a mistake."

"No, I don't think I am," Jake announced to the general room. "Tell Safan his old friend would really like to see him. It's important."

More of the avatars disappeared. In the virtual space, Jake's avatar spread his hands. "Was it something I said? Can't a man see an old companion these days? My old buddy Safan Zlata, the guy who runs this place, he and I go way back. I'm just looking to reconnect, that's all."

The quasi-Victorian sitting room disappeared in a burst of colorful noise. A moment later, Jake and Nadine stood in a sumptuously-appointed bedroom, tastefully decorated with antique furniture. An enormous four-poster bed of dark wood, polished until it gleamed, dominated the room. A white comforter adorned with gold thread covered the bed. A large box of blonde wood richly padded with white velour stood open on an antique nightstand with elaborately carved legs, revealing an array of expensive-looking designer sex toys, some of which had functions Nadine could not guess.

Nadine looked around in wonder. The quality and resolution of the rendering exceeded anything she'd ever seen before. Across from the bed, she found an intricate roll-top desk, open to display a fascinating assortment of complicated little cubbyholes and boxes. A small pot of ink and a beautifully rendered quill pen sat atop a stack of eggshell-textured paper. Every individual barb on the feather had been rendered as its own object, a meticulous attention to detail she'd never experienced in even the most elaborate virtual environment. A single candle on a brass base burned atop the desk. Beads of wax rolled down its sides.

"Do you like it?"

The woman was just suddenly *there*, an utterly gorgeous apparition of ethereal beauty, arriving from thin air. She addressed Nadine in a melodic, cultured voice that sent shivers down her spine, ignoring Jake entirely. "There's a desk just like it in my bedroom. I've owned it for years. When I created this space, I had it disassembled so I could scan every part, then put it back together here and in the real world. The bed is real, too." She walked around Nadine, looking her up and down.

Nadine gawped. The avatar, like the desk and the room, had been rendered with painstaking care more finely detailed than anything Nadine had seen before. Golden skin, large luminous eyes of soft gray, a long white dress closed diagonally in the front and tied with a white silk ribbon. The cloth flowed with extraordinary realism, moving across the avatar's body as it turned, the ribbon independently animated. The avatar moved with an effortless grace that suggested countless hours of high-end motion capture. It looked her up and down in a way that made

Nadine feel suddenly, acutely underdressed in her crude, low-fi stock avatar with its simple, janky animation.

The woman settled gracefully on the bed, leaning back slightly. "I'd invite you to sit, but as you can see, there aren't really any places to do so. Most visitors to this space aren't here for conversation." She tilted her head at Jake. "Is there something I can do for you?"

"Where are we?"

"The most private VIP suite in the virtual space you were just in. I ported you here. When you asked about Mr. Zlata, that dropped a card, you see. He prefers to remain a step removed from the day to day operation of this place, as I'm sure you understand. And you are?"

"Jake. Jake Fox. An old associate of your boss's."

"Jake Fox. Hmm. Curious that he's never mentioned you."

"Yeah, I seem to have that effect on people. I knew him a long time ago, back before he ran a—" Jake spread his arms. "Respectable enterprise like this. My friend here and I are just in town, and we could use a man of his particular talents and expertise."

"I see. As you point out, my employer is in a different line of business these days. I doubt he will have the time or energy to help you with whatever..." She seemed to look at Jake closely for the first time. "Sordid affair you may have in mind. Good day, Jake Fox."

"Wait. I think he'll want to talk to me."

"Oh?" Her tone suggested the faintest stirrings of impatience. "Why is that?"

"Because we have quite a lot of money. If he's still the man I knew, you know how he feels about money."

The woman chuckled. "Yes, he is motivated by cash, isn't he? My name is Liz. I'll tell you what. If you give me a moment, I'll see if he has any interest in re-connecting with his old friend. If he says no, then I will bid you good day and ask that you do not return."

"Fair enough."

"I'll be right back."

Some indefinable something disappeared from behind the avatar's eyes. After a moment, it unfastened the ties that held the front of the dress shut. Fabric parted to reveal a body every bit as artistically rendered as the room. It slid exquisitely modeled hands with carefully manicured nails over well-crafted skin. Dazzlingly detailed pink nipples hardened under its caress. It slipped one hand between its legs, lips parting in a soft sigh, the sound just a tiny bit generic, unnoticeable had it not been for the rich, warm quality resonating from the voice just a moment ago.

Back in the RV, Nadine felt a prickly rush wash over her. She shot a questioning look at Jake's avatar. It wore a neutral expression, though she couldn't tell if that was due to the low facial fidelity of the model or if the pixelated carnality didn't affect him. In the virtual room, Nadine-the-avatar shifted uncomfortably.

They waited there as the minutes stretched on. Liz's avatar ignored them, sliding its hands over itself, its eyes peering somewhere into the middle distance. It parted the dress wider and slipped two fingers into itself, then brought them up to its elaborately rendered lips. The prickly heat crawled down Nadine's body. She felt herself respond involuntarily, and squirmed in the shabby RV light-years away from this sophisticated, elegant place.

The avatar threw back its head and moaned, its rendered body quivering with some facsimile of ecstasy. Jake hummed tunelessly to himself. Nadine turned away from the bed to watch the candle flame dance, waiting for the animation to loop. It never did. Gasps and moans from behind her sent crawling shivers over her skin.

The cries built up, heading for an unmistakable crescendo of ecstasy, then suddenly cut off. "I'm terribly sorry," Liz said, "I left my avatar running its default idle animations."

Nadine turned. Intelligence lived behind the avatar's eyes once more. Liz re-fastened the dress, casual and unhurried. "Mr. Zlata will see you tomorrow afternoon at two o'clock. Here's the address." An icon appeared in Nadine's peripheral vision, signaling a data packet on a side channel. "Anything else I can do for you, Mr. Fox?"

"This a secure line?"

The avatar folded its hands over its knees, an inscrutable expression on its face. "Reasonably so."

"If I wanted to find out the balance on a bank chip, but didn't know if the accounts were flagged, that something you might be able to help with?"

"Perhaps. For a price."

"What price?"

"For an old friend of Mr. Zlata's? Let's call it a thousand."

"You're killing me. Would it be higher or lower if I didn't know the man?"

The avatar smiled an equally inscrutable smile. "Yes."

"Fine. Melody?"

Nadine pulled off the headset, dug around in the slim remnants of her worldly possessions, and slotted the chip into the side of the goggles. When she settled the headset back over her head, Liz's avatar turned as if looking at something invisible just beyond the nightstand with its collection of exotic sex toys. "Give me a minute."

"You know, you could leave those default animations on," Jake said.

"Most people pay extra for that."

The avatar froze into unnatural immobility, eyes blank. A minute later, a number appeared, floating in midair in front of Nadine. Her eyes bugged. "That can't be right."

"Your girlfriend was good at what she did," Jake said.

Liz returned, a sense of presence once more inhabiting the avatar. "No sign of any alerts on that account."

"You're sure?" Jake said.

An expression of amused patience crossed the avatar's face. "Quite. If you will excuse me, I have other matters demanding my attention." The avatar looked directly at Nadine with a smile that made her shiver, then the room dissolved, leaving her once more in the RV, staring at a Chinese electronics conglomerate's logo floating in an endless blank void.

She pulled off the headset. Scintillating lights faded from Jake's contacts. "That was weird," Nadine said.

"Really?" Jake looked surprised. "I thought it went rather well. I did say he isn't exactly a friend."

18

A Lot of Fucking Balls

AT ONE FORTY-FIVE the next afternoon, Jake sat in the driver's seat with a pair of binoculars in his claw, studying a small, low single-story office building set back from the road. Tall trees flanked a long ribbon of white concrete that led up to the door, where a sign read "Strategy+ Management Consulting Inc" in eggshell blue letters on a black background. Two men in black rent-a-cop uniforms stood beside the door, arms folded in front of them. Nervous energy radiated from Jake in waves.

"You seem wound up for someone who's about to see an old friend," Nadine observed.

"We didn't part company under the best of circumstances," Jake said. "Kinda hoping it's water under the bridge, but..."

"But?"

"Hope for the best, plan for the worst, right?" He rose from the driver's seat. Yellow triangles flashed, pointing to the compact handgun and taser tucked into the back of his pants. "Did you transfer some of that money onto some new bank chips?"

"Yes." Nadine tucked the squares of white plastic into her pocket. "What do we do if your frien—sorry, your old acquaintance doesn't want to help?"

"Guess I'll just have to be extra persuasive."

They stepped out into the shimmering heat. As they approached, one of the security guards, burly man with dark skin who stood nearly as wide as he was tall, spoke inaudibly into a microphone clipped to the shoulder of his shirt. He nodded to his taller, blonder companion, and the two of them stepped forward.

"Good afternoon!" Jake said in his most cheerful voice. "We have an appointment with your boss."

"Yeah, well, meeting's off," the shorter man said. "Boss doesn't want to see you. He's given us very...specific instructions." He slipped a truncheon from its belt loop.

"Listen, I'm sure we can talk about this like reasonable people," Jake said.

The man shook his head. "Nope."

His companion headed toward Nadine. "Normally, I would never hit a lady," he said, almost apologetically. "Nothing personal, you understand. Just business."

He swung his fist. Nadine just had time to catch a quick glimpse of a blurred red arc when something detonated on the side of her face. She reeled, stunned. He drew back for another punch.

His companion swung his nightstick. Jake was already moving, ducking low. The truncheon passed through the space where he'd been. Jake spun and ducked. The truncheon came down again, connecting solidly with his prosthetic arm. He laughed.

The taller of the two men came at Nadine once more, ghostly red cones springing from his fist. She dodged. The red turned green. He grunted in surprise and lunged at her, arms wide, grappling her. She went down on hot pavement, pinned beneath him.

Nadine heard a pop and an electric crackle. The man went rigid, his sweat-soaked face inches from hers, a look of surprise and pain frozen on his features. The crackle came again. His eyes rolled up.

The larger man struck again. Jake yelped in pain. The taser skidded from his fingers. Another blow and he fell to his knees. "You know," his attacker said casually, "I think I'll fuck you up extra for that."

Nadine heaved the limp form from atop her and scrambled to her feet. She snatched the gun from Jake's waistband and leveled it at the larger man. He froze, then turned toward her.

"I think you'll want to show us in now," Jake said.

"Or what? Your friend here will shoot me? She doesn't seem the type." He reached down to grab Jake by the collar, dragging him to his feet one-handed.

Nadine squeezed the trigger. The gun clicked. The security guard's jaw dropped in a comedic caricature of surprise. Jake grabbed his wrist and twisted sharply. Nadine heard the distinct crack of breaking bone. He crumpled, face a mask of agony.

"Let me kill them," Nadine said.

"No. That's not what we're here for." Jake pressed Nadine's arm down, took the gun from her trembling fingers. "Lucky for you my friend didn't know the safety was on," he said to the man with the broken wrist. "Toss me your keys and radio. His too. And your backup piece."

"I don't have—"

"You want to go home tonight? Do it or I'll make sure my companion gets to play with you instead."

He complied, face contorted with agony, drawing a compact revolver from an ankle holster with two fingers. Jake collected his gear and did the same for his friend, who lay face down on the sidewalk. "Now cuff yourself to your friend here, or I'll let my companion add another notch to her belt," he said. "I'd tell you how many people she's killed, but you wouldn't believe me."

The man fumbled a pair of folding black handcuffs from his belt one-handed and locked them around his wrist. He went to do the same to the limp form of the other guard. Jake shook his head. "No. Your wrist to his ankle."

Muttering curses, the man complied. Jake fished his companion's cuffs from his belt and cuffed them together, wrist to ankle. "Now, we'll be back in a minute. This meeting shouldn't take long. I think your boss is gonna be real happy we saw him." He tucked the gun back into his waistband. "Let's go meet the man."

Inside, they found a dingy reception room with a long, empty desk along the far wall. Above the desk, painted letters on the wall read "Strategy+ Management Consulting: Your Business Is Our Business." A single solitary camera glowered at them from one corner near the ceiling. A door in the side wall buzzed. "Let me do the talking," Jake said.

They went through into a small office. A dark-haired man in a shapeless green jacket looked up from a desk cluttered with papers, bits of electronics, pieces of drones, and what looked like a doll's head. A wide grin spread across his broad face. "Well, I'll be god-damned! Jake! What's it been, man, eight years?"

"More like nine."

"Time flies. You look good, man. Well, mostly. What happened to your arm?"

"Belarus."

"Fuuuuuuck." He exhaled and sat back in his chair. "You were in that shitshow? Jesus."

"Yeah. Army fixed me up after. I can even feel it. Direct sensory input." Jake opened and closed the claw. Servos whined. "Still itches sometimes, though. The docs say it's all in my head. What can you do?"

"Rough, man. You still working for—"

"No," Jake said. "I've been exploring new opportunities. That's why I'm here. I need a favor."

He leaned back further in his chair and spread his hands. "Hey, anything for an old friend, am I right? What do you need? A place to stay? Papers? Stims? Whatever you need, man. I owe you." His eyes flicked toward the door.

"Yes, you do. I had something else in mind."

"Like what?"

"Blueprints."

His eyes flicked toward the door again. "Blueprints? Of what?"

"The Terracone Research facility. And don't bother waiting for those Neanderthals you laughingly call 'security.' They aren't coming."

Safan lunged for the desk. The gun materialized as if by magic in Jake's hand. "Don't."

"Fuck you." Safan's face hardened. "You've got a lot of fucking balls, coming into my place after you brought the cops down on me."

"After I what?"

"'Bout four hours after you turned up in my space, the cops raided my business. 'Simulated child sex acts,' they said. You telling me you don't know anything about that?"

"Yes," Jake said. "I'm telling you I don't know shit about that. Is that why you told your boys to put a beating on us? After you said you'd see us? I'm very disappointed, Safan. Without our word, what do we have?"

"You think you'll get out of here alive? Is that what you're thinking?"

Jake shrugged. "I give myself 60/40 odds. Better than you. You ever visit Australia, Safan?"

"Australia? The fuck you talking about? No, I've never been to Australia. What the fuck does Australia have to do with anything?"

"There's this bush in Australia called the gympie gympie tree. Locals call it the suicide bush. You know why?" Safan glared at Jake, his face a mask of loathing. "It produces this toxin called moroidin," Jake went on. "Complicated molecule, very hard to synthesize. Just a tiny amount of it causes agony that lasts for months. There are these little hairs all over the plant, see, and if you touch it, they inject the toxin into your skin. The pain is so bad a lot of folks who tangle with it end up killing themselves just to make it stop."

"Yeah? And?"

"Turns out someone's cracked the synthesis, made it into a weapon. Same people murdered a friend of mine to keep it quiet. I'm really keen on finding out who and why."

"What the fuck do you want?"

"I told you. Blueprints."

"Terracone is a military contractor."

"I know."

"You really think I'll help you?"

"Yeah, I do."

"You always were a shitty judge of character. Why would I give you a goddamn thing?"

"Two reasons," Jake said. "First, you don't want to die. That's where any thought of double-crossing me or turning me in leads, so I urge you in the strongest possible terms to banish all such thoughts from your mind."

"And second?"

"Time hasn't been kind to you, Safan. Look at you, in this shithole, grubbing for crumbs. Running an online brothel? Really? I remember when you had ambition."

"Yeah, well, at least I got two arms."

"Touché. Thing is, Safan, I'm your fairy fucking godmother. You just don't have the sense to see it. Play this right and I'll make all your dreams come true. Show him, Melody."

Nadine fished out one of the new bank chips. Jake tossed it on the desk. "Go ahead. Take a look. Slowly."

Safan picked up the card with the tips of two fingers like he expected it to bite him and slotted it into a reader. Lines of text hovered in the air. He whistled. "You must be pretty desperate."

"I prefer to think of it as 'well-funded and highly motivated.'"

"Okay. Assume, just as a hypothetical, that I can get what you want. How do you know I won't just cash that and then turn you in?"

"You really think I'd pay you before you deliver? That's just the retainer, to help cover expenses. There's twice that much on delivery."

"What do you need? You're not paying that much just for site plans. You can get those for fifty bucks at the city planning office."

"We need everything. Security systems, data links in and out, security rotations, everything."

Safan whistled. "You're planning to break in."

"Something like that."

"Wow. Okay, your funeral."

"We all gotta die some time."

Safan relaxed back into his chair and tucked the bank chip in his pocket with a broad, congenial smile. "You know what I always liked about you? You're my kind of crazy. It's a pleasure working with you again, Jake."

"I'm glad we have an understanding."

"You going to give me a number?"

"Fuck no," Jake said. "We'll be in touch. By the way, your security team is lying out front handcuffed together. You might want to call an ambulance. And give them a raise."

"After they let you in? I should fire their asses."

"To be fair, you didn't give them any warning what they were up against."

"No, I suppose I didn't."

"To old times," Jake said.

"To old times."

"Oh. One more thing," Jake said.

Safan raised an eyebrow. "Hm?"

He tensed as Jake pulled a small memory card from his pocket. "DNA sequence with MHC profile. If, hypothetically, this were to belong to someone I wasn't much fond of, might you know someone who knows someone who could—"

"I'll see what I can do."

Out in the parking lot, the two security guards, still cuffed together wrist to ankle, glared at Jake and Nadine. The one Jake had tasered spat. His companion with the broken wrist sweated profusely in the heat, face contorted in pain. About halfway back to the RV, Jake stopped Nadine. "Anything back there seem odd to you?"

"All of it?"

"No, I mean particularly odd."

"What are you getting at?"

Jake frowned, face thoughtful. "We see an old associate of mine, and that very same day his business is raided by the cops. What are the odds?"

"He seems shady. I'm sure he's no stranger to police intervention."

"He's also careful. And virtual kiddie porn isn't his thing. I'd bet half the money we just gave him that he got raided because we got in touch with him."

"You're being paranoid," Nadine said.

"Maybe. From now on, watch what you say unless absolutely necessary, 'kay?"

"Yeah."

"So," Jake said when he settled into the driver's seat, "that was disappointing. I really hoped he would see reason. Still, I do have a few other contacts in Houston." He put his finger to his lips at Nadine's puzzled expression. "I'm hungry for something that doesn't come out of a vacuum-sealed pouch. You?"

"Um, sure, yeah," Nadine said.

They navigated the alien streets of Houston, so different from the streets Nadine was used to. All around them, enormous, noisy internal-combustion cars seasoned the air with aromatic hydrocarbon stew. Everywhere she looked, towering cranes swung alarmingly over the streets, erecting bland, characterless skyscrapers of no discernable purpose.

They headed away from the city core until they found a cheap Indian drive-through. Jake parked and rummaged in the back for a while. Nadine opened her mouth. "I thought—" Jake brought his finger to his lips, a quick flicker of motion.

Nadine watched him take a small, complicated-looking device from a battered box wrapped in black electrical tape. He fiddled with it for a moment, then paced up and down the length of the RV, frowning at it. He lingered for a time near the door. Any time she opened her mouth, Jake silenced her with a quick touch of his finger to his lips.

Finally he stowed the device with a grunt and beckoned her to follow him out the door. In the restaurant, Nadine said "What was that about?" between bites of chicken makhani.

"RV is bugged," Jake said. "Tiny thing stuck on the edge of the door."

"Martin Taylor?"

"Gotta be."

"How?"

"At a guess? The lot lizard," Jake said. "They probably picked us up coming through customs. Musta put two and two together, figured out you were traveling as Melody. Maybe scanned your implant when they caught you, backtracked from the ID to that name, flagged it at the border."

"That's why the raid on your friend's place?"

"Probably, yeah."

"Did you destroy it?"

"Destroy it?" Jake gave her a feral grin. "They don't know we know.

That presents us with a certain window of opportunity, if we're careful. Taylor's been a couple steps ahead of us this whole time. Now maybe, just maybe, we have a chance to change that."

"How?"

"Dunno yet. Interesting to think about though, isn't it? Meantime, be careful what you say. If you need to say anything sensitive, write it down or do it outside."

"Do they know where we are?"

"Don't know. The bug I found piggybacks on mesh wireless and cell but it's too small to receive GPS. Cutting-edge, military or near-military-equivalent. Expensive. I'll do a search for passive trackers."

That night, as Nadine lay on the lumpy mattress searching for sleep, doubt and worry gnawed at her. Jake had gone over every inch of the RV, inside and out, on the pretext of looking for a water leak and pronounced himself satisfied that whoever'd put the bug hadn't done anything else. Nadine argued for abandoning the RV, but Jake seemed adamant that it would mean throwing away the one slender advantage they possessed. In the end, Nadine grudgingly agreed. "Besides," Jake said, "it's not like they can call the police. Not without answering questions they'd really prefer not to. Especially in light of that package of digital fuck-you you uploaded. They're still in crisis-control mode."

Visions of faceless figures kicking in the door filled her dreams that night. She woke with the dawn, head still swimming with visions of blood and death. "Good morning, sleepyhead!" Jake offered from the driver's seat as she pulled the tab on a tube of coffee substitute. "You look like hell."

"It's a reflection of the company I keep," Nadine said.

"You were talking in your sleep again."

"Did I have anything interesting to say?"

"Couldn't tell."

She blinked and peered at the freeway out the windshield. "Where are we going?"

"Supplies. You're drinking that stuff like you like it. Also going to see if I can find an old friend of mine, you know, since Safan seems too preoccupied with his own problems for the likes of us." He gave Nadine a flicker of a wink, barely perceptible.

They drove for nearly an hour. Nadine had the sense they were somehow on the opposite side of Houston, though Jake seemed to be navigating using his implant; the RV's touchscreen showed only a set of controls for what passed as a sound system. He pulled into a bland shopping mall that looked as if it dated from decades ago, in front of a nondescript store with dark-tinted windows. A plain painted sign propped in one of the windows read "Army Navy Surplus" with a Texas flag on one side and a Federation of Free States flag on the other. Next to it, a garish storefront promised "Video Poker! Lotto! Keno! BIG PAYOUTS!!!" in scrolling characters above the door. Brilliant holographic ads crowding every square inch of the windows, luring them in with the promise of cigarettes, ice-cold beer, and fresh hot sandwiches.

Jake turned off the RV and hopped out. Nadine followed, rock in her shoe, fake violet hair pulled over her face, finishing the last of her coffee substitute as she stepped into the heat. A bell over the door jangled as they went in. The air inside seemed faintly disused. Filtered sunlight did little to brighten the long rows of dark-colored shelves loaded with flags, military rations, and assorted pouches, belts, rucksacks, and other things whose function Nadine couldn't fathom. A long metal clothes rack near the door bore an enormous load of military fatigues, vests in a dozen different styles of camouflage, and T-shirts emblazoned with Federation of Free States slogans. The store was bare of customers.

At the counter, a man in a leather vest adorned with embroidered patches stood behind a compact electronic register, steel-gray hair tied back in a braid. He nodded to Jake. "You serve?"

"Belarus."

The man whistled. "Don't see a lot of you here."

"Not a lot of us made it out."

"True that."

Jake lowered his voice. The two of them engaged in what to Nadine seemed like a quick, tense negotiation of some sort, just below the level she could hear. When the conversation ended, Jake gestured for Nadine to follow him.

The cashier, or owner, or possibly both, turned a key in a door in the back where a plastic sign read "No Admittance - Employees Only." Another sign below it read "Violators will be shot, survivors will be shot again" over a stylized crosshair.

The door opened with a solid, heavy *clunk*. Flat white LED panels in the ceiling flicked on. As the door swung open on enormous hinges, Nadine got the sense of massive weight. Beyond, steel walls gleamed. Racks bolted solidly to the walls held rows and rows of guns, both rifles and pistols, each held in place by a metal bar with a round, complicated-looking keyhole. The door swung shut behind them.

Jake walked down the rack of rifles. "So what was it like, man?" the steel-haired man said.

"What was what like?"

"Belarus. When the shit went down."

Jake shook his head, so slightly Nadine barely caught it. He scratched at the place where his prosthetic met his shoulder. "You don't want to know."

"But—"

Jake whirled toward him with an expression Nadine couldn't read, some feral mix of anger and pain. "Believe me when I say you don't want to know," he said, voice tight.

The man spread his hands. "No offense. Just making conversation."

Jake returned his attention to the rack with a grunt. "This one," he said. "You got a conversion kit for left-handed shooting?"

"Nope. Gotta be a bullpup?"

"Preferably."

"Got a Kel-Tec that'll do ya. Short, great balance, good in closed spaces. Costs, though."

"Show me."

Nadine tuned them out. They went on for a while before they reached some sort of conclusion. In the end, Jake exchanged the last of her cash for an odd-looking, strangely squat rifle and several boxes of ammunition. The man, who Nadine figured was more likely the owner than hired help, tried to offer Jake all sorts of freebies on top: a weird knife with three blades twisted in a sort of spiral, that made Jake snort and roll his eyes; a complicated-looking shoulder holster with a black plastic latch on top, that Jake said wouldn't fit his handgun; and finally, a case of military rations with coffee substitute, self-heating, which Jake gratefully accepted. Nadine carried the case of rations. "Thank you for your service!" the man called as they left. Jake raised his hand as the bell jangled behind them.

As they climbed into the RV, a quick flicker of gold from the cacophony of holographic ads in the window next door caught Nadine's eye. A golden-skinned woman in white bent forward alluringly and blew her a kiss. Pixelated hearts danced around her. A number flashed beneath her. She disappeared. Nadine blinked and shook her head.

"What?" Jake said.

"Just...I saw an ad that reminded me of Liz."

"She really left a mark on you, huh?" Jake said. "I must admit, she had a nice avatar. Very comely."

"That's what it was designed for. Engineered desire. The semiotics of lust."

Jake gave her a skeptical side-eye. "If you say so." He stowed the case of rations and the strange-looking gun in the back of the RV. "Struck out there," he said out loud. "Not giving up yet. I still have one more contact I can try. Gonna need some lunch first. I have a taste for greasy burgers. Sports bar sound good to you?"

"Um, sure," Nadine said.

Half an hour later, Jake pulled into a tall parking garage wedged between a warehouse and a shopping mall. The arm rose when he stuck his new Booker card in the slot. They found their way to a sports bar decorated with road signs and posters of bygone sports heroes, all just a little too polished to be real. They found seats at a small table with a wobbly leg, its top covered in scratched-up red plastic. Other than a man with a scruffy, unkempt beard sitting in a booth muttering to himself over a grilled cheese and bacon sandwich, they had the place to themselves. A large-screen TV occupied most of the far wall, showing a hockey game in English with Spanish subtitles. "May be about time to ditch the RV," Jake said.

"How? Sell it?"

"I was thinking more like leave the fob on the dash in a particularly unsavory neighborhood and walk away. I was hoping sending the Mini to Canada would throw them off the trail. Should've known coming through customs would set them back on the scent again. Figure someone might do us a favor by stealing the RV, maybe give us some freedom of motion. If—"

A beer commercial interrupted the game. Midway through, the screen flickered, then changed to a tastefully-appointed bedroom. A beautiful, gold-skinned woman sat elegantly on the enormous four-poster bed. She blew a kiss toward the camera. A number appeared beneath her.

"Jake!" Nadine hissed, pointing frantically at the screen. He turned. The beer ad appeared again.

"What?"

"It was her. On the screen. Liz."

"You sure?"

"Yes! There was a number. Gone now."

He frowned. "Should I be worried?"

"I'm not going crazy, if that's what you're asking."

"Good. Finish your food."

On the walk back to the parking garage, they passed a jewelry store aimed at a solidly middle-class market. Restrained holographic ads scrolled along the top of large windows, behind which diamond necklaces and sleek watches nestled in white satin. Nadine paused for a moment to stare at a pair of earrings, overwhelmed with sudden homesickness.

The scrolling ads flickered and changed. "Jake. Call me. 7742:4458:3323."

"Huh." Jake shot an inscrutable look at Nadine. "Will you look at that."

"What are you going to do?"

"Find a place to call, of course."

The place he found turned out to be a dingy, poorly-lit coffee shop with a row of shabby terminals on a long wooden table with little privacy dividers made of particleboard between each station. It belonged to a chain Nadine had never heard of called Keep Your Data Ltd. "Texas thing," Jake explained. "All their connections go through a no-log offshore proxy in a country not exactly friendly to American data extradition requests." He gestured to Nadine to put on the headset attached to the table with a thin steel cord. "Port in. We're paying by the minute."

Nadine fit the goggles over her eyes. The foam padding was worn and discolored from use. She tried not to think too hard about how many other people had used this same rig, and for what. The headset chimed. Static washed over her vision. She chose one of the avatars built into the headset's firmware, a blocky, low-poly female character with spiky hair and improbable anatomy, modeled vaguely after a popular character from the dawn of video games. "Okay," Jake said, "I'm dialing us in now."

This time there was no loading screen, no Spartan antechamber before they connected. One second Nadine was looking at the headset manufacturer's logo, a company out of India she'd never heard of, and the next they were in the lush, tasteful bedroom with its roll-top desk and enormous bed. The candle still burned atop the desk, shorter now than she remembered.

"Welcome," Liz, or Liz's avatar, purred. "I wondered what it would take to get your attention."

"How'd you find us?" Jake said, speaking from a blandly handsome low-resolution avatar in a boxy three-piece suit.

"Goodness, you two look a frightful mess," Liz said.

"We're using headsets from a chain that does proxy connections. Wouldn't make sense to load my avatar from cloud storage if I'm trying not to be traced."

"Keep Your Data?"

"You know it?"

"I was an early investor."

"Who are you?" Nadine said.

"I am who I am. I called you here because our mutual friend wants to meet. He has the information you asked about."

"That was fast," Jake said.

"He's efficient." The avatar turned to him with a small smile on its face. Nadine watched, hypnotized. Even its animated breathing was flawless. "Surely that's why you insisted on his help so crassly?"

"I said I'd call."

The smile grew a fraction. "He didn't want to wait."

"That was a nice trick, hacking the video feed and the ads. You still haven't told me how you found us."

The avatar shook its head. "Embarrassingly easily, I'm afraid. Our mutual friend scanned your implant when you visited, got your UUID. Your companion's appears to be offline, but no matter. From there it was simply a question of triangulating your location from pings on mesh receivers. Low resolution, but it got me to within a couple of blocks. Then I tapped into video surveillance in the area. Did you know Houston has surveillance almost as pervasive as London? It helps you're driving such a distinctive vehicle."

"If it was that easy for you to find us..." Nadine said.

"Why haven't the police done the same? They can't get access to mesh network relay receivers without a warrant, and they need a separate warrant for every camera owner. Plus they don't appear to be looking for Jake, and your implant isn't broadcasting."

"I was more thinking about Ter—"

"No names, please, even over a proxy connection. The company you speak of is dealing with internal problems. That media packet you uploaded kicked over a hornet's nest."

"I have no idea what you're talking about," Jake said.

The avatar sighed. "Don't play coy. It didn't take long to put the pieces together. But your friend raises an interesting point, and that's why our mutual friend would like to see you soonest. In person. Tomorrow. I'll send you the address. It's a little ways out of town."

"Well, you know, I'd love to, but I'm scheduled to get a haircut," Jake said.

The avatar's face hardened. Nadine wondered if Liz, or whoever was operating it, had full facial capture, and at what resolution. "Don't be a bigger asshole than you already are. You paid to be on this ride. I think you're going to want to hear what we have to say."

"We?" Nadine said, then immediately kicked herself.

The avatar looked at her. "Tomorrow. Date and time in the side channel. Don't be late, and please take a different vehicle." The room dissolved, leaving Nadine sitting on an uncomfortable chair with a shabby headset strapped to her face.

19

Too Much Insurance

THEY TRAVELED SOUTH under a steel-gray sky, following a road alongside an enormous above-ground pipeline of steel the same gray as the sky. A chain-link fence emblazoned with red-painted metal warning signs promising dire consequences for trespass enclosed the pipeline on both sides. Massive powder blue supports cradled it every twenty yards or so. "Oil?" Nadine guessed.

"Water. Lakes started to run dry when the weather got all funny. They built this enormous desalination plant on the coast. What you're seeing there is most of Houston's water supply."

They rode in a long, heavy black car Jake had summoned with his new Booker account. It had an interior larger than any car Nadine had ever seen before, covered in acres of soft brown leather. The internal combustion engine vibrated disconcertingly, even when the car wasn't moving. Jake grinned at Nadine's expression. "What's wrong?"

"It's just...I don't think I've ever ridden in a gas-burner before."

"Whole different world here," Jake said.

Houston proper gave way to the sort of sprawling industrial spaces that ringed the less desirable outskirts of many cities. Nadine watched the rental car's nav screen, where a glowing blue triangle made its way along roads rendered as thin white lines, an abstraction of the real world simplified for easy comprehension. They crossed a set of train tracks dusted with a fine patina of rust that suggested long disuse.

Eventually, their path veered away from the water pipeline and down a long, badly-paved road that opened into a small industrial park sheltered by trees. Three low one-story buildings clad in dull tan stucco huddled together at the heart of a nearly empty parking lot. Two of the three showed no signs of being inhabited at all. The car pulled into a space in front of the third, next to a large white van without markings and an electric roadster in brilliant red. A sign reading "New Horizons Data Services" hung over a narrow glass door framed in black. A camera peered down at them from a white metal bracket above the door. "You have arrived at your destination," the car announced in a pronounced drawl. "A long-distance surcharge has been deducted from your Booker account."

"Wait here," Jake said.

"Waiting incurs charges as explained on the screen. Failure to return within twenty minutes without releasing the cab may incur additional charges."

"We might be a while."

"Wait times longer than twenty minutes require reserving the cab in fifteen-minute increments. Charges for cab reservation are nonrefundable but may be applied to your return trip on a prorated basis as explained on the screen."

"Reserve us an hour."

"Your account has been billed for one hour's reservation," the car announced. The doors popped open. Jake stepped grumbling into the heat.

The door made a raspy electronic buzz as they approached. Jake went through first, with Nadine behind. Inside, they found a short hallway with a steel grate at the end that reminded Nadine of a cage door at a zoo, heavy steel bars with steel mesh between. Another camera watched them suspiciously from a bracket in the ceiling just above the door. A loud buzz greeted their approach. "I don't like this one bit," Jake said.

Beyond the door, or gate, or whatever it was, the hall stretched off for some distance before it ended in yet a third door, this one a solid, massive slab that wouldn't look out of place at a bank. Midway down, the hall branched to the right. "Come in," Safan's voice said through round white speaker grilles in the ceiling. "Hall to your right. First door on the left."

The first door on the left opened into a large room that seemed oddly disused. A long oval conference table that had once been expensive commercial chic but was now covered with the accumulation of years of scratches and stains crouched low and heavy in the room's center. On the far wall, an enormous whiteboard still bore faint smudges of diagrams gone by. An old-fashioned projector clung to the ceiling, covered in dusty plastic.

Safan rose from his seat at the end of the conference table. "Jake! I'm glad you got my message."

"Hell of a drive all the way out here," Jake said. "Booker's sitting in the parking lot charging us by the minute."

"No greeting? What's become of civility these days? How are you doing, Jake?"

"You're one to talk. How are those two goons you sicced on us?"

"They'll live. Though I hear your girl tried to shoot one of them. Not very professional."

"When you make your living beating people up, you have to account for the occasional victim who isn't a pacifist. What's so important you couldn't just tell us online?"

Safan shook his head sadly. "All those paranoid old habits of yours, but they never reach where they need to. And you, my friend, need some paranoia right now. You've well and truly kicked over the beehive, haven't you? I won't ask how you got in the shit, because you wouldn't tell me anyway, but I do admire the shit you're in."

"Did you get what I asked for?"

"And more. You know a guy named Martin Taylor?"

Nadine's blood froze. "Why do you ask?" Jake said quietly.

Safan leaned back in his chair, fingers steepled in front of him. "Let me tell you a story," he said. "It's a good story, full of twists and turns. It starts with me minding my own business, when out of the blue, this guy I knew once from years ago suddenly shows up on my doorstep wanting to speak to me." He held up his hand when Jake opened his mouth to reply. "No, wait, it gets better. And what is it he wants? I'm glad you asked. Oh, nothing much, really...he just wants blueprints for the Houston headquarters of a defense contractor, that's all."

"Do you have a point?" Jake said.

"Humor me. Now, this fellow, let's call him J, is in the company of this Chinese woman who looks suspiciously like a terrorist the police are after. And there's a funny thing about that. You see, it turns out this woman just uploaded a conversation with a fellow who seems to have been working for, or with, or under contract for, a subsidiary of Terracone Research. And this fellow, who looked rather the worse for the wear, I might add, admits on camera that this company had been very naughty. Very naughty indeed. Framing our Chinese terrorist, or so he says. Deepfakes, all sorts of things. He subsequently disappears. Not available for questioning."

"I don't see what—"

"Patience, please. This story puts a bee in the bonnet over at Terracone Research. You remember J, the guy who just showed up? He wants access to that very same Terracone Research. And then, magic! Martin Taylor, a high-powered executive directly implicated by our mysterious informant, he shows up in Houston too! Quite a plot twist, isn't it? Rather a coincidence, I thought." He squinted at Jake. "I don't like coincidences. In my line of work, coincidences are never a good sign."

"What exactly is your line of work?" Nadine said.

"That's complicated," Safan said. "It's also not part of my story. And don't think I've forgotten for even half a minute that visit from the police a day after you showed up, which is also a coincidence I don't much like." He turned his attention to Nadine. "First you're a wanted terrorist, then maybe you're a victim of a frameup by a private security company with ties to a defense contractor. You get around, too. Sightings of you in California, Washington, Pennsylvania, Canada. Conspiracy theorists are going nuts. Terracone is in a tizzy, fighting subpoenas left and right. Word is the board's near a state of civil war."

"That's not—" Jake started.

"Jake. Jake, my old friend, I don't care. I don't care why this is happening. I don't care if you're in bed with a Chinese ecoterrorist, figuratively or literally. I don't care what your angle is. I don't care about your politics. I'm a businessman. Commerce is my interest. I don't want to seem ungrateful, because you are in fact offering me quite an extravagant amount of money—almost an embarrassing amount of money, if truth be told—but I'm really starting to wonder if it's worth it. Or if I want to be anywhere near you when this all goes down. You and your Chinese terrorist piece of ass here. I'm a little surprised at you, Jake. You're not thinking with the small head, are you?"

Nadine balled her hands into fists. "Now look here—"

"No. You look here. You're radioactive. So. I told you a story, now you tell me a story. Make it a good one."

"Why?" Nadine said bitterly. "You've already decided not to help us."

Safan's eyes narrowed. "The day is young. Change my mind." He turned to a small microphone on a gooseneck stand bolted to the desk. "Elizabeth, will you come in here, please?"

A moment later, the door opened to let a bulky, powered wheelchair through, humming an electric whir to itself. The chair bore...Nadine frowned. An ancient woman, hair gone totally white, holding a tabby cat on her lap, as ancient in its way as she. Something about those gray eyes, bright and alert from a face wreathed in wrinkles... "Liz?" Nadine said.

A broad smile crossed her aged face. "In the flesh. Not what you were expecting, hon?"

"I just, I..." Nadine shook her head. When she looked closely, she could see the resemblance between this woman in the chair and the avatar in that other place, the curve of her smile, the lines of her neck.

"Why is she here?" Jake growled.

"I thought I could take advantage of her expertise," Safan said.

"The expertise of a whore?"

"Language," Liz snapped, steel in her voice. "I'm Safan's top earner, but I'm also his head of electronic security. Who do you think found you in that silly restaurant and told you to call?"

"How old are you?" Nadine said.

"That's a distinctly indelicate question, young lady," Liz said. "Though if you must know, I'm old enough to remember why some people set command line displays to green letters on black. Now, shall we get down to it? Explain why you're here."

"Martin Taylor killed my girlfriend," Nadine said.

"Ah. So it's revenge, then." Liz shook her head sadly. "How utterly tedious. My dear child, Martin Taylor did no such thing. A corporation killed your girlfriend. And not to seem insensitive, but your misery is barely a rounding error in an average corporation's weekly allotment. But I'm glad to see you've put aside the pretense. You are Nadine Jiang, possibly a wanted terrorist, not that I'm judging. Many's the time I've been tempted to spit on my hands and hoist the black flag myself." She leaned forward to pin Nadine beneath an unnervingly piercing gaze. "The question here is, what makes your pain any more special than someone who lost a loved one in an industrial accident in Bangalore because it served to move some numbers on a balance sheet, hmm?"

Nadine looked away. "It feels more personal," she mumbled.

Liz stroked the cat, which butted its head against her hand. Its stripes were almost the same color as her eyes. "It always does to the person most affected." The chair swiveled toward the door. As it turned, Nadine caught a glimpse of something black and sleek on the side of Liz's head, clinging there like some alien artifact. "You do what you want, but I am uninterested in your private vendetta."

"It's not about revenge," Nadine said.

The chair stopped but did not turn back. Words floated over its high, well-worn back. "No? What, then?"

"I want...I want to make her death worth it. Make it mean something."

"So you want to change the world."

"I don't know. Maybe." She hesitated. "Do you know anything about some project, something called Mirage?"

The chair swiveled back. "No. Should I?"

"It's something Anna found, right before she died."

"Found where?"

"In their database."

"Tell me. Leave nothing out. No detail, however small."

"That might take a while."

"Then get to it."

Nadine told the story, then, of Anna, the woman with starlight in her hair: the night they danced together, the clothes on the floor, the morning coffee, the walls that came up around certain parts of Anna's life. She told them, these two strangers, about Marcus, and his screaming, howling, raging pain, the argument with Dan-boy, the Booker to the hospital and what happened when she tried to see him, make sure he was okay. She talked of the flight from the once-proud house by the sea, the mad dash in the small inflatable boat, Anna's casual violence, the trip to Tijuana Town, what came after. They listened to her speak, without interrupting, as tears leaked down Nadine's face. She told them of Thomas, the man who suffered and died on a shabby couch in an abandoned school turned community center, and how she held his hand as he went, so he would not die alone. Not like Anna had. As the story poured from her, she became aware, in a hazy sort of way, of the twin stars about which the narrative revolved: Anna, her creature of light; the all-devouring black maw of Martin Taylor, the man in the suit who'd so casually dismissed her life, and nearly dismissed Nadine's too. She left out nothing except the ghost in the machine, the voice in her head that might or might not be her own oncoming madness.

When she finished, Liz leaned back in her wheelchair and looked thoughtfully at her. Safan spoke first. "Has Jake been giving you his magic DoD-approved anti-PTSD pills?"

"Yes," Nadine said.

Safan grunted. "Funny thing. Even if you don't get shell shock, that doesn't mean you're okay. It just means you break different. He tell you that?"

"Go back to what happened in the tunnel," Liz interjected. "Tell me everything. You said your friends started screaming before the grenade was dropped?"

"Yes." Nadine closed her eyes and shivered. "It was like...like they went crazy or something."

"Of all the things you've said, I find that the most peculiar," Liz said. "How very interesting. I would dearly love to get a peek inside their network."

"I have every confidence if anyone can do it, you can," Safan said.

Liz smiled kindly at him. "I appreciate your confidence, but they're no slouches at network security, and probably even less so now. I'd need to get physical access to their network, or near enough, and our friend here just explained how that's likely to end."

"Okay, so how do they get to it, then?" Jake said. "I mean, people like Taylor must need to work when they're on the road, right?"

"Sure. His computer probably has a way to create a private encrypted tunnel into their network," Liz said.

"Then we steal his computer," Nadine said. "Easy."

The other three all turned to look at her. "You have an interesting definition of 'easy,'" Safan said at last.

"An executive's computer is a tempting prize," Liz said, "but it would probably not do much good. They're certain to be encrypted and biometrically locked."

"But it has to connect to a network somehow, right?" Nadine said. "What if we get him to connect to a network we have access to?"

Safan snorted. "I like your spirit, but it doesn't work like that."

"Well, I mean, it could, given enough time," Liz said. "If we could control what network he uses, that gives us leverage, but it's not like he's going to port in from some hotel somewhere. Terracone has a private penthouse suite for executive visits."

"So we break into that," Nadine said. "Gotta be easier than breaking into their headquarters, right?"

Silence settled around the table. Jake shifted in his seat. Liz looked thoughtful. "So," Safan said finally. "Who wants to be the first one to poke holes in that idea?"

Nobody spoke. Jake eyed Safan, who watched Liz stroke her cat, lips pursed. Nadine looked around at the three of them, willing the ground to open and swallow her up.

At last, Liz broke the silence. "It's not a terrible idea."

"Does that mean you're on board?" Jake said.

Silence. Safan and Liz exchanged a long look. Light scintillated in their contacts, hinting at some private communication, some quick hidden conversation neither Jake nor Nadine were privy to. Then, decision apparently reached, Safan nodded, the barest hint of motion.

"I have a network intercept device," Liz said. "Short range. Programmable and remote accessible. It will masquerade as an access point. If you can get it into the penthouse where Martin Taylor is staying, I might be able to use it to get access to his computer. Look for weaknesses in his security, wait for him to get sloppy, if we are really lucky leverage some unpatched vulnerability. Company computers tend to be locked down pretty tight but you'd be surprised how often they aren't updated. I'll give it to you before you leave."

"Hang on," Jake said. "We just came up with this idea and you happen to have this gizmo you need handy?"

Amusement wrote itself on Liz's lined face. She scratched the cat behind the ears. "Consider where we are."

"I have no idea where we are, except the ass end of Houston in some run-down commercial park. What is this place?"

"This used to be a data center for a company that did high-precision mapping," Liz said. "Safan bought it when they went under. Owner got busted by the SEC. Securities fraud, I believe. I repurposed it, set it up for remote administration, it's almost entirely lights out now. Only need to come here physically a few times a year, do stuff I can't do remotely. Safan said he wanted someplace to talk to you in private, figured kill two birds with one stone. Nobody knows we're connected to this place."

"This where your house of pleasure lives?"

Amusement again, there in her face. "Live backup of it. Good rule of business: if you make your money in the virtual world, never put your eggs in one basket. I also keep some other projects here. Excuse me a moment."

The chair spun. Machinery whined somewhere in its depths, and she was gone.

"Where'd you find her?" Jake said.

"That's a long and interesting story I have no intention of sharing with you." Safan took a thumb-sized bottle from his pocket and placed it on the table before him. A colorless liquid glinted within. "For you, in regards to that DNA profile you gave me. You sure about this?"

"You can never have too much insurance," Jake said. "I didn't expect you to get it so quickly."

"Money is a powerful motivator."

Nadine looked down at her shoes, the ones Jake had bought for her so long ago, there in the hotel. She'd switched off Net access from her implant that day, and hadn't switched it back on since, for fear of some errant packet of data making its way to Martin Taylor, betraying her whereabouts to the machinery commanded by the man who, presumably, still hunted her. But if Taylor knew about Jake, now, what was the point?

The door opened again. Nadine looked up at the whirr of electrical motors. Liz, the real one so different from her avatar, returned, a small black lozenge about the size of a pack of cards sharing space on her lap with the cat. Nadine wondered for a moment whether the avatar was in some way the more genuine version of her. Certainly the woman who looked out from behind those vibrant eyes in that age-ravaged face seemed to belong in a body perhaps a quarter her age. Even in the chair, she radiated crackling vitality.

Liz placed the black lozenge and a pair of small boxes on the table. "This will hide itself from most bug sweeps," she said, "but of course you'll need to find a place to put it where it won't be seen. There's a switch on the back. Don't turn it on until you have it in place. It will search out the closest jack point and then do a bit of sleight of hand, set itself up to take its place."

"Won't the real access point be password protected?" Jake said.

Amusement flitted across Liz's face once more. "I'm sure it will be."

Jake slipped the intercept device in his jacket pocket and picked up one of the boxes. The end slid open to reveal a small earpiece like a glittering jewel wrapped in translucent foam. "Wear them when you're in," Liz said. "I'll be monitoring the security response and jamming any alarms. I'll be able to talk to you without eavesdroppers."

Jake held the earpiece up to the light. "Range?"

"About two kilometers."

"Nice. Almost as good as I had in the army."

"Better," Liz said. "The private sector isn't bound by the procurement process. Things move faster."

"Why two?"

"You know why."

Jake's face hardened. "No. No way. This is a simple in and out. She's not going with me."

"You sure you're not thinking with the wrong head?" Safan said. "You're acting like it."

"Don't be ridiculous," Liz said. "Whatever is going on between them, it isn't that. She's more likely to shag a potted plant." She grinned at Jake. "No offense."

20

Miracles Take Time

N ADINE STEPPED ONTO the pavement and looked up through the bangs of the wig she wore. The executive penthouse owned by Terracone occupied the second floor from the top of a vertical slab of black glass just outside the city's core. An immaculately terraced plaza spread out from the tower's foot, a pleasing if bland expanse of carefully manicured shrubs, gleaming white walkways, stone picnic benches, and small black bubbling fountains. A handful of people in corporate casual sat chattering at one of the tables in the manner of work colleagues who liked each other well enough but would never choose to socialize of their own accord. A burly man in a light pink shirt sweated profusely as he paced nearby shouting at some unseen subordinate. A beat-up UPS delivery drone swooped by, just above head height, one rotor buzzing ominously.

On the ground floor, holographic ads danced in the windows. A monolith of white marble jutted up from the ground in front of the doors. A security guard in a white uniform barely glanced at the ID card Jake flashed. The earpiece crackled in Nadine's ear. "I've isolated and rerouted the alarm lines from the penthouse," Liz said. "You're clear to go. Glad to see your friend persuaded you to let her tag along."

"Some people, you just can't reach," Jake grumbled. "She's insistent."

"I bet. The elevator up to the penthouse is ten meters ahead and then right. It's the small door farthest to the right."

They went through the lobby, all gilt and faux marble, Nadine feeling distinctly uncomfortable in her delivery uniform. Jake wore one just like it, nondescript blue denim with a patch sewn on the shoulder that could've been from one of any of a dozen different Houston courier services. "They all look pretty much the same," Safan had said when he'd called them to tell them the uniforms were on the way. And sure enough, the courier who'd dropped the package off wore an outfit just like it, with a patch on the shoulder advertising whatever courier service he worked for. Nadine had forgotten what it looked like the instant he was out of sight.

"Don't people normally do this sort of thing at night?" she hissed to Jake as they made their way to the elevator, studiously avoiding the gaze of the business drones waiting for the more public elevators. The smell of coffee and donuts from a small coffee shop in the lobby made her mouth water.

Her earpiece crackled. "Night's when Taylor will be home," Safan said. "He's out now. So, you go in now."

"His security?" Nadine muttered under her voice.

"Took the bait. They think you're on your way to a meeting with a friend of Jake's on the other side of town. Bad neighborhood. Gangs, drugs. Good place for an ambush."

"See? Told you we shouldn't destroy the bug." Jake took the card that had also been in the package with the uniforms and touched it to the blank white rectangle on the lonely elevator a fair distance from the others. No buttons on that elevator, no lights to let anyone know where it was, just a door of shiny brass-colored metal and the no-nonsense card reader.

A light on the reader turned green. Somewhere above them, machinery whirred. The door slid open.

Once they were alone in the elevator, Jake cleared his throat. "Sure do hope you're right about the alarms," he said.

"I'm right." Liz's disembodied voice, cool and sultry in Nadine's ear.

Jake glanced at Nadine. "I still don't know why you were so keen on coming. This is a one-person job. Easy. In and out, no muss, no fuss."

"Then it's not a problem if I'm here," Nadine said. He sighed and shook his head.

Nadine tapped her foot. The ride seemed to take an eternity. No music, here in this elevator, just three mirrored walls and the faint rattle and hum of equipment. Jake stood still, carrying the empty cardboard box emblazoned with the FedEx logo, with a detached calm Nadine desperately wished she could feel.

The elevator dinged. The door slid open into a hallway, gleaming hardwood floor, tasteful plants in bronze planters that matched the elevator trim. At the end, a frosted glass door with a squat card reader and a number key beneath.

Jake passed his card over the reader. A green light came on. "Six eight eight two three," Liz said in the earpieces.

The door buzzed when Jake punched in the number. He whistled. "You really need to tell me how you found that out."

"No, I don't," Liz said. "Alarm panel on the wall to your right, keypad on it."

Jake slid open a small glass door set in the wall. "Got it."

"Red light blinking?"

"Yeah."

"Okay, silent entry alarm just tripped. You have fifteen seconds to punch in the disarm code. That, I don't have. No matter, though. It rings to Terracone's private security room, but not to worry, there's just been a routing glitch. I'm afraid they won't get the alert."

"You're like a fairy godmother," Jake said.

Low, throaty chuckle over the comm link. "You have no idea how many times I've heard that. Usually in a different context."

"Usually?"

"Focus, please. Through the foyer into the living room. You'll see a large set of shelves on the left, little doors underneath."

"Roger that."

Nadine's heart hammered as she followed Jake through the short entryway, past a shoe rack that looked fantastically expensive and a set of folding doors she imagined opened into a coat closet, and out into the main living space.

Nadine stopped dead in her tracks. "Fuck me," she breathed. The vast space, larger than the entire house she'd shared with Olivia, looked down through floor-to-ceiling windows at the Houston skyline in the distance. Thick, dense white carpet sank beneath her feet. To the right, the room melded seamlessly into a vast, luxuriously appointed kitchen, polished granite countertops over the island sink and the huge six-burner gas stove. To the left, a square sofa group big enough for a dozen people, upholstered in white leather. Beyond it, the shelves of polished wood built into the wall, compact doors underneath, an enormous holographic entertainment system above, next to a bar set stocked with expensive-looking bottles. Past that, a door, and a hallway leading, Nadine imagined, to a bedroom, or bedrooms, all just as decadently appointed.

Jake, already halfway to the shelves, turned. "You okay?"

"It's not right," Nadine said.

"What?"

"It's not right. He murdered my—murdered Anna and the others, and he gets to live like this." Her fingers curled around the slender glass tube she'd slipped into a pocket when Jake wasn't looking. "It's not right."

"No, it's not. He's a terrible person and he shouldn't get away with it. But we have a job to do and not a lot of time. What's next?"

Liz's voice crackled through the earpieces. "Somewhere on that wall, probably in the doors beneath the holoscreen, you'll find the network access port."

Jake rummaged around for a bit. "Got it. Next?"

"Okay. Here's what you need to do. Take the intercept device…"

Blood roared in Nadine's ears, drowning them out. Her body shook. "It's not right," she repeated. Jake, on hands and knees, head inside a tangle of electronics beneath the shelves, didn't reply.

Nadine picked up a heavy bottle of scotch carved like cut crystal, the only bottle in the bar set not still sealed shut. Amber liquid filled it about a third of the way. She pulled off the absurdly large cap fastened to a long cork. From somewhere outside herself, mind blank with a mixture of static and voiceless anger, she watched her hand drift to her pocket.

"Freeze." The voice, cultured and mannered, filtered and processed by years of education in the most expensive private schools and universities the world had to offer, came from somewhere behind them.

Still without conscious thought, Nadine found herself slowly pouring a large splash of scotch into one of the heavy cut-glass tumblers. The voice came again: "Turn around slowly. Let me see your hands."

Nadine turned slowly, bottle in one hand, tumbler in the other. Martin Taylor stood there, near the hallway from the foyer, one hand holding a briefcase, the other a black pistol. A yellow triangle with an exclamation point floated in the air, stating the obvious. "You too," he said to Jake.

"What's going on?" Liz's voice came in Nadine's ear.

Jake backed slowly out from beneath the shelves, empty-handed. He rose slowly, without sudden moves, arms out, his one palm up.

"Good. Like that. Nice and slow. You two have just solved a sticky problem for me. I do believe some people on the Board of Directors were seriously considering firing me. I have to hand it to you. That was a clever thing you did with that media package. You should be proud. You played a losing hand well. Ah, ah, don't even think about it." The gun swiveled to Jake. "I know that look. It's the look of someone about to do something stupid. I recognize it because I know your kind very well."

"You don't know a thing about me," Jake spat.

"Oh, but I do. I commanded men just like you in Afghanistan. I command men just like you in the private sector. Legs apart. Hands—well, hand, I should say—behind your head."

Eyes flaming with hate, Jake put his hand and claw behind his head. "Good," Martin said. "You've caused significant inconvenience for me. But now that you've turned up at my home and I was forced to kill you in self-defense, I'd say that ties things up nicely. You played a losing hand well, but it was still a losing hand."

Nadine swallowed half the scotch in a single gulp. She set the bottle on the shelf and wiped her mouth with the back of her hand. "So what happens now?"

"Now? You die, of course. Preferably in the bathroom. This carpet is worth more than both your lives. Speaking literally, not metaphorically. You didn't think I'd move in here without putting in some extra security of my own, did you? Now move." He gestured with the gun. "Both of you. That way."

Liz's voice came again. "Fuck. Don't do it."

"I don't suppose we have much choice," Nadine muttered.

"Quite so," Martin said.

Jake and Nadine moved across the room, Jake's hands still behind his head. Martin stayed out of reach, eyes bright and alert. Nadine set the tumbler on the coffee table as she passed. Martin circled around, keeping the table between himself and the two of them. He bent to set down his briefcase, eyes not leaving them, gun tracking them with laser precision.

"So, what, you're going to just shoot us yourself?" Nadine said.

A ghost of a smile flickered across Martin's face and was gone. "My security team is on the way back. I considered holding you here until they arrive, but we all know what happened last time I tried to delegate your death. Some jobs you really must do yourself. Still, you did well. Sending them on a wild goose chase was a stroke of inspiration. You should be proud of making it as far as you did. I would love to interrogate you about how you defeated the main alarm system here, but at this point, I think I just want you gone. Back up. No sudden moves. I really don't want to have to replace the carpet, but I will if I must."

"You don't need to kill us," Nadine said.

"No? Perhaps I don't. But you do need to die, and I'm here with a gun, so..." With a shrug, he scooped the tumbler from the coffee table and raised it to his lips. "No sense wasting good scotch."

"You know what?" Jake said, lowering his arms. "Fuck your carpet."

"Jake, no!" Nadine hissed.

"No? Why not?" Jake said. "This sonofabitch is going to kill us either way. Might as well inconvenience him."

"No!" Gears turned furiously in Nadine's head. "He wants to know how we got in here. Maybe he won't kill us if we tell him about the... you know."

Martin lifted a fastidiously groomed eyebrow. "Careful now," Liz said in Nadine's ear.

"Nadine, it's over," Jake said, his voice tired. "We made it as far as we could. There's no way out." He turned to Martin. "Do it, asshole."

"Jake!" Nadine said. Then, "Listen. You asked how we got in here. There's a man, old Army buddy of Jake's." Liz said something in her ear, but Nadine paid no attention, not like she could hear over the roaring of blood anyway. "He knew a guy who knew a guy who happened to be a low-level employee of Terracone Research. You stop to think why we came here, of all places? Right into the lion's den? When we could have gone anywhere? Think, Martin! You're not stupid. Mirage."

"Nadine, what the fuck are you talking about?" Jake said. That dangerous light was back in his eyes, the one she'd seen in the abandoned subway tunnel. "Have you lost your mind?"

"Shut up, or I will shoot you in the stomach and let you bleed out," Martin said, in the same matter-of-fact tone he might use to have his car brought around. "It hurts a lot." He shifted the gun, just a fraction, pointing it at Jake. "Do please go on," he said to Nadine.

Nadine's heart pounded, roar in her ears smoothing into background static. "You shouldn't have done what you did," she said, the words coming out in a rush, no plan or intention, tumbling from her lips fully-formed before she even realized what she was going to say. *Stall him*, she told herself. *Every second he's listening is a second he's not shooting us.* She felt her face harden, become a mask of confidence she didn't feel, let a tiny note of sneering cockiness into her voice. "You've got dissension in your ranks. That video I uploaded, you said it yourself. Problems in the boardroom. Did you really think it stopped there? Just like a CEO, never thinking about the little people. Lot of folks make their living working for you, they weren't too happy about what you did. Folks like the janitors, the low-level techs. Some of them know the passcode. Some of them have keycards. The rot's spread, Martin Taylor, and you're just too shortsighted to see it. Too stuck on yourself. You—"

Martin sighed. "You're stalling. Playing a bad hand well, once again. You're smart. Determined, too. I like that. It's over now. Goodbye." He raised the gun. His expression changed, just a little. "I think—I—" His skin flushed.

Jake roared. Martin blinked, like he was distracted by something only he could hear. He blinked again and turned the gun toward Jake. The yellow triangle with the line followed. Time slowed. Nadine saw Jake rushing forward, a blurred outline in front of him, mathematical constraints on the possibility of motion, an electronic soothsayer looking a tenth of a second into the future. A fan from Martin's arm, the gun, intersecting...

Martin's lips moved. He crumpled without a sound, a split second before Jake reached him, his mouth opening and closing like a fish's. He tried to bring the gun up, moving his entire arm, awkward and clumsy. Jake's foot flashed out, following a glowing arc, connected with his wrist. The gun tumbled away, noiseless in soft white carpet.

Martin flailed on his back, eyes wide, one hand against his throat, where his spotless Oxford shirt met the flawless knot of his conservative navy-blue tie. Jake frowned. "What the hell is wrong with him?"

"Anaphylaxis," Nadine said.

"You didn't."

"We had it. I used it." She cast around, ignoring the man flopping on the floor, eyes bulging, skin going bright pink. "Where is it?" Her eyes fell on the briefcase. "Ah." She flipped it open, pulled out his laptop, touched the stud. A hologram floated in the air, white padlock on a blue background. "Goddamn it!" she swore.

"Nadine, what are you doing?"

"What we came here to do." She watched her hands fumble at the terminal, watched herself turn to Martin, whose wrists had swelled like balloons. A vein pulsed in his forehead. "No!" she barked at him. "You don't get to die just yet! There's still something I need you to do." She knelt beside him on the luxurious carpet and pried open one of his eyes. He glared at her. A red arc blurred from his fist, turning yellow as she twisted away. She knelt on his forearm as she held the terminal up to his eye. The padlock icon vanished. "Got it. Let's go."

"But—"

"We have his computer! What more do we need? Come on!"

Nadine raced for the door with Jake behind her. The electric whir of the elevator filled the long hallway outside. "Liz!" Nadine said. "Trouble on the way. Can you stop the elevator?"

"Not from here," Liz's disembodied voice said.

"Emergency exit! There must be a fire escape, something, right?"

"Fuck!" Jake said. "The intercept gizmo. It's in the penthouse. I need to get it."

"Leave it!" Nadine said.

"No," Liz said. "He's right. They can't find it there. Were you able to unlock his computer?"

"Yes."

"Good. Don't let it go to sleep. Stairway next to the elevator."

Nadine looked at the elevator door, blank mahogany walls on each side. "No."

"What do you mean, no? I'm looking right at it on the blueprints. Door to the left of the elevator. Stairs leading down."

"I mean no! No door! No stairs!"

"Look harder. It's there."

Nadine looked for Jake, who was nowhere to be seen. She tapped on the wall next to the elevator, then hammered on it with her fists. The whine of the elevator grew louder. "Jake! We need to go, now!"

Jake reappeared, shoving something bulky in his pocket. "Got it," he panted. "Got his gun too. Now what?"

"Supposed to be a door here, Liz says, but I can't find it. I think the elevator's almost here."

Jake ran his hands over the blank wall. "There's no door."

"There's a door," Liz said. "It's there."

Jake patted his pockets, looking for the card that had opened the elevator door. He held it against the smoothly polished, gleaming wall. With a dull thunk, part of the wall swung open. "Bingo."

"Stairs down," Liz said. "Now."

The elevator dinged. Jake and Nadine pushed through into a stairwell, smooth blank concrete on one side, a breathtaking panorama of Houston through thick glass on the other. Nadine held her breath. Jake closed the door quietly as the elevator door rattled open. Jake leaned against the door, panting. "I could do with a bit less of that." He glared at Nadine. "You and me, we need to talk."

"Not now," Liz said. "Down the stairs. It's 49 floors, no other exits until you get to the ground floor. If you two get caught there you're sitting ducks. I've disabled the motion sensors in the stairway but who knows what other alarms your friend might've planted. Make sure that computer doesn't go to sleep or this is all for nothing. Van's waiting."

Nadine stuck her thumb in the computer's lid to keep it from closing. Heartbeat still thudding against the white noise, one hand on the smooth rail, she pounded down the stairs as fast as she dared. The sun sleeted through the immense wall of glass glass into the hothouse of the stairway. At each landing, a motion sensor with a winking LED stared down at them. "Who designs a fire escape like this?" she panted.

"Someone who didn't think about needing to find your keycard in the middle of a fire, I imagine," Jake said.

Nadine kept her finger on the scroll pad of the computer, stroking in small circles as they raced down the stairs. Her world shrank to just this moment, this place: gray concrete, hard-edged steps, suffocating heat, the weirdly contradictory beauty of the vista through the window. Every foot placed just so, to give her the maximum possible speed without sending her tumbling down the stairs in a pinwheel of broken bones. Landing, turn, more steps, back and forth, an endless zigzag. "What," she panted between steps, "what happens if they catch us?"

"Depends who catches us," Jake said.

"What are the possibilities?"

"Police? Arrest, extraordinary rendition, enhanced interrogation, terrorism charges. Your video monkeywrenched the nice tidy narrative, but they'll probably be inclined to let the prosecutors and the courts sort it out, perhaps, if we're lucky. Meanwhile we rot in a concrete cell. Taylor's people? Taken to an undisclosed location, tortured on general principle, shot in the back of the head. They'll have heard what you did to their compatriots in LA."

Landing, turn, steps. Red LED of a motion sensor that Liz, somewhere far from this fire escape, was presumably silencing, its electronic squawk cut short for none to hear. "Then let's not get caught."

They pounded down the stairs, Nadine in the lead, endless back and forth of hard unyielding gray, until nothing existed but the hammering of Nadine's heart and the dull slap of her feet on the stairs. When at last they reached the bottom floor, she stopped short, not sure what to do. Another motion sensor looked down at them.

Four gray walls, the foot of the stairs, blue-painted metal rail, plain blue steel door with a silver lever. Jake reached for the door.

"Stop." Liz's voice, urgent in their ears.

Jake froze. "What?"

"Security. Two of them, just outside the door. I see them on the camera."

Jake held his breath. "Fuck."

"Stay put," Liz said. "Lot of chatter right now. They found Martin Taylor. No sign they think it's foul play. If we're lucky, they might not realize you were ever there. Police are en route. They'll pull the security off that door soon. No point standing in front of a fire escape if they know nobody's coming down, right?"

Jake let out a long exhale. "Okay, we wait."

A red triangle appeared above the stolen terminal. "Fuck!" Nadine said. "Fuck fuck fuck!"

"What?"

"What kind of hotshot corporate executive doesn't charge his computer? Do you have a memory card?"

Jake patted down his pockets. "Why?"

"So I can copy files off this thing before it dies!" Nadine held out her hand impatiently. Jake fished a compact card from his pocket. She took it and turned the computer around. "Fuck!" she swore.

"What now?"

"Everything except the headset port is filled with something hard!"

"Figures," Liz's voice said. "Hotshot executives sometimes get computers with all the ports disabled to keep them from doing something dumb. Occasionally they're sealed off completely at the factory. Do not let that computer sleep and don't let the battery die or we're screwed."

"If you have any ideas, I'm all over it," Jake said.

"Police inbound, ETA six minutes," Liz's voice said. "Give me a second. I have a plan."

"Make it a good one."

Nadine watched herself kick the concrete wall in frustration, as if from some place outside her body. She noted with interest the scuff marks on the boots Jake had bought for her, the fact that one of the laces had lost the little plastic thing on the end and was starting to fray. The symbol floated in midair above the computer, a red triangle with a lightning bolt in the center. "Running out of time," she muttered. "Running out of time."

"Working on it, hon," Liz said, an unseen presence in her ear. "Miracles take time."

Nadine slumped on the bottom step, concrete wall hard and warm through her thin shirt. "Not sure we got that."

"I'm on it." Burr of annoyance in Liz's normally sultry tones. "It takes as long as it takes. We succeed or we don't."

"Fuck!"

"No plan survives contact with the enemy."

"Jesus, don't tell me you're military, too!"

"Let me work."

Minutes ticked by in strained silence. Nadine stood, paced the small landing at the bottom of the stairs like a caged tiger, then sat again. Her finger jerked back and forth across the scroll pad. The red icon winked. Jake stood motionless in front of the door in a relaxed, loose-limbed stance, cool and ready. Sweat dripped in Nadine's eyes.

Finally, the earpiece crackled. "Okay, got a miracle coming up... hang on, get ready to go. Quiet. Fast. Hard left once you're through the door. Keep your heads down. Parking lot behind the building, van will be waiting between the loading dock and the dumpsters. Glitching the camera, and...go! Go now!"

Jake slipped open the door just wide enough to slide through, smooth and fast, like a ballet dancer or one of those martial artists from the movies Nadine watched as a kid. She slipped through after him. He ran, low and surprisingly fast, hugging the wall. Nadine risked a peek behind her. At the corner of the building, a Houston police car, all black angles like a shark, sat idling. Red and blue light strobed against the wall. Of the security guards, she saw no sign.

A white electric van with dark-tinted windows sat parked next to a gigantic green trash container behind the tower. The stench of rancid grease and hot asphalt rippled in slow waves through the air. The van's back doors swung open. "Go, go!" Jake said.

The moment they were in, Jake pulled the door shut. Dense blue industrial carpet covered the floor. Metal shelves lined the walls, with toolboxes and bits of equipment Nadine couldn't identify lashed down against sudden motion. A young, heavily tattooed man in a red shirt sat in the driver's seat, Safan beside him in the passenger seat. "Give me the computer," Safan said.

"Battery's almost dead,"Nadine said as she passed it to him. "Keep your finger on the pad. Don't let it sleep."

"Cables in the bin on the right-hand side. No, your other right. Yes, there, bottom tray."

Nadine tore through the tray, clumsy in her haste, sending bundles of cables sealed in white and silver zip-locked bags to the floor. The kid in the driver's seat pulled them around the building, manual control. "Here! This one?"

Safan tore open the pouch. "No. Marax, not Sendai. There."

Nadine passed up another cable. Safan plugged one end into Martin's computer and the other into the outlet on the dash. The computer chirped. Nadine let out the breath she hadn't realized she'd been holding.

"Well done," Liz said in her ears. "That should give us access and a window into the Terracone network. Now get your asses back here, and let us see what there is to see."

21

The Keys to the Kingdom

"WHAT THE FUCK did you think you were doing?" Jake spat each word like a bullet from a rifle, face contorted with rage. Crazy, dangerous light blazed in his eyes.

Nadine faced him squarely, arms folded across her chest. She thought maybe she should be afraid, or angry, something, in the heat of his rage, but she felt nothing, and marveled at the void where her emotions should be. She looked at him levelly, neither moving nor speaking.

"I knew it was a bad idea to bring you," he went on. His prosthetic whirred as he flung his arms out. "I never should have done that. I should have listened to my gut. You can't be trusted! What was I thinking? What were *you* thinking? This was about intelligence, not your petty revenge fantasy! We had a goddamn plan!"

"If you hadn't brought me," Nadine said mildly, "you would be dead right now. If we had stuck to the plan, we might both be dead right now. I improvised. We got what we were after."

"That's not the point!" he thundered. "We got what we were after because we got lucky. Again. Either you can be counted on to do your part or you're worthless. Worse than worthless!" He leaned in close, hand balled into a fist. "You didn't think. I put my ass on the line for you, and you pull a stunt like this? Did you even think to tell me? Did you think that you were putting the mission at risk? Suppose he'd come in and had a drink before he settled down in front of his computer. Where would you be then? You told me you wanted information. You said you wanted to find out why your friends died. Bullshit! You lied to me. You lied to all of us. This wasn't about information. You wanted revenge, and you didn't care who you might hurt to get it."

"She's right, you know," Liz said.

They stood in an air-conditioned office attached to a small warehouse in a decaying industrial zone north of the heart of Houston. The building boom had passed the entire neighborhood by, leaving it to squalor. Safan directed the kid, who he hadn't bothered introducing to Jake and Nadine, to drop them off. After he left, it occurred to Nadine he hadn't spoken a single word.

Liz had accepted the laptop with the reverence of an archaeologist finding a sacred object deep in the heart of some long-buried temple. The first thing she'd done was set it inside a steel cage made of grilles that reminded Nadine of the mesh inside the door of a microwave oven, behind the glass. Once it was safely tucked away and connected to power, Jake's rage surfaced.

He spun around to face her. "No. No, you don't get to defend her. What if we had placed your little network intercept whatsit in that penthouse and then Taylor had died? Did you think about that? They would have investigated. They'd have found it, and I bet there'd be something in there that would lead them back to you."

"Don't be so sure," Safan said. "And if that happened, we would deal with it. It didn't. You got what you wanted, Elizabeth got what she wanted, your friend got what she wanted."

"You know better than that!" Jake snarled. "I can't work with her if I can't trust her. She went in there intending to kill him, and could have screwed everything up."

"I didn't—" Nadine started.

"Didn't what? Didn't go there to kill him?" Jake jabbed his finger at Nadine. "Don't. Don't even. You brought the stuff with you. That's premeditation. You knew exactly why you were there."

"How do you know Terracone won't be tracing that computer?" Nadine said.

"Oh, nobody's tracing anything," Liz said. "Not with it caged away like that. Over the next few hours, we'll spoof the GPS, make them think it's heading out on a container ship to parts unknown. They'll try to remote-wipe it, of course." She grinned nastily. "It won't work, but they won't know that. They've given up the keys to the kingdom. Won't be long before all their dirty little corporate secrets are mine. All in all, a success beyond what we could have hoped for, Jake's concerns notwithstanding."

Jake's face darkened. "My concerns—"

Safan held up his hand. "Concerns I share." He turned his attention to Nadine. "I would like to hear your account. Is what Jake says true? Did you go there intending to kill Martin Taylor?"

Nadine shook her head. The strange detachment clung to her, like some emotional armor. "No."

"But you did bring the engineered poison."

"Yes."

"Poison you knew was tuned to his DNA, designed to provoke a fatal autoimmune response."

"Yes. I—" She hesitated. "I honestly don't know why I brought it. I saw it sitting there, when we were getting ready to leave. I thought, better to have it and not need it than need it and not have it. So..." She shrugged. "I put it in my pocket and forgot about it."

"But you used it."

"Yes." She looked from Safan, who watched her intently with hard eyes, to Jake, his face suffused with rage, to Liz, who watched her with aloof indifference. "I don't know if I can explain."

"Try," Safan said.

"I went into that elevator intending to do exactly what we set out to do. Get access to the penthouse, plant that network whatever it is, leave. I sorta knew, I guess, that it would be a nice place. But when we got there..." Her voice trailed off.

Safan leaned forward. "Go on," he said, voice low and dangerous.

"It's not right," Nadine whispered.

"I'm sorry?"

"It's not right!" Her hands balled into fists. "None of it! That a man like that should live that way, after what he did. It's not fair. It's not just."

"Fairness and justice," Liz said, "have never been currency in particularly high regard. Graveyards are filled with the just and the unjust alike. You want to know the difference? The unjust more often achieved what they wanted to. The easiest path to success is on other people's backs."

Nadine hung her head. "So you poisoned his drink," Safan said.

"Yes. It was the only bottle that was open. I thought that probably meant it was his."

"And if he had come home and had a drink before he used his computer?"

"I didn't think about that."

"What then?"

"When he showed up," Nadine said, "I expected him to kill us on the spot. The only reason we're still alive is he kept going on and on and on about his fucking carpet." Her fists clenched so tightly her nails bit into her palms. "Like, he told us point blank that carpet was more important than we were! So I drank half the whiskey and put the rest right in front of him. I thought, if we can just keep him yapping long enough to drink it... And he wouldn't suspect, right? He saw me, right? Lucky for us it worked."

"Yeah. Lucky," Safan said. "And if it hadn't?"

"Then I would have charged him, he would've shot me, and Jake would've killed him."

"How did you expect to survive that?" Liz said.

"Survive?" Nadine looked puzzled. "I didn't."

"People who don't care if they live or die are a hazard to everyone on the team," Jake said.

Nadine spun. "You don't care if you live or die!" she spat. "I've seen you! You were ready to jump him after he poisoned himself. Don't you dare. Don't you even."

"Maybe," Jake said, "but I have it under control. You don't. You're a loose cannon and you almost screwed the whole operation."

"I saved our asses!"

"You jeopardized our mission! You went way out of bounds, and you know it!" Jake jabbed his finger in the air. "I'm out. I cannot work with you any more. You're too much of a risk."

"Where will you go?" Liz said. "You have to assume your RV is not safe."

He waved his hand in the air as he stormed away. Liz sighed and shook her head. "That's unfortunate."

"His choice," Safan said. He sat back and looked at Nadine through narrowed eyes. "Can't say I blame him. You came out aces up, but he's right. You screwed up. The outcome doesn't excuse the methods. You should not have done what you did."

"Leave the girl alone," Liz said. "She handled herself well. Sometimes the outcome does excuse the methods. You of all people know that."

"What do we do with her?"

A smile wreathed Liz's aged face. "She can stay with me."

Two heads snapped around to stare at her. "That's not necessary—" Nadine said.

"That's not a good—" Sefan said at the same moment.

"Wrong," Liz said. "Both of you. It's necessary and it's a good idea. We stand at an extraordinary moment. Access to a defense contractor's internal systems will pay dividends for years. I don't know if you're fully aware of what a coup this is, and it's all thanks to Nadine here. Or Melody, or whatever you prefer to be called. So here's what I suggest we do. I will tuck her somewhere safe, and I will see what secrets I can sweet-talk the Terracone corporate mainframe into giving up. And if I find something that pertains to this Mirage you're looking for, so much the better."

"So what now?" Nadine said.

"Now? Now I find a place to put you, and then I start rummaging around in Terracone's underwear drawer."

"And Jake?"

Liz made a dismissive gesture. "Leave him to me. I know his kind. He'll come around."

Liz lived in a modest apartment in Bellaire. Nadine looked out the window at a neighborhood near the old interstate that had clearly fallen into squalor in the past couple of decades, but now seemed to be gently gentrifying again. New, sprawling, blandly generic houses gave way to older, quirkier houses with strangely-shaped bay windows, which in turn gave way to apartment complexes hiding behind black iron fences.

Nadine rode in the passenger seat of a Chinese electric minivan. The driver's seat had been removed and replaced with a platform that mated with Liz's wheelchair. She drove with a steering yoke outfitted with brake and accelerator levers, even though the van was clearly equipped for self-driving. "Why do you drive manually?" Nadine said.

"Child, if you knew what I know about the software that drives for you, you'd never get into a Booker again," Liz said. "Put every programmer at every automaker in the world who knows anything about security in a room together and you wouldn't have enough people to field a rugby team."

"So how come we don't hear about people's cars getting hacked all the time?" Nadine said.

Liz glanced over at her with a sour expression. "Mostly because there's not enough money in it. It's not worth hacking low-value targets, and high-value targets know better. You're a high-value target now, hon. Best start thinking like one."

"Is that what you are? A high-value target?"

Liz smiled without a word.

The apartment itself was a ground-floor unit in the back of a C-shaped cluster of apartment buildings within spitting distance of the freeway, swirling arcs of concrete and steel between the complex and the vertical towers of the Houston skyline. Liz unlocked the door with a large, heavy key with two rows of teeth along a groove down the center. The bolt retracted with a thunk. She pushed the massive door open. The chair whirred. The ancient tabby waited at the door, climbing into her lap the moment she was through. "Well, come on, child! Don't just stand there like a cat that doesn't know if it wants to be in or out!"

"No fingerprint scanner?" Nadine said. "No retinal scanner?"

"You know what's wrong with biometrics?" Liz said. "They break the first two rules of good security. Everyone knows your password, and you can't change it. If your friend Martin had used a simple password instead of a fancy biometric lock on his computer, we'd be right fucked, wouldn't we? Convenience over smarts. Gets 'em every time. Even the ones who should know better. Lock the door behind you, hon."

Nadine levered the door shut with her shoulder. It seemed curiously heavy, and reluctant to move. As soon as she latched it, Liz spun her chair to face her. "So, here you are," she said. "The big bad man who killed your friends is dead. How does that make you feel? Have the scales of justice balanced? Is your need for vengeance slaked?"

Nadine blinked. "It wasn't about vengeance. Isn't. Isn't about vengeance."

"No?" Liz skewered her with a piercing gaze. "Not even a little bit? You said it wasn't right. Have you made it right?"

"I don't even know what that means."

The chair glided toward her with a whirr. "What do you want?"

"I don't...I want to find out why."

"Why? What if there is no why? What if the why is a corporation found it more convenient to its bottom line to make you and your friends die? You think Martin Taylor was a monster. He wasn't. He was an ordinary man. And believe me, there is little on God's green earth more ordinary or tedious than ordinary men doing monstrous things for tedious reasons. He was alive. Now he's dead. Tomorrow another ordinary man will take his place, and the world will go on, same as it ever was."

"You're a cynic."

"I'm older than you, hon. Seen it all before. You didn't answer my question. How does that make you feel?"

"I guess…" Nadine frowned as she probed her feelings. "I guess I'm just surprised it was so simple. He drank the whiskey and he died."

"What did you expect? A climactic showdown? Drama and excitement? He was a man, not a video game boss. It's a remarkably simple thing, to kill a man." She narrowed her eyes. "But you know that already. You're a stone killer. It's in you, part of who you are."

"I'm not!" Nadine protested.

"You would've killed Andrew if you could've. You tried."

"Andrew? Who's Andrew?"

"The man you almost shot at Safan's office. You didn't even bother to learn his name. You would've killed him for no other reason than he was in your way. Didn't think two steps ahead, did you? You think Safan would've agreed to help you if you shot his man in cold blood on his doorstep?"

"He attacked us first!" Nadine said.

"Sure. Fine. He hit you first, so it's totally okay to splatter his brains on the sidewalk. Someday, maybe we'll have a talk about proportionate force. Can't help noticing you still haven't answered my question. How do you feel?"

"How do I feel? Angry! Frustrated!"

"Why?"

"Because you're needling me!"

"Huh. Hell of a thing, kill the guy who murdered your girlfriend, and what's got you worked up is an old woman's questions."

Nadine glared at Liz. She returned the stare levelly until finally Nadine dropped her gaze. "You know," Liz said, "Jake's not wrong."

"I saved us back there! If we'd have done it his way, at least one of us would be dead!"

"Nobody's arguing that," Liz said. "But the thing is, you didn't trust him. You didn't tell him you had another idea. You got lucky, more lucky than you realize. Way more lucky than you had any right to be. That's what saved your ass. Maybe if you'd trusted Jake enough to let him know what you were doing, he wouldn't be so mad. Everything I've seen of you, you don't think two inches in front of your nose. You're rash. You're impulsive. You make choices without understanding why."

"So what, you're on his side now? Why'd you take me here, then?"

"Hon, I'm not on any side. I'm just calling it like I see it. You want some coffee?"

Nadine folded her arms. "Sure."

"Good. Coffee's in the top left cupboard in the kitchen. Coffee maker's on the counter, cups on the hanger right above it. Make me a cup while you're at it." She scratched the cat's ears. "Black, no sugar."

When Nadine carried the steaming mugs back into the living room, Liz bade her sit on an overstuffed couch covered with a scratchy floral fabric. They regarded one another over the rims of their cups without speaking. Nadine couldn't shake the feeling that Liz was studying her the way a biologist might study a newly-discovered species of beetle, watching to see if it would do something interesting. Eventually, Nadine broke the silence. "What now?"

"I finish this coffee you've kindly prepared for me, then I get to work. There's a spare bedroom down the hall on the right. Please feel free to make yourself at home."

"I don't have anything," Nadine said. "Not even a toothbrush. Just some credit chips and the clothes I'm wearing. Everything else is in the RV, and..."

"...it's not safe to go back there," Liz finished. "I'm sure there's an extra toothbrush around here somewhere."

Nadine set her cup on the table. "So is this where you..." Her voice trailed off.

"Whore from?"

"I wasn't going to put it like that."

"Yes. I have a studio in one of the spare bedrooms. Motion capture equipment, high bandwidth net access, everything a girl needs."

"If you know so much about security stuff, why do you—"

"Pretend to fuck people in virtual space? It's okay, you can say it. It's easy, it pays well, I set my own hours, and I meet interesting people. Plus computer security is a young person's game. Not a lot of work for someone my age. You know how you can tell a field isn't a meritocracy? When they try really hard to convince you that it is." She grinned. "I've forgotten more than those kids will ever know, which is exactly why your friends at Terracone will never know what hit them. Speaking of which..." She set her own mug down. "If you'll excuse me, I have some laws to break." Her eyes gleamed.

Liz locked herself away in the room she called her studio, which Nadine gathered also served as her office. She poked around the apartment. The spare bedroom Liz offered was comfortable if uninspired, with a large soft bed neatly made and a bare nightstand that spoke of little use. A large bathroom with an enormous walk-in tub connected it to the master bedroom. Nadine poked her nose in to find a space uncannily like the room in the VR brothel: same huge four-poster bed of wood polished until it gleamed, same fussy, complicated roll-top desk. A half-burnt candle, now extinguished, sent fingers of wax over the edge of the desk.

Nadine drew a bath and sat in the tub until her fingers and toes shriveled, staring blankly at the space, probing at her feelings. Martin Taylor's anticlimactic death brought her no catharsis, no sense of release. She'd tried to make him the personification of all her pain, but Liz was right—another person would take his place, and the world would keep on in its eccentric orbit. Without Anna.

Did you think it would be otherwise? Anna's voice, a murmur in the air behind her.

"I miss you so much."

This still isn't over. Find out why I died. Find a way to tell the truth.

"Will I feel better after that?"

Probably not. The difference between vengeance and justice is that vengeance is about your feelings. Justice is about making the world better for people who don't even know you.

"What's the point of a better world without you in it?"

That's sweet, but I'm never coming back. Make it mean something.

Liz was still tucked away doing whatever it was she was doing when Nadine rose, dried, and re-dressed in the same clothes she'd worn for days. She checked her pockets for the bank chips and Melody's passport, then rummaged in the refrigerator.

By the time Liz finally emerged, Nadine had finished her first serving of eggs and bacon and sausage and was midway through her second. "Smells good," Liz said. "Did you make any for me?"

Nadine nodded, mouth full, and prepared a plate. Liz regarded her thoughtfully. "Maybe I should keep you around. You're useful."

"Don't even," Nadine said.

"I suppose not. Though I am glad to see you making yourself at home. Your friends at Terracone are sloppy. So focused on perimeter security they left their internal network in a sorry state. Typical. I've stolen some of their private security certificates."

"What does that mean?"

She smiled a ruthless, predatory smile. "Means I've got the keys to the kingdom. And I have sacked the city, oh yes. We have a lot to talk about, you and me and Safan and Jake."

"I don't think Jake's part of this any more."

"Hm. Maybe not."

That night, Nadine slept beneath clean sheets in a comfortable bed for the first time in what seemed like years. She burrowed under the blanket and in the darkness imagined she was back at home in the decaying mansion by the sea. Any moment, she told herself, Anna would come through the door, lift the covers, and slide into bed, warm and soft against her, and all her pain and grief would evaporate like morning dew.

22

Phantom Cities

THE SMELL OF coffee and bacon dragged Nadine back to grim reality. She looked around the room in confusion, still dogged by the last dregs of sleep. "Anna?" Memory fell on her like a pile of bricks. Her eyes welled with tears. She wiped them away impatiently. By the time she'd dressed in her last remaining clothes and ran her fingers through her hair, she'd composed herself enough to face her benefactor.

Liz bustled around the kitchen. She smiled at Nadine as she slid a cup of coffee to her. "Ah, there you are. Sleep well? Breakfast?"

"I suppose, sure."

"Good, good. Eat up. You have work to do."

"Work?" Nadine frowned. "What sort of work?"

"Getting back into your friend Mr. Fox's good graces. He spent the night in a cheap-ass flophouse in Edgebrook. Real shithole, even by Houston flophouse standards. Take it he's not exactly flush with cash."

"I don't think he wants to see me." Nadine pulled at her coffee. "Funny, I think I actually like the coffee substitute beverage better."

"No accounting for taste." Liz's chair extended itself, the wheels coming together with a whirr of machinery, elevating the seat. She scooped an omelet off the stove with deft motions, laid some strips of bacon and sausage next to them, and swiveled toward the table, settling back down as she did. "I reckon he probably won't be too happy to see you, but not a lot of choice. We need him, which means you need to make nice with him." She slid the plate across the table to Nadine. "Here. Eat up."

"So what, I'm supposed to just go wherever he is, say 'hey, nice place, you maybe wanna come back now'?"

Liz shook her head. "No. He's much too proud for that. I'll contact him, arrange a meeting somewhere he can pretend he didn't just spend the night in a shithole."

"Don't think he'll be too happy to hear from you, either."

"No? I'll just have to be persistent, then."

"Why do we need him?"

"Ah, now that's a story. Short version, if the two of you want your lives back, you'll need to do some work, and for that, you'll need his skills. Long version I'll explain once you've mended fences."

"And if he doesn't want to come back?"

"Well, then, I'd say the two of you are buggered. You worse than him, probably, but there's plenty of buggering to go around."

"There's no getting our lives back. He knows that."

"You don't know what I found digging through Terracone's laundry."

Nadine froze, fork halfway to her lips. "What did you find?"

"All in good time. I'll call a Booker for you. Get a toothbrush and some clothes while you're out."

The Booker, a long black internal-combustion car, pulled up in front of the apartment in a cloud of hydrocarbon fumes. Nadine stared at it in horrified fascination. "Something wrong?" Liz said.

"No. It's just...this is only the second time I've ever ridden in a gas-burner."

The car deposited Nadine in front of a small cafe, steel umbrellas with fading white and pink paint sheltering metal mesh tables in front. "This Booker cab is reserved for the afternoon," the car announced in its synthetic drawl. "Waiting incurs charges as explained—"

"I get it," Nadine said. The door popped as soon as she mashed her finger on the smudged touchscreen.

Jake waited for her at one of the little outdoor tables, a brightly-colored drink in a long-stemmed glass clutched in his claw. His face hardened when she settled beside him.

A woman in a frilly powder blue uniform appeared at her elbow. "Get you something, hon?" Nadine closed her eyes, for an instant back in the warehouse party where she'd met Anna. "I'm fine," she said when she felt she could control her voice.

"I'll get you some water, then." The oval plastic nametag on the front of the woman's uniform said "Elsie" in black block letters.

When she left, Nadine said, "Liz thinks we should talk."

Jake leaned back. "You're doing what she says now? Okay, talk."

"Look, man, I'm...I'm sorry. I didn't think—"

"Obviously."

A quick flare of anger flashed through Nadine. She watched it clinically, as one might track the course of a large and unpleasant-looking spider. "Don't be an asshole," she heard herself say.

"You're not off to a good start here."

"I'm sorry. I mean it. Listen…" Nadine took a deep breath. "I know I fucked up. I should have trusted you. But—"

"You were doing well until you said 'but,'" Jake said.

"Fine." She spread her hands. "I didn't tell you what I was doing because I didn't know what I was doing until I did it. I know you won't believe me, but I didn't have a plan going in there. I don't know why I took the stuff. I mean, yes, I wanted Taylor dead. Of course I did. And I knew we were walking into a bad situation. I know he wasn't supposed to be there, but still." She shrugged. "I should've told you. I didn't think it through. It didn't even occur to me to tell you. I was just…I was so…I don't know. I get that you're mad at me. I get why. I think—"

Elsie reappeared with a scuffed plastic tray bearing two plastic glasses of ice water. Droplets beaded on their sides. "Get you anything else?" she said.

"No," Nadine said.

"Lunch special, extra corned beef hash, Coors light," Jake said. "She's buying."

"Fine. Lunch special for me too, then," Nadine said.

Elsie disappeared. Jake shook his head. "Look at you. It still hasn't sunk in, has it?"

"What? That Taylor is gone?"

He waved the blunt mechanical claw dismissively. Servos whirred. "No. Your change in station. You're rich. I mean, not like multinational CEO rich, but rich enough. Anna's gift to you. Numbers on a bank chip. Lots of them. And you're still wearing the same clothes you were in the last time I saw you."

"I don't care about money. Besides, fat lot of good it's doing me."

"It gave you access to Safan."

"And he's going to end up with a big chunk of it."

"So? Isn't that what money is for? A resource to get what you want?" He leaned across the metal table, bits of paint peeling off onto his faded army jacket. "What do you want?"

"Liz says—"

He shook his head violently. "No. What do you want?"

"I want…I want to find out what happened. I want to understand."

"Will it bring you peace?"

"No. But I still want it anyway."

"Why are you here?"

"Because...because Liz says we need you."

Jake snorted. "You're a 'we' now?"

"She said she found something. Something that can give us our lives back. Both of us."

"When I asked you what you want, you didn't say you want your life back. So I'll ask you again. Why are you here?"

"I can't do this without you."

"Okay, listen. First, you—"

Powder blue in Nadine's peripheral vision. "Let's see. Two lunch specials, was it?"

"Thank you," Nadine said.

"Where's Elsie?" Jake said.

"On break."

Jake nodded. "Thanks."

"Enjoy."

"Jake," Nadine said, "we need you. I need you."

Jake tilted his head sideways like he was trying to solve a puzzle. "Let me ask you something, Melody."

"What's that?"

He leaned close, across the small metal table. "You notice the guy sitting to our left, two tables over?" He held up a finger. "Don't look. Corner of your eye."

Nadine glanced over. Quick glimpse of a man sitting alone, military haircut, black suit, dark glasses, reading a tabloid. "What about him?"

"He hasn't ordered anything. He's just been sitting there."

"So? Maybe he's waiting for someone."

"Maybe." Jake's voice carried doubt. "Funny thing, though."

"What's that?"

"He's been looking at the same page in his newspaper since you got here."

Nadine's blood froze. "What do we do?"

"Follow me." Jake stood smoothly. "Move quickly. This way. Alley. Stay close. Nice and calm, right?"

Heart thudding, Nadine followed Jake. He moved with surreal grace, flitting through the alley as fast and silent as a ghost. Nadine ran after him, struggling to keep up. His contacts danced with light. "Liz, you there?" He swerved around the metal skeleton of a rusty fire escape.

Smells of hot oil mixed with urine. "We're in a spot here. Could use a bit of help. Can you send us a car?" Pause. "Roger that, three minutes." He beckoned to Nadine. "Faster!"

Nadine gasped for air, arms wrapped tight around her sides. "Is he following—"

"Come on!"

They emerged from the alley into a street, heat shimmering around them. The smell of burnt hydrocarbons filled Nadine's nose. Jake swerved left. Nadine stumbled after him. A car horn sounded. Jake reached behind him. Yellow alert triangles flared. He pulled the handgun in one fluid motion without slowing down. Adrenaline surged in Nadine. She sped up, the pain in her side falling away.

He turned right at the next block. Nadine followed him down another alley, where he paused, breathing hard, gun held low. An orange cat blinked at him, cocked its head, then hissed nonchalantly before trotting away.

Jake's lips moved, subvocalizing. "Car's on the way," he said. "When it gets here, move fast."

"Who was that guy? Cop?"

"Dunno. Doubt it. He was on his own. Plus he didn't smell like a cop. Private security, more likely. Getting close to make a positive ID, meaning no drones or snipers. Maybe following me, maybe following you, probably called for backup."

"Terracone?"

"Maybe." Doubt crossed his face. "Something's weird. Seems awfully fast for them to have found us. Looking for me in surveillance cameras, maybe, but..."

"What?"

"I don't know. Just seems awfully convenient, them finding us so fast. Car's inbound. I'll take the driver's side. You get in the back on the passenger side. Ready?"

"Ready."

"Move."

A black Booker stopped at the edge of the alley. The doors popped. Nadine scrambled in, so fast she hit her head on the pillar.

By the time the car pulled up in front of the same dun-colored stucco building where they'd regrouped after the penthouse, Nadine's heart had settled back into her chest. Safan and Liz waited for them in the office. "Welcome back," Liz said to Jake. "So, you with us now?"

"Like I got a choice?" he said.

"You always have a choice. What brought you back?"

"Run-in with private security, someone, I don't know. Still trying to figure it out. Looks like someone's not going to leave me alone, though."

"Elizabeth," Safan said. "You dragged us all the way out here. You going to tell us what you found?"

"I've spent quite some time rooting around in Terracone's network," Liz said, "and it's been enlightening. We play our cards right, we'll be brokering their secrets for years."

Safan settled back with a pleased expression. "It's nice to be pleasantly surprised. From that look on your face, I gather there's more?"

"Oh, yeah." Liz grinned. "I found Mirage."

Nadine sat forward. "What is it?"

"Short version? A weaponized exploit platform. Very sophisticated, Cutting-edge, like state-level-actor stuff."

"Exploit for what?" Safan said.

"Implants. All of them, near enough. There's two parts. Injection part is a set of modules written for all the different implant models, mix and match penetrators for vulnerabilities. Customizable, easy to update with new exploits. Weapon module lets you compromise the implant, see through the paired contacts, control what the user sees and hears. Works through OTA firmware update channels, lets you plant persistent malware, remote access, tracking, whole nine yards."

Jake whistled. "Fuck me dead."

Safan exhaled, long and low. "So Terracone has something that you point at a person to make him see and hear what you want him to see and hear, and lets you see through his eyes?"

"Bit more complicated than that, but basically, yes."

Nadine closed her eyes. Pink mist. "In that tunnel," she said, "right before every—before it all went to shit, Kev...he said he saw something. They started shooting, and then Lena and Dan-boy, they just started screaming."

Safan nodded slowly. "Tactically, middle of a firefight, you turn people's implants against them, make them see or hear things that aren't there, that's big. Strategically, every implant is a potential spy. Think of the leg up it gives you, bidding on contracts, knowing what legislation's coming up...guy could get giddy just contemplating it. So my question is, how come it didn't affect you?"

"Anna did something to my implant. Killed remote firmware updates. Had to drill a hole in my head to change my ID number. Think she did the same to hers."

"Now isn't that interesting," Safan said.

"Melody here says you found something might haul our asses out of the muck?" Jake said.

"Yeah, well, that's a good news/bad news thing," Liz said. "Good news, I found indexes into their databases, and oh my, they do have files on you. Corporations, they can't help keeping records on everything. Setting you up, raw footage of the deepfakes they gave the cops, emails, it's all there."

"And the bad news?" Nadine said.

"Only the indexes, titles of internal memos, email headers, filenames. The data's in cold storage."

"What does that mean?" Nadine said.

"Your friend Martin Thomas didn't exactly want to keep a log of criminal activity on a network subject to subpoena. They have a data facility outside Houston. All of it's there, in offline storage."

"So can we get it?" Jake said.

"Offline means offline," Liz said. "Not accessible through the network. It's all there, but it's out of reach."

"So what does that mean?"

"It means if you want it, you'll need to break into the facility and pull the storage units out of the rack. No hacking, no trickery, just old-fashioned meatspace smash and grab."

"Can't we just go to the police with what you found?" Nadine said.

Safan rolled his eyes. Jake shook his head. "Assuming you can find a cop who isn't on Terracone's payroll," Liz said gently, "what would you tell them about how you found this information? I probably broke a dozen Federal laws and another half-dozen state statutes finding this."

"So we break more laws then, and maybe get killed?"

"You got something else needs doing?" Safan said.

"Well, I mean..."

"Look, it's your life," Liz said. "Just think of me as your personal oracle of information. What you do with it, that's you, right?"

"I still don't have a toothbrush," Nadine said, more to herself than to the room.

"What?" Safan said.

"A toothbrush. I still don't have a fucking toothbrush. Everything I had left was in the RV. Liz said to get a toothbrush on my way back, but we left in a hurry and I..." She shook her head to clear it. "The Booker you got for me is probably still sitting in the parking lot racking up charges. And we didn't pay for lunch."

"Don't sweat the Booker," Liz said. "I've already paid the fees."

"This is what it's going to be like, isn't it? From now until they catch me."

"Pretty much, yeah."

"I can't...this can't go on. We need to end this."

Jake frowned. "If you want my help, we need to come to an understanding. No more surprises. You can't go changing the plan mid-stream. I need to know that if I tell you to do something, you'll do it. Understand?"

"Yeah," Nadine said. Jake's glare hit her like a physical blow. "Yes. I understand."

"Good. Now, where's this storage drive?"

"Data center in a research lab in Amos City."

"Never heard of it," Jake said.

"It's a phantom city," Safan said.

Jake stared at him. "A what?"

"Phantom city. When the Federation of Free States agreement was signed, member states got certain...considerations on taxes. Corporate taxes particularly. Big windfall for the richest of the rich, but there's a catch."

"What's that?"

"Investing the money outside the FFS brings down certain tax consequences. Highly arcane, gives me a headache just thinking about it. The tax part of the agreement runs over three hundred pages. Upshot is, a lot of folks in the FFS have money they want to invest, but no easy way to do it outside the FFS. So..." He shrugged. "When in doubt, buy real estate, right? Texas has plenty of it, and it ain't like they're making any more."

"So what's a phantom city?" Nadine said.

"Gettin' to that. You can buy land, but then what? You can put cows on it, I suppose, but if there's no cows and no minerals, it's not doing much for you. So they build buildings. Lots of buildings. High-rise condo towers, mostly. Thing is, nobody's there to live in 'em."

"So why build them?"

"Because they're worth money."

"Why are they worth money if nobody lives in them?"

"Same reason everything else is worth money—because people think they are. They're an investment. Like, someday people will live in them, and then they'll be worth more. Maybe a lot more. Meanwhile, just building them employs contractors and roofers and whatever, so the economy goes up, see? And if the economy goes up, then housing goes up, even if nobody's living in it."

Nadine stared at him, incredulous. "That's insane."

Safan spread his hands. "It's Texas. Anyway, that's Amos City. Skyscrapers that nobody uses, towers that nobody lives in, and oh yeah, a little data center slash research facility owned by a subsidiary of Terracone called Data Storage Systems and Services LLC. In which is a cold storage complex for high-security data. And in that is the key to your future."

"How high-security are we talking?" Jake said.

"Manageable," Safan said.

"How manageable?"

"Manageable."

"That doesn't exactly inspire confidence."

"Is what it is," Safan said. "You can take your chances if you like, hope the change of leadership underway at Terracone right now turns out in your favor. Thing is, they know you're attached to Melody here, and they know who Melody is. Law enforcement doesn't yet, on account of certain awkward questions that raises, but now that Martin Taylor's gone, Terracone can come clean, pin it all on him, rogue executive operating off the reservation, terrible damn thing, only just became aware, blah blah blah. Maybe even spin it so they come out heroes, not that they have to do much spinning. Having a few senators in your pocket is table stakes in the defense contracting biz. In a way, you did them a favor killing him. Simplified things, anyway. Soon as they figure that out, you're a marked man."

"No way out, huh?" Jake said.

"No way out."

23

Crayon Eater

A WEEK WENT BY in nonstop activity that somehow didn't seem to go anywhere. Jake and Safan pored over street maps and structural diagrams—blueprints, Nadine gathered, of the lab or facility or data center or whatever it was where the key to her redemption could, they said, be found. Liz usually made herself scarce, off exploring Terracone's network like an archeologist mapping out some lost city.

No, not like an archeologist, Nadine thought. More like a looter. She and Safan spoke every evening about what she'd found, sometimes with Jake, sometimes without.

On one of the days Jake made himself absent from the conversation, she found him stripping his handgun on a makeshift table made of a blue plastic shipping tray across two derelict server racks in what had once been an office, tucked away in the small building south of Houston. Nadine hadn't set foot outside in days. She'd watched him re-assemble the gun, every move rehearsed as a ballet dancer's routine, not hampered in the slightest by his mechanical claw. "Thumb safety," he said, showing her a lever. "Only reason you didn't kill Safan's goon." She shivered, remembering the nameless man stripping his gun outside Mayor Tony's office, what had happened after...

"Nervous?" Liz said the next day.

"What would you say if I told you no?" Nadine said.

"I'd say you were a liar, or a crazy woman." The chair whirred, wheels coming together as the old woman rose to Nadine's eye level. "Shit gets real pretty soon."

Nadine probed her feelings and found a generalized sort of tension, but a curious lack of fear. "One foot in front of the other," she said. "I want this to be over."

"The boys are polishing up the last details now. I'm so far inside Terracone they couldn't get me out with a crowbar even if they found me, which they haven't yet, but I don't have access to the network at Data Storage Systems and Services. Different system. Doubt there's more than a dozen people at Terracone who even know DS3 exists. Highly secret, need to know, very little communication in or out. Skunkworks."

"Skunkworks? What's that mean?"

"Means we have to get a lot of information indirectly." Her chair whirred as it resumed its normal height. "We're gonna have to go in dark, of course. No implants. Jake's none too happy about it. The gunsight on that artillery piece of his is paired to his implant. Not that that's any use if someone can make him see things that aren't there." Liz's eyes, wired and alert in her weathered face, studied Nadine. "But that's not what I came here to talk about."

"What, then?"

"I came here to see how you're doing."

"How I'm doing." Nadine turned the words over in her head, like some ancient mantra whose purpose she did not understand. "How I'm doing. I'm not sure there's any 'I' to be doing, any more. You know, I always thought I'd be special, that I'd be a movie star. Even as a kid." She laughed bitterly. "Though I suppose to you, I'm still a kid, aren't I?" She sat on an empty crate that looked like it had once held something heavy and pulled her knees to her chest. Half the building housed racks of servers, their blue and green lights winking like fireflies. The rest was mostly empty, littered with trash. Jake and Nadine slept in sleeping bags on slabs of memory foam on the floor in another old office, and showered in an abandoned executive washroom. She still hadn't bought any new clothes, and the clothes she wore were starting to chafe.

Liz looked at her with a thoughtful expression until Nadine dropped her eyes. "So now here I am," she went on, "at the unfriendly end of a vast and dangerous machine trying its damndest to crush me, because I fell in love with a woman at a dance party. Wrong place, wrong time. How am I doing? I don't know how to answer that."

"I imagine you already have," Liz said. "Anyway, it'll have to do. Need you to be part of the meetings now. Like I said, shit's about to get real."

Nadine spent the rest of the day in a claustrophobic room outfitted with a shiny new holographic projector, listening to Liz, Jake, and Safan. Safan did most of the talking. "Thing about Data Storage Systems and Services," Safan said, "is it kinda feels like someone's private fiefdom."

"Martin Taylor?" Nadine said.

"Probably. Lotta money going in, and I mean a lot, routed through this whole network of subsidiaries and shell companies from here to California, but not a lot of revenue on the books." Dust danced in the air above the projector. A three-dimensional blueprint hung in space in front of them, a representation of a building, color-coded to show power lines, data conduits, water, sewer, alarms. "Place has been a money pit for years. From the internal memos Elizabeth found, board's been getting restless for a while, and I don't blame 'em. Financials are rather alarming. They always seem to be on the verge of something big, something that'll make Terracone enough money to justify their existence, but so far they've never quite delivered. And that gives us an advantage."

"How so?" Nadine said.

"Terracone's keen to reduce the burn rate. First thing any corp does to reduce burn is get rid of warm bodies, and the first warm bodies to go are usually security. They've been consolidating. Relying more and more on automated perimeter security, drones, that sort of thing, less and less on people with guns. Nobody even knows the place exists, it's out in the middle of nowhere, you can't get close without being spotted from miles off, right on the edge of a phantom city so it's not like you got people knockin' on the door. Now, getting inside without being pegged thirty miles before you ever get there, that's a problem. And since nobody to speak of lives in Amos City 'cept Terracone's own, strangers stand out."

"So how do we get in?"

"Easy." Safan folded his arms. "They invite us in."

Nadine blinked. "I'm sorry, what?"

"Kinda the same as the penthouse, only in reverse. Elizabeth cozies up to their systems, sets off an alarm. Chemical disaster, hazmat situation, whatever. For a data processing outfit, they work with some weird shit. They call the mothership, ask for help, we intercept that call, send in a hazmat team. Building should empty itself out for us. Jake goes in, grabs the storage drives, bing bang done."

"I thought Liz didn't have access to their network," Nadine said.

A muscle worked in Jake's jaw. Safan's hands closed around the armrest of the cheap office chair he sat in. "Aye," he said. "That's where you come in."

"Me? How?"

"How tall are you?"

"What?"

"Your height. How tall are you?"

"About a hundred and fifty-seven centimeters. Five foot two," she added for Liz's sake. "Give or take."

"You see?" Safan said. Jake grunted.

"What does that have to do with anything?" Nadine said.

"Amos City," Liz said, "is a very *modern* city. That means modern infrastructure. The roads aren't graded and poured. They're hauled in in prefab sections, roadway on top, service corridors underneath. Water, data, power, all in pre-formed channels in the sections. Each section is assembled, shipped out, and buried." The projection changed, became a section of road about as long as a bus, with a rectangular concrete tunnel beneath. "Whole town's built that way. Designed to let people pull cable or fix water pipes without tearing up the road. Well, I say people. Utility robots do most of it. It's a tight fit for a person, but should be easy for you."

"No." Nadine shook her head. "No, no, no, no. You can't be serious. No way. Last time I went down in a tunnel—"

"How you sleeping?" Safan said.

"What?"

"Nightmares? Sweats? Panic attacks? Flashbacks?"

Nadine hugged herself tightly. "No."

"See? No PTSD. Jake's magic pills did the trick, right? You'll have no problems. Besides, you'll have backup."

"Jake's going with me?"

"No. We need him to go in the front door. You're going under, planting a data tap that lets Elizabeth into the alarm systems. Not the whole network, that's too heavily protected, but the alarms are their own thing. Here's your backup."

Safan slid a small black case across the table to her. It reminded Nadine a bit of something an engagement ring might come in, about the same width but three times longer. She snapped it open. Inside lay a thing like a mechanical wasp, smooth glossy black, with thin wings of some clear plastic. The front was pointed, with two lenses that suggested eyes. Overall, it had a sleek, menacing look that made Nadine's skin crawl. "What is it?"

"Swarm drone. A bunch of these will follow you in, all controlled remotely. Anyone turns up to give you grief, well..." A nasty grin crossed his face. "You designate a threat. The swarm picks the closest drone, it locks on, fires a propulsive charge, tears into the target and then explodes. Core is a foot of grooved tungsten wire dipped in wax impregnated with quick-acting nerve agent, wrapped around half a gram of crystallized high explosive."

"Jesus." Nadine dropped the case on the table. "Who comes up with shit like this?"

"Subsidiary of Terracone's biggest competitor." Safan laughed as if at a private joke. "Expensive as fuck. Been spending that advance you gave me. We'll have an operator outside, piloting the swarm to give you backup. Everything goes well, you splice into the alarm controls, Elizabeth does that thing she does, they call the cavalry, we ride up, you meet Jake inside, grab the drive, get your life back."

"Just like that?"

"Just like that."

Jake clenched his jaw. "I'd still feel better if you gave her a gun."

Safan shook his head. "She's not qualified."

"Bet she's shot more people in the last month than you have in the last five years."

"She'll have the swarm—"

"She gets a gun."

Safan spread his hands. "I'll see what I can do."

"Who's the operator?" Jake said.

"Guy I know," Safan said. "Merc. Experienced."

"You trust him?"

"More than I trust you."

Jake shook his head. "I don't like it."

"You got a better idea?" When Jake said nothing, Safan nodded. "That's what I thought. Get some sleep. Both of you. I'll introduce you tomorrow, we'll run through it all, make sure we're on the same page."

That night, as Jake and Nadine laid out their sleeping bags, Jake shook his head. "I don't trust them," he said, voice low.

"What? Why?" Nadine peeled herself out of her bra without removing her shirt and pulled off her pants. A month ago, she might have felt uncomfortable half-dressed in front of him, but a month ago, she had been a different person in a different life. Now it barely even registered.

"I don't know. Something's wrong. There's something..." He frowned. "I can't put my finger on it, but something doesn't add up."

"What?"

"I told you, I don't know!" Jake snapped.

Nadine sighed. "Liz and Safan have been there for us. They've helped us—"

"They've been paid to."

"Whatever. They're coming through for us. Way more than we have any right to expect. They could've cut us loose after the thing in the penthouse, but they didn't."

"I don't trust them."

"You're paranoid."

"Maybe. But that doesn't mean I'm wrong."

"I like Liz."

"You like her because she reminds you of your girlfriend."

"I like her," and now Nadine's voice carried a sharp edge of frost, "because she's been there hauling our asses out of the fire and she's done everything she said she would do."

"Maybe." Jake scratched his chin with his claw. "But there's something—"

"What?"

"I don't know. I don't like bringing in someone new."

"We can use all the help we can get."

"Just watch your ass, is all."

Jake switched off the light. Nadine stared up into the darkness for a long time, until his breathing became snores. She pulled the sleeping bag over her head, faint musty smell permeating the fabric. Sleep eventually found her.

She woke to strident voices in the room outside. The light in the windowless room, probably once a meeting room, was still off. She fished around in the dark for her clothes, dressed, and rose barefoot.

She found Liz, Jake, and Safan in the conference room with a person she didn't recognize, a tall, lanky Hispanic man with dark hair and a beard that jutted out like a promontory from some craggy headland. He wore loose-fitting jeans with large pockets on the knee and a sweat-stained T-shirt. A black leather shoulder holster held a small black handgun.

Nadine blinked sleep from her eyes. "Who's he?"

"Crayon-eater," Jake said. "One of Uncle Sam's misguided children."

"What?"

"Pay the muddie no nevermind," the stranger said. "Name's Carlos, ma'am. Former United States Marine Corps, Second Battalion, First Marines, drone swarm operator. I'll be your backup, ma'am." He flashed her a high-wattage smile that failed to reach his eyes, where something cold and appraising and somehow insectile lurked. Nadine shivered.

"Carlos will be going in with you to Amos City," Safan said. "You'll be staying on the outskirts of town, a few kilometers from Terracone's facility. Two of you will be in a trailer, looks to all appearances like an ordinary couple of campers. You go down into the tunnels, Carlos stays behind to remote-pilot the swarm."

"Will they work underground, with all the concrete and stuff?"

"Yes, ma'am." Carlos took a small plastic from his pocket, tossed it to her. Inside, Nadine found a roll of blister wrap, each little plastic bubble holding a device about the size of her thumbnail. "Mesh transceiver," Carlos explained. "You'll stick them on the wall every few hundred meters. They'll relay comms and drone C&C back to me."

"You won't be in the tunnels with me?" Odd relief at the thought.

"No, ma'am. Not a lot of room down there. Plus it'll be dark. There's IR security but no lights, from what I'm told. We have ways to hide your body heat, but me crawling through the tunnel and operating the swarm's out of the question. You'll be in touch with me the whole time."

"I don't like it," Jake said. His claw snapped open and shut, over and over. "I don't know you. I don't trust you. I should be the one backing her up."

"You qualified on remote-piloted, semi-autonomous microdrone swarms, Army?" Carlos said. The muscle in Jake's jaw bulged.

"There you go," Safan said. "Jake, we need you in the building. You grab the data. Melody gets us access to the alarm comms, out of the line of fire. Everything goes to plan, we set off the alarm, you go in, grab the storage units, out before anyone knows any better."

"Then why do we need Carlos and his toys?" Jake said.

"In case everything doesn't go to plan."

Carlos grinned again, something predatory this time. His cold eyes didn't waver.

Nadine spent the rest of the day with Safan and Carlos, going over the diagrams of the cramped utility tunnels under the street. "State representative who sponsored the bill that requires new new roads to have these tunnels happens to own a contracting firm that makes them," Safan explained. "Each segment is shipped in on a flatbed truck, dropped in place with a crane. Parts all lock together, street beneath the street. Not enough room to stand up in, but you'll be fine. No lights down there, but there are cameras, passive infrared, twig onto the body heat of anything bigger'n a rat. You'll be blind, but not to worry, we'll guide you through."

"Won't the cameras see me?" Nadine said.

"Nope," Carlos said. "Got that covered. Disposable infrared counter-measure. Used 'em in Eastern Europe. Just the thing for sneaking past IR cameras."

"How does it work?"

"You'll see."

Safan touched the projector. As the cross-section of road zoomed out, Carlos put his feet up on the desk, pulled a knife from a sheath at his side, and started whittling a bit of wood that looked like the end of a broomstick. Yellow triangles flared to life in Nadine's vision.

The projector view soared until Nadine found herself looking at a top-down engineer's-eye view of Amos City. "You'll go in here. The prefab segments have ladders and access hatches every hundred meters or so, but we want to keep you well away from Data Storage Systems and Services before you go in. We don't know how far out their drone coverage or sensor net extends, but I'm betting it's pretty far. Probably take you about an hour, hour and a half in the tunnels to get there. That work for you?"

Nadine nodded curtly.

Carlos looked at her, eyes intent. "Heard what happened to you in LA. You good with this?"

"Yes," Nadine said. "I'm good with this."

He held her gaze for a long moment, then nodded. "Good. Lot riding on you here."

"Then why aren't you going down in the tunnels instead of me?"

"You be able to back me up if I did?" The smile flickered across his face. "Besides, I ain't gettin' paid enough for that. That's a whole different payscale than manning the drones."

"You said you were military?" Nadine said.

"Former. USMC."

"What are you now?"

Another quick flash of a smile. "Freelance."

"Let's go over it again," Safan said. "You go in here. Ladders every hundred meters, you can feel them, use them to orient yourself. Count off three, turn right. Six more, turn left. Fifty meters down, turn right, if you reach the ladder you've gone too far. You remember this?"

"I think so."

"I can help with that," Carlos said. He showed her the bit of broomstick he'd been carving. "Keep this in your side pocket. Put your thumb on the rounded bit on top. Count the notches, see? Three, then this hole here, that means go right. Six notches, then this hole on the other side, go left. Helps you remember when you can't rely on your implant."

"Thanks," Nadine said.

Carlos did something, some subtle motion with his fingers. The big knife spun once, bright flash of metal beneath blueish LED lights, and was back in its sheath. "Don't mention it."

Nadine dreamed that night of small dark places, outlined in glowing blue light, space beyond space, extending forever around her in darkness and silence. She woke restless and uncomfortable. The room was still dark, Jake's breathing slow and regular.

She slipped quietly out the door and made her way to the bathroom, where she showered, then washed her last remaining clothes under the stream of hot water. She toweled off, draped her clothes over the rod to dry, and, wrapped in the towel, went in search of breakfast.

Out in the hall, she heard talking, low and indistinct. She followed the voices to the office with its holographic projector. The door was closed, the voices still indistinct. She reached for the knob. It swung open before she could touch it. Carlos came through, knife spinning in his hand, face unreadable. Over his shoulder, she caught a glimpse of Safan and Liz before the door closed again.

Yellow triangles.

His eyes flickered over her, head to foot. His expression didn't change. "Get dressed. We get to work in an hour."

"I'm a bit lacking in the wardrobe department at the moment, on account of leaving my entire life behind in a hurry."

He grunted. "I know the feeling." The knife spun and disappeared smoothly into its sheath, without Nadine being quite sure how it got there. "Gettin' close. We move out soon. Eight hours to Amos City. You want some coffee?"

Nadine had dressed and was on her second self-heating coffee substitute when Jake found her in the old office, running through a projection of the utility tunnels over and over again while she ran her finger down the notches in the worn bit of broomstick. "Hey," he said.

"Hey."

"Listen, I— "

Nadine flicked off the projector. "Yeah?"

"We need to talk."

"Is this the bit where you apologize for storming out?"

"What?" Jake frowned. "No, I—no!" His tube of coffee substitute fizzed when he pulled the tab.

"What, then?"

"Look, something feels off. I'm getting a weird vibe from this. Something's been off since the penthouse."

Nadine pulled at her own coffee substitute. "You mean since I saved your life?"

"Yeah. Since you saved my life."

"Apology accepted."

"You're not listening. This is important. I—"

Carlos stuck his head in the office. "Truck's out front. You know how to drive a gas burner with an Allison automatic, Army?"

"Gas on the right, brake on the left. How hard can it be?"

Nadine trailed after them, out into the shimmering Houston heat. An enormous yellow fire truck sat idling in the parking lot in a cloud of hydrocarbon fumes, HAZMAT SPECIAL RESPONSE UNIT in black block letters down its flank. As she walked out into the muggy air, the doors opened. Three people hopped out, all wearing long, bright yellow jackets with reflective tape. "Ah! Welcome, welcome," Safan said. He stood at the edge of the sidewalk, arms spread wide. "Jake, meet your team."

"Excuse me?" Jake's voice went cold.

"The big guy in front is Andy. The—"

Jake whirled, pulled the handgun tucked in his waistband at the small of his back in one acrobatic motion, and leveled it at Safan's head. "You ever see what happens when you shoot someone right between the eyes?" he said. "They just stop." He clicked the claw shut. "Just like that. Like turning off a light."

"Whoa, hey, Army," Carlos said, hands apart. "No need to do anything rash." The three men from the truck, Andy and the other two, spread out in a loose triangle around Jake and Safan.

"You may have noticed I don't like when things don't go to plan," Jake said. "When things don't go to plan, people get hurt. A team wasn't part of the plan. You tryin' to get people hurt, Safan? That your goal here?"

Carlos edged closer. "Listen, Army, just be cool—"

"Shut. The fuck. Up," Jake said. "This doesn't concern you."

"Jake!" Nadine said. "Jake, stop it!"

"Yeah, be cool, Jake," Andy said. "We're all friends here."

"Was I talking to you?" Jake said. "This is just me and Safan, having a conversation about the plan, and why he's changing it without my express fucking consent. So how about it, huh? Answer the fucking question. You tryin' to get people hurt?"

"No," Safan said, as easily and casually as if he were talking about the weather. "Think about this. The alarm goes off, you roll up in an emergency response vehicle, you're the only one there, what kind of sense does that make? Your team is part of your cover. And your backup."

"He's right, Army," Carlos said. "You roll up there all by your lonesome, responding to a hazardous situation, whole thing's blown and you can kiss the mission objective goodbye."

"Jake!" Nadine said. "Put the goddamn gun down. Jesus."

"Fine." Jake raised the barrel and thumbed the safety on. "But only because she says. You and me, all this is over, we're going to have a conversation."

"That's the second time since you arrived in Houston you've put a gun in my face," Safan said mildly. "Do it again and you'd better shoot me. Jake, meet Andy, Benjamin," with a nod toward a squat, broadly-built man who gave an impression of muscular solidity even through the firefighter's suit, "and Parker. They're going in with you. We've made some modifications to your gear—"

"What kind of modifications?"

"Put some loops inside your jacket so you can carry that artillery piece you favor. You know, in case things don't go to plan." He beckoned to Nadine. "Melody. Come here. Got something for you. Might help put your friend's mind at ease."

"Yeah?" Nadine said. "What's that?"

"Here." He handed her a small, silver pistol, heavy despite its compactness. "Magazine," he said, passing her a long rectangle filled with squat cartridges, ugly things designed with ugly purpose. "Magazine goes in the end of the grip, there, like that. Slap it hard, you won't break it. Good. Pull back the slide, there. Don't point it at anything you don't want dead. Safety's here, red means ready to rock and roll. Magazine release here. Pull the magazine out, right. Remember there's still a round in the chamber. Clear it by pulling here. Good. Okay, got it?"

"Got it." Nadine pressed the ejected round back in the magazine with her thumb.

"Good. Do me a favor, don't load it until showtime."

"Right." Nadine turned back to the door. "It's fucking hot. You guys must be dying in those jackets."

Parker shrugged, awkward in the heavy jacket. "Been through worse."

24

Hack and Pray

"YOUR BOY'S COMING apart at the seams," Liz said. The chair had settled close to the floor, wheels scissoring apart from each other, legrests moving forward. She folded Nadine's new clothes and packed them neatly into a garish suitcase, a hideous hot-pink thing with a GG logo on the front.

Safan had brought her an old-style smartphone with a flat touchscreen display open to a clothing site and told her to pick out an assortment. She fumbled with the crude interface for a while before she managed to put together a collection that would, a lifetime ago, have lasted her for a week without laundry, then Safan sent Carlos to collect them. He'd come back with the clothes and the suitcase. "Fake," he said, grinning beneath a new pair of aviator sunglasses. The knife whirled in his fingers. "Not a great fake, but a good fake, Just the thing for someone out glamping."

Now Nadine was dressed in the first change of clothes she'd had in days, a light, skintight black shirt with cutouts for her shoulders that ended just above her midriff and a long pair of slinky black jeans tucked into black leather cowboy boots with shiny metal tips. Liz examined her critically, pronounced herself satisfied, and set about packing the rest of her new clothes into the awful knockoff designer suitcase. "It's not really me," Nadine complained.

"That's the point," Liz explained patiently. "That plus a wig plus this and you won't look like a fugitive who's still technically wanted, even if there's some debate about her guilt." She tossed Nadine a thing that looked like a cross between a surgical mask and a bit of impressionist art gone wrong, two elastic ear loops and a triangle of filter fabric printed with blocky black squares and brightly colored lines that reminded Nadine of what happened when a video call went bad.

"What's this?"

"Latest thing in automated facial recognition evasion. Adversarial input. Confuses the newest machine learning systems. They're getting better at seeing past dazzle makeup. High-performance facial recognition is one of Terracone's things. That shit scrawled all over the mask makes facial recognition think you're someone else."

"Who?"

"That one? Someone named Heather Monterey. Ex-girlfriend of the programmer who designed it."

Nadine stared at her. "You're shitting me."

"I assure you, I am not." Liz zipped up the suitcase. "Mask serves two functions. Confusing facial recognition's only one of them."

"What's the other?"

"Helps keep you from dying. Central Texas is a high-risk neo-parainfluenza zone."

"Fuck me."

"Ah, were I fifty years younger," Liz sighed. "Still, place you're going, not too likely you'll meet anyone, least not anyone who isn't part of Terracone, and they're all vaccinated." She lifted the suitcase onto its wheels. Some hidden clockwork mechanism in her chair whirred as the wheels pulled back together. It rose, resettling into its normal configuration. "Almost ready to head out." She glided through the door. Nadine followed her. The suitcase raised a small shaft tipped with a tiny glass camera, then trundled along behind Nadine.

They joined the others in the office. "—leave 0800 tomorrow," Safan was saying. "Ah, Elizabeth, Melody. We load out tonight. Jake, you're in the engine with Parker. Melody, you and Carlos are in the trailer, the rest of you in the van with me and Elizabeth. Eight and a half hours to Amos City. Andy, Benjamin, Jake, Parker, you gear up when we arrive. Ninety minutes for Melody to do her part, then we trigger the alarm, you ride in to save the day, grab the data, get out, done." He patted a compact white box beside the projector. "Just one detail."

"What's that?" Carlos said.

"Gotta disable your implants."

"Now that's some bullshit," Benjamin said.

"Our adversaries have deployed a weapon that can hijack implants," Safan said, "make you see and hear things that aren't there. External access will be disabled until we secure the data."

"Let's get this done," Liz said. "Who first?"

Safan rose. "Do it."

One by one, the others sat in front of the white box. Liz tapped a keyboard on top, a rod with a coiled loop on the end extended, a light blinked. "I'll re-enable network access and over-the-air updates after we're done." Finally, she turned to Nadine. "You've already disabled your implant."

Nadine closed her eyes. Takeru's voice in her head, the shriek of the drill, the awful grinding... She swallowed and nodded.

"Okay, that's that, then," Liz said.

"What about you?" Nadine said. "Are you going with us?"

"Yes. I'll be with Safan. I could do what I need to do from here, if everything works perfectly, but I don't want to take a chance on latency or interrupted comms."

"Don't you need to disable your implant?"

"Oh, hon." Liz touched the black plastic lump on the side of her head. "I got my first hardware before Neuralink was even a glimmer in that Martian guy's eye. Electrodes inserted manually, very hack-and-pray. I've added some upgrades over the years, some my own design, but nothing Terracone's best and brightest can get anywhere near. All bespoke. And I have never allowed remote firmware upgrades."

"Oh."

Later that night, as they made ready for their last night in the sleeping bags atop tattered slabs of foam in the disused office, Jake turned to Nadine. A muscle jumped in his face. "Something you should know," he said. "I did some digging."

"Yeah?"

"Your boy Carlos, he was dishonorably discharged from the Marines. Some kinda operation in Latvia, his unit killed some civilians. Shot them in the head, he helped cover it up."

"Fuck," Nadine said softly.

"Yeah. Don't turn your back on him."

Nadine slept little that night. She stared into the darkness, heart thumping, mouth dry. *Anna?* she sent into the claustrophobic void. *Are you there? Anna, I am so afraid. If you were here, would you think less of me for that? I want you to be proud of me.*

The darkness made no reply.

Morning came quickly. After a tepid shower and a bland breakfast from a foil pouch, Nadine found Carlos climbing into the cab of an enormous white Ford electric truck towing a long, retro-looking rounded silver trailer with dark-tinted windows. He aimed his smile in her direction. "Morning, ma'am!" he called. "We're ready to move out."

"That's our ride?"

"Yes, ma'am."

Liz wheeled up beside her. "It's mine. Try not to get it banged up."

"Why aren't you taking it?"

"Because the two of you are a lot more believable setting off on a camping adventure through central Texas."

"Liz?"

"Yes?"

"Thank you. For all of this."

Liz patted her arm. "No need to thank me, hon. Your money's thanks enough."

"Still, thank you."

The Ford had a large cab with plush, comfortable seats. It even had a proper back seat, not one of the little shelves most pickups had if they had anything at all. A set of oversized fuzzy dice in hot pink dangled from the rearview display, each dot a small black Playboy bunny.

Nadine's new suitcase followed her to the truck. Carlos slung it in the back seat next to a new but far less tacky suitcase in drab, reasonable shades of brown and gray. He pulled out of the parking lot under manual control, then poked at the touchscreen display, surprisingly small in a cheap plastic frame covered with fake chrome flash. "I feel half-blind without my implant," he grumbled. "Doing everything the old-fashioned way." The truck plotted a route and dinged to announce the self-driving had kicked in. "Gonna feel weird, not talking to you through the implant."

"So how do we talk?" Nadine said.

Carlos pulled a flat package from his pocket that reminded Nadine of the peel-apart pouches hospitals used to sterilize scalpels. "Old school."

"What is it?" Nadine said.

"Transduction receiver, subvocal mike." He tore open the package. Two small objects slid out onto his palm, one a flat crescent a bit smaller than Nadine's little finger, the other round. "Peel off the backing, that starts the battery. Stick this one behind your ear, this one on your throat. Five hundred meter range direct, extendable with active amplifiers or the mesh transceivers you'll be carrying."

"How long does the battery last?"

"Six hours."

"Is that enough?"

Carlos laughed. "Ma'am, if we're still there six hours from go, we ain't comin' back."

"Ask you a question?"

"Sure thing."

"Why'd you leave the Marines?"

His face hardened. "That's a long story, and one you don't want to hear. Short version, I was helped out the door to protect the careers of a coupla COs had no business being in the Corps in the first place."

"Yeah?"

"Yeah."

"That make you mad?"

"I got over it." He glanced across the cab at her. "Suggest you lie back and get some sleep if you can. You look like you could use it."

They stopped to recharge three times along the drive. On the third stop, Carlos handed Nadine a burger and a cup of coffee. "Gettin' close," he said.

Nadine stretched and rubbed the crick from her neck. "Thanks." She dug the burger from the bag, chewed and swallowed mechanically.

"Nervous?"

Nadine turned the question over in her mind, trying the word on the way she might try on a dress she found at a thrift shop even though she knew it was three sizes too large. "No," she said finally.

Carlos looked at her for a long moment. "Heard stories about you."

"What kind of stories?"

"You're a stone cold killer. Wouldn't guess it just looking at you, Nadine Jiang. Is the thing about the dirty bombs true?"

"No." Nadine took a bite from her sandwich. "Would it matter if it were?"

"I'm not a Marine any more, but I still take my oath seriously. So when I'm offered a job helping a wanted terrorist do a snatch and grab at a defense contractor, you gotta understand it raises certain questions for me."

"You know what we're after?"

"Data."

"Yeah. More than that, data that proves I'm not who the cops say I am."

The truck pinged as the charging umbilical detached itself. "The thing with the ogre, that for real?"

"Yeah."

"He didn't look so good."

"He doesn't have to worry about it any more."

"Dead?"

"Yeah."

"You do that?"

"Me and Jake, yeah."

"How you feel about that?"

"He tried to kill me first."

Carlos nodded. "Impressive, going up against an ogre. Especially an ogre in body armor. How'd you do it?"

Nadine finished her burger, stuffed the wadded wrapper in the bag. "Does it matter?"

"Just trying to get a handle on you. Make sure you won't crack under stress is all."

"I can handle myself."

The appraising look came back. "Yeah," he said after a while. "Yeah, I imagine you can."

At last, the truck's navigation dinged. "You have reached your destination," it announced in a sultry voice with a faint Midwestern drawl. Carlos took over manual control and steered the van into a small and, as near as Nadine could tell, deserted campground. Trees closed around them and, north of them, the black fingers of large towers, neatly arranged in a grid, dark against the gathering gloom.

"Go time." Carlos fished a paper strip from his pocket, tore it open, peeled the backing off the comm link, pressed the mike and receiver to his skin. "Gear up."

"Where are the others?"

"About three klicks north northeast, waiting for the call. Your entry point is about a kilometer north of here."

Nadine peeled the waxy white paper from the two bits of gear Carlos had given her to expose the adhesive. She pressed the larger one against the bone at the back of her ear and the other on her throat. "Can you hear me?"

"Loud and clear," Carlos said, voice buzzing oddly in her head. "Here." He passed her a long tube of black plastic embossed with a stylized ADS logo. "Mesh transceivers. Same deal. Peel and stick about every hundred meters or so."

"Where will you be?"

"In the trailer. Got a full suite of comms and sensor gear back there. Elizabeth has the best toys. Let's get you dressed."

Nadine climbed from the truck, earth damp and loamy beneath her feet. Around her, scent of pine needles and decaying leaves. Carlos opened the door on the sleek aluminum trailer. A platform extended itself from the opening with a whirr and lowered to the ground. Nadine stepped up into a tidy, luxurious space, efficiently laid out: small refrigerator, tiny stove with cabinets above, long table crowded with monitors. A hallway led to a spacious bedroom in the back. "Man could get used to private service," Carlos said. "You'll want to wear something warm."

"It's muggy out."

He flipped on the radiant grin, turned it off again. "Took the liberty of getting you a sweater, ma'am. Chiller in your IR suit will make you glad to have it." He tossed her a fuzzy black sweater with a thin red stripe, then tore open a dull green sealed pouch with "IR CNTRMSR 1PC DISPOS DOD LIC#15172324-2" printed across it. Inside was a long silver poncho-looking thing and a small silver gas canister with a complicated-looking valve on the narrow end.

Nadine pulled the sweater over her head. It smelled of thrift stores, an indeterminate musty odor mixed with damp cardboard. Carlos showed her how to fit the poncho. "The hood goes up, and this panel goes over your face," he explained. "Chiller gas goes in this pocket here. When you get down in the tunnels, connect this tube, twist this bit, and break it off. You'll hear a hiss. Don't do it before you get to the tunnels. The gas'll keep the material from warming up with your body heat, automatically regulates so you'll be around background temperature to IR cameras. You can wear the gloves if you want, but most likely the sensors in the tunnel won't register your hands. They're looking for anything that's warm and bigger'n a rat." He pressed a large, heavy key with a round stem into her hand. "This unlatches the cover down to the tunnel. Liz show you how to connect the tap?"

"Yes."

"Here." He handed it to her, a box of blue plastic with leads for a passive fiber optic tap dangling from the front, flat switch on the back.

Jake's voice grated in her ear, oddly distorted by its trip through bone. "Test, test, test. Melody, you hear me?"

"Yeah," she said.

"Good. Comms link is up. You know what to do?"

"Yeah. Heading out now." Nadine slapped the magazine into Safan's small, heavy pistol, worked the slide like he'd shown her, tucked it in her waistband at the small of her back the way she'd seen Jake do. She folded the poncho over her arm, gas cylinder surprisingly dense in its pocket, and stepped out into the muggy heat of evening.

A buzzing sound followed her out, low, not loud, like flies nudging around the remnants of a picnic on a lazy summer day. She looked back and saw them, six of them, glossy black bodies easy to miss if you weren't paying attention. Her guardian angels, each carrying a core of agony and death.

Nadine set off across the small, sad campground toward Amos City, named after the young nephew of a state senator who also owned several construction firms and an architectural office, and had vast sums of money that couldn't leave the Federation of Free States. The walk wasn't hard or unpleasant, and except for the steady insectile buzz of the drones, she could almost pretend she was alone, and not about to do something potentially terminal in its recklessness.

The receiver behind her ear buzzed. "You hear me?" Carlos's disembodied voice said.

"Yeah."

"Okay. With the antenna and repeater I have in the trailer, you'll be able to talk to me and Jake and the rest until you get to the tunnels. Once you get down there, things get a little tricky. You'll need to remember to drop mesh nodes or we'll lose touch with you, and I won't be able to guide the drones after you. How you doing so far?"

"Why does everyone keep asking me that? I'm fine."

"Good. Path you're on meets up with a service road fifty meters to your left."

"Got it." Nadine changed direction. The dirt beneath her feet gave way to gravel.

"Curves around a hundred and fifty meters ahead of you, ends at a bunch of Dumpsters. There's a gate and a road. See it?"

"Yeah."

"Follow the road for about half a kilometer, then turn left."

"Right." Nadine adjusted the silver suit over her arm. Beads of sweat rolled down her skin beneath the sweater. "Hey Jake, you there?"

A click, felt more than heard, then Jake's voice buzzing through her skull. "Yeah."

"You ready to roll?"

"Soon as we get the alarm."

"I guess that means it's all on me, then."

"Yeah, I guess it does."

She found the gate, two long triangles of tubular metal, yellow paint just starting to peel, mounted in bits of pipe on each side of the gravel road. A chain with a combination padlock held them together in the middle of the gravel road. On the other side, a flat slab of black asphalt, almost entirely pristine, dense grass and a handful of young trees on each side. In the distance, the still towers of Amos City beckoned.

"Hell of a thing," Nadine muttered, half to Jake and half to herself, as she headed toward the towers of a city without people, winged death in her wake. "I almost didn't go to that dance party."

"Say again?" Carlos said.

"Nothing."

"Eyes open. I don't see any drones around except the ones I'm driving, but stay frosty."

At Carlos's promised half-kilometer, the flat asphalt road ended at a T-junction, a flat ribbon of wide concrete highway off to the left and right. Nadine turned left, where the silent towers waited.

Amos City reminded her of a setmaker's prop, built at one to one scale, something designed to look like a city without *being* a city. The road, sidewalks, and even the mounts for the street lights were all cast from a single piece of concrete, regular lines slicing across the roadway where the segments joined together. Around it, nothing but bare dirt— no trees, no flowers, no sign of life. It looked to her as if someone had scraped the ground flat and then dropped the road and its sidewalk out of the sky—which was, she realized, very nearly what had happened.

After ten minutes of walking, she came to the first of the towers. They were all identical, crisp rectangles jutting up toward the heavens, story after story bristling with identical balconies, all painted the same off-white with the same blue metal rails. Windows gleamed in the late afternoon sun. Between the towers, no lawns or gardens, just parking garages and bare brown earth. No cars moved, no people leaned over the rails or walked along the sidewalks with her. Soon the towers closed around her, silent as tombstones. "This place gives me the creeps," Nadine said.

"Sometimes money finds its own expression," Jake said. "Like water flowing through a canyon, only the walls are laws and regulations. It follows the path of least resistance and leaves the landscape altered behind it."

"Closest I've heard you get to philosophical," Nadine said.

"Okay, intersection ahead of you," Carlos cut in. "You want the southeast corner."

Nadine crossed the road, following the painted lines of a crosswalk. Turn signals sat dark on poles at each corner. "I'm here."

"Should be a steel door at your feet."

Nadine looked down. A square hatch of silver metal, stamped with a no-skid pattern. "Yeah."

"Use the key. Suit up. Shouldn't be a perimeter alarm on the access door."

"Shouldn't be?"

"Always gotta expect the unexpected."

"What if there is?"

"Then they'll probably send someone to investigate."

"And if they do?"

Grating laughter buzzed in her skull. "That's why I'm here."

Nadine shrugged into the silver poncho thing. Concealed ties in the waist cinched it tight. A separate part, connected in the back, covered her legs in two baggy silver tubes, with more ties at her ankles. She pressed the gas cylinder onto a short tube that projected from the pocket. As soon as she twisted the knob, it snapped off in her hand. A hiss, and the inside of the poncho grew cold.

She knelt to fit the lock-like thing into the access hatch. It resisted her efforts to turn it. Swearing, she leaned her weight against it. The key turned with a metallic scrape. She heaved the hatch open. A simple metal ladder, painted light gray, descended into darkness. "I've spent way too much of my life lately climbing down dark tunnels," Nadine grumbled.

"Leave the hatch open," Carlos's voice said. "Stick one of the mesh nodes to the inside lip right at the surface, and another one to the wall at the foot of the ladder."

"Fine." Nadine popped open the plastic tube. A band of plastic bubble wrap lay coiled inside. As she pulled the end, a bubble tore off, depositing a gleaming black thing in her hand. She peeled the paper off the back, exposing a tacky adhesive. "Won't they find these?"

"They slag themselves when the battery runs out," Carlos said. "Little solvent capsule inside. Don't leave much behind."

"Nice. You army people think of everything, don't you?"

"Marines, ma'am, and yes, we try."

Nadine stuck the thing right at the edge of the tunnel, level with the street. "Here goes nothing." She swung a leg over the edge and climbed down into darkness.

The tunnel was small enough she couldn't stand without bending over. Concrete tubes about as wide as her hand ran down both side walls. A much larger hump, awkwardly shaped, ran straight down the center of the floor. With a low buzz, the six tiny drones dove down the tunnel after her. "You be able to steer those things?" Nadine said.

"Yes, ma'am. Active IR, passive IR, and ultrasound."

"All that?"

"Yes, ma'am."

The square of late afternoon light receded quickly. Nadine shuffled along the tunnel in an awkward crouch, one hand on the wall, feet forced by the hump in the floor into a narrow channel. "Okay, I'm going to send the swarm about ten meters ahead of you," Carlos said. "I'll guide you through the turns."

Darkness closed around her, as absolute as the bottom of a cage. Blind, Nadine felt her way along, concrete cool and slightly rough beneath her hand. "You're doing fine," Carlos said. "Can you go a little faster?"

"Only if you want me to twist an ankle."

"Don't even joke about that," Jake said.

"Signal's getting a little weak," Carlos said.

Eyes closed, Nadine fished around until she found the end of the roll, pulled off another bubble.She nearly dropped the thing before she was able to peel the backing off. She pressed it firmly against the tunnel wall, ran her fingers over it to make sure it stuck. "Good," Carlos said. "It's working."

Step by step, inch by inch, Nadine fumbled her way along through black so deep she didn't even have a name for it, so deep she could feel the weight of it pressing against her, until it stole her memory of what light used to be. She followed Carlos's voice, counted the notches in the broomstick with her left hand, mind repeating the directions over and over, making sure they all agreed. The chiller gas hissed through the tubes in her poncho, as loud as the end of the world. She heard the steady low housefly buzz of the drones, smelled the dank air of the lightless tunnel. Carlos's voice guided her along, through turn after turn, until it seemed that she'd always been here, that the world outside this black lifeless maze had never been anything more than some distant dream.

"You're getting close," Carlos said an eternity later. "Tunnel on your right, then sixty meters on. I'm pulling back the drones."

Nadine crawled over the hump down the tunnel's center and reached out for the wall. She stumbled, shoulder catching painfully on the edge of the opening to the next tunnel. "Goddamn it," she swore. The drones buzzed by her face.

"You okay?" Carlos's voice managed to carry concern, fizzing through her head.

"Yeah. How far?"

"Not far at all. You're almost to the foot of the building. According to the blueprints, there's a junction box at—"

"Ow!" Nadine ran directly into a concrete wall directly in her path.

"What happened?" Jake's voice, harsh and grating.

"Hang on. There's something..." Nadine felt her way across the tunnel. Her questing fingers found a ladder, ascending the wall that entirely sealed the tunnel. "Did I make a wrong turn?"

"No," Carlos said. "You're right where you're supposed to be."

"No, I'm not. There's a wall."

"What do you mean?"

"I mean there's a wall! Fuck!" Nadine beat her palms against the concrete. "There's a fucking wall right through the fucking tunnel!"

"Hang on. I'm moving the drones up."

Nadine knelt, pounding her fists against the wall as if trying to bash her way through. "Fuck! Fuck!"

"She's right," Carlos said. "Ultrasonics shows blank wall. No junction box, no fiber optics, just wall."

"Then you aren't in the right place," Jake said.

"We're in the right place," Carlos said. "There's no alarm junction here. Service tunnel is walled off. There's supposed to be another fifteen meters of tunnel, but nothing. It's not there."

"Okay, think," Nadine said. "We can fix this." She shivered in the parka, sweat cold on her skin. "Where am I?"

"You're right by the edge of the building. Data Storage Systems and Services."

"But where?"

"East side of the building, fifteen meters out."

Nadine squeezed her eyes shut in the black, calling up the blueprint in her memory. "What's at the top of this ladder?"

"I don't know," Carlos said. "Um...according to the site plan, just ground."

"What happens if I climb up there?"

"Twenty kinds of shit is what happens," Jake said. "They have drones, perimeter alarms, armed security, the whole lot. You won't get five meters."

"Any doors? Any way in?"

"Not on that side of the building, ma'am," Carlos said. "Wouldn't matter anyway. They'll all be locked and alarmed. Cameras, too."

"Time for Plan B," Jake said.

"What's Plan B?"

"Don't know yet. Still thinkin' it through. Right now I'm leaning toward smashing this truck through the front door and shooting our way in."

"You're not serious."

"I'm a little serious. We are well and truly fucked right now."

Nadine traced the blueprints over and over in her mind. "Melody," Jake said, "pull back. You can't do any good down there."

"Let me think."

"I'm serious. Pull back. If there's no alarm panel, there's nothing for you to do. Pull back."

"I said let me think!" Nadine slumped to the ground, her back to the unexpected wall. "I remember some round things in the back. What are they?"

"Auxiliary power," Carlos said. "They've got primary power from the grid, backup power in big-ass batteries, generators for emergency power. What are you thinking?"

"Liz, are you there?" Nadine said.

"I'm here, hon."

"You still have a way into Terracone's network, right? If the alarm goes off, you can stop them from knowing?"

"If the alarm goes off, local police will know. Without the patch, I can't prevent that."

"But you can stop Terracone from knowing?"

"What good will that do if local authorities know?" Liz said.

"Humor me."

"Yes, I can stop Terracone from getting the alert."

"Get ready to do that."

"What are you going to do?"

"Save our asses." Under her breath, she added, "Carlos, I sure hope you're watching out for me." She fumbled the heavy key from the pocket beneath the poncho, then felt around along the low ceiling, fingertips seeking the latch. After five tries, she unlocked the access hatch. Evening light streamed around her, blinding her, as she pushed it open. She blinked, dazzled. The swarm buzzed past her into the open air, tiny mechanical wasps bearing their lethal payload.

25

Move Like You've Got a Purpose

THE ACCESS PANEL opened up onto a stretch of immaculate rolling lawn. Nadine pinched off one of the remaining mesh nodes and stuck it to the edge of the opening as she pulled herself up. To one side, a white single-story building, walls of coarse stucco. To the other, a row of trees, their limbs spreading wide, then beyond that, a high, solid-looking fence of no-nonsense black metal. Above her, a dark shape against the sky, long and oval, held within a rectangle of small ducted fans. "Shit," Carlos's voice buzzed. "Drone. They've got you."

"That was going to happen regardless." Nadine started toward the rear of the building, remembering the diagrams she'd seen. Flat expanse of pavement, generators, door, all ringed by a concrete wall about head high, open in the back...

She'd made it around the wall and was moving toward the back of the building when the rear door banged open. Two figures came through, fast and low, dressed in the sort of black security uniform that suggested rapid escalation. The one in the lead drew a gun. "Freeze!" Woman's voice. "Hands where I can see them!" Yellow alert triangles danced in the air.

Nadine stopped, arms at her sides. "I'm looking for my cat!" she called. "Have you seen it?"

"What?"

Two pops, one after the other, no louder than the cork leaving a bottle of champagne. Two pale yellow flashes of light, quick bright flares, there and gone. Two louder pops, these ones wet somehow, and sharp, and then screams...

Nadine turned away from the figures convulsing on the ground, arms and legs flailing, bright arterial jets of blood spurting from their necks. The generators, three of them, sat in a silent row on concrete pads against the back of the building, tall exhaust stacks plumed with black grime. "Two hostiles down," Carlos said in her head.

Nadine stripped off the silver foil suit, dropping it as she crossed over to the tall cylinder that rose next to the generators, like an LP tank turned up on its end, supported by rust-stained metal legs. A thick steel pipe ran from its base, branching toward each of the generators, valves at each branch. She knelt, inspected the pipe. "What are you doing?" Jake's voice, tightly controlled.

"Looking for a way to dump the fuel. There's got to be a pressure release valve, something."

The drones hovered over her, her own protective swarm of hornets. "There isn't," Carlos said.

"Goddammit." Nadine rose and kicked the valve violently. "Come on! Dammit!" She kicked again, and again, bringing the boot Jake had given her down hard. "Fuck!"

On her sixth kick, the valve twisted slightly. On the seventh, the pipe started to buckle. She kept at it, kicking again and again until at last the pipe cracked. Liquid gushed out, filling the air with the pungent stench of long-chain hydrocarbons. Nadine crowed in triumph. "What are you doing?" Carlos said.

"Setting off the alarm. I need some way to light it."

"I'll use one of the drones."

"No! We only have four left." She ran to the two security guards, their blood pooling on black asphalt. The woman still twitched feebly. Nadine patted her down. "Do you smoke? Do you have a light?"

The woman's eyes followed her. Her lips moved soundlessly. She was young, only a little older than Nadine, and pretty, Nadine noted. The hole in the side of her neck had stopped jetting blood and was now oozing more slowly.

"This will be useful, thank you." Nadine pulled a security card on a lanyard from the woman's neck. She twitched one last time and lay still, eyes staring sightlessly into the sky.

Nadine moved to the other body. "Please cut me a break here," she said, patting the man down. "Tell me you smoke."

"Someone inside just tripped an alarm straight to Terracone," Liz's voice said. "Expect more company soon. Doesn't look like they've rung local PD yet."

"On it," Carlos said. The drones divided into two groups, one hovering on each side of the door.

Nadine reached into the dead man's front pocket. "Yes! Thank you."

The door slammed open. Two more pops, two more loud cracks. Screams. Nadine pulled off the sweater, wadded it into a ball. Fuel puddled around the concrete feet of the generators. Nadine wet the edge of the sweater in the torrent of fuel that poured from the broken pipe, flicked the lighter. "Jesus, Mary, and Joseph," Carlos said.

Nadine watched flames consume the ugly sweater with distant detachment. She tossed the flaming ball into the pool, watched the greedy flames spread out.

"Melody! Run!"

Carlos's urgency shattered the detachment. Nadine bolted, adrenaline giving wings to her flight. As she rounded the edge of the sheltering wall, a roaring column of flame licked at the sky. When the tank blew, Nadine heard a dull "whump." A great invisible hand pushed at her chest. Breathless heat, hard and deep, washed over her, filled the night around her. "Fuck," Carlos said in her ear. "Last two drones are down. Fried. Didn't get far enough away."

"Fuck." Nadine picked herself up and stole a peek around the edge of the wall. One corner of the building had crumpled inward, consumed by the ferocious inferno. Even from the edge of the lot, she could feel the heat like a physical weight.

Nadine picked herself up and ran toward the door. "What's happening?" Carlos said. "I don't have eyes."

"I'm trying to get inside." She held up her arm to shield herself from the heat, ran the dead security guard's card over the pad. The door unlatched. "Thank God," she said. "Is the alarm going?"

"Oh, yeah," Liz said. "Police, fire, ambulance. The only people on earth who don't know about it are Terracone."

"Good."

"Good?" Carlos said. "In what possible way is that good?"

Nadine pushed her way through the door, found herself in a narrow hallway lit by long rectangular LEDs in the ceiling. Alarms shrieked around her. She closed her eyes, calling up a mental image of the floor plan, then set off at a jog down the corridor. "All that attention, a hazmat response truck will fit right in. Hell, the cops will probably wave you in, and keep everyone else out of your way." She rounded a corner and nearly collided with a man in a black uniform. For the barest instant, their gazes locked. His eyes widened. "Oh, fu—" Nadine said.

The security guard's hands blurred. Red arcs slashed out toward her. Nadine jumped backward. The red turned green, barely grazing her. He reached for his side, where yellow triangles danced.

Without thought, without intent, Nadine lunged for him, watching herself dive for his weapon with an almost clinical interest. He reached it first, unsnapped the strap, started to draw. She grabbed his wrist with one hand, grabbed the thing's strange square barrel with the other, twisted. He let out a cry of surprise, then it was in her hands, and she was pulling the trigger...

The gun whined, light in her hands. Something shredded his shirt. His chest erupted in thin slivers like the needles on a cactus, and he screamed, a desperate shriek of agony that rose and rose until nothing human remained. He fell backward, clawing at his chest, eyes wide, legs kicking uselessly on institutional gray carpet.

For a moment, he wore Marcus's face, and Nadine was back there, in the home she shared with Anna, Marcus screaming on the floor, Lena leaning over him...

Nadine dropped the gun. Smoke crawled like a living thing along the ceiling, choking her. Jake's voice grated in her head. "Six minutes out. Pull out."

"No," Nadine said. "I'm going for the server room."

"Pull out!"

"There's no time! The fire, it's spreading fast. If the servers burn we are utterly fucked."

"Jesus Christ," Jake said. "I'm almost there. If the fire—"

"She's right," Liz's voice cut in. "Get there as fast as you can, be ready to pull her out if she gets the drives before you do."

"I have no birds. I'm blind here," Carlos said. "I can't back her up."

"Five minutes out," Jake said. "Goddammit, don't get yourself killed."

"That's the plan. Carlos! I'm in the corridor from the back door. Getting smoky in here. Could use a little help. Get me to the server room, and do it fast or this whole show's for nothing."

"Roger that. Stand by...okay, I'm seeing a corridor that comes to a T-junction. That where you are?"

Nadine looked left and right. "Yeah."

"Okay. Left leads to a bunch of...huh. Looks like a lab of some sort. You want to go right."

"Fuck. I was afraid you'd say that."

"Problem?" Carlos said.

"That's where the fire is."

"Better move like you've got a purpose, then. Security door five meters down."

"Got it." Nadine passed the dead woman's stolen keycard over the reader. An LED glowed green. "I'm through."

"Bunch of offices on your right. Server room will be on your left at the end of the hall."

Heart hammering, Nadine sped, as quietly as she was able, down the hallway, darting a quick glance into each office. The rooms sat empty, LED panels still glowing, computers still on, all abandoned in haste. In one of the room, a forsaken mug half-full of coffee rested precariously on the edge of the desk. The alarms kept up their raspy drone. Red lights blinked.

When she was midway down the hall, the lights flickered and went out. Suffocating blackness closed around her, then the panels flicked back on. Wisps of curling smoke crawled along the ceiling.

A massive, heavy door guarded the entrance to the server room. The red light on the pad changed to green when Nadine swiped her card. The door opened into a long space, narrow aisles between long black racks filled with geometrically precise silver rectangles with small blue and green lights behind glass panels. Warning lights strobed in the ceiling. Another alarm, high and shrill, battled with the insistent rasp of the fire alarm. "What now?"

"You're looking for a storage array," Liz said. "Might be at the end of one of the rows. Flat panels, divided into squares, four rectangles in each square. Blinking lights."

"Got it," Nadine said a minute later. "Looks like four racks' worth."

"Okay, here's where it gets tricky," Liz said. "I have a logical address, not a physical address."

"What's that mean?"

"Means I don't know which drive pack you're looking for."

Nadine stared at the banks of storage units, blinking behind the glass. "Lot of them here. No way we're walking out with all of them."

"Look for labels. Gotta be labels. The data's on a cluster called Mordor."

"Are you serious?"

"Yes."

Nadine scanned the cabinets. Each one had a rectangular bit of tape stuck to it, neat handwriting in felt-tip: Elysium, Gallifrey, Nostromo, Mordor. "Found it. Um..." Nadine tuned it all out—the alarms, the strobing lights, the smell of smoke. "I see a bunch of little stick-on labels, a letter and two numbers."

"Look for D-22."

The labels seemed random, no order that Nadine could see. "T-16, R-74...got it, D-22." Tiny green lights blinked on a square storage unit a bit larger than her palm. "What do I do?"

"There's a button on the upper left. Push it, wait for the lights to go out. There's a carrying handle that unfolds. It also unlocks the drive unit. Lift the handle, pull the unit straight out."

Jake's voice cut over Liz's. "I'm here. Jesus Christ, what did you do?"

"Set off the alarm," Nadine said absently.

"Well, it's a circus out here. Cops beat us. They're keeping people away."

"Good." Nadine pulled the latch to open the glass door over the drives. "Fuck. Locked."

"What's locked?" Jake said.

Nadine pulled the heavy gun from her back, gripped the barrel, swung it hard against the glass. The door shattered. "Nothing." She tucked the gun back in her waistband and stabbed the button. Lights blinked. "Come on, come on..."

With a roar, the corner of the room collapsed. Flames poured up the wall, licked at the ceiling. Instantly, nozzles in the ceiling sprayed a cloud of fog that settled around her, cold and slightly sweet-smelling. "Room's on fire. Some kinda gas coming in. Do I need to worry?"

"About the gas?" Carlos said. "No. Fire suppression system. Harmless. About the fire? Yeah, I'd worry about that."

"We're on our way to you," Jake said. "Twenty seconds."

The blinking lights went out. Nadine grabbed the handle and pulled the array free. It slid out, surprisingly deep, leaving a gaping hole in the rack. "I've got it."

"Good," Liz said. "Go back out the way you came, make your way to the front of the building. Jake will meet you there."

"Isn't it faster to go out the back?"

"Sure, if you don't mind being burned alive. Go out the front. Jake's got a spare hazmat suit for you. Just walk right past the cops, they won't even look at you."

Smoke filled the hall, hot and thick. Nadine pulled her shirt up over her nose and mouth. "Is it true most folks in a fire die from smoke inhalation?"

"Yup," Carlos said.

"Great." She crouched low, turned toward the front of the building. "Jake, I'm on my way out." Pause. "Jake? You there?"

"Northeast corner office," Liz said. "Move fast. Building's coming down."

"On it," Nadine said. "Hey Jake, that firefighter's gear is sounding really good right about now. Gettin' pretty uncomfortable here."

The hallway opened into a cubicle farm, every box the same: computer, holographic display, little squares of Post-It notes, staplers. The smoke hadn't intruded here, but the strobing alarm lights were starting to give her a headache. Two-thirds of the overhead LED panels were out, and the remaining third gave the room a surreal, gloomy air.

Still keeping low, Nadine worked her way around to the corner office. "In and out, huh, Jake? Guess you could've sat this one out."

"Cut the chatter." Liz's voice, curt, with undertones of stress. "Get your ass suited up and out of there. You're running out of time."

"I'm here, just going into the office now—"

Nadine froze, taking in the scene in one blinding instant of clarity. Oversized executive desk, dark polished wood; potted ficus in a shiny brass pot in the corner; whiteboard on the wall, financial numbers written in black dry-erase marker; and on the floor...

"Jake!" Nadine cried. He lay on his side, firefighter suit open. A figure knelt over him. "Safan?"

"Melody!" Safan straightened, turned toward her. "Over here! Quick!" He reached toward her. A yellow triangle bloomed, line following a red arc that slid like a scythe toward her.

Nadine jumped back. Red turned green, and somehow the gun was in her hand, summoned there from the small of her back by unconscious sleight of hand. She brought it up in line with Safan's face, thumbed off the safety, pulled the trigger.

The gun clicked.

Safan smiled. "Knew giving you a gun was a bad idea. Took the liberty of filing down the firing pin just for this eventuality." He lunged again. Red arcs. Nadine twisted away. "You're fast," Safan said. He leapt at her. More red arcs. Nadine spun, swung her fist at Safan's face. He cursed and ducked. She bolted for the door.

A wall of yellow blocked her way, outlined in reflective tape. "Going somewhere?" Benjamin said.

With a shriek of pure rage, Nadine swung the pistol square into his face, felt something crunch. He cried out in pain and staggered back, blood gushing from the side of his head. Then the probes of Safan's stun gun hit her neck, and suddenly her body didn't work anymore. He took the drive unit from her nerveless fingers as she collapsed.

"Bitch hit my face!" Benjamin said, the last thing she heard before blackness swallowed her.

WHEN SHE OPENED her eyes again, she wished she hadn't. Pain sleeted around her. Her stomach knotted. White light, much too bright, pressed down around her. She rolled her head to one side and vomited.

"Hey, slow, take it easy." Unfamiliar voice, blue latex gloves, dark blue uniform. "We found you unconscious. Probably smoke inhalation, miss..." He flipped up the security card that still hung from the lanyard around her neck. "Patterson."

Nadine brought her hand to her head. "How long—"

"We brought you out about five minutes ago."

"Out?" She frowned, looked around. Her surroundings came into focus: stretcher, bins, light. Ambulance. A bag hung over her head. Saline flowed down a tube through a needle in her hand. She lifted her head. Through the open door, billows of orange flame roared toward the sky.

Someone banged on the side of the door. Nadine got a glimpse of yellow firefighter gear. "Medic!" Jake's voice came through the door and into the bones of her head at the same time. "Need you outside, stat."

"I'm with a patient—"

"She's stable. We have a code blue."

The man grabbed a red and white case and scrambled from the ambulance. Jake climbed in the moment he left. "Nadine!" he hissed. "We need to move. Now." Red arc, then he yanked the needle from her hand. She yelped. "Sorry. Window of opportunity is closing fast."

Nadine scrambled from the ambulance after him. Red and blue lights shattered the evening. An inferno twisted up to the heavens. Fire trucks ringed the blaze, surrounded by yellow-jacketed men wrestled hoses that snaked across the asphalt. Jake dragged her by the hand past a row of ambulances, their doors open. People sat dazed, wrapped in blankets, fussed over by blue-uniformed EMTs. When they reached Safan's fire truck, Jake said, "Get in. Time to go."

Nadine slumped in the enormous front seat, arms around herself, as the raging fire dwindled behind them. The glow lingered on the horizon for a long time.

"Fuck!" Jake pounded the steering wheel. "Fuck! Fuck! They took my fucking rifle, too. Jumped me as soon as I got inside. Please tell me we have something."

"Safan was waiting for me," Nadine said. "He took the drive."

"Fuck!"

Nadine huddled further into herself. "Now what?"

"Now we get the fuck away from this clusterfuck. First order of business, we need to lose this truck. It's not exactly inconspicuous. We're gonna need another ride. I'll dump the truck, we'll walk a while, call a Booker—"

"How? Your implant's disabled."

"Fuck!"

They slept that night in a motel in a small town three hours south of Amos City. Jake parked the truck in the back of a vehicle auction lot, between a crane and a cherry picker. Then, rocks in their shoes and masks bearing adversarial input over their faces, they limped across town. Cold despair settled over Nadine, its weight dragging her down. "I don't understand," she said. "What was it we stole?"

"Not information to clear your name, that's for sure. They used you. Found out what you needed, told you what you wanted to hear, pointed you at Data Storage Systems and Services LLC, you got in, got what they wanted, they took it."

"What do we do now?"

"Nothing. It's over."

"But—"

Jake spun toward her, eyes blazing. "It's over! We took our best shot. We lost. Game over."

"So now what?"

"I don't know! You still have money. Use it to disappear. Right now, we need sleep. Tomorrow we rent a Booker, take it to...I don't know. Something tells me we're gonna have a tough time crossing the border. Whatever. We ain't figuring it out 'til after we get some sleep."

Nadine spent most of the night staring at the ceiling, feeling tears that would not come. Jake was already up and had loaded more money on his prepaid Booker card by the time Nadine dragged herself from bed into the shower. As they finished room service, the Booker pulled up in front of the door, a long, black, heavy thing with dark tinted windows. "We're riding in style," Jake said.

"Where to?" she said as they climbed in and settled into rich, soft leather.

"Good question. Houston, I suppose."

Nadine studied his face. Jake stared grimly forward, jaw clenched tight. His claw opened and closed, over and over, click click click. "Why Houston?"

"There's a chance Safan will head back there. They still have business interests. That shit takes time to wind down."

"Suppose they're there. So what?"

"He fucked us. I fuck back."

"And then?"

"There is no 'and then.' End of the road." Click click click. "We did well. Better'n we had any right to expect, once you went off script and said no to Canada. Hell, for a second there I actually thought we might come out of this alive. End of the day, we still lost."

"Then why go after Safan?"

"Make sure he loses, too."

The rest of the trip went by in silence. Eventually Houston came into view, glittering towers surrounded by decaying interstates. Yellow haze hung over it all, wrapping the city in fumes.

The Booker dropped them off at a tiny hotel with no cameras in the parking lot, well outside the interstate that circled the city's heart. Jake checked them in. "You know," Nadine said as they arranged a makeshift bed on the grubby couch against the cracked, peeling wall, "this is the second time I've ended up with nothing but the clothes on my back."

"And the bank chips in your sock," Jake said. "Lucky thing Safan didn't find them, or else we'd be even more fucked than we already are. He didn't have time to search you."

"Why didn't they just shoot us?"

"Don't know. Probably thought the flames would get us."

"Even with police and fire on the scene?" Nadine tossed a pillow onto the sofa. "You take the bed."

"Maybe they thought we weren't worth shooting. And I'm fine."

"You're not fine. Your leg's a mess. If you're serious about going after Safan, you're going to need to be in top form. Get some sleep, we'll figure out what to do tomorrow."

The phone on the nightstand, an antique black Cisco IP thing made of glossy black plastic, chirped. Nadine and Jake exchanged looks. "That can't be good," Nadine said.

Jake raised the square black handset. "Yeah?" Pause. "From who?" Pause. "I see. I'll be right down."

"What's up?" Nadine said after he hung up.

"Courier just delivered a package for Jake Fox to the front desk."

"Trap?"

"Bet on it."

"You going to get it?"

"Yep."

"Why?"

"Because if I don't, they'll try again. They know where we are. Might as well get this over with. What are you doing?"

"Going with you."

"The hell you are. Stay here."

"But—"

"Non-negotiable. You hear shit go sideways, you book it out of here."

Nadine sat. The sofa creaked beneath her. "Fine."

A minute later, Jake rapped on the door. "It's me." He came through the door with an envelope in his claw.

"Nobody jumped you? No shootout?"

"Nope. Just this." He dropped the envelope on the nightstand next to the Cisco phone. It was made of heavy, cream-colored paper, richly textured, with Jake's name written on the front in swirling fountain-pen calligraphy.

"What's in it?"

Jake cocked his head. "How would I know that?"

"So open it."

"Might be a bomb or a biological."

"Maybe." Doubt filled Nadine's voice. ""Easier just to shoot you when you went to the office."

"Suppose."

"So open it."

"Fine. But stay back." Jake tore open the heavy cream envelope. A small storage drive and a folded card in the same elegant cream slid out. Jake unfolded it carefully with his claw.

"What's it say?"

"It's a network address and '2 PM tomorrow'."

"I suppose this means life just got a good deal simpler."

"Suppose."

AT 1:56 THE next afternoon, Jake and Nadine sat in a Keep Your Data franchise shop in the back of a Happy Gator Ship-n-Store in Atascocita. They took seats at a square metal table in the back near the fire escape. Nadine settled the goggles over her eyes and punched up one of the built-in avatars, a big-eyed anime girl with spiky blue hair. Jake punched in the address.

At 2:00 exactly, the Keep Your Data franchise dissolved in a spray of pixels. They found themselves in an elegantly appointed bedroom, giant four-poster bed against the wall. A candle flickered on the edge of the antique roll-top desk. "Right on time," Liz purred.

Jake's boxy suit-clad avatar folded its arms. "You called us here. You must have something to say to us. So talk."

"The fact that you're here tells me you got my package," Liz said. "The drive has everything you need. Martin Taylor's instructions to set up you and Anna, raw footage of the deepfakes, everything. That man loved his memos, oh yes. He even wrote memos about your friend Marcus. Should be plenty there for even a halfway decent defense lawyer to get the terrorism thing cleaned up, assuming the prosecutor bothers pursuing charges. Which they won't. All's well that ends well, hmm?"

"I have a question," Jake said.

"Yes?"

"What was on the drives we stole?"

"Jake. I thought you were smarter than this. What do you think?" Liz rose from the bed, every motion grace embodied. She walked past Nadine to the desk, leaned over to blow out the candle. An animated ember sent up a curling wisp of smoke. "Come on, Jake, you know this. What would Terracone have in cold storage, out of reach of network access, even from inside the corporate network?"

Jake's avatar raised its hands to its face. "Mirage."

"Mirage. Now we have it."

"But why?" Nadine said.

"Why?" Puzzlement crossed Liz's immaculately rendered features. "Money, mostly. I already took it for a spin. There's a certain state senator who's using his government contacts to throw some very juicy jobs to certain contracting firms he happens to own. You know how long it took me to find that out? Less than a day. Know how long that's going to be paying dividends?"

Somewhere back in a room behind a ship-n-store, Nadine's eyes flooded with tears. "Money? You did it for money?"

"Well, that too. I have my own ideas about how the world ought to work, and maybe now I'll be able to pull the strings instead of being pulled by them. But mostly money, yeah."

"You had the information to clear my name from the start."

"Yeah." Liz seated herself on the bed again. "It was all over Terracone's network. Martin Taylor was arrogant. Didn't exactly cover his tracks."

"You could have told me."

"But then you would not have had any reason to go into Data Storage Systems and Services."

"I trusted you."

"And I delivered."

"You betrayed me!"

"Nonsense." Liz shook her head. "The way I see it, we all won. You got what you wanted, we got what we wanted."

"You left us to die."

"Oh, hon. We did no such thing. We told the responders where you were. And now, with all that money still in your girlfriend's account plus what's on the drive I gave you, you have your life back." The glowing ember on the candle wick faded. "Goodbye."

The bedroom dissolved. In the little room behind the ship-n-store, Nadine wept, great shuddering sobs without end.

Epilogue

SHE STANDS AT the edge of the water, a black canvas bag slung over one shoulder. Youthful features, perhaps late twenties, and pretty, with high cheekbones and a long wave of straight black hair. Behind her, the wreck of the *Georgina Maersk* claws jagged and broken at the rose-colored sky.

Three young men staggering home from some all-night revelry catch sight of her. The shirtless one whistles. Urged on by his companions, he approaches her. "Hey, baby," he coos in his best attempt at drunken seduction. "You here alone?"

She turns to look at him through blank shark eyes that do not belong in that face. He sees something there, bottomless and old beyond her years, that steals his breath and freezes his heart in his chest. He takes a step back, hands spread wide, then turns away, to the safety of his friends. They tease him for his cowardice. "C'mon, guys," he says, "let's get the fuck out of here."

She has already forgotten him. She kneels and opens her bag. She removes a sheet of colorful paper and with careful, deliberate motions, folds it into a small lotus flower. She places a long, thin stick in its center, pressing the point through the middle. A small torch flickers, its pale blue flame nearly lost against the rising sun. The tip of the stick glows. A thin wisp of fragrant smoke curls up. "Marcus," she says aloud. She places the flower in the scummy water and gives it a nudge. It drifts away, turning slowly.

She repeats the process, folding another flower, lighting another slender stick of incense. "Lena," she says. The flower joins the first, floating on a calm, flat, endless sea.

She folds another, and another, and another after that, reciting the names, tasting them on her tongue. Dan-boy. Jason. Kev.

She turns more blank sheets of paper into little flowers, and says the names she looked up in the news files, the ones who hadn't made it out: Mateo. Tony. Takeru. Trails of smoke hang in the still air. It isn't right, what she's doing. It isn't proper. But there are no graves to visit, no tombs to sweep. Nowhere to burn offerings or lay out food for the dead. She's doing the best she can.

She folds another flower. Another wisp of smoke joins the others. "Thomas." She's getting near the end of the stack of paper. She takes out another, fingers moving through motions made automatic since childhood, lights another stick. "Martin." The flowers bob together, bumping into each other as they gradually drift away, rocking slightly back and forth.

She hesitates, just for a moment, before she takes out the last sheet. Her hands tremble as she makes each careful, deliberate fold. She lights the stick, caressing each petal as she sets the flower gently in the water. "Anna." Her voice cracks. The tears come then, silent, from ancient broken eyes in a young face.

The sun rises higher. Finally she stands, turns away from the gleaming water that bears away the floating fragments of her wordless, hopeless ache. The voice comes to her. *He still wouldn't forgive you, you know.*

"You're not real," she says out loud.

Silence.

"Who wouldn't forgive me?" she says at last.

Thomas. The man who died on that shitty couch on that shitty stage in that shitty run-down school. This won't get you absolution. It was cruel, what you did to him.

"Maybe I'm not looking for absolution. The dead still deserve to be remembered."

She walks now, away from the water, down the dark alley between decaying shipping containers and rust-stained corrugated metal. The news channels report some new development on the horizon in the ongoing feud between the insurance companies over who will pay to clean up the mess. Perhaps this year it will finally happen.

The car waits where she left it, a red Tesla with a dented bumper and duct tape on one headlight. It pops its doors when it recognizes her. She slides into the back seat, gives it an address. "LA transit police investigate all reports of Booker cab vandalism," the car drones. "Vandalism may adversely affect your Booker score. Acceptance of transit implies assent to these conditions."

She mashes her finger on the Accept button and leans back in the seat, hands folded in her lap, the black canvas bag beside her.

So you're going to do it, then. Anna's voice in her head.

"Yes."

Is this really what you want? If my voice is some fragment of me in your firmware, you will destroy the last remnant of me that exists. You'll be throwing away the last gift I gave you.

"And if I do this, and I still hear you after, then I will know I'm insane," she says.

I just think—

"I know." Her voice carries the weariness of an argument worn threadbare by time and repetition, every exchange predictable, rehearsed. She watches the bland beige buildings flow past. "I'm so tired, Anna," she whispers.

The cab stops in front of a nondescript dental office. "Happy Smiles Gentle Dentistry," says the name on the sign.

"Wait for me."

"Waiting incurs charges as explained—"

She hits the Accept button before it can finish. The doors pop open.

Inside, she finds a cunning facsimile of a dentist's office. It has two small operatories, X-ray machines, lights, trays of instruments. It even has the smell, the twang of antiseptic she always associates with dentists. Who knows, she thinks, maybe they actually do dental work here.

A man in a lab coat greets her with a warm smile. Pale blue embroidery on one pocket reads "Dr. Talbot, DDS." He leads her past the operatories through a pair of double doors hung with a sign that says "STAFF ONLY - NO ADMITTANCE - XRAY EQUIPMENT IN USE" with a black radiation symbol on a yellow background. They pass a small open room where a woman in powder blue scrubs polishes a porcelain crown. Dr. Talbot stops in front of a closed door. "This is an unusual request," he says. "I get people in here wanting unapproved upgrades, new firmware, modifications. I don't think I've ever had anyone want it taken out before. Are you sure?"

"Yes, I'm sure."

"It's just that...I've seen your file. You have some nice gear in there. Expensive. I don't understand—"

She lays her hand briefly on his, pulls back before the warmth of his skin can penetrate. When was the last time she felt a kind touch? "Just do it. Please."

He opens the door, ushers her through. She leans back in a comfortable chair. He draws the strap around her head. "Do you mind if I ask why?"

"Maybe I'm going native," she says. "Joining a tribe of *Homo immechanica.*"

"I'm sorry?"

She smiles, but there is an endless well of sadness behind the tremulous curve, deep enough to drown in. "Something a friend said once." She closes her eyes. "I'm ready."

Acknowledgements

WRITING THE BOOK you now have before you was a massive effort, aided by countless people along the way. I tried, as much as I was able, to extrapolate from existing or nearly-here technology, politics, culture, and trends to create this vision of the near future we may be headed for if we aren't careful. Time will tell how well I hit (or missed) the mark.

I am deeply indebted to several people whose knowledge and generosity helped turn this book from a vague idea to a finished story. **Bill Otto**, whose knowledge of all things related to infrared imaging and Doppler radar is unparalleled, kindly fact-checked some of the technology for me. **Ileen Verble** provided detailed assistance with some of the medically-related parts of the story. **Jon Lowy** offered the wisdom of his experience with micro-optics, particularly contact-lens-mounted thin-film displays. **Myles Taylor** provided critique of an early draft. Finally, **Jamaika Campos** shared her valuable insight into the linguistics and culture of T-Town.

And, of course, my friends and family have been incredibly supportive. It's not always easy being close to a writer. We writers are a strange and sometimes discourteous lot, prone to retreating to the study at odd times of the day (and night!) muttering "so sorry, but I have to write this down." It takes a special kind of patience to be close to a writer, and I am grateful those around me have that patience in spades.

—E. F. Coleman, London, October 2022